(Books 1 and 2 of The Night Walkers)

Also by J. R. Johansson

Insomnia

Paranoia

MANIA

Book 3 of
The Night Walkers

MANIA

J. R.
Johansson

flux
Woodbury, Minnesota

First Edition
First Printing, 2015

Book design by Bob Gaul
Cover design by Lisa Novak
Cover image © www.iStockphoto.com/8783493/©Claudiad
              www.iStockphoto.com/21070098/©brainmaster

Flux, an imprint of Llewellyn Worldwide Ltd.

Library of Congress Cataloging-in-Publication Data
Johansson, J. R.
  Mania/J.R. Johansson.—First edition.
    pages cm.—(The Night Walkers; book 3)
  Summary: After their father's death, Parker Chipp and his half-brother, Jack, must decipher clues to locate the ingredients of their father's new formula, their last best chance to stop the Takers.
  ISBN 978-0-7387-4431-5
  [1. Brothers—Fiction. 2. Dreams—Fiction.] I. Title.
  PZ7.J62142Man 2015
  [Fic]—dc23
                                        2015005606

                            Flux
                    Llewellyn Worldwide Ltd.
                    2143 Wooddale Drive
                    Woodbury, MN 55125-2989
                        www.fluxnow.com

              Printed in the United States of America

For the Seizure Ninjas.
This book and series would never have
been completed without your mad skills.
Thank you!

ONE

JACK

Staring into the pit that had swallowed every answer I needed, I could still feel the earth shaking and the burning heat from the fire against my face. The frantic yells of the prisoners we'd set free echoed in my ears. Every shard of memory from the explosion at Benton Air Force Base—which had stolen away my mentor, my father—was still vivid. It had only happened a month ago, but I knew it would always be hard to forget something that had knocked the wind out of me and thrown me clean off my feet.

Especially when every time I remembered that night, my heart felt like it was happening all over again.

The wind blew cold at my back and chilled me in spite of the warm summer sun. I stood at the very edge of the crater, balanced on the brink. I gazed down into the deep shadows and rubble far below, wishing that the knowledge Danny—*no, my dad*, I mentally corrected myself—had taken with him could somehow drift like the dust through the air, up toward me.

Because from what I could tell, that might be the only hope I had of figuring out his damn puzzle.

"I wish we'd found another way," Parker muttered from a few feet to my right. I usually came here by myself, but he'd convinced me to bring him along this time. I was already regretting it.

This was where I always came when I ran into problems solving Dad's last riddle, his last assignment. Parker was a distraction here. Dad had given me a paper with directions and clues to piece together the formula for a new drug, and he'd told me I was the only one who could figure it out.

You'll be the answer. You'll know what to do.

Except I wasn't ... and I didn't.

And yet I was still expected to stop a war between the three different types of Night Walkers, a war that had been going on my whole life. Oh, and in order to do this, I had to solve Dad's puzzle, make the Takers stop killing long enough to listen to me, and create a magical—and I believe untested—drug that would somehow save the day.

No pressure.

"This sure is a creepy old place to decide to build a society, isn't it?" Parker asked. This time his question was directed at me and I couldn't stay silent.

"Dad picked it."

"Oh ... " My brother sounded frustrated as he added,

"See, that's the kind of detail I'd like to know about him. Why would he pick a place like this?"

The smallest groan escaped my lips before I could stop it, and I could tell from the way Parker stiffened that he'd heard it. This was why I hadn't wanted him to come. I came out here for time to think, and he wasn't helping.

"The structure is sound, there's plenty of space, and much of it is underground," I said.

Parker's reply was soft. "Now that actually makes sense. Thank you."

I sat down near the edge of the hole, then picked up some rocks and tossed them inside. The last thing I wanted was to hurt my brother, but it was hard to even look at him anymore when every detail reminded me so much of our dad. It wasn't Parker's fault that he caused me pain with everything he did.

Giving up on trying to keep him quiet, I decided to smooth things over a bit. "What else do you want to know about this place?"

"Why did the Takers keep so many prisoners here?" Parker hesitated only a moment before sitting down next to me.

"They suspected some of them of being Watchers, like us. But the rest were mostly for leverage. They wanted to force people to give them what they wanted. We should know better than anyone that taking loved ones can usually get you anything you want."

Parker nodded. "And if the base is so big and so much of it is underground, how do you know for sure the Takers left?"

"I've walked through every remaining hall—they're gone. Dad's explosion took out the majority of the space they were using," I said. When Parker squinted at the other side of the base, I went on. "Yes, it's huge. Much bigger than you'd think. There's probably two-thirds of it left. "

"So then *why'd* they leave?" Parker grabbed a handful of sand and dropped it into the hole. "They were taking more and more bodies in Oakville, so they seemed to be setting up something big. Why not move to the other side of the base and pick up where they left off?"

My voice dropped to a grim note. "Because they knew I'd come back."

Parker didn't speak, but I saw him turn his head to watch me.

"Plus, their entire plan revolved around Eclipse, and being able to set up a system nearby so a lot of Takers could take over Dreamers at will and not give the bodies back." I pulled my shoulders up and tried to loosen the knot in my neck. "Since Dad destroyed Eclipse and any hint of how to make it, right now they're scrambling. But once they get organized, they *will* come for us."

I thought of the few times in this twenty-year war when our side—the Builders and Watchers—had made any kind of headway against the Takers. The Takers always came back harder and more violently than we expected. People always died. Waiting for them to regroup felt like waiting for a bomb to drop from the sky—one you knew for certain was coming but didn't know when. And you couldn't stop it.

Brushing my hands against my jeans, I hopped to my feet. "When they come, we need to be ready."

"You think we can be ready by working on the formula Dad gave you?" Parker stood up beside me but kept his eyes on the crater. "You really feel sure this one won't go bad, the way Eclipse did?"

"Eclipse caught Dad by surprise when it let Takers take over Dreamers permanently." My gut wrenched inside me. I shared Parker's fear but was trying to keep it buried. "I'm sure he wouldn't let anything like that happen again."

I turned to walk back to Parker's car, but my brother caught my sleeve and stopped me. His questions were making me feel smothered, and it took enormous control not to yank my arm out of his grasp.

"Jack, Dad was Divided. At the end, he was pretty far gone…" Parker let the question hang in the air, and it stung to hear it.

"I trust him." I spun back to face my brother, despite the pain it caused me to look into his ice blue eyes that were so much like Dad's. Looking at them made me feel like I was ripping open wounds that were still too fresh to heal. "Maybe you should too."

"Okay, okay." Parker held his hands up in front of him as a sign of surrender and took a step back.

I immediately regretted my reaction. I considered apologizing, but instead turned to walk back to the car.

"Tell me this, though." It only took three steps for him to catch up with me. "This new formula is supposed to help the Takers sleep like Dreamers—like regular people?"

I nodded.

"Would it work on Watchers too? Could it make us not need Builders anymore?"

It was a good question, one I'd looked into myself when Dad was first trying to come up with the formula. "No. Each type of Night Walker has a different brain chemistry. It wouldn't do the same thing to Watchers because it's designed to work in the brain of a Taker."

Parker scratched his cheek. "Okay, that makes sense. Well, at the very least it should put us on more even footing, right?"

"What do you mean?" I kept walking.

"I mean, Watchers would die too without Builders to help them get real sleep. So this drug should, theoretically at least, do what the Builders do ... but for the Takers instead of the Watchers?"

"Yeah ... what's your point?" When I reached the car I opened the driver's side door, but Parker shook his head.

"You aren't driving again," he said.

"Why not?" Did everything have to turn into an argument with him? Every time we talked it felt like I was trying to swim upstream.

"Because it's *my* car." Parker lowered his chin, but I just stared at him and waited. I'd wanted to bring my motorcycle. The only reason we'd even taken this crappy car was because Parker had insisted on coming with me.

He knew it. I just had to wait for him to realize it.

With a sigh, he tossed me the keys and climbed into the passenger seat.

After I'd shoved the keys in the ignition, he continued,

obviously irritated. "My question is, if the formula we're trying to make is supposed to help them, then why don't we just tell them that? Wouldn't they want to help us help them?"

I laughed.

"What?" Parker's anger was growing. "Chloe might be the only Taker I know, but she doesn't seem *that* unreasonable."

"Yeah, sure." I shrugged and then threw him a piercing look. "She just tried to take Finn over permanently and then kill you for finding out about it."

Parker frowned. "But she also helped me set him free, and she hasn't tried anything since she's been back in her own body."

"That we know of…"

"You don't know—"

"People don't change, Parker. It isn't in them." I gave a firm shake of my head and tightly gripped the steering wheel.

"Why do you have to be so frustrating?" He growled the last word out low, but his voice still echoed across the tiny car.

"Better watch it." I put the car into gear. "You're starting to sound like *him*."

Parker deflated immediately and looked like I'd punched him in the gut. I almost regretted my words … but he needed to remember what it felt like, didn't he? How else could he try to prevent his darker side from breaking free again?

He slid down into his seat, completely silent as I drove toward the main road. Every minute of his silence added to my guilt until I filled the void with the answer he'd been asking for in the first place.

"The Takers won't help us help them because they don't

think it's as simple as choosing to 'live' or 'die.' They believe that with Eclipse they had the power to be like gods, and they want to find a way to get that back." Parker turned his head enough toward me that I could tell he was listening, so I went on. "To them, this is a choice between living like gods, or losing that ability and becoming normal."

Parker slouched down in his seat. "For so long, I would've done anything to just be normal. You're telling me there aren't any of them who would choose that?"

"Those who would are going to be hard to find, let alone organize. Dad told me they spent years basically being brainwashed by a man named Steve Campbell. He was the leader of the Takers and started this war to begin with."

Even saying Campbell's name made every emotion in me twist into a tight ball of rage. I'd deliberately kept Parker unaware of all the details about the man and what he'd done to ruin our lives.

"He's dead now," I continued, "but he did plenty of long-term damage while he was still around. He convinced the Takers that even if their lives are shorter than Watchers' or Builders' lives, being able to use other people's bodies and invade their minds is an immense power. Because of him, they believe that they truly *live* more in twenty years than a normal person does in a lifetime."

Parker shook his head. "That's crazy."

"Exactly."

TWO

JACK

The rumpled paper in my pocket felt like a branding iron waiting to mark me as a disappointment, a failure. Even from the grave, Dad was managing to give me challenges that felt impossible.

I scanned down the laptop screen that I'd already read three times, knowing that it held nothing that would help me figure this out. There was a simple truth here... either Dad had screwed up, or I was missing something important.

Moving to lean against the wall, I stared hard at all the lab equipment I'd managed to gather from Dad's warehouses over the last few weeks. He'd rented storage spaces throughout Oakville and kept full labs in each one in case he needed to work. He said it ensured he'd always have a lab he could go to, and we'd never have to lug his equipment around when we had to suddenly bolt in the middle of the night.

When Parker's mom agreed to let me use the storage room between Parker's bedroom and the door to the garage, I'm sure she didn't expect me to set up a laboratory. But she hadn't said anything.

Maybe she did expect it ... after all, she *had* been married to our dad.

But despite all of my hard work, the equipment and chemicals were going mostly unused. Nothing, including visiting Benton Air Force Base yesterday hoping for some kind of inspiration, had provided the answers I still needed.

"Jack?" Chloe stared at me as she leaned against a table on the other side of my lab, waiting. She'd asked the same question every day for the last month: when will the new drug for the Takers be ready? I still couldn't give her the answer she wanted.

The formula Dad had given me was fairly basic, nothing overly complicated. The only problem was that in place of three of the ingredients, he'd scribbled in the numbers 1, 2, and 3. Dad had always loved puzzles, and he was beyond paranoid at the end of his life, but so far I'd had no luck filling in those blanks. I'd hoped maybe to find a clue at one of his labs, but there was nothing.

And I was going to have to tell Chloe the truth sometime.

I wasn't sure I even wanted to make this formula in the first place. Takers had been responsible for my mother's death as well as my father's. Why would I want to work so hard just to save the people I'd spent my life hating?

But I knew why—it was because Dad had asked me to. He wanted this war between the different types of Night Walkers to end, and he was sure the incomplete formula in my pocket was the way to do it.

So I would figure this out … even if it killed me.

There was one extra word scribbled in at the very bottom of the formula. It was the main reason I'd gone out to the base to begin with, and even though I'd had no luck there, I had to believe he'd written it for a reason. The word was "buried."

Not my idea of hopeful, but hey, that was Dad …

"The new drug isn't ready, and it won't be for a while."

I stood with my back straight, hoping that once I told Chloe everything, she would stop asking, at least for a couple of days. She'd been around a lot since Parker had separated her from Finn's body. Some days it wasn't half bad … I mean, she was obviously hot when she wasn't pissed at me.

"I'm working on it," I added. "It's just not going to be as simple as I hoped."

"The deal was, I help baby-bro Parker save his buddy Finn and you help me survive. Right?" Chloe shifted her weight and stepped closer. Her stance was casual, but her eyes were gray storm clouds. As always, they begged for a fight.

A fight I could handle, but the darkening circles of sleep deprivation beneath her eyes made me look away. They were a reminder that this latest challenge from Dad was taking longer than either of us wanted.

Chloe was the only Taker I'd ever spent more than five minutes with and not tried to throw any of my knives at.

Actually, that wasn't true. I did throw a knife at her once, but it was when she'd taken over Finn's body, so I'd missed on purpose. I rubbed my fist against the rivets on the right leg of my jeans, trying to decide if that counted or not.

Grabbing the neat stack of clean clothes from the corner, I threw them into my duffel bag, on top of everything else I'd never quite unpacked. I kept my voice perfectly calm. "Yes, that was the deal, but—"

"But what?" she demanded. "It sounds pretty damn simple to me!"

Zipping the bag closed, I double-checked that I'd put my cell phone in the pocket of my jeans. Taking a breath, I mentally braced myself for the fight that was bound to come after I told her the whole truth. "Look, I'm trying, but what Dad left me about the formula...it isn't complete."

She stepped away from the wall, all pretense of this being a casual chat shattered. Her voice turned to a whispered hiss. "What?"

I stood my ground and met her hard gaze, despite the fact that she was a Taker and I had made it a goal to *never* meet the eyes of someone like her. "He gave me most of it, and a clue to find the rest, but I need time."

"Time isn't always something we can get more of." Chloe took another step closer. She masked it well, but the roiling emotion behind her stiff expression was hard to hide. "I don't understand. If he really created this formula to help the Takers, then why wouldn't he give you the whole thing?"

"Because he's learned through years of experience not to trust people like you."

She looked away, but I wasn't done.

"Because even when he was trying to help Takers, he felt he had to build in safeguards. He had to make sure you needed his sons alive in order to make it." I stepped a bit closer, and her eyes came up to meet mine again. "He didn't want your kind to be able to grab the formula, kill Parker and me, and make it yourselves."

"Fine," she muttered. "I get it."

"Good."

"Even so." She rubbed her eye with her right hand and the shadow beneath it stood out in even stronger contrast. "It sure would've been nice for me to know this little detail *before* we made that deal, don't you think?"

"I'm working on the problem." I pulled the duffle bag's strap over my shoulder.

"That's not good enough, Jack." Her hands curled into small fists at her sides. After our last conversation, I already knew she wasn't afraid to use them to work out a little frustration. My quick reflexes were the only thing that had kept her punch from landing.

Not that I blamed her for being frustrated; what she was facing was terrifying. To be dying slowly, your mind eroding away from lack of sleep, with no way to stop it— any Watcher could understand how that felt. That was why this formula was so important.

I walked around her toward the door. "Well, it has to be enough. This is my responsibility, and—"

"Screw responsibility! This is my *life*, Jack!" Chloe grabbed my shoulder and jerked me back until I was staring into her eyes. She took down her mask completely, wanting me to see the desperation and fear she was feeling. I drew it all in, meeting her gaze, willing her to believe I really *was* on her side.

I couldn't guarantee I would always be on her side ... but for right now, I was.

I understood too well the weighty responsibility that rested on my shoulders: the fate of not only her life, but the lives of many, *many* more. All of the Takers' lives—plus the lives of ordinary people, which the Takers could and would destroy if I didn't find a way to stop them.

Watchers my age had been raised to despise all Takers. We were polar opposites in many ways—Watchers learned how to blend in when we were in the mind of someone who was dreaming. As much as possible, we tried not to disrupt the Dreamers. Takers did the opposite. They took over the actual bodies of Dreamers while they slept, and often left nothing but rubble in their wake.

I shook the thoughts from my head. The Takers had been my enemies for a very long time, but for right now I had to focus on a different part of our relationship: the similarities. The Takers were still Night Walkers, just like me. And so no matter how much I disliked them—and yes, at times even Chloe—I would still find a way to save them. Dad sacrificed himself to save Parker and me, so I would finish the task he gave me.

As tough as Chloe always tried to act, her fingers trembled as they gripped my arm.

"I know *exactly* how important this is, Chloe." I enunciated every syllable as I backed slowly toward the storage room door, and her hand fell back to her side. "So please, let me do what I need to do. I want to keep my promise."

The door opened behind me and hit the back of my shoe, but I didn't turn when I heard my brother's voice.

"Uh, am I interrupting?"

"No." I stepped forward and shifted my bag so Parker could open the door the rest of the way. When I turned around, his gaze was on my duffel. He raised his eyes to mine and I pulled out my phone, studying it like it held some fascinating secret.

"You're leaving right now?" His face fell into a deep frown.

I didn't look up as I answered. "I told you that last night on the way home from the base."

"Yeah." He rubbed his thumb along his chin and added, "You said the same thing the night before that, and the night before that."

Finn, Parker's best friend, poked his head around the corner, shaggy pieces of auburn hair hung across his right eye. "You're really going?"

I groaned. "Yes, if you two will stop blocking the door."

Finn shuddered when he saw Chloe standing behind us and jerked backward out of the room. He'd been avoiding her—more specifically, avoiding eye contact with her —as much as possible. It had been very awkward ever since she'd taken over his body … not hard to see why.

Of course, there was a lot more to the whole Dreamer-Taker connection than just making the mistake of looking at a Taker. The Dreamer, Finn, would have to go to sleep after the eye contact, and Chloe would need to lie down and enter the Taker version of sleep—which looked like sleep, but was actually more like a light coma state. And Chloe would need to do this before making eye contact with anyone else. Although Finn basically knew all of that, it didn't seem to make him feel any better about being around her. I guess once someone has trapped you in your own mind and tried to kill people using your body, forgive-and-forget isn't really an option.

Reaching out one long arm, Finn yanked on the back of Parker's shirt until he too moved out of my way. I got one quick glance at Finn's shirt—*If history really repeats itself, I'm SO getting a dinosaur*—before it was out of sight. Although I didn't know him that well yet, even I had to admit the guy was pretty entertaining.

"Anyway, I think I know where I'm going now." I stuck my phone into my pocket and adjusted my bag. After Chloe stepped out, I locked the lab door behind me and stepped past Parker.

"Where?" Parker's expression was dark as he followed me down the short hallway. Even without looking him in the eye, I could see this argument coming from a mile away.

I looked around to make sure Chloe hadn't followed us. I'd been worried over the past month that she might be reporting back to the other Takers, even though she'd given me no hint of it. For the first few weeks I'd occasionally followed her, or grabbed her phone when she wasn't looking to check for texts or calls to her brothers. If Parker hadn't agreed to try to help her after she separated herself from Finn, I would never have let her hang around. She was a risk…and a big one.

"Dad and I lived in a trailer outside Logandale a few years back," I said. "I need to go there." I muttered the part that concerned me under my breath: "I think."

Parker said, "How will this help exactly?"

"In the formula, there are numbers standing in for three missing ingredients. And the word 'buried.' Logandale is a place where Dad might have buried something he wanted me to find later." I crossed to the kitchen counter and leaned against it, trying not to get bumped as Finn dug around in the fridge beside me.

Parker popped the knuckles on his right hand. "So you think he buried a list of the missing information out on a trailer lot somewhere?"

I shrugged. "Maybe he told people the information and buried his address book. Or maybe there's nothing there at all. It's just a place to start."

"Could he have buried actual ingredients there?" Parker looked incredulous, and I couldn't deny that I had doubts of my own.

"I don't know, Parker." This was starting to feel like an interrogation, so I did my best to shut down any further questions he might have. "I think Danny—Dad—didn't want anyone else to be able to make this formula without my help. It's an insurance policy for both of us, because if the Takers hurt either of us, then I'll burn every reference to it and they can all just die for all I care."

When I turned around, I saw Chloe standing in the doorway. She caught my eye over Parker's shoulder, and I immediately regretted my words when I saw the hurt in her expression. It's not that I hadn't meant what I said ... but I hadn't intended for her to hear me say it.

Finn sidled across the room in the awkward silence and took up a post in the opposite corner of the room from Chloe.

Parker didn't say anything, and his mouth pressed into a firm line. Then he sighed. "Fine, give me five minutes to pack some stuff."

"No need. I shouldn't be gone too long if it goes well. Logandale's only an hour away, and I'll let you know what I find." I walked around him and propped the door to the garage open with my bag while I lifted my motorcycle keys off the counter.

Parker shook his head, looking frustrated. "You want me to stay here?"

"Yes, for now." I braced myself for the argument I could see coming. "Would you move my bike out back and throw the tarp over it? It's probably in your mom's way, and I need to get on the road."

Parker shook his head before I'd even finished my question. "I'm coming."

"No," I replied, trying to make it clear from my tone that there was no room for argument.

"You need my help."

"I do, but not this time." I tossed him the motorcycle keys and he caught them on instinct before they hit his chest. Chloe had left, probably angry with me for what I'd said, but I still lowered my voice when I continued. "You can help me most by staying here in case it takes longer than I think. Keep an eye on things. Watch Chloe, and keep her out of the lab. The Takers are still too shaken to do much—what Dad did set them back years. His explosion destroyed the little bit of Eclipse he'd made, as well as their only access to the formula. But like I said, they'll be gearing up for a fight soon. You need to watch for signs of it coming."

Parker still looked like he wanted to argue, so I turned and walked out the door toward the van before he got a chance. Besides, I did have a point, whether he wanted to admit it or not. Something told me the Takers weren't just going to forgive and forget how Dad blew up half the base, all of the Eclipse formula, some of the Takers who'd held him captive . . . and himself.

My heart throbbed with an empty ache in my chest, and I pushed the thought away.

Living with a target on my back was never comfortable, but it was also the only thing I'd ever known. Dad had taught me to be smart and survive this way. He'd wanted Parker to have something different, a more normal life. I would do my best to make sure Parker still had it, even now.

As I passed through the garage, I grabbed a shovel and some rope.

"Planning to bury people, are we?" Finn asked in a cheery voice from somewhere behind me.

"Could be … or to dig them up."

I guess they could tell I wasn't in a joking mood, because no one commented again.

I grunted as I hefted everything up and placed it in the passenger side of the white van we'd stolen from the Takers' base. When I'd learned that Mason, one of the prisoners we'd rescued, hadn't destroyed the van like we'd planned, I asked him to give it back. It came in handy for projects when my motorcycle just wasn't going to cut it.

I glanced around the yard to see if Chloe had come out here. I'd wanted to at least give her a quick wave before I left, but she was nowhere in sight. She must've disappeared again; not all that surprising. If there was anything I'd learned about her over the past month, it was that she had a tendency to come and go whenever and wherever she pleased, with no warning.

In that respect, I guessed she was a lot like me.

Parker was leaning against the driver's side of the van when I walked around. I wrapped one arm around his shoulder in a quick hug that also helped move him somewhat out of the way. "Take care of yourself. They know who you are, but they'll probably be afraid to retaliate for everything when they're so desperate to get Eclipse back. They probably think we're the only people who might have a clue how to make it."

"You're the only one who might have a clue." Parker pulled back and frowned. "That formula Dad gave you looks like gibberish to me."

"First, they don't know you don't understand it, and *please* don't tell them." I leveled my gaze at him, forcing myself not to react to his eyes. "Second, without the last three ingredients, the formula isn't useful to anyone—myself included."

"Right." Parker didn't move from where he stood, blocking me from closing the door and leaving. "Are you sure you can't wait another day or that I can't come with you? I still have so many questions, and you promised to tell me more about Da—"

"I'm sure." I nudged him out of the way with my arm and closed the door. "And we'll have time for questions and answers later ... after I've finished this."

I stretched my neck to one side, forcing myself not to dwell on the hurt my brother was struggling to keep from showing on his face. This conversation was complicated, and I was itching to get moving. I was already past tired. It had been too long since I'd slept in a Builder's dreams. Addie, Finn's sister, was the only Builder I knew in this town, and since Parker and Addie had gotten their relationship problems worked out, it seemed weird to step in. Not to mention that she was busy being *his* Builder.

The more time I spent with Addie—awake or asleep— the more I had to remind myself that she was unavailable. I'd avoided her dreams except when things were getting really bad. And although her friend Mia was no Builder, her self-hypnosis-induced dreams had helped me more than I'd expected. But still, they weren't the same as a Builder's dreams.

And figuring out Dad's formula required me to be alert and rested. That meant one thing for certain—after I checked out the old Logandale spot, I would go to the

Night Walker rebel camp at Cypress Crest and see Libby. I really was tired, and she was the best Builder I'd ever met. Plus, I missed her. The two months I'd been with Parker were the longest we'd gone without seeing each other since we were kids. It felt weird being apart like this.

And, between Addie and Parker being together and the newest romantic developments between Mia and Finn, there was yet another reason I needed to get out of here. It was getting very ... *gooey* lately.

Although I had to admit it was almost worth it to watch Chloe around Addie and Mia. She would get a stiff spine and a wary look in her eyes every time they were nearby—it was like she was afraid those girls might accidentally touch her and make her soft.

I'd tell her she could use a little softening, if she asked me—which was probably why she'd never ask.

"Well, I'd better get going." I looked at Parker through the window of the van. "I have my phone. Keep me updated and be careful."

He nodded reluctantly and took a few steps back.

I waved at Finn and put the van in reverse. The vehicle was far from nice, but it belonged to me now—I'd secured it with fresh plates after I got back it from Mason. It felt like a better choice for this mission than my bike, since I didn't know what or who I might need to bring back with me. Also, I could sleep in the backseat if it turned out Dad's paranoia would make this quest long and complicated.

Parker walked back up to my open window and I kept my foot on the brake. "So, three missing pieces, huh?"

"Yep."

"You really think you can figure this out?"

I let out a fast puff of air and the speedometer in front of me fogged. The tension from that one question tightened every muscle in my upper body. If we had the key to helping the Takers sleep—and survive, then there was hope they *might* come to an agreement with us. The Night Walker Society could finally be what it was intended to be when it was founded: a place of refuge for people who lived in a world of nightmares. A place to escape to a life worth living. It could be what Dad had always wanted it to be—what I still wanted it to be.

"Dad thought I could." I swallowed hard and met my brother's eyes.

Instantly, my heart ached. While Parker had spent years getting used to the idea of never seeing Dad again, I'd only had a month...and the gaping hole Dad left didn't seem to be healing very fast.

"Guess his faith will have to be enough," I added.

Parker put his hand on my shoulder and gave it one final squeeze. "That's good enough for me."

THREE
JACK

It took an hour to get to Logandale and another half-hour to find the remote patch of land where the trailer was parked when Dad and I had lived here. That was shortly after Mom had died and he'd come back to Cypress Crest to get me. When he took me away from the rebel camp and brought me out to the middle of nowhere, I'd wondered what he was planning to do with me.

I hopped out, grabbing the shovel from the passenger side. The brush on the land was wild, having gotten way past overgrown in the couple of years since I'd been here. One particular bush was still misshapen in the back from where I used to climb under it when Dad called out for me to hide. I could almost hear his barking order echoing across the open air, bouncing off the empty land: "Jack, now—*GO*."

It happened regularly. Sometimes someone was heading our way. Sometimes he just wanted to test me.

Either way, I'd gotten very good at hiding.

It felt so weird to be able to openly refer to Danny as my dad. I'd always known he was—it wasn't ever kept a secret from me, but it was something we never shared with anyone else. He told some people that he was looking out for a friend's kid, others that he was training me; whatever lie he felt worked best for the situation.

But I was *never* allowed to call him "Dad" even in private. He was afraid I might then slip up in public and somehow reveal our secret. Parker was the only thing he felt vulnerable about; he was terrified people could use Parker to hurt him. His son, his weak spot.

He could never let his enemies find out he had more than one of us.

In the back of my mind, I remembered the only time I'd called him Dad. I was eight, and it just took two seconds for him to lift me up and pin my back against the wall.

"*Danny*—not Dad," he growled, glancing over his shoulder even though we were completely alone. "*Never Dad*...do you understand?"

My lungs burned with the need for air, but I was proud I kept my emotions in check as I nodded. He released me and I slid down the wall.

He might have been rough, but his tactics worked. I'd never made that mistake again.

I surveyed the land, trying to remember everything as it was the last time I'd been here, five years ago. Ten feet in front of me stood the remains of the makeshift fire pit where we'd cooked our meals many nights. Ten feet to my right was the spot Dad had set up a target and taught me to use first a slingshot, then a BB gun, and eventually throwing knives. About a mile over the rise to the left, he'd set up a shooting range and taught me to fire a rifle and then a hand-gun. We'd been here longer than anywhere, but almost every sign of it was gone now. How fast Mother Nature could wipe away every footstep we'd left behind.

My feet took me further into the lot without a thought to guide them. There was a clear spot here where nothing grew. No weeds, no wildflowers—no beauty of the land broke through this soil. A vivid memory came floating back; Dad had poured so much rock salt in this spot I wasn't sure if anything would ever grow here again. I smiled tightly and my chest twisted with bittersweet pain. Even nature couldn't erase Dad completely.

Dust swirled around my feet as a breeze kicked up. I could still see Dad standing across the empty lot from me, waiting for me to attack—teaching me to fight—teaching me to kill.

"Come at me high." He bent his knees and waited. His eyes, always rimmed with shadows and exhaustion, somehow still looked alert and ready for whatever attack I had planned.

I'd circled him, hands up, blocking as I searched his stance, his body, and his eyes for weakness. *Find the weakness and you've won.* He'd taught me that lesson time and again. There was always a weakness.

Then I saw it—the slight dragging of his right foot, the smallest hint there was something wrong. He'd been cornered by some Takers the day before. I knew there'd been a fight, but he'd said everything was fine when he came home. Standing up straight, I dropped my hands and stepped forward.

"You got hurt?"

He pounced before I could take a breath. I got one arm up in time to absorb the blow from his fist, but he swung his right foot out—the one he'd been dragging only an instant before—and I was on my back, his forearm cutting off my oxygen before I could blink.

I struggled against him. Pushing and shoving with all my strength, fighting for the air I knew I needed. But I was only eleven, and he had me out-muscled and out-maneuvered on every side. As always, Dad kept me trapped until my vision started to darken and my body shook with the desperate ache for air before releasing me.

Coughing, I rolled onto my side to face him as rich, sweet oxygen flowed into my lungs and through my veins. He paced in front of me with no sign of injury, the slight limp from before completely gone. My head pounded as I climbed to my feet.

"You—you're not hurt?" Still dizzy, I rested my hands on my knees to regain my balance.

"No." He looked a little sad behind his smile and I wondered how much I'd disappointed him.

"Then why—?"

"Because, Jack." He shook his head and sighed. "I was going after *your* weakness."

As I stepped across the overgrown lot now, I heard a light second step somewhere behind me. Abruptly, my instincts brought my mind fully back to the present. There was someone else here—right here, right now—and they were setting my senses on edge.

I casually moved another step forward, behaving exactly as before but now with all my focus on my stalker, whoever it was. I kicked a rock across the landscape and watched it bounce as I rested my shovel on the ground in front of me.

There ... a crunch of dirt, behind me to the left. Then a muffled footstep, two ... I waited again, another moment until he was close enough. Now—

I spun into a crouch and grabbed the two sneakered feet in front of me. I didn't recognize the vibrant purple laces until I'd already jerked up and toward me.

Chloe fell hard onto her back, and I had her pinned to the ground before she could react. Her wide gray eyes stared at me in shock as she struggled to catch the breath I'd knocked out of her. A strand of her white-blond hair was stuck to her dark eyelashes and she blinked, trying to make it fall away.

Reaching up, I hooked one finger under the strand and pulled it to the side. My motion caught her off guard, and she watched me closely as she panted. My heart beat fast in my chest and I quickly moved off her. Chloe was very smart, and she already knew how to get under my skin.

I wasn't about to show her that there were probably a few more ways she could do that.

"What are you doing here?" I kept my voice low and

my anger in check, forcing back the guilt I felt when she winced and rubbed the back of her head.

"What do you think, genius? I snuck into the back of your van because I can't get enough of the smell of oil and old upholstery?" She struggled up onto her elbows. "I'm here to help."

"You shouldn't have come." I hopped to my feet and held out a hand to her, but she glared at it and stood up on her own.

"Let me help." A weed was tangled up in the hair on the right side of her head. I stared at it, trying to decide whether it was a good idea to touch her again.

She shifted her weight to one side and rubbed her hands against her jeans to brush the dirt off. Her eyes never left me, and finally she said, "What are you looking at?"

I grunted under my breath. My hand approached and she froze, eyeing me warily.

Taking another step closer, I closed my fingers around her shoulder and reached for the weed. Once I'd freed it, I held it in front of her eyes before releasing it to the ground at our feet. "Why?"

She cleared her throat twice. "W-why what?"

"Why would you even want to come with me?" The skin of her shoulder had felt hot beneath my fingers. I flexed my hand as I dropped it back to my side.

She bent forward, flipping her hair upside down and running her fingers through the strands to shake out another weed and some dirt. Then she stood upright and was suddenly very close—too close—but I wasn't going to be the one to back away.

She finally answered. "Because I want to make sure you aren't going to disappear or back out on me, Jack. This is too important to me . . . to all of us."

I sighed. "Do you trust anyone?"

"No."

"Why don't you go home to your family?" I watched her for any reaction. After monitoring her for those first couple weeks, I'd eased up. I'd figured my options were either to let her go—and, if she betrayed us, not save her life with the new formula—or tie her up and watch her constantly. I didn't have time to do that, and Parker's mom would definitely have frowned on me keeping a prisoner in the storage room.

"I—" She looked away and withdrew a step, turning her back on me. "I just need to make sure you don't forget our deal."

"Fine, but the first time you get in my way or slow me down . . ."

"I won't." She glanced at me over her shoulder, her sudden smile distracting.

I bent over and picked up my shovel, muttering as I walked over to the spot where our trailer had once been parked. "It isn't if, it's when."

It was clear from Chloe's expression that she'd heard me and didn't appreciate it. She gestured at the area I'd been pacing on earlier. "I hate to interrupt all of . . . this, but are you just going to walk around and stare at the ground all day or are we here trying to accomplish something?"

I pushed my knuckles hard against my forehead, fighting off the wave of memories that threatened to wrap me up and wash away what was left of me. "We'll do something."

"And what's that?" She crossed her arms over her chest.

"We're going to dig, and I don't know how deep we have to go." My voice was grimmer than I intended, but her attitude was bothering me and we'd only just started.

When she walked over, I passed her the shovel and plastered a cold grin on my face. "You get to go first."

FOUR
PARKER

I sat on the couch with Finn watching a behind-the-scenes documentary on the making of an old Bruce Lee movie. Finn's shirt today was one of my favorites. It said, *Dear Math, I'm not a therapist. Solve your own problems.*

Classic Finn.

Addie and Mia were supposed to be here soon, and I was having a hard time sitting still while I waited. I needed Addie. Everything with my brother had been so uncomfortable lately, and she somehow always knew exactly the right thing to say or do to make me feel better.

Jack had been gone for over an hour. He'd probably reached Logandale by now. As always, his first instinct was to leave me behind. I was sure I could've helped somehow ... if he'd let me.

I was getting really sick of being shut out.

The doorbell rang. I hopped up immediately and went to answer it. Addie smiled at me brightly from the porch steps and my tension began to seep away immediately. Mia stood just behind her and gave a little wave.

"Are you ready?" Addie asked.

"Yeah, Jack's gone. Come on in." I leaned over for a quick kiss before backing toward my room. "I'll grab the laptop and meet you guys at the table."

Addie had her pen and notebook out by the time I came back. The TV was off and the three of them were waiting expectantly for me to return with the laptop.

Addie scanned her notes. "So, last time we were looking for references to Eclipse and came up pretty empty—"

Finn interrupted. "If you're certain we should rule out any reference to vampires ... "

"I'm sure." I laughed as I opened the computer and pushed the power button.

Mia smiled at Finn and shook her head before giving me a sympathetic glance. "And the time before that, we looked up your dad."

"Right." I popped the knuckles on my right hand and forced myself not to show how much it hurt me to talk about him. "Didn't find much there either, except for the police reports from when Mom reported him missing."

"So what do we research this time?" Mia asked.

I scratched the back of my neck and thought for a minute. "Let's look up any news about Benton Air Force Base first."

"Got it." Addie jotted my suggestion onto her list and I typed the words into my browser. Finn scooted around the end of the table and read over my shoulder.

"Most of these are about the base closing in 1987 ... " I glanced over at Finn as I scrolled down the page. "Let me know if you see anything different."

He nodded and squinted as he stared at the screen.

Midway down, I spotted an article from last month. "Here's one."

Opening it, I skimmed through, reading the important parts aloud. "*Base used to be a central training hub for new Air Force pilots ... it stood vacant and abandoned for so many years ... *" Then I stopped and stared at the words.

"What?" Addie asked, but I couldn't find my voice to answer.

Finn took over for me, sounding like he felt guilty for even speaking the words. "*Until an explosion rocked the base in the early morning hours yesterday. Initial reports indicate some kind of gas leak may have caused the explosion, but the investigation is ongoing.*"

I swallowed hard and scrolled further down.

Finn continued before I even had a chance to speak, and I was grateful. "*Reports have come in that bodies were found among the rubble, and it is believed that some of the local homeless population may have been using the base for shelter ... *"

I stared at the words. My dad could've been one of the bodies they found. They might have buried him a month ago with a plain marker and no name. The thought made me feel sick, and I pushed out my chair abruptly and got to my feet. My friends didn't say a word as I walked past them and into the backyard.

After a minute, Addie came out to sit with me. She slipped her hand into mine and sat in silence. I watched a family of bluebirds nesting in a tree a few feet away. They flitted about from branch to branch, chirping to each other—singing. It was nice. Soothing, somehow.

"Finn finished the search." Addie's voice was soft and tinged with worry. "That was the only article written about the base in the last ten years."

"What if they found my dad and buried him somewhere?" I asked after thirty more seconds of silence, looking into her hazel eyes. "What if he has a grave and we can't find him? We can't visit ... can't mourn him right. No one had a funeral or showed up for him."

"You both showed up." Addie shook her head hard. "You and Jack tried to save him, and instead, he saved you. Don't take the meaning of that away."

"I know." I sighed and leaned forward, resting my elbows on my knees. Addie rubbed her hand gently across my back. "I just wish there was somewhere I could go to feel close to him again. The base has been the only thing I had ... and now, knowing they removed some of the bodies, I'm not sure it would feel the same anymore."

"Your dad didn't sound like the type to stay in one place." Addie rubbed the tips of her fingers across my knuckles as she thought. "Given the choice, he probably wouldn't have wanted a grave anyway. Judging from the way he lived his life, he probably would've wanted to be scattered in the breeze somewhere."

I closed my eyes, feeling the truth in her words slightly mend my pain. Jack hadn't answered most of my questions about our dad yet, but still, I knew this part was true.

"And if you need a place to feel like you're close to him ... " Addie leaned over, resting her head on my shoulder. "You figure out where you want that to be, and find your own way to say goodbye. You know we'll all be there with you whenever you need."

I sat up straight and wrapped both of my arms around her, kissing her softly. "You know I love you, right?"

"You better." She grinned up at me and winked. "I'm kind of awesome."

"You're extremely awesome."

"Glad you think so." Addie tucked my hair back, then she kissed my neck lightly and my heart sped up. She whispered, "Because I love you back."

Finn cleared his throat from the doorway and we both pulled back to look at him. He was staring straight up at the sky like he couldn't handle glancing directly at us.

"It's safe to look." Addie laughed. "You know that seeing us kiss won't burn out your eyes or anything."

"Eh ... better not to risk it," Finn muttered as he walked out to us holding a large yellow envelope. "This just got dropped off. It's addressed to you, Parker."

I took it, assuming it was probably some packet of college information. Now that Mom and I agreed I had a future to plan for, I swear she'd started requesting info packets from every university this side of the Mississippi.

But when I flipped it over to check out which school had caught her attention this time, there was no return address label. And when I read my name, my heart skipped a beat. That handwriting... I may not have been able to understand the formula Dad gave Jack, but I'd looked at it enough times to recognize his sloppy scribbles.

I didn't know how or why, but I'd just received a package from my dead father.

FIVE

JACK

This spot *had* to be it. I'd been thinking about it for a while—
it was the only spot that made sense. Dad had always planned
to hide something on the lot. He tried to leave something
small buried everyplace we stayed, and we'd stayed at this
place the longest.

I stopped digging for a minute. The day was getting
warmer, and even though it wasn't noon yet, it was still
mid-summer and the manual labor made me sweat. Wiping my hand across my forehead, I looked over at Chloe.
She'd spread out my leather jacket on the dusty ground
and was sitting on it.

I remembered Dad wearing that jacket while he
explained why the spot between the tree and the barren

patch of ground we practiced fighting on was the best place to bury something.

"You can't choose your spots based on anything that will change," he'd said, pacing back and forth between the two landmarks to keep warm in the chill fall air. "Shrubs or other plants come and go with seasons. Rocks are too easy to move or kick around unless they're big, heavy boulders. Trees will grow, but that only makes them easier to find."

He'd grinned at me and I'd smiled back as he drew an X in the ground in front of him with his toe. "Right here is perfect."

I'd shaken my head, not quite following. "Why? The tree is ten feet away."

"Right below a tree is the first place I'd look, wouldn't you?" He moved to the spot where he'd killed all the plant life with rock salt and then pivoted to face the tree. "So you find two landmarks that aren't going to change. And then bury it right in the middle."

Turning to face the tree now, I knew I was searching in the right place, assuming he actually had buried the answers on this lot. I just had to keep digging. My eyes fell on Chloe again, and I noticed how dirty my jacket was getting. My brow lowered and I clenched my jaw. I guess letting her use it was the gentlemanly thing to do ... I just couldn't decide if I cared whether "gentleman" was ever a word anyone would use when they talked about me.

After all, Dad had taught me everything I knew. Fighting, shooting, picking locks, making a great Molotov Cocktail ... sure, I'd been called many names because of it, but he hadn't spent a single moment teaching me to be a gentleman.

I climbed out of my now three-foot-deep hole, reached for the edge of my coat, and yanked it hard out from under her.

Chloe swore as she tumbled to one side. It was immediately clear from her language that she hadn't received much training on how to be a lady either.

"What the hell, Jack?" She jumped to her feet, both hands already tightened into fists. We'd both taken a couple of turns now and Chloe had rolled up the sleeves of her T-shirt in an effort to cool off.

"You said you wanted to come on this little quest, right?" My voice was completely steady as I shook the dirt off my jacket and folded it in half. When I met her eyes, she nodded slowly. So I said, "It's your turn again to dig."

She grumbled and kicked the side of my shoe as she grabbed the shovel and got down in the hole. I leaned against the tree, watching her. Strands of white-blond hair fell forward out of the clip where she'd tucked them. Every time she bent over for another shovelful, she blew her hair out of her face and the strands floated up in the air like shining flags in the wind before falling back into her eyes again.

I hid my smile behind my hand to keep her from seeing it if she looked up. Chloe was smart, pretty, funny...and a pain in my ass. But deep down I was secretly glad she'd come along. It kept me from getting wrapped up in too many memories. And right now, those only held the potential for more pain.

Besides, Chloe wasn't half bad to hang out with ... when she took a break from yelling at me. That was a pretty big statement coming from me, especially about a Taker.

She pushed the shovel in again, but this time I heard a thud and she stopped short. In one movement, I jumped forward into the hole and grabbed her arm before she could try again.

"Stop! You could set it off!"

I'd pulled harder than I intended and she lost her balance, falling against me and knocking us both back against the side of the pit. Holding tight to her wrist, I pulled her straight toward me to keep her from falling down and over whatever she'd just found. Her hands landed on my chest and her forehead against my mouth.

We both froze. Her hair moved with my panting breath, and my nose filled with the smell of some kind of warm vanilla spice. She was softer than she looked, in all the right places, and our position was just becoming more awkward the longer we were in it.

Chloe raised her face and whispered, "Set *what* off?" Her tone and eyes were filled with fear and the tiniest hint of something else I didn't recognize.

I shook my head, tried to speak, but nothing came out. Clearing my throat, I circled her wrists tighter with my fingers, trying to get into a position to lift her off my chest. "Whatever trap my dad set on that box."

"There's a trap?" Her eyes widened even more. "I don't like how you're making a habit of leaving out important details I could've used earlier."

"If that's difficult for you to adjust to …" I began, ignoring the contrast between the heat from her body on one side of me and the chill sinking in from the cold and unyielding dirt against my back. "Maybe you should go home."

Her brow lowered and she shifted her weight to get off me. I had to slide quickly to the side and lift her up so she didn't end up *accidentally* kneeing me in the stomach.

"Oops," Chloe said.

I ignored her, focusing my attention on the wooden edge peeking out from below the dirt. "The last few years, Dad's been—was—kind of paranoid. Not without good reason."

"Super." She crouched down to look closer. "So what flavor of paranoid are we talking about? The 'wraps things in tin foil' kind or the 'push the wrong button and you die' kind? From your reaction, I'm guessing door number two?"

"Definitely door number two." I knelt before the box and gently brushed the dirt off the top before carefully clearing a bit of the earth from around it. Chloe followed suit and we'd mostly freed the sides within a few minutes.

I studied the large wooden buttons on the front of the box, which were covered in rough engravings. They were sectioned off from each other in large squares, and I knew immediately that there would be one right answer to this puzzle and five wrong ones. Dad was a chemist, not an artist; I tried to recognize something from the various codes he'd taught me. I realized the markings were in Russian, which made sense. Russia was the birthplace of the drug that had started it all, the home of the experiment during World War I that had led to the creation of the Night Walkers. He hadn't taught me much Russian, but it was enough that I recognized the words: семья (family), доверие (trust), лояльность (loyalty), кошмар (fear), предательство (betrayal), and боль (pain).

Now I just had to figure out which square to push.

I knew the one most people might choose, *family*, should be eliminated immediately. Dad would never choose *family*. It needed to be something related to me: I was the only one this box was intended for, so I had to have the answer somewhere in my mind. I racked my brain, repeating the words again and again.

"So, now wha—?" Chloe began.

"Shhh … I'm thinking." I cut her off, trying to stay focused.

"Ah, that's a rare thing. I'll be sure not to interrupt." She leaned back from the box and watched me.

I repeated the words over and over in my mind, trying to think of everything, of anything it could mean.

Family, *trust*, *loyalty*, *fear*, *betrayal*, and *pain*.

Chloe finally scooted over to sit beside me and stared at the words. "What do those marks mean?"

When I told her, she reached up with one hand and scratched behind her ear. "Do you have any idea which to pick?"

"Not *family*. He'd never use that to refer to me. The right answer might be *loyalty*. Being loyal meant a lot to him …" All my energy suddenly felt like it was sucked out through my feet, and my voice came out flat. "He spent a few months believing I'd been disloyal and nearly killed me for it. The answer could be *betrayal*."

I sank back against the dirt in stunned silence. Each beat of my heart was loud and rang with a piercing echo in my ears. Chloe watched me quietly. Could Dad really have chosen *betrayal* as the word for me?

The memories of what happened the last time I saw him—of him attacking me—ricocheted through my mind. He'd pinned me to the floor of his cell and accused me of the one thing I could never do. The emotion of the moment came rushing back, and I struggled beneath the painful weight. The bruises from his hands on my throat had only just faded completely in the last two weeks. If Parker hadn't pulled Dad off, Dad would've killed me. There was no doubt. He'd believed it completely. Even if it was caused in part by his delusions, he'd still believed I was capable of the worst kind of betrayal.

And that hurt more than any bruise his hands could ever leave.

Chloe didn't speak, but she lifted her hand like she was considering reaching out to comfort me—before letting it fall back to her side. That was something I never imagined seeing... a Taker wanting to comfort me.

Then something clicked in my mind. He'd pinned me to the floor of *his cell*. "Never mind. Not *betrayal*." My relief was obvious in my voice. "Dad only believed I betrayed him while the Takers had him locked up. He couldn't have put this box here while he was in that prison. So it must've been before that."

Chloe gave me a wry smile and then shook her head. "Good. I would've thought you were crazy if you tried to convince me your dad chose *betrayal* as a message for you."

"Why?" My tone was tinged with suspicion, and I was almost afraid to hear her answer. I knew if she told me she'd spent time with him while he was being held captive it might make me change my mind about helping her.

She looked hesitant, but finally answered. "Jack ... take it from the enemy. We learned everything we could about your dad and spent years trying to trap him. The one word that doesn't make any sense at all when looking at that box is betrayal."

I felt relieved at her answer, but she looked the opposite. Her shoulders sagged forward a bit and the pain in her eyes reflected part of what I was feeling inside ... I just didn't understand why *she* would feel it.

"Not *family* or *betrayal.*" The look in her eyes disappeared as she refocused on the puzzle. "So *trust, loyalty, fear,* and *pain* are left?"

"Right."

"Do *fear* or *pain* make sense at all?" She bit her lip and stared at the box.

I thought for a moment and then shook my head. "Not really. He always said those were things we had to put out of our minds if we wanted to be able to do what we had to do."

Chloe nodded. "Well, that just leaves us with trust and loyalty then ... but aren't those kind of similar?"

Leaning back against the dirt I tried to remember anything that would help me decide between trust and loyalty.

"My dad always told me to trust no one." I shrugged.

"So did mine." Chloe turned to face me with a grin. "If only we could've been like other kids and made them pay for it the normal way—by spending years watching us in therapy."

I couldn't help but return her smile. The image of some kind of Night Walker kid-support group was too bizarre not to.

"*Loyalty*, then," I said, and when she gave me a firm nod, I shifted closer to the box. It surprised me when she started to move forward with me.

"I hope this is right, but you should get back." Crouching, I gestured for Chloe to climb out of the hole.

"If you die with this box, I might as well die with you." She scooted up next to me, her jaw tight. I was even more surprised when she placed her hand on my shoulder and gave me an unyielding look. "Better to have it be quick than slow and painful, right?"

I swallowed back a tremor of fear and then pressed firmly down on the section of the box bearing the word *loyalty*. The world froze around us as I hoped, more than anything, that I knew Dad as well as he thought I did.

SIX

PARKER

"This...I think it's from my dad." The spoken words felt like they'd vibrated out of me in some strange way.

I didn't look up, but I heard Finn whisper something to Mia and they both came out into the backyard and stood nearby.

My heart pounded in my ears as I carefully opened the yellow envelope and reached inside. My fingers closed around something smooth and leathery. When I pulled it out, the first thing I saw was the symbol of the Night Walker Society staring back at me: a skull and crossbones wearing two eye patches—the Blind Skull.

Dad had sent me his old wallet. I remembered seeing it as a kid, and the same symbol was on Jack's leather jacket. But why was I receiving this now? And how had Dad arranged the delivery when he'd been in the Takers' prison?

A small, folded-up paper fell out of the wallet and onto my lap. I reached for it with trembling fingers and carefully unfolded it.

Parker—

If you've received this, it means I haven't been able to prevent it from being sent. I'm sorry that I'm not there with you now. Know that I died fighting for you and your future. Ask for Jack at the Cypress Crest Trailer Park and tell them I sent you—he has all the answers you need. Give him this note.

I missed you every single day. Never doubt that.

—Dad

Each heartbeat felt like it tore a new hole through me. Reading his words, his thoughts ... realizing he'd always had some kind of plan in place for me to learn the truth. It meant more to me than I thought it would.

At the bottom of the page, the letter continued:

Jack—

It's up to you now. Tell Randall that I said it's time to begin. Trust Parker and no one else. It's time to tell him everything and for you to work together. He is your ally and it's time to act like it. You can do this. I know you can. Do not doubt yourself.

I'm sorry for everything I couldn't do.

—Dad

I gaped at the words. No wonder Jack was so bitter and jealous when we'd first met. The difference between the way Dad acted with me and with him was clear. It was obvious Dad had been afraid some enemy could get ahold of this letter and use it against him, but wasn't that what he'd been afraid of for Jack's entire life? This was just how it had always been between them.

And that made me abruptly sad for my brother.

I couldn't imagine how hard it must've been for Jack ... to always know that Dad was his father but for Dad to never act like it. To see the way Dad talked about me and the difference in how he reacted to his two sons—it must've been hell.

But at least Jack got to know him. I'd have given anything for that simple chance.

"What did your dad say?" Finn asked, and I handed him the paper. He read it and passed it on to Addie and Mia.

I pulled out my phone and hit the power button. It hadn't rung, it hadn't vibrated, and it hadn't beeped ... but I still picked it up and watched it like it could suddenly tell me what Jack was doing and if he was okay. I scrolled through the screens like doing so might tell it I was waiting. Like now that I'd touched it, the phone would suddenly have the information I wanted ... but no, nothing.

Jack had to come back—the sooner the better—and read this letter. I wasn't sure if anything Dad had said to Jack here would help him with piecing together the new formula, but either way, he had to read it.

I pulled up a text box and sent one single message.

You need to come back.

"When do you think your dad sent this?" Addie asked.

"I'm not sure. Sometime before he was captured." I stretched my neck to one side and then the other, trying to let go of the sadness that had seeped into me from the letter. "Being exhausted and Divided for so long had my dad pretty messed up. It sounds like he's been preparing for this a long time."

"I'm sorry," Mia said, and then she bent over to hug me.

I hugged her back, grateful my friends were here with me. I opened the wallet that still sat on my lap and looked through it, but it was empty. And as far as I could tell, except for the symbol on it, it was just a normal wallet.

"Do you think you should call Jack?" Addie rested her head against my shoulder again.

"I texted him to come back. I don't think it's something I should read over the phone, and also, he might see some kind of hidden meaning that I can't. Maybe he'll have an idea what Dad's message is about. For now, I guess we just wait." I stood up, and Finn seemed to know I didn't want to discuss this anymore because he picked up the basketball and tossed it my way.

I dribbled the ball in the warm afternoon sunlight, focusing on the way it felt in my hands and how it bounced differently if it hit a crack in the cement. Anything that might serve as a good distraction. I didn't realize my friends had continued talking until I looked up and saw them all watching me.

"I'm sorry, I'm distracted. What did you say?" I took a

shot and Finn grabbed the ball after it went through the hoop. Addie walked over and draped an arm around my waist.

"It was nothing. We were just discussing whether there's anything we want to do tonight. Are you tired?" She gave me a quick sideways glance before her cheeks flushed a little.

I realized what she was referring to, and I hoped the others didn't notice. The last couple of nights in her dreams, we'd spent a little more time making out than having her actually help me sleep. It was one of the unforeseen hazards—and perks—of your amazingly hot girlfriend also being the Builder who helped you sleep and kept you alive.

"A little." I cleared my throat and sat up straighter. The truth was that yes, I was feeling kind of tired and would have to find some self-control so I could get at least *some* sleep in Addie's dreams tonight. "You come up with any ideas?"

"No…" Addie and Finn said simultaneously.

"Nothing that we can all agree on," Mia added.

"Not surprising." I gave them a half smile and stopped trying to avoid the subject we were all thinking about. "I'm worried about Jack and this formula crap."

"Our searches for information aren't exactly panning out, and he's still not answering many questions," Finn said. After making a shot, he turned to face me immediately. "What else can we do to help?"

"I don't know." I ran my hands through my hair, which I'd let grow out a little longer over the last couple of months. It curled at the back of my neck, and I tugged at the ends, using the little jolts of pain to try to focus my mind on finding an idea that might get me somewhere.

The truth was that what I wanted to do was exactly what Jack *didn't want* me to do. I'd been sitting here all day trying to figure out how to not piss him off and somehow be helpful at the same time. Maybe it just wasn't possible. Maybe I had to give up on keeping him happy. Deep down I knew it was fear that drove me. I was scared that if I made him angry he might disappear again, the way Dad did. The way he had done before.

But I couldn't live like this forever, and I didn't want to.

Brothers were supposed to make each other mad sometimes, right? I guessed now was as good a time as any to see how my big brother was going to react when I did just that.

"I can't sit here and wait for the Takers to attack us again. We know they're going to—we just don't know when, where, or how. I don't want to be here waiting for it to happen, no matter what Jack says." I looked at my friends, and although the fear in their eyes mimicked mine, none looked like they wanted to argue with the idea of taking action. "We have to do *something*. I'm just not sure what."

Mia spoke up suddenly, her voice surprisingly firm. "Maybe we need to start by figuring out what *they* are doing."

Ever since she'd begun meeting with a psychologist a few weeks ago, Mia had really started coming out of her shell. But it still surprised me sometimes. The psychologist had recommended she try taking painting lessons again. Painting had brought out a new spark in her, which was so nice to see.

Addie put her hand in mine, looking nervous. I felt the same way. Especially because every scenario I could come up with to figure out what the Takers were doing left me feeling cold inside. "How could we find that out?"

Mia shrugged. "I don't know, but your side can't be as powerless against the Takers as it seems, can it?"

"I seriously hope not." My voice sounded grim. "We have to be able to do something to fight back."

"I'm not sure." Addie's grip on my hand had tightened so much it was cutting off circulation. "Jack said you were safest here. He said you were helping him here."

"He said I was helping by moving his motorcycle." I sighed and looked at Addie. I hated seeing fear in her eyes and knowing it was because of me. But that fear would never go away until this war with the Takers was over. We could pretend that the Takers weren't out there all we wanted, but it wouldn't make it any better. "This isn't just Jack's fight. I have to help ... and I'll do everything I can to stay safe, but I am not going to just sit here and do as I'm told. Not anymore. I'll come up with some kind of plan. I'm going to help."

Addie still looked scared, but she squeezed my hand tighter and then exchanged a look with Finn and Mia, who nodded. Finally, she turned back to me and said, "Then whatever you decide to do, we're in, too."

Before I could utter my first word of argument, she cut me off. "Don't even start. If there's anything the last year has taught us, it's that our odds are infinitely better when all four of us work together. Don't try to stop us."

The breath I'd been planning to argue with sputtered out of me, and I laughed. "All right then."

Addie grinned, but the look on Finn's face was anything but pleased.

"I was just thinking..." Finn shuddered and then gave me a pointed look that told me that whatever he was about to say, he really didn't want to be saying. "Jack might not be willing to talk to us about the Takers and everything yet, but he isn't the only one we know with answers anymore."

I realized what he was saying instantly and understood his reluctance. I'm pretty sure no one would look forward to working with the person who'd taken over their body for several days. "Chloe."

Addie and Mia both looked hesitant, so I tried to convince them. "I know... but she really is the only option we haven't tried yet. Isn't it worth at least asking her?"

Finn stared down at his feet, but the girls reluctantly nodded.

"Great. Anyone have any way to get ahold of her?"

Addie and Mia both frowned, but Finn closed his eyes and groaned. "I think I remember it..."

He grabbed my phone and punched in a contact entry and number under the name "Body Snatcher" before stalking away and muttering, "I don't want to talk about it."

Right after I sent a quick text to Chloe, my phone chimed with an incoming text. I hoped it was from Chloe or Jack, but Mom's smiling picture popped up instead.

The message was short, sweet, and gave me an entirely new distraction to focus on.

> We need to have a talk about Jack. I'm heading
> home for a bit. If you aren't home, meet me there.

SEVEN
JACK

Chloe tensed when I pressed the button and the puzzle box hissed. Something inside had diffused, and the sound was followed by the click of a latch being released. The front corner of the box rose slightly, and then all was silent.

I waited a full minute for some sort of secondary trigger to engage, but I heard nothing. Moving my body low against the bottom of the pit, I peeked into the small gap below the corner of the lid, releasing each breath from my chest as slowly as possible to be sure not to disturb anything.

I stayed there for several minutes, shifting my position by mere inches, just as Dad had taught me. Patience and diligence kept us safe. That was how we stayed alive.

Be careful.

Be in control.

Always.

The third time I heard Chloe sigh behind me was also the first time I saw the shimmer—the slightest shining bit—in the empty air near the edge of the box. Chloe got to her feet behind me but I barely noticed, my attention drawn to one square inch of apparent void.

"Come on, Jack," Chloe grumbled behind me. "It's a box. You chose the right button and it unlocked. Pick the damn thing up already."

"Shhh…" I said, watching the almost-invisible wire intently, trying to figure out where it attached so I could disconnect it.

Chloe abruptly reached over my shoulder for the lid of the box, and the tips of her fingers passed straight into the tripwire before I could stop her. It looked like she felt the resistance from the tripwire just before I grabbed her wrist. Her lips formed the smallest expression of shock. A split second of regret shone in her eyes before I chucked the box out of the pit as hard as I could and pulled her down into the dirt with me.

The booming shockwave tore across the ground toward us. Chloe and I were showered with dirt, rocks, shredded pieces of paper, and bits of carved wood from the box. We ducked down low in the hole as the secrets I needed rained down around us in hopeless chaos. A few flying bits of jagged wood sliced the side of my face and I wrapped my arms tighter around my head.

The world settled back to normal and I stood up slowly to take in the destruction. There was nothing left. Anything that could have helped me had been destroyed. My jaw clenched and I swore as I stared at the dark scar on the ground where the box had exploded.

Then anger pumped like a living beast through my veins. I wanted to grab her, to hurt her for what she'd just done. Instead, I forced myself to hold perfectly still until I could calm down. Until I could be sure I wouldn't do something I might regret. I heard Chloe coughing beside me, but for once, she didn't speak.

I hadn't even thought about whether to pull her down and save her. It was pure instinct. I hadn't needed to consider it, and there wasn't time. It's what Dad would've done for me, so it's what I did.

And Chloe was lucky for that, because if I'd had time to think about it, I might've thrown her out of the pit with the bomb she'd just set off. It might have been the better option ... for both of us.

I recoiled inwardly at the thought, but it sounded crueler than it was. In reality, it might have been a kindness. At least then I wouldn't have to see her sitting at the edge of my field of vision, a mixture of horror combined with the dwindling of all hope printed plainly across her face.

At least then I wouldn't have to confirm for her that she'd just ruined the only chance I had of saving her life.

"I ... I'm so ... " She didn't finish, but her eyes were wet and she was blinking rapidly. "I didn't think ... "

Unless interfering with my plan had somehow been her intention to begin with.

"Why did you come?" With immense effort, I kept my tone as flat as I could.

"I ... I told you ... " She shifted away from me, looking uncomfortable.

"No. Why did you *really* come? What did the Takers send you to do? Slow me down? Make sure I would fail?" I moved over until she was sitting in my shadow. For the first time ever, Chloe was nearly cowering. She was afraid of me. She should be afraid. I took several deep breaths, deliberately restraining myself, keeping my anger in check like I'd been taught to do. "I will *never* agree to even *try* to make Eclipse again, whether this new formula fails or not. You know that, right? You know that whatever you're trying to pull just ensured the destruction of you and every other Taker?"

"Believe whatever you want to about me, I don't care. I came because *I want to help*." She jumped to her feet, her anger abruptly matching mine.

"*That* was your idea of help?" I growled. Her hair moved from my breath on her face.

She lifted her chin, determined not to show her fear. "Hitting the wire was an accident and I'm sorry—but I'm not ready to give up yet. Are *you?*"

I didn't respond. There was no need. She knew what she'd done. I walked toward the car. Not that I had anywhere to go now, but I had some water bottles in the back and I needed something to drink. *If* she was telling the truth ... then she could probably use a drink, too. If water was our only option, then so be it.

When I came back with the bottles, Chloe was kneeling

in the debris, crouched so far forward it looked like she was trying to smell the earth. For a moment, I thought she was crying, but then I saw her hands moving right below her face.

"What are you doing?" I sat her water bottle on the ground beside her and twisted the top off of mine.

My phone chimed in my pocket. I pulled it out and groaned. Parker's message was cryptic. I hoped whatever he wanted was important. When I put the phone away, Chloe finally answered my question.

"I think... I think I might have something." She looked up at me, but her face was guarded like she was afraid to hope again. In front of her was a pile of the shredded paper she must have gathered from the box. A couple of larger pieces were in her hands, and they shook as she held them out toward me.

I squinted and knelt beside her, trying to make out the words I could already tell were repeating over and over. I was ready to dismiss it as part of Dad's plan to mislead whoever set off the explosion, but then I thought of the gravity of the task he'd given me. He wouldn't have wanted what he'd written to be lost forever just because some Taker had gotten here before I could. I focused on his words, in that handwriting I would never be able to forget.

The second's skull contains the key—
The second's skull contains the key

My mind locked on the words, trying to decipher their meaning.

Chloe's phone went off, and when she read the message she laughed and held it out to me. "Your brother sure is persistent."

This is Parker. I have questions and I think you might have the answers I need. Can you come over?

I laughed softly and shook my head. Persistent was the perfect word to describe him ... sometimes to a fault.

"I'll answer him in a minute." Chloe tucked the phone back in her pocket.

I nodded but kept my eyes on the shredded papers she still clutched in her other hand.

Chloe read the words aloud, and then asked, "What does it mean, Jack?"

"I think it means we can still find the answers we need." I stood up and stretched my back before putting on my sunglasses. "It's just going to be a lot harder now."

"I'm sorry." She got to her feet beside me and this time looked me straight in the eye. "That was stupid. I should've waited."

I looked back at her, surprised by her sincerity, and realized that despite going through two explosions together, I knew very little about her.

As I turned back toward the van, I responded. "You're right. You should have waited, but I'm not ready to give up either."

"Where are we going?" She picked up her water and jogged to catch up, then climbed into the passenger seat.

"My brother wants us to come back, so we're going back." I glanced over at her and said, "Besides, you know how it refers to 'the second' in the message?"

"Yeah?"

I shoved the van into gear and put my foot on the gas. "That's what my dad used to call Parker."

———

As I gripped the handle to Parker's front door, I hesitated. Since I'd left with all of my stuff this morning, I technically didn't live here anymore. A pang of sadness hit me at how much of my family was gone. I was like a plague—anyone who got too close wound up dead. Given this, Parker and his mom were probably safer without me around. I shook off that morose train of thought and jabbed in the doorbell.

I heard footsteps, and when the door opened I was surprised to see Parker's Mom, Mrs. Chipp. One thing I'd learned while staying with them was that she really wasn't home very often, at least not nearly as much as she wished she could be.

"Hi Jack!" She smiled and held the door open, but there was still a bit of hesitation behind her expression.

Ever since Parker had told her everything about Dad and who I really was, she'd gone out of her way to be kind, but there was still that knowledge in the back of her mind that I was her husband's kid with another woman. From the couple of times I'd watched her dreams since she found this out, it seemed like knowing that Dad had left my mom to be with her had shaken her a little. She felt both guilt and some jealousy, which was probably normal...

Or, at least, I guess it would be normal if we could use that word to describe anything about our situation.

"Hi, Mrs. Chipp," I said as I walked in, and Chloe snuck in behind me, keeping her head tucked low. I couldn't help but notice that Parker's mom didn't even acknowledge Chloe's presence. She'd had a hard time even letting her in the house at first, knowing Chloe was a Taker and what she could do, but Parker and I had convinced her that we'd keep Chloe from causing any more damage.

"I said you could call me Emily." Mrs. Chipp put on a fake-stern expression that softened as she smiled. "But do whatever feels comfortable."

She placed a hand on my shoulder. It caught me off-guard and my spine stiffened a little, unsure of what to expect next.

"I'm really glad you came back. I wanted to talk to you today, but then when I talked to Parker, he said you'd left." She glanced behind me at Chloe, who took the hint and scooted past us to wait. It was hard not to feel bad for her, even if she was a Taker.

"Yeah. I'm hopefully only stopping in for a few minutes. I just need to talk to Parker about something." The conversation felt uncomfortable already, and I wasn't sure why. I wondered if I should assure her that I'd be out of their way soon. I'd definitely already overstayed a normal welcome at their house.

Her hand dropped from my shoulder. "Do you have to go?"

That wasn't a question I'd been expecting, especially not from her. "I . . . have something I need to do."

She nodded slowly and brought her eyes back to mine again. She already knew enough about me to understand there were things I wouldn't—and couldn't—tell her. I wasn't certain which details Parker had given her, but she knew our dad had given me a job to do. And that was really all I wanted her to know for now—from me, at least.

"Okay. Well, what I was hoping is maybe when you're done, or when you feel ready, or whenever, really . . . " She shifted back and forth on her feet in obvious discomfort before finally blurting out, "Would you like to stay with us permanently?"

My eyes blinked and my mouth opened, like it knew it was supposed to respond but my brain wasn't supplying it with anything to say. I wasn't prepared for this. She wanted me to *live* with her and Parker? Here—in an actual house without any wheels on it? In a place where you didn't already have a plan for where you would go when you next had to run? My palms began to sweat at just the thought. The idea sounded at once like both heaven and hell. I couldn't give her an answer, though, because I honestly didn't have one.

"I don't . . . "

"Please don't answer right now," she said, like she could read my thoughts. "Just say you'll think about it?"

I straightened my shoulders and tried to act like this

wasn't the most difficult question I'd ever been asked. "Okay, I will."

She smiled widely this time and then abruptly hugged me. It took me a few seconds to recognize that I knew the correct response to this action and awkwardly hugged her back. She laughed lightly into my shoulder and then pulled away. "I know we still don't know each other very well, but as far as I'm concerned, you *are* family. Parker is your brother, and you know what he's going through, being a Watcher too. I'm not like you two...it's hard for me to understand. I spoke with Parker about it and he agrees. We need you. You should be here with us."

"I...thank you." My throat felt tight and those were the only words I could get to come out.

Parker's mom squeezed my arm and then turned toward the kitchen. "I'm heading out to do a showing, but I'll grab Parker for you. Come in and have a seat."

I stood for a moment in the empty entry and was surprised when my balance skewed slightly and I had to steady myself on the door frame. Wow...it had been awhile since I'd been this sleep deprived. I'd lost track of how many nights I'd been without a Builder, but it had obviously been too long. I needed a Builder by tonight. I decided to call Libby as soon as I was done talking to Parker and tell her I was heading to Cypress Crest next. I knew she would leave with me if she could; she always did. We'd grown up together. When I needed her, Libby was there—always.

Once I'd regained my equilibrium, I shook my head and straightened, relieved no one else was here to see me.

This was definitely one of those moments of weakness Dad warned me to never let anyone see.

I moved down the hall, walked around the corner, and ran into Chloe—hard enough that her face hit my chest. She bounced off and knocked a lamp toward the edge of a nearby end table.

"Whoa." I reached out with my right hand and caught the lamp before wrapping my other arm across Chloe's back, pulling her against my chest to steady her. Just from her being so close, my heart doubled its pace. The side of her face was pressed against my neck and I could feel her warm breath inside the collar of my jacket. She pulled back with an awkward laugh and turned her face up to mine. Her eyes looked like dark and light eddies of gray marble from this close. They were absolutely beautiful.

She was a Taker. Her eyes were deadly.

I pulled away so fast her mouth fell open slightly. Then I acted supremely focused on the lamp I held in my other hand, safely returning it to its spot on the table. When I thought this moment couldn't get more uncomfortable, I turned toward the archway in search of a reason to leave.

Instead, I found Finn and Parker standing there watching us, each with a very different emotion stamped across their faces. Finn's expression was slightly horrified, while my brother was trying unsuccessfully not to laugh.

EIGHT

PARKER

"Well, that didn't take long." I smiled and tried not to look too amused. It was hard not to enjoy the thoroughly uncomfortable expression on Jack's face. Taker or not, ever since I'd gotten her out of Finn's body, Chloe was starting to grow on me. Anyone who could make Jack respond with human emotion was good for him.

Finn managed to slip quickly from shocked right back into natural Finn form. "Agreed. This is definitely in the running for the easiest quest ever."

"Not quite." Jack frowned as he walked past us to the dining room and slid into a chair at the table. "Where are Addie and Mia?"

I followed suit, taking the seat across from him. "Mia is taking a painting class and Addie went with her."

Jack looked surprised. "Oh, that's great."

"Yep, it is." I nodded briefly and then got back to the point. "What happened in Logandale?"

Jack studied the wood on the table as Finn sat down on my right. He looked at Finn, out the window, at the floor, anywhere but at me. He was avoiding eye contact with me more and more lately. I just wished I understood why.

"We had a ... problem," Jack said, finally.

I saw a movement behind him and realized that Chloe was the only one who hadn't joined us at the table. She had a tendency to always stick to the shadows around here anyway, probably because of the way Finn reacted to her simply being in the room. But she physically winced at Jack's last word and slipped into a recliner in the living room where she could still see us.

"What kind of problem?" I asked.

"The kind that complicates everything." Jack's words were stiff, but they softened as he continued. "The problem doesn't matter. What matters is that I have a clue for where to keep searching, but I don't really understand what it means."

Finn opened his mouth, but I spoke faster. "I might have something that could help too, but let's start with yours. What was the clue?"

Jack raised his eyebrows in surprise and actually looked me directly in the eye. He must've decided my suggestion was a good one though, because he kept talking.

"'The second's skull contains the key,'" Jack said, his gaze searching mine for some kind of recognition ... or understanding. I repeated the words under my breath.

"'The second's skull contains the key'... what second?" I shook my head, shoulders slumping forward a bit with the heavy weight of disappointing him. My brother had finally turned to me. He wanted to let me help... and I had nothing to offer.

"Cryptic," Finn muttered, raising one eyebrow. "Why isn't anything with your family ever simple?"

I sighed, my brow furrowed. "What am I missing? Do you understand that at all?"

"You." At my blank stare, Jack continued. "When Dad would talk about you, he referred to you sometimes as 'the second,' meaning his second son."

"*I'm* the second?" I sat back in my chair and tried to make sense of the message.

"Wait... so you're saying there's a key in Parker's skull?" Finn's voice went up at the end, and he looked like he couldn't decide if he should put on his best horrified expression or start cracking jokes.

"Yeah... that's the part I don't understand." Jack leaned his head onto his folded arms. He was starting to show signs of the familiar exhaustion that was the worst part of being a Watcher. I tried to remember if he'd mentioned getting any sleep in Mia's dreams lately. I'd been keeping Addie all to myself.

I felt a little guilty for that, but I still had a touch of jealousy that welled up at the idea of Addie and Jack sharing dreams. It wasn't fair of me, and the logical part of me understood that—he needed her dreams as much as I did. But we all knew she'd chosen me, and Jack respected that. However,

I would need to stop being selfish and share if Jack agreed to stay with us long-term like Mom and I both wanted.

I shook off the distraction, refocusing my attention on the task at hand. I needed to up my game if I wanted him to keep letting me help. I tried repeating the clue again to myself.

"The second's skull contains the key..."

Then I stood up so fast I knocked my chair over. Those words... 'the skull'? Of course!

"Parker?" Jack lifted his head and watched me.

I turned, stepped over my chair, and ran to my bedroom shouting, "I'll be right back!" over my shoulder.

I wasn't even down the hall before I could hear Finn picking up my chair and muttering something about "Ungrateful kids never cleaning up after themselves."

The door to my room was shut, and I twisted the handle and ran into it with my shoulder at full speed, flinging it open. I flipped on the light switch and dove for the wallet I'd placed on my desk when Jack hadn't answered my text earlier.

It might not be what the clue was talking about, but it was definitely my best guess.

Springing to my feet, I caught my reflection in the mirror. My breath stopped in my chest for just an instant when I felt an awful sensation screaming that something wasn't quite right.

Every time this happened, I followed the same steps. It was the only thing that could work to set my world back in place again. I closed my eyes, waited for my heart to stop pounding, and listened inside my head for any indication that he was back. For any sign that Darkness had somehow separated from me and we'd become Divided again.

There was none.

It was only me...and my fear.

I opened my eyes and looked in the mirror. Everything was normal.

He was gone—and I seriously needed to get a grip.

I caught my breath as I walked back down the hall. When I rounded the corner, I saw Jack kneeling down by Chloe's recliner. They were speaking quietly enough that I couldn't make out any words.

My eyebrows shot up. This conversation already looked more juicy and personal than anything I'd ever seen from Jack. I felt like I was eavesdropping on something even though I couldn't hear them. Still, I couldn't help smiling a little to myself. Wasn't this kind of what younger brothers were supposed to do? Find ways to gather dirt on their brothers for blackmail purposes down the road? I could totally use some blackmail on Jack. Although I suspected he would be impervious to anything so...mortal.

Jack's eyes caught mine. He stood up immediately and walked over to the table to meet me.

"What's going on?" His brow was deeply furrowed and he watched me close.

"This came in the mail today." I held the wallet out toward him, but he sucked in a quick breath of air and a couple seconds passed before he reached out and took it.

"Dad's wallet?" He slipped down into his seat and touched the worn leather gently, reverently.

I sat down next to him, somehow relieved his reaction to the wallet wasn't much different than mine. Maybe deep inside we weren't so different after all. I reached out and turned the wallet over, exposing the opposite side where the NWS symbol was embroidered. It was strange to be staring at it with Jack, when "Blind Skull" had been the nickname I'd given him when he kept following me, before we'd officially met. That felt like a lifetime ago.

"'The second's skull'?" I smiled, hoping the wallet was somehow tied to the clue like my gut was telling me it was. "Maybe this is the one he meant."

"Good," Finn said. "This option sounds much better than trying to dig out something that's been hidden in Parker's head. It seems like a mess in there."

"You're one to talk…" I barely heard Chloe's words from her spot in the recliner, but I hid my grin when Finn threw a slightly offended glance in her direction.

Jack grunted with the slightest hint of a smile, checking the various pockets of the wallet for any kind of clue or hint that this was what we were looking for. "It just showed up today?"

"Yes. It's empty now, but there was something in it…" My words trailed off. Reading the message from Dad could hurt Jack, and I really didn't want that. Maybe I should just tell him what it said?

"Show me." Jack put the wallet gently down but kept his eyes on it.

There went that option. Reluctantly, I reached into my back pocket and carefully pulled out and unfolded the note before handing it over.

Jack read through it carefully. Except for the slightest muscle twitching in his jaw, there was no indication that it bothered him.

"He must have had this set up and ready to send. Some sort of last resort plan in case he … he … " Jack stopped, looking embarrassed for a second before even that flash of emotion and weakness was gone.

My voice shook, sounding frail next to his strength. I hated both of us for it. "Yeah, that's probably how it got mailed, but why send the wallet? Why not just the note? Is it something to remember him by?"

"No … he wasn't ever what I'd call sentimental." Jack studied the stitching in the wallet for more than thirty seconds. I was almost ready to rip it out of his hands in frustration when he finally smiled and said, "There. I found it."

Standing, I came around the table. He showed me one corner of the wallet where the stitching didn't quite match the rest of it.

"I never would have seen that … " The stitches were nearly identical. You almost had to be looking for the mismatch, or know what to look for. "How?"

Jack gave me a tight smile. "It's nothing. Just a trick Dad taught me a long time ago."

I waited as hope filled me like a giant bubble too hard to swallow or breathe around, but Jack didn't go on. After a second, he turned back to the wallet and started picking at the stitching again.

I pushed aside the pain of knowing just how much better this near-stranger knew our dad than I did. Clapping him on the back, only slightly harder than necessary, I grabbed him some scissors out of a drawer in the kitchen. As Jack carefully unstitched the mismatched section, Finn asked if anyone else wanted food. I didn't respond, but Finn never really needed a consensus when it came to the prospect of food. A few beeps later, I heard the sound of popcorn popping.

"Jack?" I asked, forcing my voice not to sound tentative even though this felt like the millionth time I'd made this request. Finn stood silently behind me, and I could feel his support even though he didn't move or say a word. "I have to know more..."

Jack kept picking at the stitches and for a second I wondered if he hadn't heard, or didn't understand what I meant.

"More about him—"

"*I know.* You're going to have to keep waiting, Parker. This still isn't the time." Jack's voice was sharp enough to slice without the aid of the scissors in his hands. He looked up at my eyes and then literally ducked away, turning his back on me. His voice was softer when he went on, but he'd already inflicted enough pain to leave me reeling. "I'm just not... there's a lot going on. You have to learn to be patient."

It wasn't the first time since I'd become one with Darkness again that I wished I still had the power to unleash my double at will. His anger was still my anger. And now I had a massive dose of hurt, frustration, guilt, and embarrassment to go with it. Was it wrong for me to want to know my dad? He was dead—I would never have the chance that Jack did. We were flip sides of the same coin, different choices one man had made in his life that now collided and kept ricocheting off one another. With each impact we only continued to pick up speed.

And I didn't know how to slow us down, let alone even begin to understand him.

The worst part of it all was the pain. My own brother couldn't look me in the eye. Was he ashamed of me? Did he think I was soft because I wasn't a robot? Everyone was soft compared to him. Did he still hate or resent me because Dad left his mom for mine?

Did he blame me for Dad's death?

Did I blame him?

I hadn't moved, but I could tell from the way Finn was shifting his weight that he was getting ready to jump to my defense, and I honestly couldn't think of anything I wanted him to do less at the moment.

"Dad said to tell me everything," I stated simply, hoping Dad's words would give me the leverage I seemed to need.

Jack raised his eyes and squinted at me. "He meant everything about our *world*, Parker. About what we're facing, about our enemies—not what he was like to be around or what his favorite color was. Knowing those things won't help you now ... they never helped me, anyway."

And then his eyes and focus were back on the stitching, and there was very little left I could say.

"Right ... well, someday then," I grunted, stepping over

to the microwave to watch the rapidly expanding popcorn bag. Fighting to calm down, I couldn't deny that with each day, the gulf between us grew.

By the time the microwave beeped, the room had filled with the smell of buttery goodness and Jack was pulling out the last stitch. I watched from a few feet behind him, holding my breath as Jack reached inside and pulled out a single slip of paper like a fortune from a fortune cookie. I hoped it would at least attempt to tell us what would happen next. Instead, it held a simple message:

You're together now. That's the best gift I could give to either of you. Value that above all else, my sons. I'm so proud of you and I love you both more than anything.

—Dad

NINE

JACK

Now that Parker knew I was going to Cypress Crest, it was impossible to convince him not to come this time. Especially when he threatened to jump in his car and drive there without me. And because I still felt guilty for not answering his questions about our dad, I didn't exactly fight him very hard. Of course, once I'd agreed to allow Parker to tag along, Finn decided to join us. And Chloe was waiting beside the van when we walked out to it the next morning. I was relieved Addie and Mia weren't around to turn this into an even bigger circus.

"I really think it needs a name." Finn turned to look at us like somehow we were all supposed to understand exactly what he was referring to.

"What do you want to name now?" Parker asked with a laugh.

"Anything and everything," Chloe muttered as she opened the van door and climbed into the far backseat. But I saw her hide a small smile behind her hand.

Finn pretended she hadn't spoken as he climbed into the middle seat. "The new drug we're working on. Eclipse had a name . . . maybe we should name this one something similar, about the sky or stars or something, you know?"

I looked at the others. I didn't know Finn well enough to tell if he was kidding, but either way, he had a point. "Like what?"

"Maybe . . . Sunstorm, or Aurora, or . . . "

"If I remember right, Aurora is the name of a Disney princess." Parker looked back at him over top of the front passenger seat, his face more than skeptical. "And Sunstorm sounds like some kind of superhero."

"Exactly! Who doesn't want a name that sounds super?" Finn pointed his finger at Parker's chest for added emphasis.

"Drive now, name things later," I suggested as I climbed into the driver's seat.

Parker turned his attention to his ringing phone as soon as his seat belt was on. He put it on speakerphone so he and Finn could tell Addie, together, about our plan. By the time I got to the corner, Finn was lecturing his sister on what to do with his car, which she was using. "Okay, so don't leave Brewster anywhere weird."

"I still refuse to call your car Brewster, but just for

kicks, where exactly would you consider a weird place to park?" she asked, her tone warm with laughter.

"I don't know … in the middle of the street … or in a farmyard … a government facility … or in a no parking zone." Finn's frown deepened and he looked out the window for any other possibilities worthy of his disapproval.

Addie gave an exasperated sigh. "But I was going to head out to a farmyard right now, pick up a few chickens and a rooster, throw them all in the backseat with some straw … "

Finn didn't respond and when I glanced in my rearview mirror, he didn't look amused.

"I'm kidding," Addie said. "The car is a piece of crap anyway. I don't know why you're being so protective."

"Because Brewster is MY piece of crap!" Finn acted like this was the most logical argument in the world.

"Next time, just borrow my car, Addie," Parker advised with a grin.

"I might, thanks." I heard Addie sigh. "Finn, I promise I'll drive *Brewster* straight home and be very nice to him."

Finn didn't look entirely convinced, but he said. "Very well."

"Thank you," she said. She sounded like she might say more but didn't get a chance.

"Remember, you can't turn on his windshield wipers and blinker at the same time or his engine will start on fire!" The corner of Finn's mouth jerked up in a wry smile.

Addie groaned and said, "Can I talk to just Parker now?"

Chuckling, Parker took the phone and turned off the speakerphone before saying hello. I focused my attention on the road ahead of me. He and his friends were kind of a mystery to me. I could see how much they meant to each other, but I'd never been close to anyone quite like that.

Actually, maybe that wasn't true. My relationship with Libby was probably close, although I always thought of her more like a sister than anything else. My mouth curved up at just the idea of seeing her again. I needed her kind of optimism right now.

Parker hung up the phone and then turned to face me. "So, who is this Randall, and why is it so important we go to this trailer park?

"Cypress Crest isn't just a trailer park. It's a rebel camp full of Night Walkers who are fighting against the Takers." I turned on my blinker and headed toward the highway. "Randall is the Builder currently leading them. He's an old friend of Dad's. Hopefully he'll be able to provide us with some answers about this formula."

Cypress Crest looked pretty run down from the outside, but it still felt more like home to me than anywhere else. The front half was a normal trailer park; no Night Walkers, just average people—Dreamers like Finn, Mia, and Mrs. Chipp. The back half was filled with Night Walker rebels. Some of the group meetings and security we'd organized had made the Dreamers in the park start to believe we were some kind of cult. They quickly learned to keep out of our business and look the other way whenever possible. That suited the rebels just fine.

I'd lived here for years before Dad came back for me. Even after we'd left, and during our years on the run, Dad and I visited the camp often. It was where my mom had lived and where she'd died. It was where Dad had first found out that I existed.

I drove the big van carefully down the narrow, winding road between the trailers, being careful not to run over anything or anyone. It was just before noon and a beautiful day. People were out chatting and working in their tiny patches of garden. I parked all the way in the back near a big field of tall grass. Parker, Finn, and I opened our doors. Even as I climbed out of the van, I could feel eyes on me.

I smiled to myself. Good. They'd finally taken my advice and tightened up security around here. Before this they'd been too vulnerable, as evidenced by the times people had disappeared in the middle of the night, or worse, when the whole camp had been attacked.

I stopped just short of shutting my door when I realized Chloe was frozen in place, ducked low in the back of the van.

"Are you staying here?"

"I think getting out and walking around here would be a *very* bad idea for me." She peered over the seat and gave me a hard look. "Don't you agree?"

I nodded, glad she'd been the one to bring it up instead of me insisting on it. Even if she truly was on our side now and trying to help us, ours wasn't an easy situation to explain.

"Agreed." I gave her a grim nod. "I'll try to hurry."

I joined Parker and Finn in front of the van.

"Everything okay?" Parker tilted his head toward Chloe.

"Yeah." I didn't elaborate, just started walking. Parker and Finn kept pace with me immediately.

"I'm still thinking... what about Wormhole?" Finn rubbed his hands together, seeming determined to solve the only problem he might actually be able to help with.

Parker nearly choked. "You want to name the drug Wormhole?"

"Too simple?" Finn frowned and then suggested, "Wormhole 3000!"

"Nothing with the word hole in it... or worm, actually," I said as I sped up a bit. A group of rebels, led by a smiling Randall, had just turned a corner thirty feet ahead and were walking out to greet us.

"So the Takers had a massive base... and the rebels have a trailer park?" Parker asked quietly. When I didn't respond, he said, "No wonder our side has been losing."

My spine stiffened and I stopped. I took a slow breath before responding so he wouldn't hear my anger. "It's more complicated than that. Our side was being hunted. Our side was trying not to abuse the power we have. Our side wasn't out to destroy every Taker on the planet."

"Right." Parker swallowed, giving a sad shake of his head. "I'm sorry. I didn't mean it like that."

"I know." My eyes searched the group approaching us for Libby, but she wasn't there. "This is part of why I agreed to let you come. You need to see what the rest of the Night Walkers have been dealing with. You need to know that Dad really was doing what was best *for you*."

Parker seemed surprised, but I saw something different

behind his eyes now, something closer to sadness than disdain. Good. That was what he needed to feel. He needed that feeling to understand why Dad's new formula was so important, why all this had to change.

Randall walked up, his grin even wider than before. He was in his fifties and had been close to my mom, keeping an eye on me when I was younger. He had black hair that was balding on top behind a rather severe forehead, but his face was softened by the smile lines around his eyes. When he got close I moved to shake his hand, but instead he pulled me into a tight hug.

"I'm so sorry to hear what happened to Danny, son. He was a good man, and we all miss him."

Randall's embrace shook loose a piece of my shell, leaving me feeling vulnerable and exposed. It was difficult for me to get a grip on my emotions again.

"Thank you," was all I could say, knowing even one more word could break me.

After a moment Randall released me, staring into my eyes as he backed away. Intentional eye contact meant something here. It was the true symbol of trust in a rebel camp.

"This is Danny's son Parker." I gestured over my shoulder. "And his friend, Finn."

Randall nodded and reached past me to shake Parker's and Finn's hands. I watched as he looked at the air just above their heads. They hadn't earned that trust yet. "It's nice to finally meet you, Parker. I've heard all about you, of course, from your father. I'm very sorry for your loss."

Parker shook Randall's hand, murmured a thank you,

and nodded, but I could feel his gaze on me. None of these people knew that Danny was my dad. They thought he was my mentor, and they knew we were close ... but they didn't know the depth of our relationship. My mom had told them my dad rode a Harley and died in a crash before I was born. As Dad had instructed, I never corrected her story.

Most of the time, truth was an inconvenient nuisance. At times it could set you free, but more often it would ensnare you in a web with no hope for release. When you lied and it hurt people, you could always make amends with the truth. When it was the truth that caused pain, there was no escape. After all these years, now wasn't the time to confess all the lies my parents had told these people in order to protect each other ... and me.

Marisol walked out from behind a nearby trailer. She smiled wide and a chuckle escaped my chest. She was a Watcher and had been my mom's best friend. Though I lost my mom young, Libby had been even younger; she was only five when her mother was killed fighting the Takers. Marisol had taken care of the two of us like we were her own. It was just who she was. She'd been unable to have kids, so she became the mom of the whole camp.

Randall smiled too and gestured to the rest of the group to go back to a large common area they'd set up in the middle of the trailers. Turning back to Marisol and me, he said, "We'll let you two catch up, but come find me again before you leave."

I patted him on the shoulder. "Count on it. I have a question for you, anyway. I'll see you in a minute."

Marisol wrapped her arms around me, led me a few steps to one side of the path, and whispered in my ear.

"I've always kept your parents' secret, but I know you mourn for more than a mentor right now, child." Her dark eyes wrinkled around the edges and her slight Jamaican accent was so serene that her words caught me off-guard. She pulled back just enough to look me in the eyes with her piercing gaze. "The question is, does he know?" She inclined her head toward Parker and raised her eyebrows.

My back stiffened and I couldn't keep my eyes from widening. Marisol had known that Danny was my dad all this time? I had no idea, and I'm not sure if Dad even knew. Still, if my parents were going to trust someone, Marisol was without question the best choice. She'd certainly been trustworthy, and she'd always tried to watch out for me. She kept me safe.

I nodded slowly. "He does."

She smiled and then hugged me again. "Good. This is the perfect time to cling to family."

"Marisol..." I gave her one last hug and then pulled away. "This is Parker and his friend Finn."

"So nice to meet you, boys." She smiled wide, again looking at the air over their heads. This time Parker glanced at me with a slightly amused expression. I gave him a small smile, not at all surprised that he'd noticed the custom. He was more perceptive than he gave himself credit for.

Marisol gestured toward me. "You know, Jack's mum and I go way back to when we were small. Just like Jack and Libby."

"Speaking of…" I was tall enough to see over almost everyone, but I still hadn't seen Libby's dark curls in the group. "Where is she?"

Marisol smiled at something over my shoulder, then gave a little wave and turned to follow Randall. In the next instant, someone jumped on my back and I heard Libby's laughter in my ear. "At least you still come looking for me occasionally."

I chuckled and reached behind me for her waist, tugging her around to stand in front of me. "You've got better things to do than worry about where I've gone off to anyway."

She stopped laughing, but her brown eyes sparkled the way they had in her dreams when we were kids. "You know I always worry."

Then her eyes shifted to Finn and Parker and she smiled again, staring them straight in the eyes without hesitation. Same old Libby, always too trusting…she'd never been as cautious as she should've been. "You found other friends? Finally. I've been wondering when someone else would be able to put up with you."

I put my hand over her mouth and said with the straightest face I could manage, "Parker and Finn, this is Libby."

She spoke through my fingers as she reached out to shake their hands. "N-ice to m—feet, y-ouf."

I dropped my hand to my side but couldn't help smiling. There was something infectious about Libby. You couldn't be near her and not notice it.

Parker and Finn were smiling back at her already. Parker said, "It's nice to finally meet someone who can keep Jack in line."

Libby's expression turned very serious and she said, "It isn't easy, but I teach a class on Wednesdays and Thursdays at midnight. There might be some ritual sacrificing involved, but I promise results."

Finn shook his head and chuckled. "I like this girl already."

"Everybody does," I said, draping an arm around Libby's shoulders. "So, Lib, do you feel up for going on an adventure?"

"With three hot guys?" She put her arm around my waist and grinned at Parker and Finn. "Always."

"Hot, huh?" It felt weird to have Libby calling my little brother hot.

She swatted at my chest with her free hand. "Don't act like you don't know it."

I shook my head and decided to move on before she went any further.

"We may be gone for a few days...maybe weeks." I felt the smile fall from my face and watched Libby's expression grow more serious in response to mine. "It's going to be dangerous."

"With you, it always is." The small smile that remained didn't waver. "What kind of trouble are you stirring up this time?"

I gave her the wickedest grin I could manage. "Chemistry trouble."

She froze in place, eyes widening as her back straightened. "Please tell me we get to melt something huge."

Finn burst out laughing. "Are you telling me that in the adopt-a-Night-Walker program, we picked Jack when we could've had this girl?"

Libby giggled and then shook her head at Finn. "What a big mistake that was."

"You don't have to tell me that." Finn gave her a mockingly sad face and an exaggerated sigh. Parker just stood there laughing and watching me.

"Too late now." I shrugged with a half-smile and Libby linked her arm through mine. I didn't care that they were teasing me. Everything felt so much lighter with Libby around that it didn't bother me in the least. But with Libby, I'd learned a long time ago how to tease her back. "I should've known better than to let you around these two. You're going to corrupt them."

"Who? Me?" She struck an angelic pose, her hands pressed together like a prayer, and winked at Parker.

I wrapped an arm around her shoulder and whispered low enough that only our group could hear. "You remember that he's my little brother, right? Take it easy or I'll feel duty-bound to protect him from your ... charms."

Libby had been the only person I'd ever trusted enough to tell my family secrets to ... until Parker. And with him, it wasn't so much because I trusted him at the time as because he *was* one of the secrets.

"You know no one is safe from my ... charms." Libby put one hand on her waist and repeated the word back to me exactly the way I'd said it. Parker's eyes widened, and Finn looked like he was having the best day ever.

"And of course I remember," she continued. "You think I could forget a juicy bit of gossip like that?" Slipping out from under my arm, she backed toward her trailer. "I'll grab my pack, and then we can say goodbye to Marisol and Randall together."

When I nodded, she turned and jogged away. We walked up to stand in the shade of a nearby double-wide and waited. The rebels had set up their trailers in something resembling a circle, which left a big open area in the middle. Dead center in the clearing was a huge fire pit that I'd sat by and roasted marshmallows over when I was little. Lawn chairs of all shapes and sizes sat in front of the trailers, some empty, some full.

Many familiar faces gathered together, talking in low voices and watching us from those seats. When I caught their eyes they waved, but they watched Parker and Finn with undisguised curiosity and a little fear. If I didn't have Parker and Finn with me, most of the rebels probably would've come over to say hello by now. But with strangers here, they kept their distance and watched us. This camp had learned to be less than welcoming, and to distrust new people.

But it was good. They were safer this way. When I glanced back to see if Parker and Finn had noticed how much attention they were getting, I saw them both staring at me.

"Wow..." Parker said as he and Finn stepped up beside me. "Libby was..."

"Refreshing," Finn filled in.

"Yeah, she does that to you." I stretched my neck to one side and shrugged.

"No." Parker's smile widened. "*She* does that to *you*."

Finn laughed, but tried to smother it when I turned my gaze on him.

"I've never seen you smile so much or be so ... relaxed." When I frowned at him, Parker turned to look in the direction Libby had run. "I don't mean it in a bad way," he added. "It's a very good thing. It's nice to see you have another mode besides drill sergeant."

Finn muttered under his breath, "Having some emotions didn't kill you either."

I felt frustration flare up inside me. I didn't know what Parker really wanted from me, but apparently what I was doing wasn't enough. So instead of responding, I turned away and saw Libby step out of her trailer on the other side of the clearing.

Just as she headed toward us, I heard the first gunshot. I watched as Marisol crumpled to the ground. Screams replaced laughter as the rebels ran. Chairs toppled over as they scrambled for cover behind the nearest protection they could find.

My instincts kicked in. I leapt toward Finn and Parker, grabbing their arms and slamming them both into a safe spot behind the closest trailer. The instant I had them around the corner, I heard two more shots; one hit the tree behind where we'd been standing.

"Stay here!" I shouted and peeked around the corner. Libby was bent over Marisol on the ground, and another man lay nearby. The rebels were quickly organizing to fight back, and I heard Randall shouting orders from somewhere on the other side of the clearing. There were already more guns firing, from inside and behind the trailers. The initial shots had come from my left, but now they came from everywhere. With everyone shooting, it was only a matter of time before someone hit Libby—on purpose or by accident.

Either way, I *couldn't* let that happen.

Taking a breath, I stayed low and ran out after her. She had her hand over the wound on Marisol's chest, but it was clear the shot had already done its job. Marisol's lifeless eyes stared up at me and branded my soul. It was like I could hear her in my head: *Get Libby out of here.*

Reaching out with my right hand, I closed Marisol's eyes and then wrapped Libby in my left arm. She fought me, but she weighed so little there wasn't much she could do to stop me. I felt the air move when a couple of bullets whizzed by, but we made it over to Parker and Finn safely.

"No, Jack!" Libby shouted the instant I put her down. She started to run back out, but even in her grief, she was smart enough to stop. "Marisol can't be … I can't just leave her there … "

I pulled her against my chest and smoothed the back of her hair. I tried to swallow my own shocked pain as I looked for the safest path back to the van. I couldn't help Marisol anymore. I needed to focus my attention on keeping Libby, Parker, and Finn alive.

"I know, Lib … but I have to get you all out of here before someone else gets hurt."

"No! Leaving is what *you* do!" Libby yelled at me, tears streaking down her face. I forgot everything around us and just stared at her. I'd never seen her like this. "But not me. I can't just leave right now, Jack. I won't!"

Libby always showed exactly what she felt, plainly on her face. Right now her eyes were filled with pain and rage. I knew I couldn't take her out of here right now or she would never forgive me. I wasn't planning on running out on the rebels in the middle of all this—I just wanted to get Libby, Parker, and Finn to a safe place first.

But I didn't argue with her. Libby was suffering, and if lashing out at me helped her deal with this, I could take it. I closed my eyes for an instant and rubbed the bridge of my nose with my right hand.

"What's going on, Jack?" Parker yelled. "Who's doing this?"

Opening my eyes again, I leveled my gaze at my brother and gave him a hard look. "Who do you think?"

He paled and looked past me at Marisol's body. "I—I didn't think it was this bad."

"I didn't share all the gory details of this war with you, but I told you it isn't a game. I told you they kill people." The truth was, I'd left out a lot of the more horrific specifics. I'd never told him about the appalling things their leader, Steve Campbell, had done to those he'd caught. I'd never explained the things I felt he didn't need to know.

Pulling Libby in for another hug, I stared at my brother over the top of her head. "This is what reality looks like, Parker."

"I know. You told me." His voice was so soft I could

barely make it out over all the commotion. "But seeing it is different."

"It is." I suddenly felt guilty for bringing him here. Maybe I should have forced him to let me come alone. It was a stupid mistake. "You shouldn't have seen it. Dad didn't want you to see this."

"No." Parker's eyes had fresh fire in them. It surprised me, even though it probably shouldn't have. He wasn't ready to run. He was ready to fight. "I needed to see this ... and now I need to help. You *have* to let me help, Jack. What can I do?"

"Libby, you stay with Finn." When Libby started to protest, I just talked over her. "You want me to stay and help. To do that, I need to know you're safe. We won't leave until we stop this, Lib. I promise. Parker, come with me."

Finn stepped forward next to Libby. "Shouldn't we call the police or something?"

I couldn't stop the harsh laugh that escaped. "Yeah, sure. Go ahead and call them. That should help."

Finn looked offended. "Why not?"

I peeked around the corner of the trailer toward the area where the shots were coming from. Two police cars were parked there. I hoped maybe I'd been mistaken, but no. When I'd run out to get Libby, I'd caught a quick glance at flashing lights on top of a white car out of the corner of my eyes. "Because, Finn, the Takers aren't stupid, and they can take over anyone they want. The police are currently the ones shooting at us."

TEN

PARKER

"What? They took over cops?" Finn said as both he and I gaped at Jack.

I turned my eyes on all the rebels around us. None of them looked at all surprised. Libby just looked devastated. But Takers were obviously responsible. It was the only option that made sense. They hadn't announced themselves. They hadn't told us all to come out or tried to arrest us.

They had just started shooting.

And they hadn't been trying to scare us—they'd been shooting to kill.

The rebels were shooting back. Hiding behind cars, trailers, and metal walls. They appeared to have plenty of ammo. They had seen this, and worse, before.

"It's a definite possibility. You guys keep forgetting. They can use *anyone*, Finn." Jack lowered his chin and gave Finn a hard look. "You should know that better than anybody else."

Finn shivered and nodded. Thinking of Finn made me remember something I'd almost forgotten ... *someone* I'd almost forgotten ... Chloe. Was she still in the van? I could see in Jack's face that he'd had the same thought.

"Finn, take Libby and head back to the van. Check on Chloe and make sure she isn't causing any trouble and doesn't go anywhere." Jack's eyes darkened. "I'm going to need to have a little chat with her when I get back."

I shook my head. "You think she had something to do with this?"

"Maybe ... but I'm certainly going to ask." He shrugged and tossed Finn the keys. "If anyone heads in your direction, or the shooting stops and we aren't there within fifteen minutes, drive away until we call you to come back."

Finn hesitated and looked at me. When I gave him a firm nod, he took Libby's arm and started toward the van. She wasn't resisting anymore. Her eyes were vacant, her mind elsewhere.

Jack put both hands on my shoulders until I locked my eyes on his. "Stay with me and don't get shot."

"Uh ... okay," I barely got out before he took off. We dodged in and out around trailers, through trailers, and under trailers until we got over to where Randall was holed up with two guns and a huge bucket of ammo.

"What can we do?" Jack asked, pushing me back until I felt like I'd been plastered against the side of the trailer. My heart was banging a staccato rhythm in my ears. A couple of feet in either direction and they could see me. It was surreal and terrifying.

Randall eyed us both, then spoke to Jack. "Can he handle a gun?"

"No," we both said at the same time.

"You said these guys are being controlled by the Takers?" Everything about what was happening in this camp felt wrong, and I couldn't find a solution that felt right.

"They could've been blackmailed into it or something else, but it's more likely they've been taken." Jack hesitated, like he could see my argument coming from a mile away.

"How can we kill them?" I asked.

"Easy," Randall scoffed before firing off another six rounds. "They're shooting at us."

I gave Jack a hard look. "If they've been taken over, they're like Finn. *They* aren't doing this. If we kill innocent people, then we're no better than the Takers."

Randall spun around with his eyebrows impossibly high. "What did you just say?"

Jack groaned and put a hand on Randall's shoulder to mollify him. "What do you want us to do, Parker? I know what you're saying, but we have to defend ourselves."

Randall waved dismissively in my direction and started shooting again.

"Find a way to stop them without killing them," I pleaded. "If anyone can do that, I know it's you."

Jack stared at me, expressionless, for several seconds but I could see the battle raging behind his eyes. He reached into both boots and pulled out a knife in each hand. "I can't promise not to hurt them…but I promise not to kill them. Good enough?"

I nodded. "That'll work."

Randall looked back at us like he was getting ready to argue.

"I'm going to have to get closer." The muscles in the side of Jack's jaw clenched so fast it looked like a spasm. "Try not to shoot me, Randall."

The rebel leader shook his head. "I'll do what I can. You be careful, Jack."

"I'm going with you," I said. Jack didn't respond, so I followed him as he darted past the backs of several trailers, circling around to where we could see a single police car parked.

"We'll knock them both out and let the rebels sort out whether they are innocent or guilty later," Jack said.

I listened intently and followed Jack's movements like my life depended on it—which it probably did.

When we got behind them, Jack held up his fist to tell me to stop and wait. It was the same communication he'd taught me when we attacked the Takers' base. I watched him carefully, waiting for his next instruction. The two officers were by the car, firing over their doors with a ton of ammunition scattered in boxes across the front seat. I counted to ten, watching and waiting.

Jack seemed to be listening for something specific, but I couldn't tell what…until I saw Jack find him. He pointed to a third officer twenty feet to our left. The third man had ducked behind a tree to reload.

Jack gave me a confident nod and I could tell exactly

what he was thinking: *Three armed men? When we have no weapons? No problem.*

How on Earth could we be related? My thoughts were more along the lines of, *We don't outnumber them. We obviously need more people to help ... and bulletproof vests.*

When the third guy finished reloading and started shooting in a different direction, Jack signaled and we moved. The shooter behind the tree had his sights on his victims in the clearing. He didn't hear Jack sneak up until it was too late. Jack wrapped his arm around the cop's throat and squeezed tight until, a few seconds later, the man stopped fighting back.

Slowly lowering the guy to the ground, Jack felt for a heartbeat. When I heard the guy take a breath, I finally felt like I could take one too.

"H-how did you know when to stop?" I whispered, so quietly that I wasn't even sure Jack had heard me until he answered.

"Three seconds." He grabbed a thick but short stick from nearby and stood up, handing it to me. "Dad taught me those three seconds are the difference between being a fighter and being a killer, between victory and defeat—and for your enemy, those three seconds are the difference between life and death. Three seconds after they pass out is enough time to be sure your enemy is fully unconscious, but it's *usually* not enough time to kill him."

"Usually?" I took the stick but didn't even look at it. My stomach felt a little uneasy about our conversation.

"Yeah ... " Jack's mouth formed a grim line, and he started inching toward the shooters by the police cars before finishing quietly. "It's the 'usually' part that can make things a little tricky."

He gestured for me to follow him behind a tree. Once there, he kept peeking out and then ducking back in.

His frown deepened every time he looked out until I asked, "What's wrong?"

"I can't find a good position to get the older officer based on where he's standing. The only place I can hit him from here is neck or head . . . both lethal." He tapped the hilts of his blades together and shook his head. "I need to make him move."

Sneaking a glance around the tree, I could see what he was talking about. I swallowed back a rush of fear, knowing what I had to do.

"Be ready," I said, knowing Jack would argue with me if he knew my plan . . . but what was all my running good for if not a situation like this?

"What?"

"Don't let me die. Now go!" I whispered, then bolted out from behind the tree in a direction where the older officer couldn't help but see me and would have to step away from the car to get a good shot.

Before I even made it ten feet I heard the zipping noise of Jack's blade slicing through the air. The younger officer cried out. I didn't look back, but I heard footsteps as the older officer stepped away from the car and followed me. My heart pounded thunderously in my head. Everything was moving so slow—yet so fast that I couldn't move or do anything to protect myself.

Another zipping noise sounded just before the next gunshot rang out. Pain burned through the left side of my head; I tripped and fell to the ground as everything around me slowed down. Visions of Addie laughing, my mom smiling at me across the kitchen counter, Finn goofing off in the backyard ... they pelted me from all angles.

My life, here and gone in an instant.

The gun fell from the officer's fingers as he yelped out in pain. I just caught sight of a whirl of motion near the car before a crowd of rebels with guns surrounded all three men.

I couldn't move. I couldn't breathe. I couldn't blink. Out of the corner of my eye, I saw Jack running toward me. I thought I could hear him yelling my name.

"Parker! Parker, are you hurt?" His voice began to slice through my haze. "Parker! Did he *hit* you?"

I slowly turned my face toward my brother. The sheer wild panic I saw on his face was nearly as shocking as the fact that I'd been shot. Drawing in my breath, I felt the world start moving like normal again, and color rushed back into Jack's face when I finally said, "I—I'm okay ... I think I'm okay."

Jack reached out to the left side of my head and his fingers came back with a drop of blood. "He just nicked the top of your ear. You're one lucky idiot."

"I guess I gotta be lucky at something," I groaned as I rolled over and up onto my knees. Relief flowed through me at the knowledge that it could have been so much worse. "Besides, it worked, didn't it?"

Jack smiled and I saw respect in his eyes. "It did."

The chaos all around us had stopped. There were no

bullets, no yelling. Even the wind seemed to hold its breath as it watched our fight end.

Jack helped me up and then jogged over to a nearby trailer. He came back with a couple of dishtowels in his hands. He crossed to the older officer, who glared at him over the top of his gag. Some rebels stood ready with rope to tie him up, but were waiting for Jack as he carefully retrieved his knife from the man's biceps, wiped it off on one of the towels, and sheathed it. He tied the cloth tight around the man's wound. By the time he'd finished, I'd taken Jack's other dishtowel and walked over to the younger officer. This one looked more scared than angry and was in quite a bit of pain.

I considered repeating Jack's steps, but the knife was embedded in the man's forearm. I was nervous that if I pulled it wrong, I might do more damage than good.

Jack stepped up, grabbed the hilt of the knife, and looked at me. "Ready?"

I nodded. When he pulled out the knife, I quickly tied the cloth tight around the man's arm. The wound was still really bleeding, but the towel did its job. The rebels tied this cop up as well. Jack wiped the knife on the makeshift bandage before sticking it back in his boot.

"We're not a bad team, you know?" I spoke the words hesitantly, but I felt I needed to say it. Jack needed to recognize that I could be more than just someone who always got in his way.

He nodded but didn't look at me. "I know."

Randall approached us. He'd taken a bullet to the shoulder since I'd seen him a few minutes before, but someone had already wrapped it up and he looked like he'd be fine.

"That was incredibly brave—and incredibly foolish. But thank you, both of you." Randall shook his head and looked over his shoulder at a few of the others, who were covering Marisol's body with a white sheet. "I'd hoped things might get better after . . . after what Danny did."

"They will." Jack was trying to sound confident, but the hesitation in his tone was hard to miss. "I just need more time."

Randall leaned toward him. "What are you working on, Jack?"

"Danny gave me something I have to sort out." Jack spoke the words quietly, looking around us as though there might still be someone we couldn't trust who was listening.

"God, please no." Randall paled as he spoke, and it took me a moment to catch up. "Please tell me he didn't give you the formula to Eclipse. I thought we were finally done with that. If he gave it to you—"

"No, Randall." Jack reached out and placed his hand on the man's shoulder to reassure him. "Danny made sure no one can make Eclipse. That plague is gone, for good."

The color returned to Randall's face. I wondered if maybe I should quietly slip away and go check on Finn and the others at the van, but then Jack gave me a look that glued me in place.

"All I can tell you right now is that *we* are trying to help, and that it's very important." Jack looked me straight in the eye for several seconds. His message came through: something had changed back there and he meant what he was saying— *we*. Then he turned back to Randall. "Danny left me a message. He told me to tell you that 'it's time to begin'? I know he was pretty paranoid by the end, but does that mean anything to you?"

"Yes," Randall said without hesitation, and deep sadness fell over his face like a shadow. "I have something to give you. Wait here while I go get it."

"We have to go check on our friends." Jack looked reluctant to leave, but we both knew we needed to make sure everyone else was all right. "Meet us at the van?"

Randall nodded and walked away as we turned back the way we'd come.

I looked at the people shuffling around the clearing. They looked damaged, but resilient. Marisol was the only one they'd lost. Even the other man they'd hit was awake and bandaged. It looked like he would make it, too. They'd been lucky.

"Maybe they should all move away?" I spoke without thinking, but then pushed on because it felt like a valid question. "It obviously isn't safe here right now."

"They have nowhere to go." Jack looked around sadly and kicked a rock across the road in front of us. "All of the rebel camps have been compromised in one way or another. There's nowhere the Takers can't find us anymore. We can't leave, not without scattering to the wind and abandoning the sense of community we've fought so hard for. At least here, when we're a group, it's impossible for them to steal a couple of us away at a time and throw us in their prisons without anyone noticing. They have to fight us all together or not at all. Plus, running is exhausting. It doesn't make for an easy life. Prey don't get to relax. If they relax, they die."

I didn't know what to say. On the one hand, I was so surprised that Jack was telling me any of this. Maybe this was his attempt to do what Dad asked in his message. I hoped so. I'd never been through what the rebels had. I wanted to understand, and at the same time I was so grateful that I didn't. How could I relate to their lives?

Fortunately, Jack didn't wait for a response. "We're all so tired of being hunted, Parker. That's what it's about for me. Hopefully the new formula will give the Takers something to lose. It will finally give *us* the leverage for once. It's about time someone gave us a weapon strong enough to help us keep them in line, something to make our predators fear us. I'll find that weapon or I'll die trying."

The fierce anger in his tone made me worry for the first time that giving him this quest might be the worst thing our dad ever did to Jack—and, as I was beginning to discover, that was really saying something.

ELEVEN

JACK

As Parker and I walked back across the clearing toward the van, I stopped with the group of rebels standing around Marisol's covered body. Most were weeping and murmuring as they comforted each other. It felt like an informal funeral.

So many memories floated to the surface of my mind: Marisol sitting at a table with us, teaching Libby and me to play card games. Marisol laughing at the silly stories Libby used to make up to tell me before bedtime. Marisol crying with me as we knelt beside my mother's broken and bleeding body. She'd always been like family to me. She'd watched out for me and held me during my tough times and struggles, even when I tried to pretend I didn't need it. She'd seen through my lies and loved me for the secret weaknesses I thought I hid so well. Being strong didn't matter to Marisol; it never had.

"You aren't doing everyone a favor, you know," she'd told me one night about a week after my mom died. She'd caught me crying in the darkness, hiding by myself in the field behind the camp. I'd tried to wipe the tears from my face before she saw, but she hadn't even had to look at me to know.

"What do you mean?" I'd asked, hoping she was talking about me being away from camp or something.

"Pretending you don't feel anything." Marisol sat beside me and stared up at the stars. "When you pretend like this, it poisons *you*, deep, but more than that, it steals away how important she was."

A few tears fell down her cheeks, and when mine fell again to match, I didn't wipe them away.

"We miss her because she mattered so much to us." She finally turned and smiled sadly at me through her tears. "Don't take that away from your mama. Let her loss matter."

Then she wrapped one arm around me and we sat together in the darkness until I fell asleep against her side in the middle of the field beneath the stars.

Reaching down now, I squeezed her lifeless hand where it stuck out from one side of the sheet. My throat closed up as I fought back emotion. I couldn't keep losing people. It was tearing me apart, and at some point soon there wouldn't be enough left to pull myself back together again.

"I'll watch over Libby, and I won't let my dad down. I promise you, Marisol." I spoke the vow so low that no one else could hear it, then took a breath and got to my feet. "Your loss matters to all of us."

I looked at the people in the camp. A group of rebels were moving the three cops to Randall's trailer. They would find out whether they'd been taken over or were just being bribed or blackmailed, and then decide what to do with them based on that. Randall was as fair as possible whenever he could be, and the people in the camp followed his lead.

The other rebels all moved around slowly, trying to clean up, to help each other … to accomplish something. They moved with purpose but their eyes were vacant, and even the ones who weren't standing around Marisol couldn't stop their gazes from straying back to her body beneath the sheet.

This was far from the first time they'd been attacked, but this was the first time the Takers had gotten to Marisol. And that wasn't something any of the rebels would recover from easily. She'd been the heart of the camp to more than just me.

Libby and I were suffering the same loss. Losing a parent was a terrible kind of pain, and Marisol had been like that for us. It morphed you instantly into an adult at a time when you'd never felt more like a child. Nothing could make you feel as scared, vulnerable, and alone as the loss of a parent.

Parker followed behind me as we made our way toward the van. As hard as it was for me to admit, even to myself, I needed him here with me today. Especially right now, I needed him. Dad had told me to treat him like an ally, but it was hard to argue that I'd been doing that. I kept losing people I loved. I was barely getting to know him, but he was my brother.

It was time to start acting like it.

I never should have waited as long as I did to come find him. I never should have let jealousy, or even Dad's original rule that I stay away from Parker, keep me from getting to know my own brother.

I could've lost him with that gunshot today. I very nearly had. Just that thought made my chest burn with pain, and I struggled to breathe.

So Parker wanted to know about Dad? Fine. I would start answering his questions. No more secrets. No more letting memories of our dad make me push him away. I would start keeping him close.

Close enough that I could make *certain* he stayed safe.

As if he understood my thoughts without me ever having to speak them aloud, Parker stayed just behind me as I walked. He was silent as my shadow, but still his presence stabilized me in ways I couldn't have explained to him if I'd tried—which, of course, I didn't.

And I was eternally grateful that right now, at least, I didn't have to.

———————

We were just rounding the corner of the trailer nearest to the van when we heard Libby yelling. Parker and I exchanged one quick glance and then broke into a sprint. By the time we got close, the yelling had stopped, but I could still hear weird scuffling noises. Parker was a faster runner than me, but when he reached the end of the van, his legs locked up and he stopped in place almost like his feet had frozen to the ground. I tried to slow down, but I slammed into him and we both went sprawling across the dirt.

He sputtered and rolled over to help me up, muttering "Sorry" as I tried to take in the scene that had stopped him in his tracks. Chloe was kneeling beside the van, her expression slightly bored as she pinned Libby facedown in the dirt. Finn was half-hanging out of the driver's side window, grunting as he tried to pull Chloe off Libby from that extremely awkward position.

I shook my head and hopped to my feet immediately. Finn had zero leverage from that angle. No wonder his efforts were getting him nowhere.

This was really not the time for Chloe to be making trouble. "Get *off* of her," I snapped.

Chloe looked up at me with a half smile, but it vanished when she saw my face. Fear filled her eyes, but she didn't respond or move fast enough for me. In two steps, I grabbed her shoulders in my hands. Within two more steps, I'd lifted her off of Libby and pressed her back against the side of the van.

"What the hell are you doing?" My sorrow over Marisol's death fueled the rage in my veins, and I growled and squeezed her arms tighter, releasing some of my pain on Chloe. Why shouldn't I take it out on her? She was a Taker and she was here, right now, causing problems.

Chloe's skin paled to a shade similar to her gray eyes, and she tried to push me away, but I wouldn't budge. Her expression flashed indignation and she raised her chin, glaring back at me with as much anger or more than I was feeling. The fire in her confused me. What right did she have to this kind of outrage?

"I asked you a question." Her stubbornness was only making things worse. "Why did you attack her?"

"You're asking the wrong person." Chloe's voice dripped venom.

Parker's tone was sharp as he called my name, and I released Chloe's shoulders.

"You brought *her* here?" I heard Libby yell. "And then the Takers start shooting up the place? Marisol is dead now. Because of her!"

I was slammed from behind by Libby's small form before I could even turn around. The impact rocked me to one side and forced me to stumble toward Chloe again. Then Libby stopped attacking me and sobbed. "How could you do this?"

I glanced back at Chloe. She held perfectly still, barely blinking. What I saw in Chloe's eyes wasn't the confusion I expected, confusion that should've been there about Libby's accusation ... but wasn't. There was something else—a hint of understanding? Recognition? Maybe even clarity?

"No ... " I stared at Chloe, and only pure restraint kept me from wrapping my fingers around her throat. If she had betrayed my trust and Marisol was dead because of it, there wouldn't be anywhere safe for her to hide from me. "Tell me you didn't signal those Takers to come here."

Chloe's eyes went wide and she looked genuinely hurt. "*Never.*"

I watched her for any hint of a lie, but if she was lying, then she hid it well. As I reached for Libby, my throat tightened with emotion at seeing her in so much pain. She'd been so little when her parents died, I don't think she remembered it. This was her first loss when she was old enough to understand what had happened—to really feel the pain of it.

"Libby, what are you talking about?" I asked her.

"How could you bring her here, Jack?" Libby repeated. "Don't you know who she is?" Her choked sobs made it difficult to understand her. "She's a Taker. She must've called the others and told them you had her here."

"I don't think that's what happened." I kept my eyes on Chloe, hoping my words were true as I rubbed my thumbs across the inside of Libby's wrists in an attempt to soothe her. Libby was always kind, always composed; this wild rage made my teeth ache. This kind of emotion felt so wrong coming from her that my world felt dissonant because of it.

"Oh my God, you *don't* know who she is..." Her voice lowered to a crazed whisper like she carried a heavy secret.

"I know she's a Taker, but she's been trying to help us."

Out of the corner of my eye, I saw Chloe move slowly toward the back of the van, and I couldn't blame her. Libby looked murderous.

"Like hell she has," Libby snarled, reaching out to grab Chloe's shirt before she moved out of range. "She isn't *just* a Taker, Jack. Her dad is Steve Campbell."

All my thoughts focused on Libby's words. My brain

tried to sort them into a logical order that would fit with what I knew to be truth: Chloe had been trying to help me. Chloe made mistakes, but she'd also saved Parker and Finn. And Steve Campbell was the closest thing to evil I'd ever known, the reason the Takers began hunting my dad. My mother died by his hands.

My skin turned ice cold and my mouth moved, but nothing came out until I finally said, "You must be wrong."

Libby's tears began to fall again and she nodded fiercely. "I'm not wrong. She *is* his daughter. Campbell may be dead, but they still follow what he taught them ... we just found out his oldest son has taken over leadership of the Takers. How could you bring *her* here, Jack?"

My mind was spinning, still trying to make this concept fit. Libby's information had to be a mistake. Chloe wasn't Campbell's daughter. I hadn't been driving around with the girl whose dad had obliterated everything I'd ever cared about. It couldn't ... "I don't—"

"Cooper? The new leader—is his name Cooper?" Parker was standing beside me now, staring hard at Libby.

"Yes. It's Cooper." Then she pulled herself in tight against my chest and I rubbed her back, trying to comfort her as my head spun. As she released Chloe's shirt, she whispered, "Cooper must have sent those shooters here. He murdered Marisol."

When I looked up, Randall and a few other rebels were standing a few feet behind me. Randall had a gun pointed over my right shoulder.

"What's *she* doing here, Jack?"

Following his gaze, I saw Parker and Finn standing on either side of Chloe and looking at her like she might run or attack them. She wasn't arguing or defending herself. Instead, her head hung down low and she stared at the ground.

I stepped gently away from Libby and moved over to Randall, placing my hand on top of his gun until he lowered it and looked at me.

"Is what Libby said true? Chloe is Campbell's daughter?" I asked. "But how? The family's last name is Thornton."

That was why Parker and his friends called Chloe's other brother "Thor." The possibility of these three Taker siblings being Campbell's kids wasn't something I'd *ever* considered.

My voice was soft, but I still couldn't mask the anger I felt as I watched Chloe. And even without Randall's answer, I could tell the accusation was true just by looking at her. It was like the truth held physical weight and pinned her down. Her white-blond hair hid her face as I tried to read something from her stance, her posture. Everything screamed defeat. Was she trying to show me that? Trying to gain my sympathy somehow? Had she been playing us from the beginning—playing me?

"Yeah, that's her." Randall kept his gun lowered, but I noticed he didn't take his finger off the trigger. "The kids went by Thornton to try to stay hidden from us. It worked for a while, but we found out the truth a couple of months ago."

Libby moved to lean against the front of the van, her eyes staring right through me.

I walked up to Chloe but before I could speak, I heard Chloe's voice. It came out raw and devastated: "I came because I want to help with the new formula. I never wanted to come to this camp."

"Why didn't you tell me who you really were?" My frustration came through in my tone, no matter how hard I fought it, but it was a mere drop compared to the lake of fury I was feeling inside. Without Chloe's father, my mom would still be alive. Dad would still be alive. Maybe we could have had a normal life, lived in a real house. The war between the Takers and the rest of us might not have even started at all.

So many lost lives, and Chloe's dad was ultimately responsible for every one of them.

"Answer me!" I roared, grabbing the hair at the back of her head and lifting her face so I could look in her eyes. When I saw they were glistening with tears, it caught me off guard. I released her hair, but she continued to stare at me. The tortured pain in her face was not what I expected, and I motioned for Parker and Finn to step away.

"I didn't tell you about my dad because it doesn't matter anymore who I am or where I came from." Chloe spat the words out like they disgusted her.

"You are Steve Campbell's daughter," I sneered. "How can that possibly not matter?"

"It just doesn't." She pulled her shoulders up high beside her ears and crossed her arms, as though her posture could somehow protect her from my questions.

"That kind of answer can't protect you, Chloe. People were hurt today. People *died* today. Where you come from matters *a great deal* to *them*."

Her eyes flew up to meet and hold mine. I knew she

could hear the pleading note in my tone. I didn't want it to be true—I wanted desperately for there to be something we didn't understand about her situation. But just as she opened her mouth to respond, someone else's voice spoke, from a few feet to my right.

"It doesn't matter, Jack, because she gave all of that up when she chose your filth over her blood." Cooper's voice sounded smooth, cold, and utterly in control as he stepped out from behind a nearby tree and placed the barrel of a gun against the back of Parker's head.

Randall immediately raised his gun, but Cooper grabbed the back of Parker's shirt and sank down a few inches to use my brother's entire body as a shield. "Drop it!" he barked, jamming the gun so hard against the base of Parker's skull that he winced.

Parker's ice blue eyes were on me. The eyes identical to our dad's, the eyes that always made it hard to look at my own brother or answer his questions about our father's life. I could see fear in them, but also some sort of reassurance. It was like he was trying to tell me it was going to be okay. But *I* was the older brother. It was *my job* to protect and keep him safe . . . not vice versa.

Dad had given me the job over a year ago, when he'd asked me to follow Parker and determine whether he was a Night Walker or not. It had been a drastic change from all those times before, when he'd said we had to keep our distance. And ever since he'd put me in charge of Parker's safety, my brother had not only experienced several close brushes with death, but he'd become Divided, tried to run away, been shot, and now was being held at gunpoint by the enemy... all on my watch.

I'd obviously been doing one hell of a job.

TWELVE
PARKER

"Let him go!" Jack's voice cracked across the empty space so loud and hard it almost scared me more than the cold metal pressed against the back of my head.

Forcing your body to hold perfectly still when every instinct is screaming at you to *RUN* is a seriously underrated skill.

"I don't think so." Cooper's voice came from behind me. "Since your pain-in-the-ass chemist decided to blow up our base and most of our leadership with it, I've taken on more of a...decisive role. I'm in charge now. I'm finally going to make things happen."

Jack gestured for Randall to lower his weapon, and Cooper relaxed the pressure a bit. Seeing a possible opportunity, I tried to jerk forward, but his grip on my shirt was too tight and he dragged me back, smashing the gun even harder against my already-throbbing skull.

"Not smart," Cooper growled. "Don't do it again."

I could tell from the expression on Jack's face that finally getting a good look at Cooper wasn't making him feel any better. I glanced backward and caught a glimpse of him too, before Cooper nudged me with his gun to turn back around.

It hadn't been much of a glimpse, but it was enough to see what was bothering Jack. The skin on Cooper's face hung loose and the circles under his eyes were so deep and dark that they could've been tattooed there. Those details weren't what scared me the most, though. The worst part was his eyes.

They reminded me of Darkness's eyes. There was a desperate madness to them that was terrifying. I released an involuntary shudder.

I didn't miss looking in the mirror and seeing that.

Finn spoke up. "What did you mean when you said that Chloe chose *us*, Cooper?"

When I slid my glance to him, his eyes were glued to me. His voice and hands were trembling, and I immediately shook my head in a slight *no*. I knew him well enough to be certain that he was working himself up to do something brave and stupid. Somehow Chloe seemed to recognize it too, because she reached out and grabbed the sleeve of his shirt. Finn was so intent on me he barely noticed.

Cooper shifted his weight, and I could tell he'd turned his demented gaze on Finn from the way Finn's skin paled. Spitting the words out like they disgusted him, Cooper answered. "She turned her back on her kind and her family when she helped set you free. She knew she shouldn't, but she did anyway. Being in your mush of a brain made her weak."

Moving his gun to my back, Cooper released my shirt, grabbing my arm instead as he stepped next to me. When he turned his eyes back on Chloe, they were ice cold. "And we don't tolerate weakness."

Finn eyed Chloe with surprise. None of us had known what she'd sacrificed when she helped us free him. She hadn't even hinted about it, and now that I knew, I didn't understand why she'd cooperated with us. Yes, she'd been trying to save herself, but she also knew that the odds weren't great of the separation actually working. It could've killed both her and Finn, and a lot sooner. Chloe had held all the power, being in his brain. Sure, we could have tied up Finn's body or killed it, but I'd seen it firsthand—we never would have gotten Finn back alive if she'd chosen to fight us. Yet helping us had cost Chloe her family and everyone she knew.

Why *had* she helped, at such a cost?

I lifted my eyes to Chloe and what I saw stopped me. She wasn't cringing and looking down anymore. She stood up tall, her shoulders pulled back. Dropping Finn's sleeve, she stepped in front of him. "Let Parker go! Right now, Cooper."

"Oh, he's coming with me." Cooper smiled lazily and took a step backward, pulling on my arm until I had no choice but to move with him. "If you want him back, I need something in return."

"What do you want?" Jack took a stumbling step forward. His face was pale, his mouth a grim, painted line. Jack was always confident, but now he looked ... scared. The thought of Jack not being prepared for something was terrifying.

"I want Eclipse."

When Jack frowned and started to shake his head, Cooper kept talking, leaving no room for anyone else to speak. "Don't tell me you can't do it. I know you worked with Danny. I even know you lied to everyone and that he was actually your father."

A soft groan came from Chloe, and Cooper gave her a wicked grin in return as he said, "That bit of information was the last useful thing little sis ever gave us."

Jack's gaze hardened, and his hands clenched and unclenched at his side. He'd wondered about if and how much Chloe had contacted the Takers, and now we knew it was at least enough to tell them this.

I saw Randall and the rebels with him turn questioning stares on Jack, but no one spoke. They all knew that questions could wait.

Jack's shoulders slumped forward slightly. "I can't make it. He made sure I couldn't."

"Ah, but I have more faith in you than that. If there's one thing *my* father taught me, it's that your ... *family* is very stubborn." He dragged me back another couple of steps—away from Finn and Addie, away from my brother, away from my life. "I'm sure you can figure it out. With the right motivation ... "

Jack whipped his knife out of its sheath and I jerked back, thinking he might be throwing it again. Instead, he grabbed Chloe. Wrapping his left arm around her shoulders, he held the blade against her throat. She didn't struggle at all. She didn't even look surprised.

"I can't possibly do what you're asking, but I'll trade you. You know he's my brother, good for you, but I have your sister—a sibling for a sibling." Jack's jaw clenched so tight his words came out rough as the gravel beneath our feet.

Chloe closed her eyes and I saw a single tear roll down her cheek. I wasn't sure if it was because Jack was offering her up on a platter to a monster ... or because she already knew what Cooper's answer would be.

I listened, and waited. Afraid to breathe or even blink. I hoped Cooper was bluffing, that his heart wasn't this cold. When he started laughing, my heart dropped to the earth at my feet. Each cruel chuckle only crushed it farther into the dirt.

"Keep her, use her, kill her ... I don't care. Your sibling is worth so much more than mine." Cooper's expression filled with what could only be described as disgust as he looked at Chloe one last time. Then he jerked me back toward the end of the trailer. "Don't try to stop or follow us or I'll shoot him." He glanced pointedly at Libby. "You obviously have other people I could use to motivate you."

A low growl came from Jack and I knew Cooper had hit a nerve.

"Better get focused, Jack." Cooper kept backing away, pulling me with him, and there was nothing I could do to stop him. "It only took your dad four days to mix up some Eclipse after we convinced him that Parker's life depended on it. I'm feeling generous, so I'll give you ten. You have ten days to bring me Eclipse, or Parker is dead. Don't call me, I'll call you." And then he was pulling me back even faster.

In one brief moment of clarity, I remembered who was taking me…and that I was a Watcher. I quickly made eye contact with the only person I knew for sure in this group was a Builder—Libby. Her teary eyes watched me from beside the van. They were distant, almost looking through me. The connection only lasted a second, but it was long enough for me to be certain it had worked. Then Cooper yanked me around the end of the trailer.

Twenty feet away, two headlights turned on in the shadows beneath a huge tree and shined straight in my face. I squinted and tried to slow down so my eyes could adjust, but Cooper dragged me toward the old model Ford as it pulled into the sunlight. I caught sight of Thor's hulking form behind the wheel and groaned.

As if things weren't bad enough already. Joey Thornton, a.k.a. Thor, seriously had a knack for showing up anytime I was in deep trouble. He'd attacked me in the hall at school, in the parking lot at the mall, and even once on the soccer field. If there was anyone in this world I wanted to see even less than Cooper, it was Thor.

Cooper forced me into the backseat and made it impossible for me to see anything or anyone by shoving a paper bag over my head. I felt the car lurch into motion as the guy who hated me drove us away from the people I cared about.

THIRTEEN

JACK

My brain and chest were on fire. Breathing was painful, thinking was a struggle—this couldn't be happening. I couldn't let Cooper take my brother away, and yet he was doing it.

Dragging Chloe with me, the knife still at her throat, I rounded the end of the trailer in time to watch the car drive away.

Now that they were gone, the dust settled.

And I still couldn't move.

From somewhere far away, I heard Finn's voice, but the words weren't within my reach. I was certain the heat from Chloe's back pressing against my chest was the only thing that was keeping my heart beating. The Takers had Parker.

No, not just the Takers. It was *Steve Campbell's son* who had him. And Parker didn't truly understand who he was dealing with, since I'd tried not to share much about the monster who'd ripped our father away from us. Like the fact that Campbell had personally ordered the manhunt for Dad. Like the horrific experiments he'd ordered, the way he enjoyed causing pain and damage. I didn't want Parker to have to think about the man responsible for that kind of pain … the person who'd made Dad live his life on the run, leaving Parker and his mom on their own.

I knew better than anyone that this knowledge wouldn't help. It couldn't … not unless you could reach out and strangle the person responsible.

But now, I wished I'd told Parker everything. I wished I'd answered his every question, given him every awful detail, because at least then I'd feel I'd prepared him for the type of people he was now facing—for what they could have in store for him. These people were known for using *any* means to get information or to bend and manipulate people to their will. And that was when they had an agenda … when they were bored, it could be much worse. The Takers made the plight of a lab rat look like a Caribbean vacation.

I didn't know Cooper, but just from the last few minutes he seemed very much his father's son, and that didn't bode well for Parker. I wished I'd trained my brother, found the time to really follow Dad's instructions and tell him everything about our past. I wished I'd prepared him to face something like this.

I wished I'd handled a lot of things differently.

And I hadn't moved since they drove away with Parker, because moving made all of it final. Moving meant agreeing to let time move forward, which would force me to concede the one thing I wasn't ready for yet—that I hadn't been able to stop them from taking away the most important person I had left.

I knew I needed to act, to do something, but all I could hear was Dad's voice in my head yelling at me, bellowing my name and telling me to do something to save him—to save—

"Jack? Jack!" Finn pulled my wrist with the knife gently away from Chloe's throat. Her shoulders were completely relaxed against me and I could hear her speaking.

"Finn, it's fine." Her voice was surprisingly soothing. "He isn't going to hurt me—just wait for—"

I whipped my arm down and re-sheathed my knife, clearing my throat.

Chloe almost fell over when I stepped away. She started examining a small bruise on her arm.

Finn nodded and his eyes went to where Cooper's car had disappeared down the road. "Okay. Do you know what we should—"

"No, Finn. I don't have a plan." I sighed and rubbed both hands across my face as I stared out at the distance and tried to force my brain to come up with something useful.

Then I turned on Chloe. "How did they know we were here?"

She blinked, and then frowned. "I don't know."

"You didn't call them?" I stepped closer, studying her face for any sign of deception.

She looked offended. "I already answered that question."

"I don't know if I believe you." I glanced back in the

direction the car had gone, then tried a different possibility. "Is it possible they've been following you?"

She started to shake her head, but hesitated. I saw doubt, and then a touch of horrified realization, in her eyes.

"Chloe, did they know you were with us?"

Her face went from flushed to ashen and her eyes were haunted when they met mine. "They—they know I have nowhere else to go. They could've followed me. I'm so sorry, Jack. I had no idea."

Without a word, I turned and walked a few feet to where Randall now stood with one arm cradled around Libby's shoulders. She stared straight forward with empty, exhausted eyes. Before I could figure out what I wanted to say, Randall spoke.

"We have more questions than there is time for. I guess secrets run in your blood?" Randall's lips were pressed in a firm line, but he didn't look angry. The emotion I saw in everyone's faces right now was fear.

"Yeah. You knew him as well as anyone. I won't bother explaining Danny's reasons for keeping his secrets. You can guess them." I stood with my eyes slightly downcast, taking my cues from the leader of the camp.

Now that he'd found out that my entire family had lied to him about Danny being my dad, I couldn't assume Randall would still trust me. He was levelheaded and smart, but trust wasn't easy to get back once lost.

"I'm sorry we didn't tell you," I said. "You know it wasn't ever about trusting you. Danny just felt like secrets were the best way to protect people."

Randall's expression echoed a bit of the loss I was feeling as he slowly nodded.

Standing next to him, Libby looked like a hollow shell of her old self. No longer crying or yelling, just staring. I was distracted, worrying about Parker and our quest to complete the new formula, but it was hard to resist the urge to go to her and wrap her up in my arms, do anything I could in a futile attempt to heal the cracks...anything to make her feel better. Yet I knew it wouldn't help. I knew her pain. I may not have shut down to mourn in the same way that she was mourning Marisol, but it didn't mean I hadn't felt the same loss.

It didn't mean my whole soul didn't still threaten to turn into an aching pit every time I remembered my dad, mom, Marisol...and now maybe Parker. I'd lost too much.

Randall slowly bent over until his eyes met mine. The skin around them crinkled, and I saw the same warmth and kindness in them that had always been there. I felt a rapid wash of relief. After all of this, he still trusted me. Having Randall's trust still meant more than he could know. He and Dad had been friends for six years, and he was always someone I could rely on, someone I cared about and respected. After everything else, at least I hadn't lost him today as well.

He gave me a slight smile before nodding grimly and getting down to business. "What can we do to help get Parker back?"

My brother's name sent a cold chill down my spine and brought me firmly back from the memories of our father. "I don't know. I can't do what Cooper wants."

"Of course you can't."

"Even if I wanted to, I can't." I stuffed my hands forcefully into the pockets of my jacket and closed my eyes. "And with only ten days, my only option is to follow my original plan. I need *something* to offer them to get Parker back. Something they need—even if it isn't what they think they want."

When I opened my eyes, Randall was watching me, waiting for me to continue. Libby relaxed against his side, her eyes barely open as she stared at the ground in front of them.

I lowered my voice so no one else could hear me except Randall and Libby. "Before my dad died, he figured out another formula—the real one he'd been searching for all along."

Randall's eyes widened and he whispered, "The real one?"

"Yes. He figured out how to make a drug that would allow the Takers to sleep like regular Dreamers." I kept my voice low and my eyes on Randall, but at the edge of my vision I saw Libby's head jerk up. I was relieved to see that such a detail could snap her out of her grief a bit. "He wanted to make sure I was the only one who could put it together, so I don't have the entire formula yet ... but I think you have what I need to start."

Randall nodded quickly and reached in his pocket. He handed me a military dog tag with words on it. "Here's what I'm supposed to give to you. It's all he gave me. Does it help?"

"Like I said ... it's a starting place." I studied the silver metal, reading the name *Wendy King* and the name of the city, *Brimley Terrace*, before sticking it into my pocket. "And now I only have ten days to find the finish line."

As I walked back to the van to make sure we had all the supplies we might need, Libby walked up to me.

"Your brother is smarter than you think." She spoke with more life than before, but still like a ghost of her former self. And she still kept her eyes on the ground. It hurt me to suspect she might be so angry she couldn't stand to look directly at me.

"I don't doubt it," I said with a sad smile.

"He connected with me, Jack." She reached out and put one hand on my chest. "Right before they took him, he looked straight at me. I didn't even realize what he was doing for a minute, but I'm certain it worked."

"He did?" A balloon of hope filled up in my chest and I couldn't decide whether to cling to it or pop it to save myself the pain it could bring if it popped on its own. "He's brilliant! All we need to do now is have you go to sleep and he can tell you in your dreams where they've taken him."

She gave me a tired smile. "I'm glad I can help."

"In more ways than you think..." I hesitated, knowing how much she was struggling, but I actually thought that coming with us right now would be a good distraction for her. It might help. "Will you still come with me, Lib? It might be good for you... and I need your help and want your company."

"You know I love you, Jack. But how can I come when your entire 'adventure' is about helping the *Takers*." She hissed the last word, her voice dripping hatred in a way I'd never heard before. It took me several seconds to respond, even though I'd already made up my mind.

"I want to end the killing." I spoke the same words she used to say to me, hoping they would sink in through her grief. Just in case they didn't, I gave her my more pressing reason. "More than that though, I want to help Parker—to save my brother."

Her anger eased and after a few seconds she nodded. "I'll come, for him and for you. Nothing and no one else—"

"Fine." I hugged her tight against me and she melted a bit more before I added, "That's all I want."

When we reached the van, Libby got in and climbed all the way to the back. She grabbed my pillow out of the pile of supplies and then spread out across the back seat. I grabbed an extra blanket I kept tucked under the front passenger seat and tucked it around her.

"Thank you." I squeezed her hand again. "Find out everything you can about where they're keeping him ... and tell him I'm coming."

When she closed her eyes, I studied her face. She looked exhausted now, so vulnerable.

She'd always had Marisol's strength to lean on.

Now I would make sure she had mine.

Once I'd hopped out, I walked around to the back of the van. Chloe was sitting on the bumper, waiting, and mostly doing her best not to draw any additional attention to herself. From the violent looks a couple of the rebels were throwing her way, I think she probably had the right idea.

I stepped in front of her and Chloe lifted her gaze to

mine. She looked at me like I was about to deliver some kind of death sentence.

"You need to go to your brothers and convince them that I can't do what they want." I kept my voice soft, hoping if we hurried, our chances of getting her out of here alive might improve.

Chloe was shaking her head before I'd even finished my sentence. "The Takers won't listen to me. They won't even let me in because he's ordered them not to. You saw him." She gestured toward where Cooper had gone. "You saw him. He's too far gone to listen to reason."

I had my mouth open to argue, but I closed it. She was right. Cooper was nowhere near the vicinity of rational. "Then there have to be others," I said. "You know the other Taker leaders. Who else can you talk to?"

"No, they're afraid to go against him. Plus, no one trusts me now. I didn't just go against Cooper—I was their hope for a future, and they blame me for that hope being gone now." She was still shaking her head. "I can do much more if I stay here with you."

"No." The word came out with an unintentionally biting edge. I gestured for her to move off of the bumper, and she got to her feet and stepped next to me.

"I can help!" Her tone was near begging. "Let me help."

"No, Chloe." I walked to the driver's side door and put my fingers around the handle.

"Why not?" She reached out for my sleeve.

"Because how can I trust you now?" I jerked my arm away and spun to face her. My fear of losing Parker was spilling out in the form of anger, and I stepped forward. She didn't move back, so I was nearly on her toes and she looked up into my face as I spoke. "You lied about *who you were* and then your brother suddenly shows up here? I swear, if you're lying and you *did* plan this, I will make you pay."

"I am *not* lying, Jack." She didn't flinch and she didn't back down, but I saw pain as deep as my own mirrored in her eyes before she responded. "I don't know how Cooper knew we were all here. He could've been following me, like I said, but he has spies everywhere. It's very likely he has one in this trailer park."

I opened my mouth to argue that the rebels would never do that, but she cut me off before I had a chance.

"Not among your friends—among the residents on the other side of the park. The ones near the entrance. The Dreamers, Jack. You and I both know they're easy to manipulate. I've seen Cooper at work, and the worst thing you can do is underestimate him. He can convince anyone that he can and will utterly destroy their lives in a single night if they don't do what he says." Her eyes searched mine, begging me to believe her. "For your average Dreamer, that's a pretty strong motivation."

I studied her expression, her eyes, her mannerisms, trying to see any hint of deception as she continued.

"You may not want me here. You can believe whatever you want about me, I don't care. I will follow you. I will find a way. And I *will* help you whether you want me to or not. I have reasons that are as strong as yours for wanting to complete this formula. Maybe even stronger." Her words spilled out so fast now that her breath came in panting bursts and her eyes burned with determination. "You can say no, but you can't stop me unless you want to kill me yourself for something that *I did not do*. I promise you, though . . . that if you let me, I *will* help you get your brother back alive."

I searched her eyes for any reason to think she would betray me again . . . and I knew she could. I'd been stupid to believe she couldn't. She was a Taker. Wasn't that what they always did? With them it was nearly inevitable.

When I thought of her as a Taker . . . I didn't want to trust her.

When I thought of her as Chloe . . . I really, really did.

"How can you possibly help me by staying with me?" I leaned against the van, sighing and massaging the back of my neck with my right hand.

"Have you ever had a Taker helping you before?" Chloe stepped in front of me, and that familiar wicked sparkle was back in her eyes.

"No."

"You'll see." She smiled wide.

Finn stepped toward us. I'd noticed him standing near the front of the van, listening, and he looked very relieved to see me fully in motion again. "So what's the plan? Rescue operation? Dark of night? Stealthy ninja attack? Whatever it is, I'm all in."

I shook my head firmly and turned to face him. "No, Finn." I heard Chloe give a low chuckle.

"If you keep saying no"—Finn's voice was light, but the determination in his expression was undeniable—"everyone will keep ignoring it and that might not be wise. No offense, but I think it undermines your ability to lead."

"Finn…"

"Parker may have been your brother for a month, Jack." Finn turned to face me and was so close I could count the lightest freckles on his nose in an instant. "But he's been mine my whole life. *Do not tell me no again.*"

FOURTEEN

PARKER

Cooper and Thor had only been driving about a mile before they got tired of me pounding on the windows and kicking their seats. They took my phone and put it under the front tire, then threw me in the trunk. I heard the crunch of my phone and grunted, trying to pull the bag off my face. I'd asked Cooper to take it off when they put me in the trunk, but Cooper refused with a cruel chuckle. Time had become pretty hard to track since then, but I guessed we'd been driving for a few hours minimum.

I spent much of the time trying not to puke. The bag over my face smelled like it had been filled with something rotten at some point. I tried to keep my breathing even and level because when I panicked and breathed in too fast, my lungs filled with rancid dust and I choked and coughed so hard my head ached. Besides, there was no reason to panic. I knew three things for sure.

1. The Takers were going to keep me alive for at least ten days.

2. Jack knew they had me, and had a somewhat unreliable track record for coming back when he promised.

3. All he needed to do to get me back safely was figure out the formula Dad had used to make Eclipse. The formula Dad completely destroyed, which Jack said he couldn't piece together again on his own even if he had ten *years* to do it.

Right … definitely no reason at all to panic.

The car finally stopped moving just as I started to doze off. I could tell by the chill in the air once they opened the trunk that the sun had gone down. Rough hands dragged me onto my feet. I didn't know how many of them were around me; I was guessing at least four. My hands were tied, but the rope was loose. My feet weren't bound at all, and I figured that since they probably didn't want to shoot me and risk losing their leverage, this might be my only chance.

Drawing in a shaky breath, I did something I hadn't dared even think about since Darkness and I had unified again. I reached inside of my head for a part of myself I knew was there, the part that wanted to survive more than anything. I tried to believe in that strength. I couldn't hear Darkness's voice anymore, and, thank God, he no longer had any control or power ... but knowing I had that kind of dark, desperate grit inside me actually helped more than I'd realized when facing something like this.

Maybe sometimes life called for a little madness.

Calling on that sheer will to live, I felt my body humming with adrenaline and tried to sense movement and sound in the air around me. Footsteps to my right, a shuffling of feet in front, someone murmuring to my left and a bit forward—I listened so close my ears ached with the strain. I gave myself twenty seconds as I heard Cooper talking with someone a few feet away to my right—if they finished their discussion and took me inside whatever building I assumed we were near, my chance would be lost. Behind me and to the left sounded the most vacant. I was eighty percent sure that spot was empty ... and twenty percent sure the world's quietest thug had decided to hang out there.

Silently tensing the muscles in my legs without yet moving an inch, I simultaneously turned and leapt straight through that spot. Reaching up for the paper bag, I yanked it so hard it ripped and fell off behind me. I crossed my fingers that I wouldn't barrel straight into anything too pain-inducing before my eyes could adjust to the dim light. I blinked and narrowly avoided running into a pole of some sort. My captors started yelling but I was already ten feet away, sprinting as fast as my cramped up legs would take me.

All around me, bizarre shapes loomed out of the darkness. Jagged archways, dark tunnels, and shady outlines of people beside metallic lumps on the ground. My eyes searched the blurred figures as I ran, desperate to identify anything familiar. But everything felt foreign. The only thing I recognized was the sky of twinkling stars spread out above me.

Ignoring my surroundings, I tossed up a silent prayer of thanks that I'd always been an avid runner, because I easily put a decent amount of ground between myself and my captors.

Suddenly, the shouts of Cooper's men cut through the air, becoming louder, more urgent.

"No! You're heading into—"

"Stop!"

"Idiot! You'll hurt yourself!"

My toe ran into something hard and metal. Searing pain shot up my leg and my whole body vibrated with the impact. The whole world spun as I tumbled through the air, landing hard on my hip and hands. Every nerve in every limb radiated with raw pain as I skidded across gravel, hitting metal tracks that ran across the ground until I finally came to a stop. I slowly raised my eyes, following the tracks to where they entered a tunnel into what looked like a massive human head sitting on the ground twenty feet in front of me.

What kind of hell had they brought me to?

I sat there, panting, staring at it. Through the darkness I could just make out huge eyes. They glowered at me. My knees and hands bled freely as I tried to decide if I should get up and run the opposite direction.

Then huge hands wrapped around my shoulders and pulled me back up onto my feet. Cooper jogged up after the others, carrying a flashlight. The beam illuminated the giant head and I realized it was a clown ... it was a huge, creepy clown face and the tracks went into its open mouth.

It was some kind of ride, I realized with a small amount of relief. Judging by the chipped paint and the piece of broken track in front of me, they'd brought me to an old, abandoned—and extremely creepy—amusement park. Cooper's flashlight brightened the clown face enough for me to see that inside, the tracks disappeared and the tunnel went into a straight drop for who knew how far. If I'd kept running...

Thor dragged me away from the giant clown face and I went willingly, panting and wiping the blood off my palms and onto my jeans. I hoped the Takers didn't see the way my legs trembled beneath me. My instinct upon catching my breath and not being eaten by a massive clown face was to say thank you, but Thor threw me so roughly back toward Cooper that the words stuck in my throat and felt as ridiculous as they would've if I said them out loud.

One of the Takers I didn't recognize grabbed my arms and held on so tightly that even taking a deep breath was painful. I was careful not to look into Cooper's eyes, but his general sentiment hovered somewhere in between bored and exhausted. "Please try not to kill yourself before we even get the chance. We're supposed to wait ten days, and if you keep doing stupid things like that, you won't last through the first one."

"An abandoned amusement park?" I panted in confusion. "This is the new Taker camp?"

Cooper grabbed on to the rope that bound my hands together and jerked me along roughly behind him. He gestured toward a ragged sign near the place where they'd parked the car. "It was called Funtopia. I like it."

"Of course *you* do," I muttered. One of the Takers kicked my foot from behind and nearly sent me to the ground again.

Everywhere I looked sat rotting metal cars and rides that had long since been grown over with weeds. I shuddered ... forget nightmares. *This* was where children's imaginations came to die. I forced my mind to focus on what I should be doing. I knew Jack couldn't make Eclipse like they wanted. The trade Cooper wanted was not an option ... so now what? What would Jack do if he were here?

That was easy. He would find a way to escape.

And that's exactly what I would have to do.

I decided to try to keep Cooper talking. Maybe I could learn something.

"Why here? Doesn't look like there's much room for shelter," I said.

"It's deceiving on the surface, like many things," Cooper grunted as he led me down a path toward the entrance of a squat, rounded building with a big double door. It looked more like storage than anything.

Four large, armed guards stood on either side of the entrance. When I got closer, I squinted and then gaped at them. Using the word "armed" to describe them was like when doctors used to write in my file that I was a "teenager with a minor sleep disorder."

When we went to their last base, the security guards had belts on with a gun at their hips. Apparently the Takers had learned their lesson, because these guys looked more like commandos. They had rifles over their shoulders, bullet-proof vests, grenades at their hips, knives of every size hung from their vests and belts, and each had a hilt sticking out of the side of his boots—and these were just the weapons I recognized. There were many more that looked completely foreign to me.

"I'm sorry ... did you move this base into North Korea when I wasn't looking?" I tried to laugh it off, but my voice sounded shaky even to me.

Cooper looked straight at me, and I barely managed to shift my gaze away before our eyes connected. I *had* to be more careful.

"This is only the part of our security we've let you see." He opened the door and stepped inside, and one of the Takers behind me pushed me through it. Cooper went on to say, "We don't make the same mistakes twice. And now when we have intruders, these guys shoot to kill."

As I followed Cooper into an entry, I was surprised to find an empty room that looked as big as the size of the entire building as seen from the outside. At the back of the room was an extra-wide set of stairs going down. My captors led me down the stairs and then through hallway after hallway after hallway. The construction went from being a few years old to progressively older and older the further we went into this underground labyrinth. I'd given up on talking to Cooper. The conversation wasn't getting me anywhere anyway. Instead, I tried to pay attention to the path through this maze and any weaknesses I might find in their security.

More armed guards were roaming around in the halls,

which didn't seem promising. I kept my eyes open for any other exits, but I saw zero alternate hallways that seemed to lead back toward the surface. In fact, everything only led deeper into the Earth. How was I going to get out of here?

My heart sank as I realized the better question was: how could I tell Jack where to come get me when the only entry I'd seen would get him killed?

The whole plan of avoiding eye contact with the Takers would only help if I had information that would help Jack. Right now, asking him to come for me would be like giving him a death sentence.

And I would not let my brother walk into that.

Of course, none of it would even matter if the Takers forced me to make eye contact with one of them before I could go to sleep. My chances of getting out of here without Jack making some kind of payment were getting slimmer with every armed guard we passed. Minute after minute ticked by with no end to this maze in sight, and after about the fiftieth turn, I felt hopelessly lost. Even if I'd believed Jack had a chance in hell of getting into this place without getting shot, I still wouldn't be able to tell him where to find me.

Finally, we reached a hallway that must've been the oldest one so far. The walls were made of stone, the floor of cracked cement. Fluorescent lights hummed and flickered overhead. The left wall had many doors, each spaced about eight feet apart. The doors had tiny, dusty windows in them, but before I got a chance to look inside one, I noticed the only thing in the hall that looked new.

Bright, shiny locks hung on the outside of every door.

Prison cells—the Takers had created their own little prison wing, just like the one they'd had at the old air force base. These cells were built to replace the ones they'd kept my dad and the other captives in.

Because what was a new Taker base without a good, solid place where you could lock up and torture your enemies?

Cooper led the way down to one that had extra locks on the door.

"Aww, extra locks just for me?" I tried to sound braver than I felt. "You shouldn't have."

He opened the door and threw me inside without bothering to untie my hands. I sprawled shoulder first onto the concrete. There was no light in the room aside from what came through the tiny window in the door. The cot against the right wall must've been brought from the base because it looked nearly worn through. The fabric was so thin I was afraid it wouldn't hold my weight. The bucket in the back corner was disgusting enough that I didn't dare stare directly at it. There was a dead rat just inside the door.

I'd never thought of myself or my life as spoiled or privileged. I'd never understood how very lucky I was to have a nice home. How great my bed was—whether I actually slept while I was in it or not. How much I missed Addie, Finn, and Mia. How amazing my mom was, and how upset and scared she was going to be when I didn't come home tonight...or tomorrow night...or the night after that.

And then I just desperately wanted to go home. I tried not to let my dread of being left in here show on my face as

Thor untied my hands. For an instant, I almost thought I saw a hint of sympathy in Thor's face, but just as fast, it was gone.

"Welcome home, Parker." I could tell from Cooper's smirk as he closed the door and left me in the dark that he knew exactly how awful this was for me. And that he loved every minute of it. "I hope you enjoy your stay at our new base as much as your father enjoyed his time at our old one."

FIFTEEN

JACK

Libby's exhaustion after the events of the day actually helped, and she was asleep in only a few minutes. Knowing she could be our best hope of finding Parker, we all stayed as quiet as possible to avoid waking her up before she had a chance to get us the answers we were so desperate for. Still, I couldn't stop myself from glancing again and again at my rear view mirror to make sure she hadn't woken up too early.

Chloe sat completely silent in the front seat. She looked like she feared that if she breathed too hard someone might kick her out.

At least we were on the road now, and I was more than relieved to be out of Cypress Crest. There was nothing else I could do for them. Nothing else I could do for Marisol or even for Libby. More importantly, there was nothing else I could do to help Parker … at least not there.

The only thing I could do right now that held hope for any of us started with finding Wendy King and ended with completing my dad's new formula. As much as I missed Dad, at the moment I wished I could punch him. This time, of all times, couldn't he have just given me all the information? Why did everything have to be so complicated?

Beneath my anger, I remembered that this was one more piece of insurance we'd get out of the base alive. If they tried to kill us, they'd never have a chance to live. His paranoia had saved us time and again over the years.

Still, right now, with Parker's life at risk. I just wanted answers.

As soon as we were on the road, Finn proved how helpful he could be by immediately running a search for all Wendy Kings in the Brimley Terrace area. There were three. He quietly called all of them, pretending to be collecting information for the local school board.

"Why the school board?" I asked.

Finn gave me a sad smile. "It's something Parker taught me once. He said most adults are more willing to help if kids are involved. It ties in to some kind of survival instinct."

I nodded, impressed.

Before we were even halfway through the hour drive, Finn had eliminated one of the Wendys because she'd died last year. He eliminated the next because the number was disconnected—she was still a possibility, but since she'd just became much harder to find, we hoped she wasn't the right one.

So now, thanks to Finn, we had an address for the best candidate *and* we knew she was at home. Parker had only been gone a few hours, but with a deadline of only ten days, every minute counted. Finn had saved us at least an hour.

"Thank you," I said softly without looking at him.

I could hear the surprise in his tone when he answered. "You're welcome. But I did it for Parker."

"I know."

Brimley Terrace was where Dad had grown up. Maybe he and Wendy had known each other for a long time. Maybe she'd known Dad before he'd become the man I knew. Maybe he'd known Wendy before he had to hide and run all the time to stay safe.

I couldn't even imagine my father as a man without secrets.

Casting a glance at the others in the van, it was pretty obvious I wasn't the only one feeling distracted. Finn was staring so hard out the window that he could've been trying to shoot lasers out his eyes to blast the road before us. Chloe kept peeking back at Libby like she thought she might suddenly wake up and decide to pounce on her again.

My eyes were starting to feel the strain of too many nights without a Builder. I blinked hard and rubbed them with the back of my hand. I honestly didn't know how Parker had survived like he had with just Mia—and then I swallowed back a fresh wave of guilt. I'd never really told him how sorry I was, or how terrible I felt, that he'd become Divided on my watch. Dad had told me to keep an eye on him, and I should've watched him closer. But he hid being a Watcher so well. Most of us couldn't go on functioning that long without sleep. Parker had still been going to school and making passable grades. He'd looked a bit like a druggy, but so do a lot of the guys in high school.

And then he'd managed to do the impossible and somehow merge his mind back together. It had literally never happened before. Not that I'd ever heard of anyway.

I gripped the steering wheel so tightly the leather creaked under my fingers. If any Watcher could survive being held captive by the son of Steve Campbell, it was Parker—the son of Steve's worst enemy, Danny Chipp.

My brother would be fine, and I would make sure of it by getting to him this time before it was too late.

"Did that steering wheel offend you in some way?" Chloe whispered.

I blinked and looked over at her, but didn't respond. Chloe just rolled her eyes and peeked into the back at Libby again.

"You don't have to watch her. She won't attack you again—not right now anyway." My eyes were mostly back on the road, but I could still see Chloe's eyebrows shoot up to nearly hide behind her bangs.

"I'm not afraid of her." Her tone made the idea sound completely absurd.

"Then why do you keep looking back there?"

"Because I just wonder..." She hesitated as she again turned to glance at Libby. "I just wonder what it's like to be able to sleep like that. And to control their dreams the way they do. You know?"

I frowned, my eyes straying from the road over to Chloe's face, but she seemed sincere. "I guess so."

"I don't know." Chloe settled back into her seat and tucked her legs up under her chin, wrapping her arms around them. She looked very small and vulnerable in that position, especially when she continued. "I just think that out of all of us, the Builders definitely got the best deal in this whole scenario."

I barely hid my reaction. To have a Taker, the daughter of a man who compared their kind and their abilities to gods, sitting here saying that the Builders had it better? Even after everything else, Chloe continued to surprise me.

Finn's phone rang and we both jumped. He pulled it from his pocket and held it forward to me in a panic. "It's Parker's mom! What do I tell her?"

"Send her to voicemail," I answered quickly, hoping we could avoid waking Libby if we didn't have to. Finn frowned deeply and shook his head, but then did as I asked before the phone had a chance to ring again.

"Okay, done. But we don't have long before she calls back. I guarantee it." Finn looked at me in the rearview mirror, keeping his voice low to match mine. "We can't just ignore her calls for ten days."

"I know we can't," I muttered. My mind raced for answers. What could we tell Mrs. Chipp? If we told her the truth, wouldn't she want to go to the police? The police would only cause problems here, as we'd already seen. The Takers had the advantage in every way when it came to Dreamers. Why hadn't I already been thinking about this problem?

Because I'd never had to deal with a mom before? Because my mom was—well, because my mom was dead. Because of that, she hadn't been around to worry about me when I'd gotten into trouble...I had no clue what to do with a worried mom.

"Text her." I focused my eyes on the road. "Tell her Parker's phone is dead and the reception is bad, but that we're fine and spending the night at the camp with the other Night Walkers. Pretend to be him. You can do that...right, Finn?"

He didn't respond, but I could hear him punching the message into his phone so I knew he was doing as I asked. After a few seconds, I repeated, "Right?"

Finn gave me a non-committal grunt before hitting one final button and putting his phone away. "You know that is going to buy us one day at best, right?"

"I do."

"Well then I hope you have a better plan for tomorrow." Finn sighed and slouched back against his seat to look out the window.

"I think I do."

In the mirror, I saw his head swivel to face the front and then he leaned forward again with interest.

"What is it?"

"Look." I put my blinker on and moved the van toward the freeway exit that said *Brimley Terrace*. "I don't know anything about moms. That should be obvious to everyone. So, my plan is to put you in charge of the problem."

"Me?" Finn's voice squeaked a little.

"Yes. I've seen you convince both Parker's mom and your mom to do something they weren't originally ready to

agree with. You get them. You're the expert. You tell me."
I held his gaze in the mirror. "Tomorrow, when we talk to
her again, what should we tell her?"

Finn's mouth pressed into a firm line. I was surprised
when he and Chloe answered in unison: "The truth."

Chloe clamped her lips shut and her cheeks flushed red,
but Finn's expression went quickly past surprised and onto
validated.

He nodded and continued, "She isn't just any mom.
She isn't in the dark anymore. Parker has told her everything
about his dad and about being a Watcher now. She knows
about how his dad died. We can tell her this. She'll be terrified, she'll want to help, but she won't cause problems if we
tell her it will risk Parker."

Then Chloe spoke again from her seat, but her words
were barely loud enough to hear. "Parker trusted you, Jack.
So she will trust you."

"Exactly!" Finn nodded, and then shot Chloe a weird
look. Chloe was staring at the floor, the door handle, anywhere but at Finn. This conversation was taking a really
strange turn.

"All right. If you're sure, then that's what we'll try . . .
tomorrow." I took my second left and parked thirty feet up
the street from the house that currently belonged to a woman
named Wendy King. It was small and gray, but there was a
fresh coat of green paint on the fence in the backyard.

"So Wendy King has an ingredient?" Chloe asked.

"Or, she *is* an ingredient?" Finn's eyebrows shot way
up. "Maybe *people* are the missing parts of the formula?"

Chloe rolled her eyes and ignored him, so I followed suit and said, "I'm hoping Dad gave her the information we need."

Finn leaned back in the front seat and muttered something about being underappreciated in his time.

It was hard to believe that Dad had stayed in touch with someone he'd known growing up, but maybe that's why she wouldn't have been at risk. He could have known her before he was even aware he was a Watcher. "Let's go see if we're any closer to solving this formula."

SIXTEEN

PARKER

The cot was exactly as worn as it looked. I'd tested the weight with one foot and it collapsed into a pile of rags and bent metal. Gathering the pieces of cloth, I spread them out across the grimy concrete floor and made a spot to sit or lie down on. It wasn't much, but it didn't make my skin crawl as much as the ground around it.

"Hello? Is someone in there?" The man's voice felt like it was coming from the wall behind me. For a moment I wondered if I'd imagined it, then it spoke again. "Please tell me if you're there."

"I'm here," I whispered softly in response, keeping my eyes on the door. "Who are you?"

"Oh, thank God..." His voice cracked with emotion.

"No one has spoken to me in over a week. I feel like I'm going crazy in here."

I waited for him to actually answer my question, wondering if this could be some kind of trick or Taker mindgame they were playing.

"Sorry, my name is Shawn." He spoke quickly. The poor guy sounded afraid of the silence when I didn't answer.

"You've been in here for a week?" I asked, careful to keep the skepticism from my tone.

"No. I've been in here since we moved here a month ago." His words came so fast I had to focus to understand him. "The silent treatment they've been giving me has lasted a week... before that, they tried different things."

Even though I was already cold, this last part made me shiver. "What kinds of things?"

There was a long-enough silence that I was afraid he might have decided he preferred silence to conversation with me. When he spoke again, his voice sounded haunted. "I hope you don't ever find out."

I didn't know what that meant, but from his tone alone I knew that I hoped the same thing.

"Listen, I'm going to go to sleep for a bit, but I don't expect I'll be going anywhere anytime soon." My voice was gentle. I didn't want to upset this man if he was the only person I might have to talk to over the next ten days. "Can we talk more when I wake up?"

"You can sleep? You aren't like them?" he asked, sounding hopeful.

"What do you mean, 'like them'?" I decided not to actually answer the question until I knew more about him.

"You aren't someone who can take over other people while they sleep?" His voice sounded scared and I couldn't blame him.

"No, I'm not like them," I said, before finishing with, "Good night."

"Good night." His whisper sounded dejected, and I couldn't help but pity him.

For now, though, it was time to sleep. I was still surprised I'd managed to make it all the way to this cell without making eye contact with anyone. I was still connected to Libby. And even though I no longer had any intention of telling them where I was—for the sake of their safety—I could at least make contact with Libby, let them know I was okay, and ask her to get a message to Jack.

And the sooner I accomplished that goal, the better.

I tried to settle my long legs into a comfortable position on the small piece of floor. It wasn't easy. Cold seeped through the floor and into my skin. I couldn't help the shivering. I tried sitting up against the wall instead and it was slightly better... even if I could hear the skittering movements from rats in the wall behind my head. Finally, the stress and outright exhaustion of the day caught up to me and I drifted off to sleep.

———

Libby's dreams were chaos, and she sat at the very center of it. The only Builder whose dreams I'd been in was Addie, and she always strived to make them controlled and peaceful.

Libby's couldn't have been farther from that if she'd been trying.

The entire dream was a storm. The wind blew and there was the tang of coming rain in the air...but no actual drops. Lightning cracked and the ground shook. It was more than just a dream of a storm, though. Something more was happening here, and it physically hurt me to be in the middle of it. My brain ached. It felt like sandpaper was being used inside my skull. What was so wrong? What was Libby doing?

Then I realized she wasn't just building a chaotic storm dream. The chaos was a by-product of a much more intense kind of damage. Every dream had layers—this was one of the first things I'd learned about them. The only exceptions had been Mia's self-hypnosis dreams, or Addie's dreams when she was in control and forced them into one layer so I could sleep.

Libby was using the layers in a completely unnatural way. It was something I wouldn't have even thought possible if I wasn't seeing it myself.

She was separating the dream into more and more layers. Shredding it into so many I couldn't even keep track— and then smashing the layers violently against each other.

This entire dream was like the ocean during a massive storm. Each layer was a wave crashing this way and that, smashing into other waves and shattering them apart.

My brain hurt as it was being pelted by bits and pieces of fragmented dreams. Libby was unleashing all her pain and anger on this dream, and the devastation from it was mind-boggling.

Several memories of a significantly younger Jack came through, and the emotion tied to them was intense. She loved him, but that strong emotion was blended with a longing and sadness that could only mean one thing—to Libby, it was more than just a sisterly kind of relationship, and it had been for a long time.

I knew that feeling too well. I was just lucky that Addie had loved me back.

Another bolt of lightning struck nearby. The ground shook as memories of Jack shredded before me. I pressed my hands against my head in an attempt to stop the pain.

Libby was only a few feet away. Her back was to me, her body curled down on the floor with her head resting against her knees. I stumbled closer and could see her fingers. They were gripped in her hair in tight fists of fury. The pain in my head became excruciating. It was unbelievable that she could hurt me this much using only her mind.

Focusing on touching her and not letting my fingers pass through, I rested my right hand on the back of her head. Desperate, I yelled her name. "Please, Libby! You have to stop!"

Immediately, everything around us went still and quiet. I withdrew my hand and fell to one side as I tried to catch my breath. My head was still pounding, but it wasn't with the same ferocity as a minute ago.

Libby shifted around slowly to face me. Her eyes were

wet and she still looked devastated, but she was focused on me now instead of bent on destruction.

"I didn't feel you enter the dream ... I'm sorry." Her shoulders hunched forward and her entire body trembled like it was trying to let go of something dark that had attached itself to her. "Very smart, by the way, you meeting my eyes before they took you."

"It was the only thing I could think of to do." I rubbed at my temples with my fingertips, willing the headache to fade even more, but it didn't.

"Where are you? You're still with *him*, right?" Libby stared at me, and her brown eyes looked darker and colder than I remember them being. "Has Jack trained you?"

"If by 'with him,' you mean I'm being kept locked up in a cell by Cooper, then yeah." I lowered my brow and finished. "Trained me how?"

"Can you kill Cooper?" Her words came out too fast, too eager.

Her words shocked me. "*Kill* him? You think Jack has trained me to kill people?"

She watched me for a minute before her shoulders slumped so far forward I worried she might cave in on herself. "No ... he wouldn't."

"No," I responded firmly. "And even if he had, I wouldn't do it ... not unless I had no other choice."

Libby obviously didn't want to talk about this anymore. "What do you want me to tell Jack?"

"Tell him I'm okay for now, but it is too dangerous to come in here to get me."

"Where do they have you?" Libby squinted at me like she didn't quite understand what I was saying.

I dropped my chin and stared at her. "You know if I answer that then he'll come in after me. I'm trying to keep all of you safe too."

She frowned. "You know he isn't going to like that you're taking this out of his hands."

I shrugged. "That isn't new. He doesn't like a lot of things I do."

"At least tell me why it isn't safe?" Her gaze was appraising.

I chose my words carefully, knowing Jack would analyze each and every one of them. "The Takers are heavily armed and have me in a place where it will be nearly impossible to get to me."

Libby watched me for a minute before nodding. "And you're sure you'll be okay in there for a few days?"

My brain wasn't so sure, but I gave a firm nod anyway. "Yes. Just tell Jack to spend his time working on Dad's new formula instead of worrying abou—" Then I couldn't finish speaking.

Libby's eyes went wide. There was a violent yanking sensation in my gut and I heard her scream my name just as I was dragged forcefully out of the dream.

———

"I don't remember saying it was naptime." Cooper's face was so close to mine that I could smell something that reeked of over-ripe tomatoes on his breath. My body sputtered at the water he'd dumped on my head, but I remembered to keep my eyes closed so I wouldn't lose my connection to Libby.

"How long was he out?" I heard him asking someone else in the room.

"Maybe an hour."

"That should've been long enough … " He shoved me against the wall so hard my forehead smacked against it and my headache was back to full force immediately. I slid to the floor and raised both hands as I coughed and sputtered, wiping the water off my face. Keeping my eyes closed wasn't an option if I wanted to be able to protect myself. I opened them, but kept my gaze down on Cooper's black sneakers.

"Did you get a chance to chat, then?" He sounded satisfied. "Got to catch up with your big brother, did you?"

My blood ran cold. "You wanted me to talk to them?"

Cooper chuckled. "Let me guess. You told them you're okay and that he shouldn't try to come save you?"

I didn't answer. The long maze-walk down to my cell, all the armed guards we'd passed on the way … he'd orchestrated this whole thing. I'd done exactly what he'd wanted, played right into his hands.

I'd made sure that my brother had no other choice than to work as hard and fast as he could on the formula—but Cooper didn't know that Jack was working on the new formula, not Eclipse.

Well, at least he wasn't the only one who had secrets.

Cooper watched me, waiting for a response. But I'd be

damned if I was going to give him exactly what he wanted again today.

Waiting in silence worked just fine with me.

The seconds stretched to minutes. My eyes grew heavy. I wanted to close them again, but I only did so when he came close enough to threaten eye contact. I forced myself not to act on all my impulses to attack him. No reason to add fuel to this fire.

"You know this isn't going to work anymore, right?" Cooper surprised me when he spoke, because he didn't sound angry or even frustrated now . . . he sounded like he was trying not to laugh.

"What?" I growled out the word.

"We take over people's bodies by making eye contact with them." Cooper did laugh now, but it sounded more crazed than amused. "Come on. You honestly think we haven't perfected ways to force people to meet our eyes?"

My spine straightened as I wondered what kind of methods he might be referring to.

I heard additional footsteps and knew other people were in the room. Closing my eyes again, I braced myself for whatever they had in mind.

Out of nowhere, they grabbed me. Someone held me down and another person opened my mouth and filled it with some kind of rancid-tasting liquid.

My body spasmed and I coughed, fighting to stay calm and breathe through my nose. If I stayed calm, it would be fine. Until someone clamped their fingers over my nose. Instantly, my eyes and my throat opened in panic. I locked eyes with Cooper before I even had an instant to think about it … but that didn't matter anymore. I was drowning. I couldn't breathe, and they dumped more and more of the liquid into my mouth. My head was pounding even harder and my throat burned. Each breath that I couldn't get made my chest ache like an empty pit I could never fill.

Jerking my arms and legs against their grip, I got one shoulder free and hit Cooper hard with my right fist before my vision started to blur. There were voices from what felt like a long distance away, but my body suffered from tremor after tremor as they argued. This was the last of the fight left in me, the last of my life, and they were washing it away with this putrid water.

Forcing my consciousness to stay aware was too difficult when the smooth oblivion that wanted me instead felt this welcoming. My last thought was to hope Jack might watch out for my mom when I was gone … and to wonder why I'd never asked him to do that before Cooper threw me into the back of his car.

SEVENTEEN

JACK

My fingertips felt numb as I knocked on Wendy King's door for the second time. I looked over my shoulder at Chloe and Finn, who looked even more nervous than I did. We'd left Libby still sleeping in the car. Chloe bounced forward onto her toes and then back onto her heels in a nervous kind of bob and weave. Her short hair swung with the motion: forward into her eyes, and then back out of them again. After a few seconds, Finn reached out with both hands and pushed down solidly on her shoulders until she settled onto the balls of her feet.

"Sorry," Chloe muttered, and Finn went back to frowning deeply at the door handle.

This Wendy had to be home. We'd just called her. It was only nine o'clock at night. The sun had just gone down half an hour ago. One day gone already. If she wasn't here, we'd just have to wait until she came back home. And we didn't really have time for that...

The door handle turned and the door opened, but the face that greeted us definitely wasn't someone named Wendy. It was a man in his forties with neatly combed brown hair. He looked at us with a wary frown, the kind people wore when they didn't know what you were going to say but they were still relatively sure they didn't want to hear it.

"Can I help you?" he asked pointedly, as we all just stared at him without speaking.

"Yes." I spoke up fast. "We're looking for Wendy King. Is she here?"

He took a step back like he was going to get someone, then hesitated and said, "You aren't selling something, are you?"

"No." All three of us spoke at the same time, which only made him more suspicious.

"I think she might have known my—my dad." I went ahead with the truth, thinking that we were desperate and it couldn't hurt anyone anymore ... not in the same way, at least. No one could use him against me, or threaten to hurt me to make him do things. He was free of that now—I guess we both were.

The man nodded and partially shut the door as he turned toward the interior of the house. "Wen! There's a group of kids at the door for you!"

There was no response, and after a few seconds he looked back out at us. "I'll go get her."

I nodded and Finn said "Thank you" as he shut the door.

A few minutes later, we heard voices coming from inside.

"Kids?" a hushed female voice said, and all three of us leaned closer to the door, listening.

"Teenagers," the man's voice responded.

"What do they want?" she asked, sounding confused even through the door.

"I don't know. Did you want me to have them fill out a questionnaire?" The man was clearly exasperated. When I looked over at Chloe, she was grinning.

The door swung open and we all stood up straight, trying not to look like we were eavesdropping. Wendy was around the same age as the man and had jet black hair pulled away from her face in a ponytail. She had flecks of red on her hands and shirt, and it took me a minute to realize they were paint. I wondered if she was an artist like Mia, or if she was the one responsible for the green fence outside and was now working on some other project.

"My name is Jack, and these are my friends Finn and Chloe. I think you might have known my dad. I'm trying to get some information." I smiled smoothly, trying to mimic the way Parker used his charm to convince people to see his side of things. It was a genuine talent...one I apparently lacked. She looked even more skeptical than before.

"What makes you think I know him?" Her words came fast. It was like she wanted us to know we were interrupting something and she needed to get back to it as soon as possible. She still stood in the doorway, her hand on the knob in case she decided to slam the door in my face.

I really needed her to not do that.

"He grew up around here and had your name written down in some old papers. His name was Daniel. Daniel Chipp."

As soon as I spoke his name, her hand rose up to her chest and I knew we'd found the right Wendy. Suddenly it was more like she was holding onto the door handle for support.

"You remember him." I stated it quietly, a fact, not a question.

"Yes, of course." Wendy was slightly pale, but she looked much more welcoming now than she had before; definitely a good sign. She gestured toward a picnic table and chairs on one side of her front yard. "Why don't we sit down for a minute?"

Finn went to check in on Libby to see if she was awake yet. Chloe and I followed Wendy over to the table. Her husband, who she introduced as Aaron, joined us.

I studied them closely as they spoke. Could they both be Night Walkers? Which one was a Builder?

Wendy asked the question I knew was coming.

"You're talking about Daniel in the past tense..." She didn't look like she wanted to finish the question.

"He passed away a few weeks ago." My stomach rolled within me at the words I'd just uttered. It felt so wrong to use that phrase to describe an ending so violent. It felt like it dishonored him somehow.

"That's terrible." Wendy shook her head and reached out to pat the back of my hand. "I'm so sorry for your loss."

"Thank you," I mumbled. It was difficult to resist the urge to jerk my hand away. I knew she was just trying to be nice, but I didn't like accepting comfort from others. I didn't need their comfort... or at least, I didn't want it to look like I needed it.

Chloe was sitting beside me, and although I didn't see her move, I felt a slight squeeze of her hand on my wrist beneath the table. It was completely unexpected and caught me off guard. The warmth of her fingers felt like an electric current to my skin, sending tingles shooting up my arm that were incredibly distracting. But more than that, it was the way she was doing it that made my head spin. Under the table where no one could see and no one knew but me— the message of it had an impact on me. I didn't know how this girl could possibly understand me like she did... but she really seemed to. Did she get all this from, as she had put it, studying her enemy?

When did I stop being that enemy to her?

More importantly, when would she stop being mine? Or had she already?

I cleared my throat, surprised and embarrassed by the sudden confusing emotion I felt rising inside me. Immediately, Chloe's hand lifted away and my skin felt naked where it had been. I missed it... and I kind of hated myself for it. I forced my mind into motion. Parker was counting on me. "Do you mind if I ask how you knew him?"

"Not at all." Wendy gave me a sad smile. "We went to school together. I would say he was my first love. We were young, only in middle school, and it was very innocent...but he was brilliant even then." She turned and winked at Aaron. He reached out for her hand. "I've always been attracted to smart men."

I calculated in my head—middle school. Dad would've developed his Watcher abilities around that age. She knew him at that time. Maybe she was another Watcher and Aaron was a Builder she'd ended up with later...or vice versa.

Wendy continued. "As we got a little older, though, we drifted apart and he moved away. I saw him the last time a couple of years ago though. I'm a pharmacist at a local pharmacy and he came into my shop. It's such a small world, and it was so great to see him again! He said he'd become a chemistry professor. I wasn't at all surprised."

She stared off into the distance behind me, reliving some pleasant memory as I analyzed every word she said. Wendy was a pharmacist, and Dad wasn't on any regular medication. So unless he'd actually been sick and just happened to wander into her pharmacy—unlikely—he'd probably planned out seeing her again to reconnect and tell her about the ingredient. In fact, he often worked with pharmacists to obtain ingredients for his compounds and formulas that were difficult to get otherwise. Maybe she was even a source he'd used?

But then why not just come out and tell me? Why the act?

Maybe she didn't trust that I was who I said I was? Or maybe...her husband didn't know? Maybe he wasn't a Watcher; maybe he actually wasn't a Night Walker at all. He could be normal and married to a Night Walker and have no idea. That happened all the time. If she was a Builder, that would make perfect sense—Builders didn't need Watchers; some didn't even ever realize what they were. It was absolutely possible he had no idea what she was.

I gave a slight cough and put my hand to my throat. I deliberately looked away from Wendy and straight at Aaron. I knew she might volunteer to get it anyway, but I thought if I made it obvious enough, that he might do it. "I'm sorry. Is there any way I could bother you for a glass of water?"

He raised an eyebrow and then glanced at his wife. She started to stand, but Chloe reached out directly in front of her and pointed over Wendy's shoulder toward the fence. "I noticed you have paint on your hands. Did you do the fence? It's a beautiful color of green."

Wendy froze in a half-standing position looking at Chloe's arm in front of her nose for a half a second before smiling widely and sitting back down. She glanced over her shoulder toward the vibrant fence. "Yes! I just finished that last week. It used to be white, but the paint was chipping and it really looked more gray than anything. I thought a splash of color could liven it up."

Chloe nodded vigorously. "It's gorgeous! Are you planning to paint the house, too? I think it would look incredible with a brick red or something to compliment the fence."

I turned my eyes on Aaron and gave another slight cough. He got to his feet and walked toward the house, mumbling, "I'll be right back."

As soon as he was out of earshot, I turned back toward Wendy and knew I didn't have much time. "You know what he was, right?"

Wendy looked jolted by the sudden change in the conversation and her mouth was frozen in an odd half-smile in response. "I'm sorry, what?"

"Daniel, my father." I spoke fast, leaning forward and keeping my eyes on the house in case Aaron came back. "You know he was a type 2."

She stared at me blankly. No recognition in her brown eyes, no response from her lips.

"He was a Watcher?" I said the only other words I knew to identify it, but still nothing even hinting of understanding came from Wendy.

"What are you talking about?" She leaned backward, looking at both of us now with a newly suspicious quality to her expression.

"Forget about it." Okay, so she either wasn't a Night Walker or she was an extremely good liar. I was getting desperate.

Through a window, I saw Aaron walking toward the front door with an armful of bottled water. "When you saw my dad, did he tell you anything important?" I asked quickly. "Did he ask you to remember anything or talk about ingredients at all?"

Wendy was frowning now and starting to look upset. "What are you talking about? No, he never asked me to remember anything like that."

"Did you supply him with any drugs or chemicals from your pharmacy without a prescription?" I spoke the words hastily as I watched Aaron walk out the front door. When I turned my eyes back on Wendy's furious brown ones, I knew I'd made a big mistake.

"How dare you?" She got to her feet and glared across the table at me. "I don't know anything about you, but I know Daniel would've been ashamed to have raised someone so rude."

"I'm sorry, Mrs. Ki—" I sincerely hadn't meant it like that and her words stung, even though it was clear she hadn't known Dad like she thought she did.

"No. Please go." She turned and stomped back toward her house, just as Aaron dropped the water bottles on the table.

I picked one up and opened it without looking at him. "Thank you."

Chloe stood, and I was a little surprised as she made apologies for us and shook Aaron's hand as I walked back toward the van. Why did everything have to be so difficult? I didn't know what to do now. How could Dad's clue have led to such a dead end?

I pulled sunglasses out of my pocket and put them on as a last ditch effort. I'd made eye contact with Wendy last. I would try to find out something from her dreams tonight. Maybe she was a Builder or a Watcher and she was lying about it. Maybe she wasn't either, but she was hiding something else. Either way, if there was anything she wasn't telling me, I would uncover it in her dreams.

No one could hide anything from me in there. It was the only place in the world where I had all the power.

EIGHTEEN
PARKER

Life came back with violent bursts of burning from my toes to the tips of every piece of damp hair. Each cell in my body screamed in unison in response to the vicious attack. There had almost been peace, and now there was nothing but agony. My stomach and lungs clawed at my internal organs, their contents eager to escape. I coughed and threw up every ounce of the liquid Cooper had forced down my throat. It seared, and the air gave intense relief in baffling bursts in either direction—liquid out, air in, liquid out, air in. I felt ill. My body had been poisoned and it wanted a way to force all of the toxin out ... but it couldn't find one.

Cooper's method had been effective, I had to admit. My eyes had opened out of reflex. I'd had no choice. By passing a message to Libby that Jack shouldn't come here for me, I'd let Cooper use me exactly the way he wanted, without even recognizing it. And now my connection to Libby had been severed.

I rolled to my side again and clutched my stomach as another stabbing pain went through my gut. In the darkness of the room I heard someone laugh. I'd thought I was alone; I don't know why, but I had. I opened my eyes, trying to make them focus, but it took several blinks before everything wasn't cloudy.

Cooper was in here, alone. He leaned against the wall next to my threadbare cot.

"I thought I said we weren't going to kill you," he said lightly.

"So did I," I grunted out against another flash of agonizing pain.

"Then you shouldn't try so hard to die." Cooper smiled and leaned forward until his face was in the shaft of fluorescent light coming through the window on my door. It was disturbing how much every passing hour affected him. He looked more exhausted now than he had when I arrived, which couldn't have been more than a few hours ago.

"If you want me alive..." I tightened my hands into fists, dealing with the pain in that way instead, so my voice could come out with more strength. "If so, you should stop trying to drown me, or at the very least don't use contaminated water to do it."

Cooper didn't respond, but he squinted and leaned a little closer to me. It was like he didn't hear or understand what I'd said.

"That water was bad and I think you've poisoned me. And this means I may have to reevaluate my position." I leaned up on one arm and met his eyes. No reason to avoid the eye contact now that he'd already forced me to do it once.

Even with the dark, sunken circles beneath his eyes, he still looked fascinated. His eyes sparkled as he said, "What position is that?"

"I always assumed Thor was the dumbass in your family." I grunted as an especially intense wave of pain hit and I couldn't hold it at bay anymore. I curled back onto the floor and my voice was strained as I finished. "Now I'm certain that it's you."

Cooper's laugh was cold this time and I watched him stand up straight against the wall. "Oh, don't worry about contaminated water, Parker. It wasn't water at all."

I raised my head slightly, a shiver going through me at the menacing tone suddenly filling his words. "Then what was it?"

"I'd call it … the beginning." Cooper walked slowly toward the door and I saw his left hand start to shake with a tremor that went all the way up to his shoulder before he gripped it with his right hand and made it stop. He turned to face me, pretending like it hadn't happened even though we both knew it had. "We're just getting started."

"The beginning of what?" I asked, and then my whole body started to shiver. The shaking only made the pain more intense and I couldn't stop myself from cursing against it.

"You can't fight it. We gave you our own special concoction designed to make your body react this way." Cooper watched my agony with a wide smile on his face before continuing. "We may not be able to kill you, but while you're here, we're going to make you wish we could. You'll be begging for it before your brother gets back here with Eclipse. I guarantee it."

Then he walked out and locked the door behind him. The room grew colder in the minutes after he left. No, the air around me wasn't colder, *I* was hotter. I had a fever. My body was fighting whatever they'd put in me. I just had to hang in there and keep fighting.

That's what Addie and Finn would want me to do. That's what my mom would want.

Another blinding wave of pain crashed through me and a hoarse cry tore free from my throat. Time passed, but it was impossible to tell how much. One wave of pain would be so intense I couldn't stay conscious through it. And the next would bring me back to awareness as it tore through my body with the force of a natural disaster. I could feel Darkness there. He lay beside me. He carried the pain too.

And I didn't feel as alone.

My eyes were closed during a point when the pain dulled for a minute. In the quiet, I thought I heard someone breathing. Opening my eyes, I saw a female figure outlined against the light that came through the tiny window in the door.

"Hello?" I croaked out, wondering what kind of twisted girl would choose to be in here watching me suffer through this.

"Oh, Parker." She whispered my name but kept her distance. The voice, though . . . I would know it anywhere.

"Addie?" I tried to raise my head but couldn't. "How did you find me?"

She didn't answer. Instead, she moved over to kneel beside me in the quiet. A match flared and she lit a small candle she held in her lap. Her face was illuminated, looking ethereal by candlelight, and her hair glowed like dying embers around her.

"I'm here," she said.

"You shouldn't be." My protective instincts kicked in. "If they find you ... you need to leave, Addie. Maybe we can both find a way out of here now. Is the door still unlocked?"

"No. We aren't going anywhere." Her tone made my heart ache. Her expression looked distant, almost cold.

I tried to prop myself up on my elbow, but my head started pounding again and I lay back down. "What do you mean? How did you get in?"

"I came here to help, but I'm not sure what I can do with this ... " Addie gestured toward me. "Cooper was right. You're weaker than I thought."

"Cooper?" My already feverish body filled with a new chill. "What do you mean, Addie?"

"You're too trusting." She leaned over and ran one finger over my forehead and down my cheek. Near my chin, she suddenly pressed harder and scratched me. "You never even suspected me."

I pulled back, watching her in complete shock. Shaking my head, my heart pounding in my throat. "No ... "

"Oh yes," she whispered, giving me that vibrant smile I loved so much. "You're so easy to play. Almost too easy."

My heart shattered into a million pieces and I asked the only word that mattered: "Why?"

I heard a thumping sound and the distant echo of someone yelling.

"You knew you weren't good enough for me, Parker. Now maybe your bad choices have rubbed off on me a little too much." Her face twisted into a snarl and I was actually a little afraid of her. Closing my eyes, I tried to convince myself this was just a nightmare, that it couldn't be real.

Except I knew that I didn't have nightmares.

"Addie … this isn't you." Tears ran down my face now and the pain rushed back with them. "You can't mean this. What did they do to you?"

"I chose this, Parker. I chose this over you … and now you have to deal with that." She spoke low, near my ear, but it didn't sound like her. I'd never heard Addie filled with so much hate. Had I known her at all? Had this been buried deep inside her all this time?

I heard the thumping and distant yelling again, but this time I recognized it. Shawn … the guy I'd spoken to earlier, was yelling at me.

"Hey man, can you hear me?" he bellowed as if from a mile away, then said, "I wish I'd gotten your name."

He kept yelling. Another wave of pain hit and made me cry in agony. "Parker," I finally spat out when it improved slightly. "My name is Parker."

Shawn didn't speak for a few seconds, then said. "Damn, they finally got one of you."

I opened my eyes and saw that Addie now stood at the

window looking out, her back to me. Every time I'd held her, kissed her, looked into her eyes—they all came rushing back and I couldn't believe they'd all been a lie. Was this another cruel trick of my mind?

"Addie, please…" It was all I could say and all I had to say.

She turned to face me and then shook her head and turned away.

"Parker." Shawn's voice was urgent and sounded closer, like he'd moved along his wall to the spot where I rested against mine. "They forced some nasty liquid into you, right?"

"Yes," I said, but I only half heard him.

"Listen to me. Whatever you're seeing in there, it isn't real," Shawn yelled, and this time a shadow crossed past my small window and someone pounded on his door.

"Quiet!" a voice shouted from the hallway.

"That stuff causes hallucinations," he continued, this time speaking at a more normal volume. "It messes with your head. Don't believe it."

Addie turned to face the wall Shawn was hiding behind and frowned. I watched her, blinking as the truth fell into place. Of course it wasn't her. In my feverish haze of pain I'd actually believed it, but I knew her better than that. It made no sense for her to be here… and she would *never* say these things.

Not *my* Addie.

She shot me a rueful look, like she knew I'd figured her out. Then she shrugged and dissipated into a million shards of shadow.

I lay there alone, catching my breath. "Thanks, Shawn."

"No problem." He sounded relieved even through the wall.

"One question, though … " Exhaustion swept me and I hoped to pass out again because at least it would give me some relief from the pain.

"Yeah?"

"How do I know that you're real?"

It was silent on the other side of the wall for a few seconds, then said, "You might not know … but I was here before, if that helps. And I won't disappear."

"Fair enough," I grunted out.

"Hang in there, man." He sounded miserable. "It'll pass."

But it didn't feel like it ever would. Waves of pain went on endlessly, easing here and there but never going away. My feverish brain argued with itself. Ten full days of this and I wouldn't be begging for death—it would be surprising if I survived. I'd probably be actually dead. But Cooper said this was the beginning. What else did he have planned? Could it be even worse than this?

I heard movement in my room. Someone else was here again. Would it be someone real this time? I prayed it wasn't Addie. Even knowing she hadn't been real, having her say those things to me was so painful. She seemed so real.

Something touched my mouth and poured more liquid down my throat. I fought to push them away. No more poison. No more pain. But then I stopped fighting. This was definitely fresh water and it had a medicinal tang to it. It brought an instant relief so sweet I nearly cried.

My visitor moved away and I tried to blink as my pain

continued to fade. I tried to focus my eyes before this person got away. Whoever this was had helped me, maybe even saved me. They were a friend, and if I had a friend in here, then I *had* to know who it was. When I finally got my eyes to focus, the door had closed and locked.

Several minutes later my shivering had almost entirely stopped and the door opened again. This time Thor came in. I watched him, unsure if I should fake the kind of pain I was probably supposed to be in. I moaned and shivered for effect. He never met my eyes, but as he walked past, he kicked my leg hard enough that I was sure it would leave a massive bruise. I grunted and considered kicking him back, but my body literally wasn't capable of that movement. Rubbing at my newly injured thigh, I rolled into a tighter ball. I pretended to close my eyes and waited for him to finish whatever he was in here for.

Once he thought I wasn't watching him, Thor grabbed a garbage can from the hall, shoveled the dead rat into the can, and then left.

NINETEEN

JACK

After driving to a nearby picnic area, I parked the van. I climbed out and took a seat on the van's back bumper, trying to get my emotions under control. Parker was in more danger every minute that I couldn't save him. Maybe I'd made the wrong decision. Maybe trying to get the new formula together first wasn't the best plan.

Maybe I was wasting time when I should've already been trying to find a different way to get to him. I wished Libby would wake up and tell us what she'd learned, but I definitely didn't want to interrupt them.

My lungs felt tight and hot. It was like fire was filling them instead of oxygen. I leaned forward, propping my elbows on my knees and trying to calm down. I was stronger than this. I had to be stronger. Dad trusted me to be...he'd trusted me to take care of Parker and to solve this formula puzzle.

I pushed aside the aching loneliness that thoughts of Dad always left me with and tried to focus. For now, the only thing I could do was spend tonight in Wendy's dreams and hope they held more answers than our conversation had provided.

As I sat up straight and leaned against the cold metal of the van, I realized Chloe had gotten out and was standing in front of me. Most people couldn't sneak up on me like that. She had dark glasses on, too, and I wondered if she already knew what I was thinking and had protected me from making eye contact with her just in case.

"Have you decided?" Chloe's voice was low, and I wasn't sure if she was trying not to wake up Libby in the van or just attempting to keep the conversation quiet enough that the few other people hanging out in the park this late couldn't hear us. Then Finn climbed out of the van and walked back to lean against it on my left side.

"Decided what?" My voice and body were both starting to match up with the level of my total exhaustion inside. I'd wanted to watch Libby's dreams tonight and get some real sleep, have her help heal me ... but that wasn't looking like an option right now.

"What we should do now," Finn said, raising his eyebrow and looking at Chloe in confirmation. She nodded and they both waited for my answer.

I'd grown used to being put in charge. Dad had trained me to lead most of my life. I wasn't afraid of it. The only thing that scared me was the thought that Parker was at risk.

Losing him would be too much for me when I already had so little left.

"We have two choices," I said. "I can go into Wendy's dreams tonight and see if she's hiding anything." Standing up, I stretched my back. "Or I can accept this for the dead end it seems to be, wake Libby up, and go after Parker...like I probably would've preferred to do from the beginning."

"Why do you always use this word 'I'?" Finn said lightly, even though his stare could burn metal. "I do not think it means what you think it means."

Chloe giggled, grinned widely at Finn, shook her fist, and said, "Inconceivable!"

I shook my head, trying to force their words into any sort of sense, and then Chloe turned back to face me. "It's from a movie, don't worry about it. But I vote option one. You don't even know where they have him."

"I'm awake." Libby's voice came from inside the van. I looked up and saw her staring out at us. She moved toward the front to climb out, and I met her before she was even out the door. She looked pale even under her olive skin. And she still appeared devastated, but much better and saner than she had been before she'd slept.

"Are you okay?" I asked, and then wished I could bite my tongue and immediately steal the words back. Of course she wasn't. Neither was I.

She pretended I hadn't spoken, and I was grateful. "Your brother was there. He was okay..."

A massive swelling of hope rose up in my chest and I saw Finn's face spread with a wide smile.

"What did he tell you?" I asked her, starting to worry that her reason for looking so grim could be tied to Parker and not Marisol.

"He refused to tell me where they have him. He asked me to tell you there are heavily armed guards everywhere, Jack." Libby reached out to hold my hand, her eyes filled with nothing but misery.

"So?" I shrugged, adjusting my dark sunglasses tighter against my face with my free hand. "I've dealt with situations like that before."

"I know, but he still wouldn't tell me. He said it would be nearly impossible for you to get to him without being caught."

"Why is he so stubborn?" I groaned and stepped back, shoving my hands into my pockets.

"There's more, Jack."

I heard tears in her voice and my heartbeat stuttered. She reached out for my arm and I almost pulled away. I knew there was more she had to say, but from the look on her face, I was terrified to hear it.

"He said to tell you not to come. He said it's too dangerous, that he'll be okay and you should stay focused on figuring out the new formula." She trembled all over. "But then they pulled him out of my dream and broke the connection. I'm not sure what they did to him, but I f-felt him go, Jack."

An icy rush of fear went down my spine and I jerked my arm out of her grip. "No. It's impossible for you to be sure."

Libby moved to the bumper and slumped down on it. She didn't even notice that Chloe stood only a few feet in front of her. That alone showed how devastated Libby was from what she'd seen. That alone showed me that she believed Parker was dead ... and that made my body shake with a wave of paralyzing fear and loss from the inside out.

Libby's words were hesitant when she spoke again. "I was still connected to him. He wasn't fully free from the dream. It felt like ... it felt like much more than just a break from our connection. I wanted you to know what I felt. But you're right. I can't be sure that he's dead ... that it wasn't just ... "

"Okay." I walked to the front of the van and took a seat on the grass. No one joined me, but I could hear Finn asking Libby questions. He sounded terrified. He sounded like I felt.

Parker couldn't be gone already ... they said they would trade him. According to their plan, they had to keep him alive.

I gripped the grass between my fingers and ripped it from the ground. If they didn't keep that promise, then screw the formula ... I would kill them all.

Chloe sat down beside me and I nearly jumped. Somehow we felt even farther away from finding the formula than we had this morning. Parker wouldn't tell me where he was and now I wasn't even sure if he was alive to be saved. My hand trembled. The blades of grass I'd already ripped free flew out in a passing breeze and landed all over Chloe's lap.

"Sorry."

Her eyes widened so much that I could sense it even behind the sunglasses. She seemed genuinely surprised. "You don't need to be sorry. Why are you sorry?"

"A million reasons ... I'm sorry that I don't know what

to do. I'm sorry that I may never finish the formula like I promised you. And I'm sorry that your brother is an ass and I'll probably have to kill him."

My hands balled into fists and I rushed to go on before she could tell me not to. I wasn't sure if she would, but still, I couldn't hear anyone defend Cooper right now. "You should probably leave us now."

Chloe's face fell like the crest of a wave. "Why, Jack? Where am I suppo—"

"Why?" My voice was too loud, and she stiffened, so I lowered it before I kept going. "Seriously, Chloe? How can you ask me why? It's unlikely that I can even make the formula, so there's no point in you sticking around here. Your brother might be killing my brother as we speak. Your dad was responsible for everything bad in my life. And you—you knew this about your dad from the beginning and never told me. Where do we even go from here?"

I turned my back, but she shifted around in front of me. "When exactly should I have told you about my family, Jack? When I was pretending to be Finn? No … that wouldn't have made sense. What about after I helped you and betrayed everyone I've ever known? I only went back to see them once and *even then* I'd been trying to help you. I told them Parker was your brother and you were just trying to save your family. I asked them to understand that and leave you alone. The next time I came back, they'd moved out of the Benton base and didn't even tell me where they went. They all blamed *me* for the explosion and losing Eclipse, Jack. Should I have told you then? Should I have volunteered the piece of information that would've made you kill me or kick me out of Parker's house? Should I have done that right then...when I had *no one* else left to turn to?"

When I didn't respond, the silence between us filled with the huffing sound of her uneven breaths. Her eyes filled with tears, but she never allowed them to fall.

"Every time I thought of telling you..." Chloe stopped and pulled in a long breath. Resting her hands on her knees, she faced me directly. Her stance, her expression, her body—everything about her overflowed with honesty. "There never was a time when you wouldn't have reacted this same way. There's never a good time to tell a friend you're the daughter of someone they hate, someone who destroyed their life. They don't make cards for that."

I watched her. It was like she'd been poised, waiting to talk about the truth, and now I'd finally given her the chance to get it all out. I couldn't help but wonder how anyone as crazy and brave and unexplainable as Chloe could possibly have come from a monster like Steve Campbell. If genetics play any role in who we become, her mom must've been incredible.

I couldn't help but return the small smile she gave me. Even if she had a point, none of this changed anything. Knowing that Cooper might have already killed Parker brought home what it meant to be dealing with Steve Campbell's kids. I'd thought maybe Chloe could help, but I was wrong. "It doesn't really matter. I can't have you with me."

"Why not?" She was starting to sound less devastated and more argumentative. Finally, a Chloe I knew how to relate to.

"Because of *who you are*." I emphasize the last three words, exasperated. "I'm not saying you're like them, but you're still one of them. How do I trust someone whose dad brought together the enemies I've been fighting against my entire life?"

"Don't you see?" Chloe scooted closer to me, but when I leaned back, she stopped and stared up at me. Her short hair fell back against her ears. "That's exactly what you are to me, Jack. Are you saying that I can't trust you?"

There was something so magnetic about her, but I forced myself not to be drawn in. "Considering I had a knife to your throat only a few hours ago, I'd probably say that you shouldn't."

She didn't move. "You wouldn't have hurt me. I know it and so do you."

"Did Cooper know it?" I asked.

Chloe grimaced, and I could instantly see how much pain my question caused her.

"I'm sorry."

She didn't answer, but she scooted a few inches back.

I went on. "I'm sorry about all of it, Chloe. Whether I should believe it or not, my gut tells me you aren't like them. I'm grateful you helped Parker to set Finn free and..."

"You think I did it for them?" she asked softly as she bent forward, studying the ground between us.

As her words sank in, I was surprised to pick up on a secondary meaning. But we hadn't even really gotten along at the time...she didn't mean...

"You didn't do it...for me?" My words were so quiet I

could barely hear them, and I knew I'd misunderstood immediately when her head whipped up, her mouth curved into an expression stuck halfway between shock and amusement.

My spine stiffened and I shifted my weight onto my knees, preparing to get up. "Got it. Not for me."

"Jack." Chloe grabbed my hand and the contact felt like being hooked to a static machine—all the tiny hairs on my arm felt like they stood on end. It froze me in place as I turned back toward her and forced myself not to let the sensation show on my face.

"Chloe, you just need to find somewhere else to go, okay? I'm not sure I can trust Cooper to keep Parker alive. I don't know if I can trust you to even be here right now. He is too important." I felt stupid. I hated feeling stupid.

"Jack, listen to me." The frustration in her voice made me stop everything and listen. "I didn't do it for any of you, but the reasons, *my* reasons, for helping set Finn free instead of fighting it might matter to you ... they meant everything to me."

"I'm listening."

"Being in Finn's head while on Eclipse like that ... it was different than ever before. Normally, when I take a Dreamer, I can access bits and pieces of information that I need: bank PINs, names, stuff like that. But Eclipse changed the connection. With Finn, it was like he became pure emotion and memory. My dad spent years convincing us all of *his* truth, you know—brainwashing us. He always taught us that we were more than normal people, we were like gods ... we were *evolved*." Her words sounded choked out and surprisingly repulsed as she spoke her last sentence. It was the way I'd have imagined myself sounding if I'd been saying those words.

"But I'd always believed him, Jack," she said. "I believed he knew better than me and that he was right. He was our leader and my father. Everyone else believed him; why wouldn't I? But with Finn ... the connection felt so different, I could see immediately that my dad had been so wrong."

I wasn't sure what I'd been expecting Chloe to say, but it hadn't been this.

She lowered her voice and continued. "Finn cares so deeply about everyone—his parents, Addie, Parker. I witnessed firsthand just how much they would all do for each other. I've never seen a Taker sacrifice for someone like that. Never." Chloe ran her hands up the back of her neck and pulled on the bottom of her short hair as she looked away from me. "My own kind sacrificed me to an experiment that easily could have killed me. They used me like a lab rat to test a drug that would help them steal other people's lives, Jack. I didn't want to be the test subject for an experimental drug and I hated that they made that decision for me. I had to choose whether to fight for the way I'd lived—the way my family taught me to be—or to choose something new, something terrifyingly different. I wanted what Finn had in his life, and it was hard to deal with the idea that I'd stolen that from him, willingly or not."

Chloe closed her eyes for a moment before speaking again, her voice very soft this time. "And now I'm choosing to help you, Jack. Because I want better for my people than the choices my family has given them. I want better for myself. My brothers left me here with you. They would let our enemies do whatever they wanted to me. That isn't more than humanity, if you ask me. It's so much less."

She shifted onto her knees and then looked straight at me. "Please, Jack. My kind have to stop what they're doing. My father led us toward becoming monsters. I *need* to be a part of stopping that from going any farther. I *have* to help end it."

Before I could answer, I saw a movement out of the corner of my eye and raised my eyes to see Finn standing a few feet behind Chloe, obviously listening.

She didn't notice him and finished with, "You can trust me because no matter what happens, no matter what or who is at risk, I would *never* let you give Eclipse to Cooper. I know you say that isn't possible anyway, and I want to believe you, but if you get desperate and find a way to do it, I'd need to stop you. Even if it meant losing your brother and both of mine, I'd find a way. *Nothing* is worth what my brother having Eclipse would cost the rest of us."

It was silent for a few seconds before she said, "You watch Wendy's dreams tonight. I'll take over her husband's body. I might not be able to access his past with the clarity you can, but I can root through his mind and his recent memories, make sure there aren't any secrets he's deliberately hiding from Wendy."

So that explained *her* need for sunglasses. But I didn't want to support her taking anyone. I opened my mouth to argue, but she jumped in before I got a chance to speak. "Relax. I promise not to hurt him at all. I'll make sure he only feels like he tossed and turned a bit more than usual. That's it."

Then she stood and walked back toward the driver's side of the van before I could say anything else. After she'd gone, Finn blew out a giant breath of air and stepped quietly over to sit beside me.

"She saw everything in my head, huh?" He shuddered.

"Apparently. You didn't know?" I raised my eyebrow.

"I'd suspected. And it really explains a lot. She knows exactly what I'm thinking so often." Finn frowned and reached up one hand, tugging on the bottom of one ear. "For what it's worth, I saw some of her memories, too."

I turned toward him in shock. I'd had no clue it could work that way. "You did?"

"Yes, and she isn't lying." He picked up a rock on the ground nearby and threw it out in the road like it had somehow offended him. "I think she could help us find the ingredients. I think you should let her help."

The surprise on my face must have showed, but Finn just shrugged and hopped up to his feet. I sat for a couple of minutes more as I tried to find the right answers. Eventually I decided that if the guy who Chloe had taken over was saying I should trust her, maybe it was time to start really listening.

I heard Dad's voice in my head telling me not to trust anyone. But Chloe's reasons had shaken me. Maybe it was time for me to learn something from her. If I didn't want my life to turn out the way Dad's had—keeping secrets from all those closest to me, always being on the run, and sacrificing myself at far too young an age—then didn't I need to try not to make the same mistakes?

That was yet another thing I could tell Parker about our dad, once I got Parker out of this mess—and, assuming he was still alive, I *would* get him out. For right now, there was nothing for me to do but hang on to hope and believe my brother was okay. There was no other choice.

Finn stood looking at the now-empty park in silence, waiting for an answer or clue from me as to what I was intending. When I shifted my weight to get up, he extended his hand down to help and I took it.

"At this point, Finn...I suppose I'm not in much of a position to say no to anyone who still wants to help me figure this out. I'm making zero progress, and time keeps moving no matter what we do."

"Good." He gave me a look of pure determination. "That's what I thought."

Maybe I needed to learn to be more like Parker instead of trying to teach Parker to be more like Dad...and more like me. A good way to start this, I thought, might be to rely more on Finn. He'd already saved Parker in more ways than one. Maybe he could help me find a way to do it again.

I thought carefully, trying to pick the right way to reach out to him...the way Parker would do it. When it came to me, I smiled. "By the way, I've been thinking, and you're right. This new formula really will need a name. Any new ideas we should consider?"

Finn's face glowed with the widest grin I'd seen since

we'd lost Parker. Seeing his face like that made our whole situation feel strangely more hopeful.

"I have *SO* many ideas…"

TWENTY

PARKER

The white nothingness of the Hollow felt like peace and oblivion after the waking nightmare in that awful cell. It didn't smell like rot in this not-really-sleeping limbo, and I wasn't cold or shivering. I wasn't in pain, or hallucinating my own heartbreak. I didn't feel like I was drowning.

Apparently my standards had lowered a bit in the last few hours.

I tried not to heed the dread that I felt sinking like an anchor deep into each of my bones. Maybe when Cooper had forced me to make eye contact with him, he'd only been making sure I wasn't still connected to Libby; maybe his goal *wasn't* to connect to me. Since he was a Taker, there were plenty of normal people who were much more useful for Cooper to make eye contact with than a Watcher like me. And if he *had* made eye contact with some Dreamer, he wouldn't be connected with me anymore and I'd be on my own.

At least I thought that was how it worked. To be honest, some of the details of how the Takers operated were still a mystery to me.

The edges of the Hollow began to expand and contract and I kept my eyes closed, knowing what was probably coming. When the minds of a Taker and a Watcher merged, it created an inky, suffocating blackness. I'd spent two nights trapped in it before: the solid black nothing of Chloe's coma-like state, which had allowed me to unite with Darkness and separate Finn and Chloe's minds, and before that, Cooper's sleep-state, which had released Darkness in an entirely new way. In both cases, Taker-Watcher connection had messed with my brain and made it hard to breathe, and I hated it.

And it appeared it was about to happen again.

Our sleepless states merged, Cooper's smothering shadow overcoming my white void until the blackness was complete and without end. It was like the ocean and I was a tiny raft. I couldn't see where it started or ended. It was just everywhere, leaving me no escape.

It was even worse than I remembered. It was like an ink well that overflowed until it filled everything up, including me. My lungs were heavier; my eyes blinked, but I couldn't tell if they were open or closed. Everything about me was drenched in it.

But I'd been trained on how to control dreams now. This was at least half my space, my mind. If part of Cooper's plan was to keep me locked up in his thick, dark sludge all night, I wouldn't make it easy on him. Thanks to Jack teaching me how to manipulate regular dreams, I knew how to fight back now, and I was definitely going to use that knowledge this time.

I forced my pounding heart to slow its pace and then pictured the darkness lightening and fading to a violet. It started working. I pictured myself sitting on a dark floor with air around me instead of floating in the black nothing. This was more of a struggle; my brain ached and it felt like I was stretching a sore muscle, until it finally worked.

I sat in a small bubble that glowed with a slight light. I took a long breath of cool, clear air. It was sweet and the ache in my head started to subside.

Before I took in a second breath, everything I'd created unraveled. The air around me collapsed mid-breath and the sudden thickness in the air made me cough and struggle in a choking fit. The suffocating pressure intensified dramatically. The density around me squeezed every inch of my skin before my surroundings started vibrating with laughter. Cooper was aware. He was squeezing me, hurting me, and enjoying it.

One panicked thread in my brain unraveled and my furious need for air shoved back, with ferocious strength, against Cooper's changes to the atmosphere. The air suddenly cleared around me again and I curled up, panting on the ground, focused on keeping the darkness at bay for a few minutes to catch my breath. My head was pounding. There was a growling sound, low and furious. It echoed throughout the dream and I couldn't tell where Cooper was. Then I realized the sound came from me.

A drop of red landed on the back of my hand, and I realized my nose was bleeding. I'd learned while trying to separate Finn and Chloe that these kinds of battles in the mind had physical consequences on the body. Cooper had to know that. He wasn't stupid. So what was he doing?

His laughter rippled through the black air I'd pushed back. I wasn't sure, but he sounded a little tired too.

"Just stop," I yelled out, and the laughing stopped before I went on. "This isn't easy for you either. You're going to kill both of us."

"You act like we're the same." Then Cooper's voice shifted from amused to cold and calculated in an instant. "We're not the same, Parker. Not yet."

He slammed his dark fog over me again and I had to struggle to fight him off.

We spent all night like that. Hours that felt like days that felt like weeks. The battle became a reflex. Each time Cooper closed his thick black liquid over me, it became more difficult to push back and it was even more painful. Each time I did manage to push him back, he closed it up immediately. My hope shrank as I realized that maybe I'd been wrong. Maybe this was easier for him than me.

There was no more laughing or talking anymore, only pain and extreme exertion. By the time the dream ended and we finally escaped to being awake again, the pool of blood next to my face was big enough that it scared me.

My nose and ears were still dripping. I was so weak I could barely lift my head, and my lungs burned like they'd been fighting for air all night long.

Each breath, each heartbeat, each thought took more effort than ever before. How could my body be this exhausted after only a day and a half here? How could I possibly survive for eight more days like this?

Opening my mouth to speak, I only ended up coughing at first. Finally, I managed to croak out, "Are you there?"

Shawn answered immediately. "Yes. Are you okay?"

"No ... did they do all of this to you at first?"

"Not all of it. Cooper seems hell-bent on making you suffer." Shawn's tone was almost angry. "They have so many drugs they've been experimenting with—far more drugs than you've seen yet. You should brace yourself for whatever they have next. Cooper even has one that makes his mind more powerful."

"What do you mean by 'powerful'?" I didn't understand. Did they have their own version of Eclipse?

"He thinks it's keeping him alive longer, and it might be ... " Shawn's voice trailed off before he said, "But there are definitely some very bad side effects."

"I noticed that it's nearly impossible to fight him off." I rolled into a ball as another wave of pain hit and then gritted out through my teeth, "Is that related?"

"Probably. But it also seems like it's driving him crazy." Shawn's next words were so soft I barely heard him. "He's losing his humanity."

I couldn't keep from crying out as a pain hit that seemed like it was trying to force my spine onto the outside of my body. After it passed, I was left trembling in its wake. "I didn't realize h-he'd ever had any humanity."

It was silent for a couple of minutes before Shawn said, "Listen, I've witnessed the worst they have to give out, and if what they've done to you so far is any indication, they aren't holding back. You aren't done yet ... you need to be strong."

Cooper had said he wouldn't kill me, just make me wish I were dead. I now believed he was absolutely capable of making it happen.

"Was there someone in here before me? Is that what you mean by 'witnessed it'?" I asked.

Shawn hesitated, and then I finally heard him again. "Yeah. You're stronger, though. I think if you just keep trying, you might be okay."

I slid away from the wall, staring at it like I might somehow be able to see through it. "Why are you in here?"

"Because I stopped saying yes." His voice seeped through the wall, drenched in genuine remorse.

"You worked for them?" I whispered, horrified.

"For a while." Shawn didn't sound like he was defending himself, just explaining. "Until I finally told them no. I said I wouldn't anymore."

I waited for him to go on, but he was silent so I finished for him. "And that's how you ended up in here."

"It is." He sighed.

I curled into a tighter ball and shivered as I fought the urge to fall back to sleep. Shawn said I wasn't even to the worst of this yet. By the time my brother came back here to help me, would he even recognize me anymore?

Would I?

TWENTY-ONE

JACK

Wendy was definitely just a Dreamer ... and kind of a boring one at that. Her dreams layered one upon the next upon the next. They were filled with mostly mundane tasks like cleaning, running errands, having dinner with her husband. It was like swimming through a soup of normalcy.

I rubbed my eyes again and tried to focus on the details—looking for anything that felt odd or out of place. But there didn't seem to be anything to find, nothing to see.

Moving through the dream, I braced myself and reached out for Wendy. It was almost a habit now, knowing how and when to blend in and stand out from a Dreamer's dreams. Still, when I was *this* tired, it required some focus. I imagined myself as part of the scene around me, blending in perfectly with the kitchen until I was almost invisible. Then I nudged her mind in the direction *I* wanted; guiding her thoughts to memories of my dad.

Usually, when sifting through memories, the most recent ones were the ones that came first. So I frowned when a memory from when they were teenagers rose to the surface instead. Wendy had said she'd seen him more recently than that, hadn't she? I sorted quickly through each memory, making sure it wasn't important before moving on to the next one. It wasn't until I got through almost all of them that I found her most recent memory of dad. For some reason, it wasn't coming to the surface the same way the others were, but I could feel it in the corners of her mind...yet I couldn't make her remember it fully, which was weird. This was so easy with other Dreamers.

Standing there in confusion, I watched her revert again to one of the earlier memories. This didn't make sense. Something weird was happening here.

I frowned and focused, trying to guide her thoughts where I wanted them to go, but stopped when Wendy winced. When I pulled harder, it caused her physical pain. Carefully withdrawing my hand, I let her whirl through all the memories of my dad I'd pulled up as I tried to figure out what was going on here. This wasn't right. I'd never encountered *anything* like this in dreams before. Could a Taker have messed with her memories like this?

No, that didn't make any sense. Takers couldn't enter, let alone control and manipulate, memories and dreams.

But Watchers could.

Dad.

My heartbeat sped up, and I felt for the first time in hours like I might actually be close to making some real progress. I took a slow, calming breath, and reached out for Wendy again. I sorted back down through the other memories and grasped for the one I knew I wanted. When it resisted again, I closed my eyes and felt around the edges with my mind.

All of a Dreamer's memories were intertwined. They're tied to other memories, thoughts, and feelings, all making up one convoluted ball of personality. Dad had taught me to find those connections, to locate the place where one memory bonds with the next.

I'd never encountered another Watcher who could navigate a Dreamer's mind the way Dad could—and he'd taught me well.

So this could be another one of his traps. Some new way he'd devised to make sure no one else could get the information except for the one person he'd fully trained. Just one more way to be certain that *only* I could uncover this answer...

One spot in the memories was a little more flexible than the others. I pulled on that spot and it gave way while the rest stayed in place. My eyes flew open to see what thought or memory I'd released...but my breath caught in my throat and my lungs froze at what I saw before me.

It was like I had become the frozen memory—while a living, breathing version of my father had broken free and now stood before me.

He smiled at me but didn't speak.

My chest burned in response to a lack of oxygen, and I finally remembered to pull in a ragged, painful breath. "Dad?"

As if my speaking gave him the cue he needed, he said, "I make you weak but also keep you safe. Your hands sweat when I am near and your heart may grow cold. I often sit with the weak, but rarely the bold."

I blinked at him and shook my head in utter confusion. "What?"

He said again, "I make you weak but also ... "

I walked around him in a circle, ignoring the words but noticing everything else. The way the clothes hung the same on his body no matter how he shifted to face me, the way his eyes stared at the same spot, even if I moved a couple of feet to the left or right. A sad smile curved up the corner of my mouth. Dad had always wanted to be able to insert something like this ... he must've finally figured out how.

"You planted a looping memory," I whispered, and he stopped speaking. The word "buried" written on Dad's paper came to mind, and I shook my head. It looked like he'd been referring to more than just the puzzle box.

Dad's image waited for me ... this was a riddle. He'd always loved riddles and puzzles, sometimes violent ones with real consequences if you made the wrong choice—as had been so clearly demonstrated by his exploding box.

I focused toward Wendy again, since all of this had been planted in her subconscious mind. "Please repeat it."

Dad did as I requested. "I make you weak but also keep you safe. Your hands sweat when I am near and your heart may grow cold. I often sit with the weak but rarely the bold."

We'd played this game a lot when I was younger. He only

gave me one chance to get the right answer. If I didn't get it, I lost.

I repeated the riddle to myself a few times until I understood how to make sense of it.

"You are Fear." I spoke the words quietly, and suddenly the image smiled and my heart filled with the overwhelming pain and loss that I'd been trying so hard to keep at bay.

My correct answer unlocked the full memory. It opened around us like an image spilling from a giant paint can and seeping over every surface until it coated the inside of the dream. I released Wendy as I watched it unfold.

Dad and Wendy stood next to a car in a grocery store parking lot. He was speaking softly to her.

"I need your help. My sons are in danger and if anything happens to me, they're going to come to you. You need to remember to tell them this." He held out a piece of paper in front of her. In big letters he had written, three times: $C10H13N5O4$—$C10H13N5O4$—$C10H13N5O4$.

My brain whirled through all the compounds Dad had taught me, and I knew this one looked familiar. It had been a while since I'd really studied up on them so it took me a minute before I recognized it: adenosine. It was a purine nucleoside that dealt with energy transfer. That actually made sense.

Finally, I'd found one of the missing ingredients!

Wendy, however, looked confused. "What am I supposed to do with that, Daniel? How could I use it to help them?"

"Don't worry about how. If they find you, Jack will understand. Also, remember this." Dad flipped the paper over and the other side read: *Veronica Nelson—in Franklin.* Then he lowered the paper.

"Danny, I can't possibly remember all of that." Wendy looked sincerely worried, and of course her concern made perfect sense. Given the few seconds she'd seen it, no person would be able to retain that information for long without writing it down or something. But the truth was that Dad didn't expect her to remember it. He expected her *brain* to remember... and then he'd gone into her dreams that night to make certain it would. He'd reinforced the memory and protected it in a way that made sure it couldn't disappear or get into the wrong hands.

Even when he was Divided, with an entire war weighing down on him, he was still smarter than anyone else I'd ever known.

Another detail I swore I would tell Parker... as soon as I got him back safe.

Dad smiled and hugged Wendy. "Don't worry. You'll remember. I promise." Then he looked her straight in the eye and said, "Tell them both that I love them and that I'm so sorry for everything."

Wendy patted her hands across Dad's shoulders. "I'm sure you can tell them that yourself."

He gave her one more hug and then, as he helped her into her car, the memory faded away. I fought to push back the grief. The pain was fresh again and I suddenly remembered Marisol's words about losing my mom: *We miss her because she mattered so much to us. Don't take that away from your mama. Let her loss matter.*

My chest burned from trying to hold back my grief, so I slowly released it. It was definitely time for me to let Dad's loss matter.

The quiet of the mellow dream that followed reflected my sense of loss. Wendy was painting her fence in the afternoon sunlight, birds chirping overhead, and I finally let myself remember everything about my dad and what I'd lost... what Parker and I had both lost.

Here, in this dream world he'd altered, I'd found Dad's last-ditch effort to save the Night Walkers. And this was the perfect place to really say goodbye to him. I bowed my head low as sobs racked my shoulders. Seeing him again was much harder than I could've imagined.

As Wendy's dreams carried on without me, I let go of the fight. I'd been trying so hard to keep my painful memories of Dad from floating to the surface. It was a battle that needed to end now, and I felt the burden of it lift, piece by piece. The memories hurt me, but they helped me too—and I desperately needed his help. I wouldn't ever stop missing him, but at least now, thanks to this clue, I had real hope that I'd found the path Dad wanted me to follow. There was a real chance I could see Parker again.

And for now, that was enough.

———

Chloe didn't learn anything new from Aaron... mostly because, as I'd learned in Wendy's dream, they really hadn't been hiding anything.

But my dad had.

Since we'd slept in the van, we stopped at a full-service truck stop to shower and grab some food before we got on the road. Interestingly, the person who was complaining the most about this arrangement was Finn.

"Ugh...I thought I'd finally gotten away from public showers when I finished my last gym class," he groaned, and then went in anyway.

The city of Franklin and the two Veronica Nelsons who lived there were only three hours away. Finn called their numbers, but since he only got voicemail, he couldn't really eliminate either one of them. And then he insisted we swing home and explain what was going on to Mrs. Chipp, Addie, and Mia before driving any farther.

As much as I really didn't want to tell Parker's mom what had happened to him, I'd promised to let Finn make this decision. And since Oakdale was technically on the way from here to Franklin, I couldn't find a good reason not to do it...no matter how hard I tried.

Besides, the more I thought about it, the more I realized I should get Parker's mom out of that house. The last thing I needed was for Cooper to decide he needed more hostages.

Chloe grabbed the keys from me as we walked out of the truck stop, back toward the van. In two steps I caught up with her, but she put them in her pocket and shook her head when I held out my hand.

"What do you think you're doing?" I asked.

"Driving." She looked at me like that was a really stupid question, and maybe it was.

"Why would you think I would let you do that?" I put my hand on the driver's side door, holding it closed as I stood over her, trying to intimidate her into giving me back the keys. From the way she crossed her arms, it didn't appear to be working.

"You need to get some sleep. From what we saw with Wendy, you may need to go into this Veronica person's dreams tonight. You need to spend the drive letting Libby heal you a bit." She raised one eyebrow and tilted her head forward. "And don't try to tell me you aren't tired or you don't need it. If anyone can recognize exhaustion, it's a Taker."

I started to argue about being tired, but she was actually dead-on in her assessment, so I changed tactics. "You're exhausted too."

Chloe swallowed and looked down. "All the more reason we need to get on the road. There isn't anything here that can help me with *my kind* of tired."

I drew in a sharp breath. It felt like I'd been hit across the face with her mortality. As much as I wanted to get the formula to save Parker … I wanted it to save Chloe, too. The idea of her dying because I couldn't find all the pieces of this puzzle in time made me feel oddly nauseous and panicked. I hated that feeling—and I really disliked how confused it made me to feel it about Chloe. Suddenly I just needed to do something to fix the situation, but I knew with certainty that I was already doing everything I could.

So I simply stood there, looking as useless as I felt.

Finn walked around the end of the van. He was wearing a new, clean shirt that read, *And yet, despite the look on my face, you're still talking.* He nudged Chloe just hard enough that she fell against me. "You two stop arguing. I'm driving. You both should get some rest—or whatever it is your kind calls it."

He held out his hand for the keys. Chloe righted herself and stood up straight, digging the keys out of her pocket. I thought I saw her cheeks flush before she jogged around the front of the van and climbed in the front seat.

Libby was already sitting in the backseat when I opened the door. She patted the seat beside her and gave me a half-smile, but it didn't reach her eyes. I wondered if she would ever be the same again. If there was anything I could do to help bring her back. She went back to staring straight out the side window as I moved in and put on my seat belt.

"Libby?" When she didn't answer, I asked, "Could you help heal me on the drive? I'm getting pretty tired."

She slowly nodded and then turned to look straight into my eyes, ensuring our connection. Immediately, she leaned over against the window, closed her eyes, and went to sleep. It didn't take me long to join her.

―――――――

Libby sat quietly in a cloud of white when I entered her dream. There was nothing happening, but I could feel a heavy tension in the air. It was like she was holding back every emotion, thought, and feeling so I couldn't see it. It stabbed at me. I knew she'd occasionally held back a thought or memory, but she'd never held back everything from me before—not ever.

"Libby, what are you do—?"

"We need to get started. We don't have much time," she interrupted, grabbing my hand. She pulled me down until I was lying in the cloud next to where she sat. She reached out and put her fingers on my head.

"Wait." I sat up and her hands fell away. "Talk to me first, Lib. I'm worried about you."

She watched me in silence, like she didn't trust herself to respond.

I sighed. "Would you be happier back at Cypress Crest? I thought bringing you with me would help you, but if not..."

Libby pulled her knees up under her chin and wrapped her arms around them. Her eyes sparkled with the stubborn fire I was definitely familiar with.

"You need me here," she stated simply.

"I need you to be okay." I grabbed her hand. She looked down at her hand in mine and ran her thumb slowly across my knuckles.

"You can't always take care of everyone around you, Jack." She spoke so softly I could barely hear her.

"I can take care of *you*." I bent lower until she met my eyes. "You're my best friend, Lib. Let me help you."

She shook her head, slowly pulling her hand out of mine before replying, "I'm fine."

"Libby..." I gave her a pointed stare that said we both knew she was lying.

"Okay, I'm not." Libby groaned long and low before continuing. "But, I'll be fine when I'm sure this Taker girl isn't wrapping you so far around her finger you can't see the truth right in front of you. Until you can see what she's doing, I'm not going anywhere."

I shook my head in confusion. "You're staying here with me because you think I need you to protect me from Chloe?"

She didn't look at me, but she didn't reply either.

"I'm not wrapped around her finger." By my tone, I made it clear that the idea was ridiculous.

"You need to relax or this is pointless." Libby seemed determined to end the conversation. Her voice was clipped and angry as she patted the cloud next to her so I'd lie down again. I wanted to make her talk to me, but I knew that might only make her push me further away. I resigned myself to stop fighting her and reluctantly put my head on the place she'd indicated. I'd have to wait until she was ready…whether I liked it or not.

Her fingers pressed into my brain and I tried to release all the worries that had balled up into masses of pain inside me. I didn't want her to have to feel that…or at least I wanted to protect her from as much of it as possible. I was partly responsible for there being too much death and pain lately. Would Libby, my oldest friend, be the one who would finally start blaming me and holding me accountable for the destruction I left in my wake?

Releasing a deep breath, I tried to relax as I felt her start pulling on threads in my mind. She began to loosen the tension and fear. There was an immediate sense of relief, but the fact that Libby was the one healing me felt backward. I wished I could heal her instead. She could hate me if it would somehow help her feel better. Anything that would bring back the Libby I'd always known would be absolutely worth it.

As I eventually drifted off to a peaceful sleep, my final thought was that I just wanted Libby to be Libby again.

If I could somehow make that happen, then maybe the rest of the world could sort itself out.

———————

Libby shook me awake a few hours later with a hint of a smile on her face. It disoriented me, like maybe I'd fallen asleep and woken up in a parallel universe where everything was better . . .

Actually, maybe I was *hoping* it was what had happened.

"We're at Parker's house." She spoke softly as I sat up. "Do you feel better?"

I stretched a few kinks out of my muscles, but it was miraculous how vastly improved I felt in such a short space of time. "Much. Thank you, Libby."

"You're welcome." She nodded and then squeezed my hand. "And thanks for reminding me that I'm not the only one hurting right now."

My cheeks felt hot, but I squeezed her hand back. It wasn't like I could keep secrets from a Builder . . . but I hadn't been trying to dump my pain on her. She had enough of her own to deal with. Somehow she looked much better, though . . . and if my showing her how worried I was and the pain I'd been feeling had caused that, I was happy for it.

Before we were even out of the van, Addie and Mia

were on their way out to greet us. Finn had called and asked them to meet us here—he said if they all heard the bad news together it would help them deal with it better.

I didn't understand it, but as with all things pertaining to normal families, I just nodded and went along with it.

When they saw that Parker wasn't with us, Addie's skin paled and she turned on Finn.

"Where is he?" Her pitch went up a little at the end. Parker's mom was standing on the front porch, but I saw her hand grip the railing next to her.

We managed to get everyone inside and seated before the questions—i.e., demands to know what was going on—started flying in a wild barrage. I was trying to figure out who to answer first when Libby helped take care of that problem.

"Stop!" Libby raised her voice and everyone turned to look at her. She seemed wild, with her hair still messy around her shoulders from sleep. Her eyes landed on each of us around the circle—at least, everyone but Chloe. "We believe Parker is alive right now, and we're trying to save him, but if you don't all slow down and let us explain, then Jack is going to run out of time."

Finn shuffled his feet from side to side in the awkward silence that followed. "Mrs. Chipp, Addie, Mia—uh, this is Libby. She's a Builder and a friend of Jack's. She's trying to help us."

They all sat in shocked silence as Finn and I filled them in on everything they'd missed: that Cooper and Thor had Parker, that they wanted Eclipse, and that we were trying everything we could think of to get him back safely.

When I finished, Parker's mom stood and walked over to me. She looked up into my eyes. Her chin quivered and her eyes were wet, but there were no tears on her cheeks yet. "Parker is your *brother*."

Her reminding me of this, like I could've somehow forgotten it, felt like a sucker-punch.

"Yes. I'm so sorry." I met her eyes and, without her speaking a word, her raw pain robbed me of my ability to breathe. My throat closed up and suddenly the emotion was hard to control. I was responsible for him. Whatever pain or damage they were inflicting on him right now was all on me. I gritted my teeth and looked away from her, unable to face the grief that I should've been able to prevent. My voice trembled when I spoke again. "I—if I could take his place, I would. *Please* believe me, I would."

"You don't talk about taking his place anymore. Understand me?" Her brown eyes commanded me so strongly that I felt I had no choice but to obey.

I nodded.

A small sob escaped her and tears rolled onto her cheeks. "Can you *save him*, Jack?"

I nodded again, forcing my voice to sound confident when I said, "I think I can."

"Then don't you talk again about taking his place. You just make sure you both get back here safe." She reached up and wrapped both arms around my neck, bringing me down into a tight hug.

At first my arms simply hung out in midair beside me; then I closed my eyes and hugged her back, releasing some of the tension, pressure, and weight from all of this being on my shoulders. Taking an instant to share the burden with someone else. I'd worried, before, that becoming close to Parker's mom might feel like I was trying to replace my own. But instead, it just felt like she was someone I could trust and rely on, someone who cared about me and wanted to help me.

When I pulled back, she smiled at me and then wiped a tear off her cheek. "Okay then, what else can we do to help?"

TWENTY-TWO

PARKER

Exhaustion was settling deep into me, encompassing and surrounding me like a second skin. Every blink of my eyelids took effort. Lifting my arms or legs felt like moving mountains. Soon this endless fatigue would brand itself into my DNA, becoming a part of who I was—a piece of my identity.

I had been fading in and out of the Hollow all day. It had been a struggle to move at all earlier, but now I was feeling slightly better. I'd never missed Addie so much ... not the nightmarish version of her I'd seen last night, but *my Addie*. I wanted to see her smile, kiss her and hold her hand—more importantly for right now, though, I wanted to *survive*. I desperately missed her dreams and her healing touch.

To have any hope of escaping to her, though, I'd first have to figure out what Cooper was trying to accomplish with everything he was doing to me. Was he simply some kind of sick sadist, or did he truly have a goal in mind? What did he want from me while he had me here as his prisoner?

If I could figure that out, I might have a chance at finding the weakness in his plan. Jack would be able to figure it out, if he were in here instead of me. And once he did, I was certain he would find a way to escape. Since we were at least fifty percent similar, genetically speaking, I figured I would have about a fifty percent chance of escaping without getting myself killed.

Right now, that felt like a risk definitely worth taking. Especially if it meant avoiding any more nights spent battling Cooper in our minds...or them trying to drown me with that toxin again.

Even half-asleep, I shuddered. There were very few things they could do to me that would be worse than what they'd already done.

Coming fully awake again, I cringed against the brightness of the room around me. I couldn't see anything. It felt as blinding and hot as if they'd made me roommates with a miniature sun. At first, I couldn't make out any details of the room around me.

Raising my right hand to shade my eyes, I blinked a few times, trying to force my vision to adjust enough to see clearly. The first thing I noticed was that the blood that had been on the floor next to me, after the dream earlier, had disappeared. Then I realized it wasn't the blood that was gone, but the concrete floor I'd been lying on. No, the entire room was different. They must've moved me while I was unconscious. The floor beneath me was white tile, the walls were white, the ceiling; everything was white.

I had no idea where I was now, but hopefully it was someplace not so far underground. With all of the tile, it could've been a kitchen originally. Maybe this room was closer to an exit. Maybe being moved here was my chance to find a way out.

The light seemed to be coming from everywhere, but I realized quickly that it was more of a special effect in the room than an actual truth. Very bright fluorescents nearly covered the ceiling. Plus, several large work lights hung from short cords all around the room. The work lights were pointed toward my spot on the floor. The lighting, combined with the stark whiteness of the room, made the tile nearly glow.

Weird... but still a massive improvement from the room I'd been in before.

At least it was fairly clean in here. That was nice... although it did make me notice how much dirtier *I* had become in the last twenty-four hours.

I climbed painfully to my feet, my head pounding. My hands stayed on my knees until the room stopped spinning. Slowly making my way to the door, I tried to turn the knob, but it was locked. I pulled on the handle, then pounded on the door until my hands hurt... no one came. Putting my ear up to the door, I listened, but there was only silence on the other side.

Moving back from the door, I curled into a ball on the floor, facing it. I studied the hinges and looked around on the floor for anything I might use to pry them out.

The only thing in the room was me.

Disappointed, I put an arm over my eyes and tried to get a little more rest in the Hollow until someone came to get me. But with the light this bright, it took a few minutes for me to settle down. As I started to drift off, a loud blaring horn echoed through the room and I sat up straight against the wall, my pulse racing, my eyes searching for the source of the noise.

Nothing changed, and it was silent again. After a few minutes, my eyes started to close and I began to fall asleep again. Again, the horn blasted the instant I was almost asleep.

Perfect. This was another sleep deprivation tactic. They were trying to keep me from even entering the Hollow. If my head was pounding before, every time the horn sounded it felt like it was being split open.

Then the door opened and Cooper strolled in. My eyes scanned the hallway outside, but it didn't give me any clues about how far I'd been moved. It looked identical to the hall outside the other room ... so my guess was that they hadn't moved me far.

My shoulders slumped and I watched Cooper warily. A short man had followed him in, carrying a small white case; they left the door open behind them. Before I could even look for any chance to escape, I saw the shoulders of two guards standing outside the door, and my heart sank.

Turning my attention to the stranger, I saw he wore all white and had a sickly pallor to his skin that nearly made him blend right into the room itself. It took me several seconds to recognize him as the doctor who'd been watching over Chloe's body the night we'd gone to the base to get Dad.

When I squinted in his direction, he turned to glare straight at me, and I gasped.

His neck, the right side of his face, and his right hand were covered with raw skin and still-healing burns. He must've been caught in Dad's explosion. The sheer hatred in his gaze as he glowered at me was so intense I slid closer to the wall.

"Oh, that's right. You've met Dr. Rivera, haven't you?" Cooper smiled, and when he turned toward the doctor I saw a trickle of dried blood below his ear. At least I knew for certain that I wasn't the only one who'd suffered in our battles last night.

With a wicked grin, Cooper continued. "I'm pretty sure the doc remembers you."

Dr. Rivera opened his case. Inside there were dozens of vials, a myriad of colors and consistencies. He lifted out a syringe and a vial with some kind of sinister black liquid in it. He started to draw a large dose into the needle. His eyes kept darting over to me, like I might blow stuff up like my dad if he didn't watch me close enough.

I only wished I had those kind of skills.

But since I hadn't been near anything as dangerous as a matchbox the entire time I'd been here, it was clear they weren't taking any chances with me. I shifted myself closer to the wall, trying to get farther away from Cooper and the angry doctor.

"What is all of that?" In spite of my efforts, my voice

sounded as scared as I felt, and I saw Cooper's smile widen in response.

"The black one is your medicine, Parker. The other vials do different things. It all depends on what Dr. Rivera and I are trying to accomplish."

"Accomplish?" My voice came out a little strangled. When Cooper didn't respond, I glanced at the white tile room around me. "Why did you bring me here?'

"I put this room together because it's really very lazy of you to try to take naps all day. We just want to make sure you have a more regular sleeping schedule." Cooper nodded. "It's always healthier, you know."

"Right. So nice to hear you're concerned for my health," I said, sarcasm oozing from every syllable. "Tell me that black goo is for you and I might actually believe you care."

"Oh, that?" He chuckled to himself. "That particular drug wouldn't work at all on me."

Then he gestured behind him, and two of the Takers who'd helped drag me in from the car entered the room. I tried to crawl away, but they were too fast. They grabbed my arms and lifted me up to my feet. The motion was too quick, and once they had me up, the room swayed as the blood rushed to my feet. My vision went dark around the edges before finally settling back into place.

Dr. Rivera finished filling the syringe and slipped the bottle back into his pocket. He walked up to me and held the needle in front of my face until I looked at it. Then he smiled, handed it to Cooper, and pulled out an alcohol wipe to clean a spot on my arm.

"It's really too bad your father isn't here to see this." Dr. Rivera's voice was as nasal as I remembered from the first time we'd met. "At least some part of him might have enjoyed this experiment."

"What are you giving me? Wh-what do you mean, *experiment*?" I watched him take the needle from Cooper and lift it toward my arm.

Adrenaline pulsed through my veins, lending me temporarily renewed strength. I kicked off the ground, driving the guards holding me back into the wall behind us. One lost his grip, and I used the opportunity to punch the guard who still held me in the nose with my newly freed hand. I heard a crunch, and he cried out and released me. Pain shot through my wrist after the impact, but I felt a grim joy as his nose immediately started bleeding.

The guard who'd lost his grip on me first now recovered enough to jump on my back, knocking me down onto my hands and knees. My arms crumpled beneath his weight and my face ached as he pushed it into the tile floor. Two more guards ran in. They rolled me over, each pinning down an arm or leg.

I held my breath as Dr. Rivera stuck the needle into my arm and then watched him press the plunger, sending the terrifying black goo into my body. I tried to breathe evenly, but my pulse felt like it had doubled before he'd even put in the needle.

Then the other effects hit me with the force of a semi on the freeway.

The room around me slanted slightly one way and then

back the other. Everything around me looked deeply shadowed in unnatural ways. I focused on Cooper's face, trying to understand what was happening.

"What did you just do to me?" My voice echoed oddly, my words slurred.

Cooper laughed. "Your dad might have caused a lot of problems, but he was also a genius. He had this theory, you see, that the different kinds of Night Walkers really aren't all that different biologically."

My body felt like I wasn't inside of it anymore. I was floating above it, but I heard my garbled voice speak. "Biologically?"

"Yes." Cooper smiled wide and gestured to Dr. Rivera, then squatted down beside me. "The doc here isn't even a Night Walker. He's just an average doctor who, nine years back, got caught up in one of your dad's schemes. Your dad asked him strange questions about chemical differences in the brain—what things could be changed without damaging brain tissue, what kind of effects different chemicals would have. Eventually, your dad told Dr. Rivera our big secret."

My dad didn't work with this awful doctor. The thought echoed back at me a million times, like I was standing at the mouth of a cave and screaming it. I hadn't actually spoken, but I was definitely trying.

"No." Finally the word worked its way from my brain, down my face, and out of my mouth, but it was barely recognizable.

"Yes, Parker." Cooper grinned and leaned down over my slumping body. "It's taken Dr. Rivera time to learn to understand us, but now he more than understands. He's learning to manipulate our brains. Your dear old dad's research really did help him quite a bit, though. The dad you always think of as such a hero actually worked with Dr. Rivera to try to test his hypothesis that Night Walkers are biologically mostly the same. The main differences they noted were related to elevations of various hormone levels and accelerated activity in different areas of the brain. They were even able to isolate the differences they found, down to a few select chemicals, and so believed that if you found the right way to do it, you could flip a switch inside our brains. They thought that with different drugs, you could turn one type of Night Walker into another—permanently."

Cooper reached into Dr. Rivera's coat pocket and pulled out the almost-empty bottle of black goo. He held it out before my vacantly staring eyes. "And if we could find the right drug for each specific type of change, we could all *choose* what we wanted to be. All we'd have to do is *flip— that—switch…*"

His last word echoed to me as if from far away … *itch— itch—itch—*

I tried to understand what he was saying, but my brain was foggy and Cooper seemed very far away. I couldn't make sense of things the way I wanted to. Nothing in my body or mind was working right. One thought floated through like a passing idea on a breeze, and I heard my lips mumbling the words: "Watchers could become Builders to survive."

My voice strained, like the words mattered so much, but

I wasn't entirely sure I was the one speaking them. Everything was incredibly fuzzy and full of echoes. My body felt numb from head to toe. "And Takers could, too...and Takers, like you, could..."

"Become something less than we are meant to be? Just to *live*?" Cooper said, spitting out the last word hard like the taste in his mouth was bitter. "We're better than that."

Dr. Rivera brought over a stethoscope and was listening to my chest, but I couldn't feel the pressure I should feel as he pushed it against my skin. I couldn't see through my eyes anymore. It was like I was floating above them instead of watching them. I stared at my body, crumpled in a ball on the floor, and tried to make sense of it.

"But then your dad had a another breakthrough. He found a formula that would help the Takers survive as Takers: Eclipse. It helped us in a different way—a better way." Cooper recited the words as though they were a memorized story. "But instead of giving it to us, he turned on the Night Walkers, betraying us all and taking the only solution the Takers had to save their lives with him."

Part of me wanted to argue with him. I knew this was not the story Jack had told me. I knew my dad was good—I just couldn't remember any of the reasons why I knew this. Arguing was too hard. Not right now...later. I'd defend Dad later...

Cooper spoke again, but this time much of the bravado was gone. He was talking to Dr. Rivera, not to me.

"Do you think it worked?"

"We have to wait and see," the doctor said, packing up

the medicine and syringe. He used a remote to turn off some of the work lights in the room. "It may not work the first time. For now, though, you should let him rest for at least a few hours or he won't survive it."

Cooper nodded. "We may not have Eclipse yet, but if this works…"

As he followed Dr. Rivera out the door, Cooper paused and hit a switch in the hall, turning off the only remaining fluorescent light in the room. His final muttered words echoed to me through the darkness: "I'm sure Jack will be much more motivated to help us once we can tell him for certain that his dear little brother has become just like us."

Then they left me all alone in a brand new nightmare.

TWENTY-THREE
JACK

An hour later, we left Parker's house and hit the road again. We now had food, clothing, supplies, and money. More importantly, I'd convinced Mrs. Chipp to go with Addie and Mia to one of Dad's safe houses for the next week or so until I could fix this mess. Dad had two safe houses left when he died; each was under a different name, everything paid for in advance and in cash. There were no phone or Internet lines there that could be used to track anything back to the addresses. The houses were the most boring, non-noteworthy homes he could find ... and for now that was exactly what I needed

I'd worried that Parker's mom wouldn't be able to leave her work as a realtor behind. I'd seen for myself how much effort she put into her job.

"It's important you not contact anyone but me," I explained as I gave her a burner phone. "Including work."

"I couldn't work right now anyway, not when I'm this worried about Parker." She shook her head. "It won't be a problem. Don't worry about me—just get him back safe. *Please.*"

"I will."

With Addie and Mia, it had taken some serious convincing from Finn, but he managed to persuade them that the place they could help Parker the most was watching out for his mom. This *was* true, but mostly, I just couldn't put anyone else at risk—and I felt better knowing they would all keep an eye on each other.

"You text me every day." Addie's eyes were full of tears, but she was too busy giving Finn orders to cry. "Don't you dare get hurt, and you have to—have to get *all* of you back here safe, Finn. Promise me."

"I promise." Finn pulled her into a tight hug, and for once he didn't make any kind of joke.

I fought my impatience as Finn said goodbye to Mia in the backyard. She looked scared, but he held her hand and whispered to her. I decided to wait in the car, because this definitely seemed like one conversation I shouldn't be eavesdropping on.

As much as I knew they all loved Parker and wanted to help, my main focus was on keeping them safe. That was the very least I could do for my brother right now.

I hoped that since Cooper had Parker he wouldn't need

to bother with anyone else—but there was nothing I'd put past him.

The first Veronica we checked out, Veronica O. Nelson, lived in a nice apartment building we had to be buzzed into. I pressed the button next to her name and waited... after thirty seconds, I pressed it again. Still no answer. Almost a full minute later, as I turned toward the others to discuss our next step, an older female voice came through the speaker.

"Yes?"

"Is this Veronica?" I spun around and spoke quickly into the intercom.

"Yes... what can I help you with?" She already sounded annoyed.

I blurted out my next words before she could disconnect from me. "I hoped you might have a minute to talk. I think you might have known my father—"

"I doubt it." She was curt, bordering on rude, and it was obvious I wasn't getting anywhere.

Libby tapped me on the shoulder and whispered in my ear. "Maybe a girl voice will set her at ease."

I moved back from the intercom and she stepped forward to take my place. "Hi, Veronica? My name is Libby. The guy you were just talking to is Jack, and we're sorry to interrupt you, but—"

"You *are* interrupting, and I really don't have time for this," Veronica huffed. "I'm sure I don't know his father. Please leave me alone."

"But how can you know that? We haven't even told you

his nam—" Libby said quickly, but it didn't matter. There was a buzzing sound as Veronica turned her intercom off.

Libby sputtered and then growled as she lifted her hand to punch her finger into the button again. I caught her hand before she could.

"No use. Talking to her over the intercom isn't good enough. I need to see her eyes."

Stepping back from the building, I looked for a way to get Veronica to come out. If I could find a back entry that wasn't locked, at a loading dock, maybe … or some external way to set off the fire alarm would work. Some way for me to make this stubborn Veronica woman come to me.

"Libby, come around the back with me and we'll check for another way in." We started to walk away, but I looked back when I realized Chloe had stopped. She rolled her eyes, tucked her arm through Finn's, and then limped back to the front door of the building. By the time she rapped her knuckles against the door, her eyes were wet with tears and I could hear her whimpering.

Finn stood beside her, looking shocked, which only added to the effect.

After the second time she knocked, a doorman came to the door and opened it. His gold nametag was hanging at an angle, and printed in nice letters was the name *Brandon*.

"Can I help you?" He looked down at her with obvious concern and then stifled a yawn.

Chloe blinked her pretty gray eyes up at him. "I think I sprained my ankle. Do you have anywhere I could sit down so I can rest it?"

"I'm sorry, miss." Brandon was genuinely upset by what he had to say. "The building rules don't permit me to let anyone in unless one of the residents puts in a request or buzzes them in..."

"Oh, that's okay. I thought you probably couldn't." Chloe swatted at Finn. "See? I told you he wouldn't be able to help. I'll be okay." She tested some weight on her supposedly injured ankle and winced.

Finn looked from her to Brandon and back. An exaggerated frown spread across his face. "I'd hoped he could do something..."

"Do you need me to call for an ambulance? Or I—I could get you some ice?" Brandon seemed eager to find a way to help. Next to me, Libby scowled. I covered my smile with my hand as we watched Chloe work him. Was she going to be able to get us into the building this easily? Once we were in, I should be able to knock poor Brandon out pretty quickly, and then...

"I don't think I need an ambulance, but ice would be great. Thank you!"

I frowned. Okay... now what?

Brandon ducked back inside while Finn helped Chloe to a bench nearby. Reaching into her bag, she pulled out the dark sunglasses, and then I understood. She was going to take him over, like she did with Wendy's husband. I still wasn't sure how comfortable I was with using her abilities, but I couldn't deny how useful they could be.

After Brandon brought her the ice, Chloe thanked him and said she thought she was actually feeling a little better.

She rested her hand on his neck and gave him a quick peck him on the cheek. Brandon stepped back into the building, blushing, rubbing the back of his neck, and looking like he fully believed he'd saved the day.

After he was gone, Libby and I walked back over to them.

"Okay," I said. "So … we have to wait until tonight for him to go home and fall asleep—"

"Please. I know we don't have that kind of time." Chloe laughed and shook her head before letting Finn "help" her toward the van.

"Then how?" I frowned.

"He was probably napping when I knocked on the door. It took him a minute to respond." Chloe shook her head at me like I should pay better attention. She lowered her voice. "Plus, I might have given him a little extra help for insurance."

I grabbed her arm and pulled her around to face me, fighting to keep from arguing with her until I knew for certain what she'd done. "What does that mean?"

Chloe kept her eyes down, but she extended her hand, and I realized that a small ring on her pinky finger was twisted upside down. It bore the infinity symbol, which was now turned toward the inside of her hand. When she lifted it for me to see, I noticed a tiny needle poking out of the metal. As I watched, she pushed one end of the symbol and the metal slid down. The needle disappeared from view, and she turned the ring back around until it faced outward again.

"You poked him in the neck and drugged him?" Libby snarled from beside me, looking surprisingly dangerous.

"Only a little." Chloe shrugged. "It won't hurt him, and it's very short term. He'll be back asleep in five minutes and it only lasts for about a half an hour—"

"That doesn't matter! We can't go around drugging innocent people. What if he has a bad reaction to it? Or loses his job for sleeping in the middle of the day?" Libby turned to face me. "Right, Jack?"

"Well, I think he was *already* sleeping in the middle of the day," Chloe muttered, half under her breath.

I looked from Chloe to Libby and back. As much as I normally would have agreed with Libby, how different was this from me sneaking in and knocking him out? This could technically be considered even less damaging to him. But I really didn't want to disagree with Libby in front of Chloe... not right now, when Libby needed me. Before I had a chance to speak, Chloe saved me.

"It doesn't matter what you guys think. I wanted to help and I'm going to make sure I take advantage of this chance." She climbed into the van, then stopped and looked out at Finn. "You know I'm not trying to hurt him—I just want to help Parker while he still might have a chance. I'm going to sleep. Please, Finn. Go to the front of the building so someone will be there for Brandon-me to let in."

Finn shrugged, then turned and walked toward the front of the building.

Chloe closed the van door softly without another word, and I turned to see Libby watching me with a frown. "She's a *Taker*, Jack. You can't trust her. I hope you aren't forgetting that."

I pushed my hands into my hair and then met Libby's eyes. "I hope she's telling us the truth ... but I'm prepared for the fact she might not be."

"Good." Libby nodded, but she didn't look entirely convinced.

Libby and I followed Finn back to the front of the building, and it only took about two minutes for Brandon-Chloe to open the door to us. She led the way to the elevator. "Hurry. It won't be too long before he wakes up."

"I only need to see Veronica long enough to make eye contact," I stated a bit gruffly. I couldn't decide whether I was mad that Chloe hadn't waited for me to agree with her plan before taking this kind of action, or impressed that she'd come up with it and executed it perfectly all on her own.

Either way, I had to admit that she was right. Having a Taker on our side was definitely proving to be more helpful than I'd expected.

"I know. Good luck," was her only reply as she walked back to Brandon's desk. We got on the elevator and pressed the button for the eleventh floor.

Finn knocked on Veronica's apartment door, on the off chance that she might recognize my voice from before. When she answered, I wasn't surprised at all to find she was thin and very severe. Everything about her was hard.

"Yes?" she asked. I faked a loud cough until she looked over at me and made the eye contact I needed. Then Finn stepped in.

"Oh ... do we have the wrong apartment?" He shook his head in confusion and leaned back to look at the placard next to her door, which was clearly marked with Apt. 11B. "Is this where Mr. Williams lives?"

She shook her head quickly and already had the door half closed as she replied, "Wrong floor. He's in 12B."

"My mistake. Sorry."

Libby raised her eyebrows at Finn as we turned back toward the elevator. "How did you know to ask for Williams?"

"I saw it on the directory outside and thought it might come in handy." Finn smiled, looking quite proud of himself. I knew exactly where he'd learned it, but I was impressed he'd remembered it all the same.

"Smart." Libby smiled and let him lead the way to the elevator. As soon as he was a couple feet ahead of us, she nudged me with her elbow and whispered, "Looks like you're starting to rub off on your brother's friends. Let's hope Parker has picked up a few things from you too."

I tilted my head, not sure if that was a compliment or not.

"Don't worry. I'm saying it's a good thing." Libby put one hand on my arm and rested her head against my shoulder. Her actions comforted me even as her words made me feel cold inside. "If he did, I guarantee it will increase his chances of making it through this alive."

————

All that work ended up being for nothing. When I went to sleep that night, there was no sign that there'd ever been a Night Walker of any kind in the dreams of Veronica #1.

My effort to pull out any memories of Dad came up with nothing. This Veronica had never even met him.

And because of her exasperating reluctance to even answer our simple questions, we'd lost an entire day. We were now down to eight days left until Cooper's deadline and still missing two ingredients of the formula. I was trying very hard not to crush the steering wheel beneath my fingers on the drive over to the second Veronica on our list.

It was obvious Finn was blaming himself for the lost time. "I'm sorry I couldn't get more information about her online." His shirt for the day fit the Veronica #1 situation well: *I used to be a people person, but people ruined that for me.*

Chloe was sitting in the front seat beside me, and I saw her glance over at me when I didn't say anything. Once she caught my eye, she inclined her head toward the backseat and raised her eyebrows.

I forced myself not to sigh as I responded to Finn. "It's fine, Finn. We didn't lose that much time, and you saved us a lot of time by being able to eliminate the Wendys the way you did. You really don't need to apologize."

The part about not losing much time was a flat-out lie, but at least the second part was true.

Chloe smiled, and as much as it confused me to react this way, her smile made me feel better somehow. Then she turned to face the window and rested her head against it. With the light shining in on her, it was hard to miss the dark circles under her eyes.

Thinking about that made me grip the steering wheel even tighter again.

Veronica #2's house was a pretty condo in a nice part of Franklin. A little girl who couldn't have been more than six or seven years old answered the door. She had giant brown eyes just a shade lighter than her skin. Her hair was pulled up in a bun on top of her head, and she was wearing a purple ballet leotard.

There were only three of us on the porch, since when Chloe climbed out of the van, Libby decided to stay behind. I wasn't at all surprised, although I'd hoped at some point she might start warming up to Chloe a little.

"Is your name Veronica?" Finn asked the girl with a smile, bending down. I rolled my eyes at Chloe. We wouldn't have found this Veronica in the phone directory, not to mention that my dad probably hadn't left his deepest secrets with a tiny ballerina.

"No, I'm Ruby!" She grinned and showed us her missing front tooth. "Veronica is my mommy's name."

"Can we talk to your mommy, then?" Finn straightened up and raised his eyebrows at me like he'd proved some kind of point. "Is she at home?"

Ruby bounced up onto her toes and then disappeared into the house, yelling, "Mommy! The door people are for you!"

A couple of seconds later a woman walked down the hall toward us, holding a large spoon in one hand and a phone in the other. She had Ruby's exact eyes. "May I help you?"

I stepped forward. "Veronica?"

"That's me." She hit a button on her phone, slipped it into her pocket, and looked at me expectantly.

I introduced myself, explaining that she might have known my Dad and I was looking for information.

Veronica looked bored at first. But she stopped fiddling with her spoon and looked horrified when I told her that Dad had died. "Oh, honey, I'm so sorry. The name doesn't ring a bell, but do you have a picture with you or anything that might help me remember?"

My heart stung with a quick, piercing stab. I wished I had a picture of him. He'd never let me take one…

"I have one," Finn said quietly, giving me an apologetic look. "Well, it's not of him, but it's his other son, and I guess he looks a lot like a younger version of their dad."

Finn pulled a picture out of his wallet. In it, Parker, Addie, and Finn were sitting at the table in Finn's kitchen. They were all laughing so hard it looked like they could fall right out of their chairs at any moment. It was a great photo. It made me miss both Parker and our dad, all in one glance.

Veronica studied it closely. "Yeah, he looks familiar, but…"

"Picture him in his forties," Chloe jumped in, and I glanced at her in surprise. She shot me an apologetic look, and I remembered that she and her family had spent a decent amount of time at the base while they were holding Dad. I looked down with a shake of my head as she continued. "He had graying hair around his temples, and—"

Veronica suddenly clapped a hand over her mouth, grabbed the picture, and pulled it closer before letting out a small squeak. "Oh no!"

"You remember him." The answer was obvious from the

look on her face. I felt a spark of hope that at least we now had the right Veronica.

"Yes." She nodded, lowering her hand. "He went by Dan, but I swear he said his last name was Richards. He used to live in my building. He seemed like a nice guy…"

It was quiet for a few seconds before she got a look of sudden panic on her face.

"Why did he change his name? Was he dangerous?" She leaned back and looked into her house to make sure Ruby wasn't close enough to hear, then put one shaking hand to her heart before asking, "He spent time with Ruby…he wouldn't have hurt my daughter, would he?"

"No, no, no," all three of us said in unison, and Veronica looked significantly relieved.

I stepped forward. I'd spent all night pushing away my fears about what might be happening to Parker, and I'd come up with what I hoped was a better way to get answers from these strangers. Now it was time to try it out and hope for the best.

"We're trying to puzzle together some stuff he was looking into," I explained. "He left a bunch of papers behind and it doesn't make a lot of sense. Maybe you can help us?"

Finn threw me a surprised glance behind Chloe's back, but I pretended not to notice. I just needed them to let me play this out.

Veronica shrugged. "I don't know what help I can be, but if I recognize anything, I'll tell you."

"Good. That's all I need." I smiled and felt genuinely relieved. "My father had some strange words jotted down near your name on the papers I found." I tugged my phone out of my pocket and pretended to read off of the notepad app. "Do the words 'NWS,' 'Night Walker,' 'Eclipse,' or 'Type 1, 2, and 3' mean anything to you?"

I spoke slowly, watching Veronica's eyes closely for even the slightest spark that she'd heard something familiar. If there was one, hopefully we'd see it without tipping her off.

She bit her lip like she was thinking hard, but I didn't detect even the slightest flicker of recognition on her face. Then she said, "Maybe he was … a diabetic? Aren't those called type 1 and type 2? Could it be something like that?"

Finn's shoulders relaxed and Chloe looked at me with one brow raised.

I acted like this could be important even though it seemed pretty clear Veronica didn't have a clue about our world. "Hmm … he wasn't a diabetic, but we'll check out if someone he knew was. Thanks for your help."

"Sorry, again, about your dad," she said, shaking my hand.

"Thank you." I made sure to make solid eye contact with her one last time before we started back toward the car.

Ruby came out to wave goodbye and I saw Chloe bend down to smile at her and tell her what a pretty ballerina she was. Ruby was beaming by the end of their short conversation. I'd never seen a Taker who could really relate to people. One more surprise about Chloe.

When she walked in my direction, I looked away and slipped on my sunglasses. Before I got a chance to speak, Chloe sighed. "I know."

That stopped me short. "You know what?"

"I know you're worried about Ruby, and I promise that when I take over her, I will not harm her in *any* way." She looked hurt that we were even having this conversation.

I actually hadn't been thinking that at all, and it made me wonder if I should've been. Did I trust her more than I should—or less? Every day, Chloe threw something I thought I knew about Takers out the window. Until I could figure her out, I'd probably be better off just keeping my mouth shut.

So I didn't say anything about her plan for Ruby. I just shrugged and led the way back to the van. When I got there, I saw that Finn was already in the driver's seat.

He had a determined look on his face. When I jumped into the back next to Libby and shut the door, he said, "We're staying in real beds in a motel tonight. I miss pillows and showering. I don't want to hear any arguments about it."

TWENTY-FOUR
PARKER

Time passed so strangely. It could've been hours or days or weeks... I couldn't keep track. I was in the white room for a long time, the lights off until I started to fall asleep and then they would all come blaring to life. If I started to doze off into the Hollow, even with the brightness, then a loud horn would go off and wake me up.

They came in with so many injections. Sometimes it was the black goo that made me feel like I was a living, breathing echo of myself. Other times it was different chemicals that seemed specifically designed to make my body freak out in various ways. I swear one was straight adrenaline; my heart would pound so hard it felt like it was trying to break free from my chest and I couldn't get enough oxygen to keep up with it.

I longed for the days when I was simply exhausted. I'd never thought that could be possible.

They always gave me the injections in the white tile room. When they were done, they moved me back to my filthy old cell, dumping me there before the adrenaline-like medicine fully wore off. I opened my eyes in confusion each time I was moved. In the old cell, my blood remained on the floor, but now it was old and dried.

Whenever I had a moment alone, my thoughts went back to the last thing Cooper had said to me. They were trying to turn me into a Taker? I'd never imagined something like that could even be possible.

But apparently, if what they said was true, then Dad had originally come up with an idea about messing with our brains—and now Dr. Rivera was trying to make it a reality.

So far, I was still a Watcher—so maybe they hadn't really figured out how to do this yet. And I would hold on to that hope until they proved otherwise.

In the quiet of my cell, I heard the whispers. Shawn spoke to me sometimes. He encouraged me, told me I was strong enough to handle this, that I would be okay. I began to believe he wasn't real, but I appreciated the company anyway. He was kind and patient, and he never showed up in my cell and tried to kill me... and that was really all I needed to know.

Besides, even if Shawn was a hallucination, I much preferred him to the hallucinations I had of Addie. In those, she kissed me and then told me she was disappointed in me; she said she loved me and then said she hated me. If I told her I knew she wasn't real, she would sometimes laugh and sometimes attack. Once, she stabbed me. I felt the pain, saw the blood…and then it was all gone, including her.

I began to really resent my own mind and the cruel tricks it was playing on me.

The next time I woke up in my cell, my head was pounding so hard I couldn't lift it. My mouth felt so dry I wondered if opening and closing it could rip something. I pressed my forehead against the cold cement, fighting to catch my breath. My heart was racing and I felt like I might throw up or pass out.

"Parker." Shawn's voice reached out to me through the wall. "Take slower, deeper breaths. I know it feels like your body can't get a full breath, but you need to focus on slow breaths first, okay? In through your nose and out through your mouth."

I did as he said and within a minute my reaction to the medicine eased. "H-how…how did you know what to do?"

He didn't answer for so long that I called his name, afraid he might have actually disappeared this time.

Finally, he let out a long breath and answered. "Like I told you, I worked for them before I ended up in here. I've had a lot of medical training. I used to be Dr. Rivera's assistant…"

I felt the wind get sucked out of me. This person, who'd helped me so much, had helped Dr. Rivera do these same terrible things to other innocent people.

Then something clicked into place. This was exactly what kept happening with the Addie hallucinations. She would show up, pretend to help or say something nice, and then end up hurting me.

"You aren't real," I said.

"What?" Shawn sounded extremely confused, but so did Addie every time I confronted her.

"It doesn't matter." I sighed and rolled over, trying to close my eyes and rest now that my pulse had slowed down.

"It was awful. I couldn't live with myself after I saw what some of the medications could do." Shawn sounded like he was pressing himself up against the wall, trying to force his voice in so I could hear it. "They threw me in here because I finally refused to help them anymore."

"Uh huh...I'm going to try to sleep for a minute now." I did my best to sound bored. This conversation didn't matter. If Shawn was real and telling the truth, I didn't want to talk to someone who'd ever inflicted this kind of torture on anyone. If he was a hallucination, my time could be much better spent clinging to whatever bits and pieces of rest I could get.

"Okay," Shawn said after a minute, and then, "I'm sorry. I wish I could help you."

I didn't reply. I just closed my eyes and let the exhaustion sweep over me.

It could've been minutes or hours that passed before the door to my cell swung open again. It was impossible to tell. All I could feel was fear closing up my throat; I ignored the pain that came with each movement as I scrambled further into the corner.

It was Thor who had stepped into the open doorway.

He swore, quiet and low, before bringing in a paper bag and closing the door behind him.

When he stepped closer to me, I growled instinctively and hunched lower. Thor stopped. He opened the top of the paper bag and pulled out a bottle of clear water, a sandwich, and a banana, showing each to me slowly before putting them back inside and tossing the bag to a spot on the floor next to me. Then he backed up and stood by the door. I watched him turn to stare out the window before I ripped the bag open and poured some much-needed water into my mouth.

My stomach snarled, but I forced myself to take slow, small bites of the sandwich so I didn't get sick and throw it back up. I sipped some more water, watching Thor's back.

"Why are you helping me?" My voice was raw and quiet, but I could tell he'd heard me by the way his back stiffened.

"I'm just trying to keep you alive," Thor grunted.

He'd always been such a silent, scary force on our soccer team, and he'd never really spoken to me before. Now that he was actually talking, I was afraid to interrupt him in case he decided to stop again.

"There won't be a trade if you're dead," he added.

"Maybe we're more alike than you think..." I said finally. He'd been the only one to help me in here. Maybe I could convince him to help more.

"We're not."

"You're Steve Campbell's younger son, right? Cooper is older..." I ate slowly and spoke softly, doing my best to think through each word.

Thor shifted his weight and peered out of the window in the other direction.

"At least your dad raised you, though," I continued. "Mine went back to my older brother and left me behind." I took another small bite, trying to mask how much it stung to speak those words aloud. No matter how much I tried to believe that Dad's choice didn't mean anything, there was still a fear deep inside me that it did.

Thor turned away from the window to look at me, but I couldn't read the expression in his eyes.

"I didn't even know my dad was still alive for four years," I said, fighting not to let exhaustion and the emotion from my own words overwhelm me. Maybe this had been a bad idea—trudging up this pain that I'd been fighting so hard to put behind me. But I instinctively felt that Thor might relate somehow to that side of me...although I could be wrong.

I tried one more time. "He was always there to help my brother...but not me."

Thor flinched like my words stung him, and then turned back to the window again.

"Shut up and eat." His voice was softer now, but I couldn't miss the way his hands clenched—maybe my words had hit their mark after all.

Not wanting to push him too hard, I finished the food and water in silence, afraid to anger the only person who didn't appear to want me dead. As soon as I held out my garbage, Thor took it and was gone.

Then I was alone for a while, but as always, it was impossible to tell how long I'd been here or what time it was when there was no natural light in my cell. Had it been two days? Three? More? Was Jack making any progress figuring out the new formula?

As much as I fought my doubts, my conversation with Thor about fathers had hit closer to the mark than it should have. Here, in this dark and horrible cell, it was hard not to question what Jack was doing. Had Jack turned his back on me, just like Dad had so long ago?

Or was I doubting someone who would never betray me—just like Dad doubted Jack when the Takers locked him up in a cage not much different from this one?

Later, Cooper showed up with his minions to drag me back to the white room again. The food and water Thor had brought gave me a little more strength, but I didn't let Cooper see that. The last thing I wanted was for Cooper to know I wasn't quite as weak as he thought... or for Thor to get in trouble. That could cause me to lose the only ally I might have in here.

TWENTY-FIVE
JACK

That night, I tried everything in Veronica #2's dreams that I had in Wendy's, but I found nothing. A few old memories came back easily, but nothing that Dad had buried or tampered with. Either he'd hidden an ingredient with Veronica in a completely different way, or else there just wasn't anything buried in her mind for me to find.

By the time I sat down in the sand in Veronica's beach dream, it took all my self-control not to lead the dream down a destructive path. I felt so trapped it was suffocating. I was running out of time. By tomorrow morning, I'd be down to seven days left. How would one week ever be enough to sort through this puzzle, especially with so many parts still missing? Would Dad's paranoia and this scavenger hunt he'd put me on end up costing me the only family I had left?

But what other option did I have than to keep trying? I couldn't—and wouldn't—give Eclipse to Cooper. Without another alternative to at least offer him, how could I convince Cooper to hand over Parker, who was essentially the only leverage he had?

And I couldn't even try to come up with a different plan for rescuing Parker because he'd refused to tell me where he was. He'd gotten into the terrible habit of trying to protect me lately—didn't he know it was interfering with my job of protecting him? I was the big brother here … this was what *I* was supposed to do.

When I finally woke up the next morning, I'd spent the entire night digging through Veronica's mind and my brain felt like mush. The healing Libby had done in my mind two days before had been thoroughly undone … and I'd found no new clues to help us set Parker free.

Groaning, I rolled over in my motel bed and found myself face to face with Finn. He was snoring with such force that it moved my hair off my forehead.

I sat up straight and moved quietly toward the door. Still feeling mildly surprised at how Libby had only maintained a stony silence about having to share a bed with Chloe, I looked over and saw that not only was Libby the only one *in* the bed, but Chloe's side was still made up.

Chloe hadn't slept there.

Rubbing my hand against the stubble on my face, I tried to think where else Chloe could've gone. Last night, around the time everyone else went to bed, she'd said she wanted to go for a walk to calm her mind. If she'd done as planned and entered Ruby's dreams, then she must've laid down somewhere.

Or else she gave up and decided to leave us completely.

Swearing under my breath, I didn't even stop to put on my shoes before racing silently out the door. If Chloe had decided to turn on us now and go back to the Takers to tell them what we were doing…

Our van was still parked in the same spot, so at least she hadn't left us here with no vehicle. I scrambled across the rocky parking lot, ignoring the stabbing pains on the bottoms of my bare feet. When I got to the van I threw the back door open to see if Chloe had stolen any of our supplies.

Instead of supplies, I found Chloe herself sleeping in the back, shivering under the corner of one thin blanket.

She sat straight up when the door flew open and gave a startled yell before kicking me hard in the chest. The impact knocked me onto the gravel and scraped up my hands. She was on her hands and knees in an instant, looking out of the van at me with wide eyes—frightened eyes.

"Jack?" she whispered, then pulled her sandals onto her feet and jumped out. She extended a hand to help me up. "What are you doing out here?"

"Me?" I tried to get the rocks off my hands by brushing them against my jeans, but I winced as it only pushed some of the jagged pieces farther into the torn-up skin on my palms. "What are *you* doing out here?"

Chloe looked at me like I was crazy. "Um, I was sleeping. Now it's your turn."

I looked away, wishing I could be as capable of change

as the girl in front of me appeared to be. I was an idiot and felt incredibly guilty about how quickly I'd jumped to the conclusion that she'd betrayed us. "Checking on our supplies," I mumbled.

Both her eyebrows shot up as she looked me up and down. "In your sweats, with no shoes on ... before anyone else is even awake?"

I didn't meet her eyes as I clambered to my feet without any assistance. She didn't ask any more questions, but the silence between us felt awkward and heavy.

"Come on. Let me grab the first aid kit and help clean you up."

I shook my head. "I can do thi—"

"Shut up."

She grabbed the first aid kit from the front of the van and spread it across her lap, working in silence. I watched her fingers move deftly across my hand. She cleaned out the scratches, then put on ointment and a clean bandage. She'd obviously done this before.

Her face was hidden behind her hair as she bent low over my other hand. When I lifted her chin, her cheeks were streaked with tears and her gray eyes were filled with raw pain.

"Chloe ... " I could see in her eyes that she knew what I'd been thinking. It was still hard for me to believe that doubts or suspicions from me could hurt her so much. But I owed her more than this. She deserved better than me.

"I s-slept out here because Libby obviously doesn't want me in the bed—in the room—in her life." She wiped the tears roughly from her cheeks like she was furious at them for even existing, but it did little good. More fell immediately to replace them. "My family hates me. Libby hates me…and no matter how much I try with you, you—you will never—"

She shook her head hard and pulled back until my hand fell away from her face, then pushed my other bandaged hand off of her lap. She turned and started packing her few belongings into a plastic bag.

I cleared my throat and tried to find something, anything, to say that would get us back on track. "My search last night failed," I told her, forcing myself not to wince at a jolt of pain in my palms. "The second Veronica doesn't know the ingredients either. I'm not sure why Dad sent me here."

"You need to try Ruby," Chloe whispered. She spoke the words fast and furious, her back to me, her voice choked off and shaky.

"What?" All I wanted was for her to stop—stop moving, stop being angry, stop pushing me away.

"I think Ruby has your answer," she muttered, still not looking at me. "When I took her over last night, I found out your dad did more than just spend time with her—he babysat her almost every day for six months. My guess is he buried the ingredient in her dreams."

Picturing Dad as a babysitter threw me, but I'd seen him pretend to be stranger things when he had a reason. And that meant there *was* a reason. Chloe was right. I had to enter Ruby's dreams.

Relieved to have a plan, I focused again on how angry she seemed and how much that scared me. The thought of her leaving me now, with my time to save Parker rapidly disappearing... her Taker abilities *had* helped us. There was no arguing that. But just her *being here* had helped me in a completely different way—and the thought of trying to save my brother without her felt impossible.

In fact, even though I'd tried to send her away more than once, her leaving now was the last thing I wanted.

"Stop, Chloe." I reached out and gingerly put my bandaged hands on her shoulders. She froze but didn't turn around.

"Why?" Her voice cracked with emotion, and she waited.

I didn't know what to say or how to say it. All I knew was that I *had* to convince her to stay.

"I can't figure you out," I growled, finally saying the only words I knew were true. Dropping my hands, I let my frustration show. "What do you want from me? You just said, 'You'll never.' What will I 'never' do?"

She shifted around until she was looking straight at me. All her toughness was gone and she looked broken down, completely vulnerable. "You'll never see me as anything but the daughter of Steve Campbell."

I flinched when she said his name, and I could see immediately that it only confirmed for her what she was saying. She recoiled, packing things into her bag even more forcefully. But I reached out again to stop her and she pivoted to face me.

Her eyes were on me, pain written plainly for me to see. I knew she was right; I couldn't ever get past what her dad did. But I didn't blame *her* for that. Did I? I believed she'd been trying to help us—she'd already helped more than I ever expected she could. But I'd never told her I appreciated it ... never thanked her. My chest ached as I realized I hadn't treated her much differently than I might have if I'd thought she was exactly like her father.

Reaching out, I brushed the tips of my fingers gently across her dark lashes. She froze. I knocked one teardrop off at a time, onto the back of my hand, until they'd all been set free. She looked at me with those big gray eyes, and I really saw her. The fierce determination that usually hid her pain, the pure loyalty that I'd done nothing but doubt and question, the absolute exhaustion that she carried so much better than any Watcher I'd ever known. I stared at the dark circles beneath her eyes. The knowledge that they were getting darker all the time sent a fresh wave of panic gripping my heart as I realized I had even more to lose than I'd thought.

Tentative, I pulled her into my arms.

For several seconds, she tightened up in shock and I wondered if she might pull away—if I'd made a mistake. Suddenly, she wrapped both arms around my back and pulled me tight against her.

There was nothing else for me to do or say, so I whispered the only three words that meant anything against her tear-streaked cheek: "I see *you*."

Any remaining tension drained from her and she buried her face in my neck, setting my skin on fire with each breath. "I'm scared, Jack."

I thought about finding words that might make her feel better. About telling her that everything was going to be okay and trying to sound like I meant it. Or maybe I could just tell her I would be here no matter what... because that was true.

Instead, I decided to tell her she wasn't alone in a different way. In a way I wished my dad had told me—so I'd have known the fear I felt living in this messed-up world everyday was okay.

I pressed my lips against her temple, held her even tighter, and whispered, "I'm scared too."

We sat there, together, in the quiet early morning light. We held tightly to one another while everyone else in the run-down motel was asleep, and for the first time in as long as I could remember, I wasn't wishing I could be too.

———

As soon as everyone was up, we drove to pick up some more supplies and then to a new motel. This one had two beds and a pull-out sofa, so that Chloe wouldn't feel she had to stay in the back of the van again. We spent the rest of the day checking in with those we cared about—at least the ones we could. I called Mrs. Chipp, Finn called his parents, and Libby called Randall. That evening, we headed back to Veronica's, and as soon as she opened the door, I recited the excuse Finn and I had come up with earlier.

"I'm sorry to bother you again. I don't have the address my dad used to live at written down in his papers." I gave her my best apologetic smile. "Do you happen to remember which condo was his?"

Veronica nodded quickly, accepting the excuse. "He

lived in the one on the corner." She pointed to a front porch two doors down.

"Thank you," I said as my stomach tightened. I was surprised it still affected me the way it did... I knew he'd lived around here, but seeing which condo he'd actually been in felt different somehow.

Ruby peeked around her mom's legs and waved up at me, reminding me of the reason we'd come back here to begin with.

"Hi Ruby." I squatted down slightly, just enough to make eye contact with her, and she smiled. I gestured to her purple shorts and striped T-shirt. "Not a ballerina today?"

She frowned at me. "These are just normal clothes, but I'm still a ballerina whenever I want. See?" She went up on her toes and did a little spin.

"Oh, my mistake." I laughed and then looked up at the sky. Pretending to squint at the brightness of the sun, I pulled out my sunglasses and put them on. I turned back to face Veronica. "Thank you for your help. I really appreciate it."

"No problem." She gave a quick nod and pulled Ruby back inside. Just as she was closing the door I heard her say, "I hope you find what you're looking for."

Walking down the path toward the van, I whispered to myself, "I really hope so too."

———

Ruby's dreams were a myriad of strangeness. They were filled with faceless adults, disappearing playgrounds, and other children who didn't see her half the time. She went to a zoo with animals that initially seemed mostly normal in shape, but then there was always something off about them: a purple horse with no hooves, a giraffe with two heads, and penguins with black stomachs and white wings. I realized about halfway through that I couldn't remember the last time I'd watched the dreams of a child. They hadn't completely absorbed the laws of reality yet, so everything was even more strange than usual.

Somewhere, buried in the middle of everything bizarre, I found my dad, and the next riddle. Dad said, "I weaken men for hours day by day. And display bizarre visions while you're away. I steal you by night, by day return you home. None suffer who have me, but they do when I roam."

This one took me almost no time to figure out. "Sleep."

He hadn't left a message for me this time, simply the next ingredient, which I recognized as a type of acetylcholinesterase inhibitor: $C24H29NO3$. I remembered Dad had told me once that it had some kind of an effect on REM sleep and lucid dreaming, but that was all I knew.

Still: two ingredients down, only one to go.

After that, Dad revealed the next name: Mason Butler.

I drew a quick breath. Mason was the man we'd saved from the prison at the Benton Air Force Base, who'd ridden out of the base in Parker's stolen van. What a twisted chase this was becoming, with the final clue to saving Parker and Chloe's lives hidden with someone we already knew. This ornery old man hopefully had the last piece of the puzzle that might bring some kind of peace to all of the Night Walkers.

And I'd had his phone number and address on a paper in my wallet for over a month.

————

Only six days remained now, but with two ingredients down and only Mason left, we were finally making progress. Maybe Parker would be okay. Maybe all of us would.

After checking us out of the motel and turning in the key card, I tried to calculate how long it would take to get to Mason's address. I'd tried calling him twice since waking up, but there'd been no answer.

I made my way alone through the parking lot, toward the end of the building where we'd parked the van. Quick footsteps sounded behind me, but before I could even spin around, I got hit from behind, hard and fast.

Thor and I were rolling across the ground before I even got a good look at him. His fist pummeled my face and I tried to get my arms up to block his blows. I'd been distracted by my own thoughts, and now I was paying for it.

Finally my instincts kicked in, and the next time he was on the bottom, I kicked up with my knees, shoving into his gut in an effort to push myself out of his reach. It was a little awkward because he grabbed hold of my shirt, but I got myself into a squatting position before he could pounce on me again. My eye was throbbing, but most of the other damage was superficial.

"Where's Chloe?" Thor growled out.

Something in me reacted violently to the idea of him

coming here for her. "Why? Do you guys want to throw her away like garbage again?" I spat a little blood out of my mouth and onto the ground.

"I'm here to remind her where her loyalty should lie." Thor moved in for another swing, but now that I was ready for him, his movements were lumbering and easy to avoid. I jabbed out and punched his side with two quick swings before he could back away. This was exactly what I needed right now: a good fight to take out all my frustrations in. I smiled when he gave me another opening and landed an uppercut against his jaw.

Thor winced in pain and staggered back a bit, trying to draw in a full breath. "All your family does is hurt my family," he gasped. "You all lie and steal and kill."

I stopped for a minute, dropping my hands in confusion because he seemed to actually believe what he was saying. "Whoever has been telling you *that* is the one you should be after..."

Footsteps were approaching from behind and I didn't want to be surrounded, so I took two quick steps to my left. But it was Finn and Chloe who ran up. Finn looked like he couldn't decide whether he could help more by jumping in or by just staying out of my way. Chloe's skin had paled to the point where she looked like someone had drained all her blood into her feet.

My excitement for the fight dwindled. If beating up Chloe's brother would hurt her, then it wasn't worth it—not anymore.

"Thor stopped by for a visit," I said with a grim smile,

dabbing the blood dripping from my eyebrow with the bandage on my right hand.

"His name isn't Thor. You know that." Chloe looked at me with eyes that begged me not to add fuel to this situation. "Please call him Joey."

"Joey? Ah, yes...Joey, then." I kept my tone even and calm. This would probably end better for everyone if Chloe could talk Thor down before he ended up getting hurt.

"Joey..." Her voice was soft, like she was trying to be gentle with the hulk across from me. "What are you doing here? How did you find me?"

"That doesn't matter." Thor's—Joey's tone lost a little of the bravado.

"Of course it matters. How did you know I was here?" Chloe sounded a lot sad and a little angry.

Her brother didn't respond this time, just glanced down at the phone in her hands. It was quick, but I noticed it and so did Chloe.

"You didn't..." Chloe turned her phone over and pulled off the back, a look of shock crossing her face. She pulled a tiny metal tracker out, threw it into the gravel, and stomped on it.

Joey's posture shifted to defensive, and he grunted, "You expected me not to be worried about you? You're my sister—"

Chloe whipped up her head, her face twisted into a snarl. "Funny how you and Cooper only remember that when it's convenient for you."

Joey flinched back like she'd struck him. "I came to bring you back where you belong. You shouldn't desert your family, no matter what." He spoke forcefully, but there was a whine beneath his tone that made him sound surprisingly vulnerable.

I kept my hands up, waiting to see what he'd do, preparing in case he tried to grab Chloe and run. My jaw clenched tight enough to make my sore cheek ache. If she didn't want to go back, then he would have to go through me before he could take her away.

"Cooper doesn't want me there." Chloe stood up straighter and a spark of anger fueled her words. "Besides, I think I'm doing more to help everyone from here."

"But how can you want to help them?" Joey howled, pointing at me. "How can you want to help *him?*"

"So many things Dad told us weren't true, Joey. He was wrong in so many things he said, so many things he did. Think of the way he treated you." Chloe's voice softened a bit and she walked over to stand beside me. "I'm helping Jack because I think it's the best way to help everyone else I care about—including you."

Joey looked completely confused. I almost felt sorry for him ... almost.

"You need to *trust me*," Chloe pleaded, and her eyes were a storm of emotion.

I could see Joey's conviction wavering. He lowered his hands to his sides and looked at me again. Then, abruptly, his anger flared. His hands clenched into fists and he spoke from between gritted teeth. "I trust Cooper."

He was about to run at me when I heard a solid thunk. Joey fell to his knees, grabbing the back of his head. Libby stood behind him, with a dark smile and a piece of wood she must've grabbed off the ground. I saw a trickle of blood dripping down Joey's neck, and he shook his head like he was trying to clear his vision.

Chloe ran to his side. But he staggered to his feet and backed away, eyeing all of us warily. Seeing that he was very outnumbered, he turned and ran.

"Joey!" Chloe yelled after him, but he got in a car at the other end of the lot and drove away.

Chloe turned on Libby, and I recognized the fire in her eyes. Before she could say a word, I grabbed her around the waist and guided her toward the van. "Thank you," I mouthed over my shoulder at Libby.

Once we were several feet away, I spoke low into Chloe's ear. "Your brother is fine, and Libby didn't have a choice. Don't pick a fight with her for trying to protect the rest of us."

She glared at me as we reached the passenger door of the van, but she seemed to be fighting to keep from saying anything she might regret. Her expression softened as she reached out to gently touch the puffy skin that was beginning to swell around my eye. "Does it hurt?"

I blew out a big puff of air and pulled her hand down, squeezing it inside both of mine before releasing it. I opened the passenger door for her and waited for her to climb inside. "No. Let's just go finish this. It isn't going to be easy … but you're starting to make me believe it may actually be possible to convince some of the Takers to think about a new formula. We can worry about getting everyone to play nice after we all survive the next month. Okay?"

She took a slow breath and then nodded. "Okay."

I walked to the driver's door, but before I could open it Libby walked up and grabbed my shoulder. She looked in my eyes.

"You really think she didn't know her brother could find us at any time? She found that tracker awfully quick, don't you think?" Libby shook her head with a sigh. "I know there's something going on between you two ..." She trailed off, like she was waiting for me to argue with her.

But I couldn't. Mistake or not, mutual or not—I was definitely developing feelings for Chloe. And I wasn't going to lie to my best friend about it. I'd seen with Parker how many more problems that could cause.

When she realized I wasn't going to correct her, Libby's shoulders drooped forward. I almost regretted my decision to stick with the truth.

"Just don't let her make you a fool, Jack. You're smarter than that. You're better than that." Libby's hand fell away from my shoulder and hung by her side. "Takers have done nothing but hurt us all our lives. Don't give this one a new way to do it."

Then she left me and walked around to climb into the back of the van without giving me a chance to say anything in return.

TWENTY-SIX

PARKER

My body suffered through tremor after tremor on the white tile floor. My eyes burned. Every muscle ached. In addition to trying to turn me into a Taker—which thankfully still didn't appear to be working—they'd also found ways to speed up the effects of sleep deprivation on Watchers. Our bodies and brains had been built to withstand being sleep-deprived longer than regular people, but eventually it would catch up with us. That's what was happening to me when I met Mia. And now, in *significantly* less time, they'd taken me from slightly tired to the worst I'd ever felt.

How long until I started to lose my mind? How long until sanity alone became something I couldn't reach anymore?

How long until I begged for them to just kill me?

The door to the white room opened and I recoiled against the wall until I saw it was Thor, carrying in an actual working cot and a blanket without any holes in it. When his back was to me, I noticed a lump and small cut on the back of his head. And he looked slightly off balance when he walked, like his ribs or back were hurting him. I wondered what had happened.

I knew better than to say thank you or look grateful, because those things would only make him angry. So I just rolled slowly out of the way and waited for him to finish setting it up.

Then Cooper appeared in the doorway. He was swaying from side to side with exhaustion, barely managing to focus on what Thor was doing. Once he did, he looked livid.

"What the hell is this, Joey?"

Thor—maybe, because he was my only ally, I should stop calling him that—*Joey* looked even angrier than Cooper. Instead of turning to answer his brother, he reached up and ripped one of the work lights in the room down from the ceiling. It went out immediately, the plug falling out of the hole. One corner of the room went a little darker than the rest and I did my best to slide into it.

"*This* would be me making sure we have something to trade when the ten days are up." Joey gestured angrily back at Cooper and said, "What about you? What the hell is *this*, Cooper?"

Cooper frowned in confusion and his nose started bleeding. He wiped it on his sleeve as though nothing had happened. "What are you talking about?"

"What you're doing here isn't going to accomplish anything. You're going to kill both yourself and him before we even get a chance to make the trade for Eclipse!" Joey glanced over at me and then pulled his brother out the door, closing it behind him. I breathed as quietly as possible and listened to his voice, which still carried through the closed door. "You have to know you aren't thinking straight right now."

And here was my main consolation in all of this. Cooper was in bad shape when they'd first brought me here, and he wasn't getting better. Overseeing the experiments, and all the battles we had in our minds every night, were having much the same effect on him as on me. Breaking me down like this was a lot of work, and he'd already been nearing the end of his path. Every time I saw him he looked worse and worse…

Just like me.

The only new plan for escape that I'd been able to come up with actually hinged on that fact. If I could just find a way to hold out longer than Cooper, then maybe Joey would be put in charge and I might have a better chance of surviving.

Cooper's tone when he answered was cold, stubborn, and tired. "I'm doing what Dad would've done."

"I know you are!" Joey's voice rose, loud and clear with desperation. "Don't you see? This is *exactly* what Dad would've done. *That* is the whole problem with this situation!"

Cooper's words became positively acidic. "You don't understand. You've never understood because you aren't one of us and you hate that."

I heard one set of footsteps walk away, and I wasn't sure

who'd left until I heard a groan and then Joey mutter, "Well, at least my weak human genes aren't going to kill me."

I had to stop myself from physically reacting to his statement. From the moment I'd found out about Cooper and Chloe, I'd assumed Joey was a Taker too. We all had. And apparently we'd been wrong.

Jack had told me that having a Night Walker parent didn't guarantee a Night Walker child; it just increased the odds a lot. It looked like their family was two for three—which actually explained quite a bit. Joey wasn't that much younger than Cooper, but he had none of the telltale signs of exhaustion that Cooper did. Those symptoms should've been showing up by now if Thor—Joey—was a Taker.

It took a lot of effort, but I managed to pull myself over onto the cot. I sighed as the material eased the ache in my muscles after so many hours on the hard floor.

The door opened again suddenly, and when Joey looked my way, I thought about saying something to him. Something to let him know that not all Night Walkers thought humans were weak or inferior to us. But it was like he could see that I was thinking about talking to him and wanted to make sure I didn't get a chance. Careful not to actually make direct eye contact with me, he tossed a new paper bag with food at my chest, hard enough that it definitely squished my sandwich. Then he dropped the water bottle on the cot beside me and hurried back out of the cell, closing the door behind him.

I opened my bag and brought out the slightly deci-mated sandwich. Even if I couldn't thank him, I hoped he knew how much I owed him. My vision shook as my eyes had one of their mini seizures, so I closed them tight in an effort to make it stop.

Taking another bite, I chewed slowly for a full minute before opening my eyes again. Relieved to see that the shaking had stopped, I watched the newly dim corner of the room where Joey had torn the work light down. It started to darken, shadows gathering together.

I focused my gaze on that spot, my head pounding, but it was already gone. Nothing.

I released a shaky sigh.

I'd lived through this before. It was only a matter of time before it all happened again. No one else had ever put themselves back together after being Divided the way I had. It was pretty safe to assume that no one knew what would happen if a person became Divided twice in one lifetime. Given how awful and terrifying it had been living with Darkness the first time around, I didn't want to face that again. Not now, when I was already this weak.

Lying back on the cot, I closed my eyes and rested one arm across them, trying to soothe the pounding ache I'd had behind my eyeballs for hours—or days now. The pain never stopped anymore. It just moved from one location to another and changed intensity. I was so tired ... and every movement was becoming so hard.

I didn't move when I heard Joey come in later and collect the garbage from my lunch. As he left, he reached into the hallway and hit switches to turn out every light, one by one. The relief from the heat and the cool darkness on my aching head was too much. A grateful sob escaped my chest. I decided I didn't care if it made him mad. This one time I had to say it.

"Thank you, Joey," I whispered into the quiet.

"Get some rest." His tone wasn't angry. He just sounded surprised and confused, and then the door closed behind him.

With Joey helping me like this, the Takers might even be less of a threat to me than what I had lurking within my own mind. After everything Cooper had done to me, I'd lost so much of my strength.

If Darkness came back again now ... I doubted I'd have anything left in me to keep him from taking over completely.

TWENTY-SEVEN

JACK

Mason had a cabin so far outside of Fairview that it wasn't technically considered part of the town. The area was filled with dense natural forests and roads that were barely usable. We bounced along the roads in tense silence. I'd tried to call Mason a few more times from the van, but he still wasn't answering. I wasn't sure what that meant, but I couldn't imagine it was a good thing.

Finn pulled his phone out. "I'm going to tell Addie and Mia we got the second ingredient and are on our way to the third. That okay?"

"Sure." I turned on my blinker, relieved that Finn had taken on the task of keeping the girls in the loop this time. If I had to name things I was terrible at, first on the list was probably communication—as I'm sure Parker would attest to—and second would be reassuring others.

Finn was obviously the clear choice for this job.

We'd been driving for a couple of hours and were getting close now, but I still didn't know exactly what I was going to say to Mason. Since he'd been kept in the Takers' prison, it seemed a safe assumption that he at least knew about the Night Walkers. But other than that, the man was kind of a mystery.

Libby had a book open. She was stretched out across the very rear seat, reading and trying to ignore the rest of us. Finn, finished with his phone call and looking bored, leaned up from the middle seat to talk to Chloe and me. His shirt of the day read, *What I really need are minions.* The shirt had a point. Minions could really come in handy with the way things were going lately.

"So, this Mason guy—he can't be a Taker?" he asked.

I glanced over at Chloe, but we both were shaking our heads no even before I responded. "He's gotta be at least fifty. No Taker has ever—" I cut myself off, realizing what I was about to say and how much I didn't want to say it, especially not in front of Chloe.

"No Taker has ever lived that long," Chloe finished for me, then shrugged it off as though it didn't matter at all. "It's okay to say it. It isn't new information."

"Okay. But he could be a Builder, though?" Finn looked eager to move on to a different possibility.

"Probably," I said, and Chloe nodded in agreement.

"And you don't know anything about why he might have

been thrown into the Takers' prison?" I asked Chloe, not for the first time. It really wasn't about trust—I just hoped she might finally remember something about the base.

"No. I didn't have anything to do with all that." She shifted uncomfortably in her seat. "I told you, they didn't trust me enough. They didn't even tell me where they moved to when they left it."

"So you say..." I heard Libby mutter not too quietly from the backseat.

"Why couldn't Mason be a Watcher?" Finn asked.

"Because he's usually alone." Libby dropped her book and spoke up. "And Watchers don't live that long either unless they can *use* someone like me."

I looked up sharply into the rearview mirror and met her eyes, but she quickly looked away. The word *use* felt specifically selected to hurt me. The Libby I knew would never want to do that. She'd been broken by all of this... and I didn't know how to fix it.

By the time I finally pulled to a stop in front of Mason's cabin, it was late afternoon and the sun was rapidly moving across the sky. The house looked quiet, but there was an old car parked next to it and I hoped Mason would be home.

We jogged up the front steps and I knocked loudly on the door. We listened as some robins took flight from a large oak tree by one end of the house. They flapped around the tree a few times before deciding that everything was probably okay and settling back down on whatever branch I'd disturbed them from. A full minute passed before I raised my hand to knock again... and then I heard a creak from inside.

"Mason? Are you in there?" I called, hoping he was being overly cautious and didn't know who was outside. In response, I heard a few louder creaks and then locks being thrown back on the opposite side of the door.

A few seconds later, the door opened a crack—then an inch—and then all the way, to reveal Mason squinting out into the sunlight at us.

"Well, this is quite the surprise…" Then he pulled out a rifle and pointed it straight at Chloe's head. "You're picking some strange traveling companions these days, Jack."

"Whoa, whoa, Mason." Every instinct in me told me to tackle him, to take him down and get him away from Chloe. Instead, I shifted slowly in front of her until the gun was pointed at me instead. "She's *helping* us. You can trust her."

Mason looked at me with watery eyes, and then peered at Chloe over my shoulder before lowering his gun back to his side. "I just hope you know what you're getting yourself into."

"I do," I said as I heard Chloe release a shaky breath. I felt her place one trembling hand against my back.

"Well, come on in, then." Mason opened the door wide and gestured for us to enter the shadowy interior. "I imagine you wouldn't have come all the way out here if you didn't have something important to discuss."

"I might not have had to come out here if you answered your phone ever." I gave him a rueful smile as we walked past him. Chloe stuck so close behind me she was nearly a shadow. I couldn't blame her. Plus, feeling her presence this close felt kind of great.

After we were all inside and settled, I started from the

beginning and gave Mason the abbreviated version of what we'd been doing. Since it was clear from his reaction to Chloe that he knew plenty about Night Walkers, I didn't hold anything back. I told him about Cooper and Parker and my dad's new formula and the ingredients we'd been tracking down. He appeared surprised and eager to help at first, but the more I explained the details, the quieter Mason became.

"Yours is the last name I was given, Mason." I watched for any sign of surprise, but his face was like a brick wall at this point, so I just continued. "We know that somehow my dad left the last ingredient with you. You're a Builder, right?"

Mason leaned forward with a loud sigh and rubbed his hand through his beard. "I wish I'd answered my phone. I'm afraid you've come all the way out here for nothing." He somehow looked visibly older than he had when we'd gotten here. "Your dad didn't leave me with any secrets, kid. I think you must've gotten your information mixed up somewhere."

I gave him a quick shake of my head, thinking he'd misunderstood. "The others didn't think they had anything for me either, but they were wrong. The information was buried somewhere they didn't know they ha—"

"I'm not like them, Jack. This isn't the same situation. I'm sorry." Mason was on his feet and moving toward the door.

"No!" I grabbed his shoulder, trying to force him to face me, but he pulled away. "We aren't leaving here. I can tell you know more than you're saying, Mason. We saved your life. Parker did. He risked his life and saved yours, and you aren't going to send us away and leave him to die until you tell us everything you know."

Mason wavered, closing his eyes and shaking his head. Finally, his shoulders crumpled forward and he turned away from me. His voice had lost all gruffness when he spoke again. "I don't have your answers, Jack. I wish I did, but I don't."

I shook my head, panic gripping my heart at the idea of getting this close only to have it all slip away over Mason being unwilling to listen. "How can you even know that?"

"Because I do, okay?" Mason spun on me, but his eyes were guarded like he still was holding a secret. But what kind of secret? If he was a Builder, he could use the dream he created to craft a dream to hide his secrets from me....

So he wasn't a Builder.

Going into another Watcher's void would be a battle for me... I'd have to fight him if I wanted to find out anything, both of us struggling to take control. At his age, Mason would have more experience, and that could give him an advantage. But where was the Builder who kept him alive?

Which only left me one option—an impossible one.

I shook my head and took a step away from him. "You can't be..."

He whipped his eyes up to meet mine, obviously shocked by my words. I could see immediately in his face that I was right.

I just didn't know how it could conceivably be true...

He moved back to his chair and settled into it again. I stayed rooted in place as I stared at him, dreading whatever he might say next to prove me right.

"Your dad couldn't hide anything in my dreams... because

I don't have them." Mason inclined his head toward Chloe and finished, "I'm like her. I'm one of them. Type 1."

Libby scoffed behind me and I heard her mutter, "They're everywhere."

Chloe's eyes widened. I tried to process this information into something that made any sense. I'd never heard of a Taker living this long.

"How?" I growled out the word, furious that he would've kept whatever was keeping him alive a secret for this long.

"I helped your dad with his work for years. He spent so many nights studying my mind, Jack. He wanted to know why Eclipse did what it did. Danny tried to figure out how the connection worked between my kind and the Dreamers. He wanted the real answers to find the real cure he'd been looking for from the beginning." Mason looked past me like he was lost in a memory. "I was the only one of my kind he could still trust. The only one he could know for certain wouldn't ever share anything he discovered. Not until we were both sure it was the right cure this time around."

"Why would he believe you wouldn't betray him?" Libby asked, a sharp edge of doubt tingeing her voice.

"Because I was the one who helped him destroy Eclipse after he first created it and we realized what it could do." He sank deeper into his chair and closed his eyes, with a frown so intense it looked like it might brand his face permanently. "No one should have that kind of power."

I repeated the only question that mattered right now. "How are you still alive?"

"Helping your dad had some benefits." Mason opened his eyes and gave me a tired smile. "We found some herbs and specific kinds of meditation that helped create a kind of hypnotic sleep. It's helped prolong my life quite a bit ... but even that can only help so much. It's why I missed your earlier phone calls, actually. It's gotten to the point that if I don't do that ritual for at least twelve hours a day, I'll be dead in a week."

Chloe's mouth hung open as she looked at him. This information was pretty amazing to me ... but for her, it must've been on an entirely different level.

"But all of this just doesn't feel like living anymore." Mason moaned slightly and shifted his weight in the chair again. He saw the way I watched him, and grunted. "Look, I've told you all I can to convince you that I don't have your answer. Only thing left is to enter my mind while I go into my resting state. See it for yourself, if you still don't believe."

"No." Chloe spoke up faster than I could, and it surprised me.

"Why not?" I asked.

"Because if he's really a Taker, it could be dangerous for you in there." Chloe's pose was relaxed as she leaned on the arm of her chair, but she looked at me with concern obvious in her eyes.

"She's right, Jack." Finn nodded. "Isn't overexerting an already-exhausted mind pretty much what made Parker become Divided?"

"I'm tired, but I'm nowhere near Divided." I spoke confidently.

Libby ratted me out anyway. "He's more tired than I've seen him in a very long time."

"The last few days have been rough, but I'm still fine. I've been through worse," I said, dismissing her concern along with everyone else's. We didn't have time for any other options. And it really was the truth—it had only been a couple of days since Libby had healed me. And while everything I'd taught Parker about being in a Taker's mind was from what Dad had taught me rather than from experience, I was sure I could handle it.

Besides, even if I became Divided while saving Parker, I'd never regret it. Despite knowing what having your mind broken like that had done to my brother...and to Dad.

Parker was my brother. I had to save him. I *would* save him. Completed formula or not, I would not let him die.

No matter what it cost.

"I'm ready." I met Mason's eyes again, and after asking Finn to wake us up in four hours if we didn't wake up sooner, we both went into separate rooms and lay down. It was time to enter the mind of a Taker.

And it was time to discover if Dad had really spent all this time leading us down a dead end road with no hope of finding the answers we so desperately needed.

————

Mason must've beaten me to sleep, because there was no stop in the Hollow to ease me into the inky blackness where our minds merged. It was just straight into the dark, the air so thick it was nearly liquid. It pressed in on me, pressed down until I was struggling beneath it. Everything was pain and agony. It was hard to move or breathe or even think. Fighting against it was so much harder than I expected. It used parts of my mind I'd never had to use before.

It took me some time to orient myself to the truth. Mason was absolutely a Taker, and he was right. There was no way Dad could've hidden the last ingredient in here. So how could I get myself out of this mess? I pushed out with my mind as hard as I could and created a little bubble of clear space to breathe in. It was so strange in here. It was exactly as Parker had described it.

I tried to picture my dad spending so many nights in this awful place. Why would he? What could he discover here? What could he learn? I reached one hand outside my bubble, feeling the thick weight of the murky air. It just didn't make any sense.

Dad might have made mistakes... but he never would've come back here night after night with nothing to show for it. There had to be something here—some reason for it.

And now that I was in here, I had to find it.

I slowly released the bubble and let the dark, thick air rush over me. My first instinct was to panic, to feel like I couldn't breathe and to struggle against it. So I fought that instinct. Instead, I relaxed into it. Trying to absorb it in different ways, to meld into it the same way I would a dream. I tried to become part of the thick haze instead of trying to push it away.

I was so shocked when it started to work that I nearly choked on a cloud of the thick air.

Relaxing further, I tried to picture myself spreading out and becoming as thin as the smoke. I tried to imagine Mason's mind opening up to me, and the air thinned even more. I reached out for the smoke, reaching my hands into it and picturing my dad being here. I pictured him floating beside me and doing the same things I was doing. It wasn't easy, and it felt like it took a long time, but eventually he appeared beside me.

I shook my head as my body vibrated from the effort. So Dad *could* hide his riddle in here. He always was brilliant.

He sat in the dark mist and smiled at me before saying, "He who makes me doesn't want me. He who buys me doesn't need me. He who uses me doesn't care."

My face suddenly felt wet and I wondered if it was tears, but when I brushed my hand across my face, I realized I was bleeding. Like Parker had ... and it scared me more than I expected. I wiped it quickly away.

"Say it again?" I spoke aloud, while also sending the thought through the dark mist into Mason's mind.

Dad repeated the same strange phrase and I knew this was one he'd told me before. I tried to focus even though my head was pounding and my nose dripped blood on my hand. I knew if my nose was bleeding in here there was a good chance it was happening in reality. If it was ... then Finn might not give me the four hours I'd asked him for.

"A casket!" I finally found the memory I'd been searching for and shouted out the answer. "It's a casket!"

Dad grinned wide and then reached out and pulled me into him for a hug. It stole my breath away and I hugged him back like I never wanted to let go. I knew he wasn't real but I didn't care. He looked, felt, and smelled like my Dad, and I would never have another chance to hug him like this again. I had no idea how Dad had managed to plant a memory this real in here, but he'd always known how to surprise me.

"I'm so proud of you," he whispered as he patted my back. "The last ingredient is blood from a Builder. You can do this, Jack. Now go."

And with that, somehow the planted memory of my father kicked me out of Mason's dream and back into the early morning light shining in through the window. Back to reality...a reality in which my brother was still missing and possibly dead, and where I missed my dad even more than I'd thought possible.

TWENTY-EIGHT
PARKER

I'd been back in my old cell for a little while, and even though my head appreciated the coolness and dimness, I missed the cot and blanket I had in the white room. When Cooper stumbled in, I opened one eye and was surprised to see that he was alone.

He rarely came alone anymore. I never asked why. In fact, we never really spoke now; I think we were both too exhausted to make any kind of effort. If I had to make a guess about his usual entourage, it would be that the others didn't ever leave him alone anymore. He often had at least Joey or the doctor with him, who were halfway responsible for keeping him upright.

This time, Cooper pulled a syringe out of his pocket, and even in the dark I recognized the black goo they'd given me so many times before. I struggled to move away, so he brought in some guards to pin me down. He bent over and didn't even bother with sanitizing anything before stabbing the needle into my arm.

Perfect... because the conditions in here were so clean. If everything else they were doing wasn't enough to kill me, then I'd get to die of some putrid infection.

I didn't even think I cared anymore. I just wanted it all to be over quicker than this. It had been a while since I'd done anything but ignore my hallucinations of Addie and Shawn. I'd started wondering if Joey's help wasn't actually just prolonging Cooper's torture. The last time he'd brought me food, I didn't touch it. I was too exhausted to do more than swallow a little of the water, anyway. He'd frowned but hadn't said anything.

Cooper got back on his feet, made it over to the door, and he and the guards left. I stayed there in the quiet, waiting for the now strangely familiar echoing of this particular medication. It usually took a few minutes to kick in, but they were giving it to me in bigger and bigger doses.

My door had a strange sliver of light on one side that I hadn't noticed before. That struck me as important, but I couldn't remember why. I blinked a few times and then lifted my head to focus my vision more firmly on the door.

It was still open. Just a crack. Cooper hadn't realized it hadn't shut tightly, and now he was gone and it was still open...

I'd been waiting what felt like an eternity for an opportunity like this, but it took nearly that long to get my body up and into a standing position. I leaned against the wall, panting, willing my body to find whatever strength it had left and make one final effort.

I had to get out of here, and I had to do it right now.

Shuffling my feet as quietly as I could, I moved from the cell into the hall and shut the door tightly behind me so no one passing by would see it standing open and notice. I had no idea where to go from here, but I knew everyone turned right when they walked out, so that's where I would go first.

The first hallway was a little difficult because I was so dizzy and stiff, but by the second hallway I was beginning to loosen up. Getting my blood pumping a little was helping bring back some clarity.

I spotted a chunk of brick on the ground to the side of a hall. It looked like it had fallen from a piece of wall that was crumbling a bit near the ceiling. I paused to pick it up, hefting it in my hand. It wasn't much of a weapon, but it was something. I had no idea where I was going, but I tried to keep track so I didn't wind up lost in this seemingly endless maze. I turned right when possible unless it felt like it would take me in a circle.

There were almost no people in this section of their compound. I heard voices once or twice, but I was able to slow down in time and wait for the people to go away, or take the hall leading the opposite direction. After what felt like my hundredth right turn, the medicine was really starting to kick in and it became impossible to keep track of my turns. It just felt like one echoing hall after another.

My body kept moving without much guidance from

me. My mind felt like it was floating somewhere above. I couldn't think which way to go. I couldn't listen for anyone up ahead. All I could do was keep walking and hope I'd get somewhere good eventually.

Instead, I ran straight into Cooper's back, sending us both sprawling across the floor.

My body felt like someone had turned it on autopilot. I watched as I climbed slowly back to my feet and started staggering down the hall again.

"How did you get out here?" Cooper watched me in confusion, huffing and panting still from the collision. I glanced at him and saw that his eyes were focused beyond me. At the end of the hall I saw what he was looking at ... doors with outside light shining through them. Had I finally found the doors to the *outside*?

Cooper got to his feet and jogged after my body, jumping onto my back and slamming me into the ground. My head hit hard against the concrete floor and the skin above my eyebrow split open wide. Blood started flowing down across my face, but still my body kept fighting to get back up.

Floating above myself, I watched it all as if from a distance, vaguely thinking I should stay down. That would probably be the smarter thing to do. Instead, my survival instincts started running the show. I took the brick in my hand and slammed the sharpest tip into Cooper's shoulder. He screamed out in pain and rolled off me. My body got up into a standing position, but then fell against the wall.

At the end of the hall, the doors to the outside burst open and several heavily armed guards ran in. They stared at the scene in shock until Cooper yelled out, "Shoot him, you idiots!"

They each unholstered their weapons and pointed them at me, but I didn't exactly look threatening as I slid slowly along the wall toward them. One of the guards grazed my arm and the other my leg. Being shot twice finally brought my body down, and I collapsed into a heap on the floor. My eyes were still open, but it didn't feel like I was really here anymore. Everything felt so far away.

There was a lot of blood and I was pretty sure I should be in pain, but all I heard were the echoes of Cooper yelling and cursing my name.

Then Joey came running by and pushed Cooper off of me. He called for the doctor and asked the guards why they'd shot me. Cooper's eyelids kept closing and he had to shake his head to get them to open again as he sat down beside my not-wounded leg.

Before I faded out and lost consciousness completely, I heard Cooper's voice coming through loud and clear, even though the words were barely above a whisper.

"I should just let you die. Let you die like your dad has let so many of us die," he threatened, and I honestly hoped he meant it this time.

TWENTY-NINE
JACK

As soon as I told Mason what I'd found in his head, he went to pack a bag while I ushered Libby, Finn, and Chloe out to the van. We got ready to head back to Parker's house, to my lab in the storage room. Mason said he knew enough from working with my dad to help out with putting the formula together, and he even had adenosine, the first ingredient, on hand because he'd used it to help keep himself alive. We only had five days left, but ... we'd find a way to make it work.

Finn jogged over to me, and I stopped sorting the supplies in the van once I saw the grim look on his face. "What's wrong?"

"The safe house." His words spilled out over each other. "Is it near Oakville?"

I thought for a second, then inclined my head. Everything about his demeanor was making me nervous. "Yeah, it isn't far from here, only about thirty minutes away. Why, Finn?"

"I texted earlier to update Addie, but she didn't answer. I just called her and it goes immediately to voicemail." His pitch got a little higher with every sentence. "It might be nothing... but I feel like something's wrong, Jack."

"We'll go," I responded immediately, closing the back of the van. "Even if they're fine, we need to check."

When we pulled up in front of the safe house, the hair on my neck stood on end. It was a tiny one-story with faded green siding that wasn't much to look at even on a good day. But now, even though it looked mostly normal, little things felt strange. The front porch light was on in the middle of the day. Parker's mom was generally pretty aware of those kinds of things. The front door looked like it wasn't quite closed. Mostly, though, it just looked too quiet. I parked in the shade of a tree two houses away and hopped out.

I told myself it was just the fact that I hadn't been here in a while that made the house look like something was off... but I still motioned for everyone else to stay in the van just in case.

Finn's jaw tightened, and I could tell he recognized my concern when he immediately moved to follow me. The look I gave him made him hesitate, but he said, "My sister might be in trouble—and Mia."

I would have much preferred to give orders in a situation like this. But for Parker's sake I tried to explain, even though I sucked at it. "I'll be right back to get you, Finn. If we're walking into something dangerous, I'll be better off alone where I don't have to worry about you getting yourself—or *anyone else*—killed."

Finn looked slightly offended.

Mason patted him on the shoulder and pulled him gently back into his seat again. "Go ahead, Jack. I'll keep an eye on things here."

"Thanks." Ignoring Chloe's worried look, I turned toward the safe house and made my way as casually as I could around to the back.

As soon as I saw the back door hanging wide open, I knew something had gone very wrong. Slipping one of my knives from my sleeve, I gripped the hilt tightly in my right palm and moved silently toward the back of the house. Plastering my back to the wall beside the door, I listened for any movement from inside.

There was nothing but silence.

I reached out and slowly pushed open the back door. My heart pounded in my ears when the hinges squeaked so loud that anyone in the house should've heard it. Moving fast, I slipped into the dark interior. The room was empty, so I ducked behind the tiny dining room table and waited.

I counted in my head, 1 ... 2 ... 3 ... and listened for the sound of running footsteps. But everything was silent. Standing up, I looked around the room. One of the chairs was tipped over. A barely touched plate of fruit, probably a snack for one of the girls, sat forgotten on the kitchen table. Then I saw the thing that confirmed all of my fears:

Mrs. Chipp's purse and the busted-up burner phone on the kitchen counter.

Anger and fear moved through my veins like a living, breathing thing. I'd considered this as a possibility, but it had felt unlikely. *Why?* I didn't understand.

Once I'd searched the house, I made my way to the front door when I heard a noise from a hallway closet. Loudly closing the front door, I moved silently back down the hall. Pulling out one of my knives, I braced myself and pulled open the door.

There was a started scream. I barely had time to raise my arm and block the broomstick coming down hard toward my head. Wrapping my fingers around the broom handle, I twisted it and pulled hard. A pale and terrified Addie came out with it.

"Addie." I slipped my knife back into place and tried to slow down my adrenaline-fueled pulse.

She looked up at me through the hair hanging over her face and breathed my name. "Jack!"

Then she leapt for me, wrapping both arms around my neck and knocking me back against the wall. Her whole body was trembling, and I awkwardly reached around and patted her back. I was suddenly extremely aware of how much I would've enjoyed this moment only a month ago. Now it just felt wrong, like a betrayal of my brother.

"What happened?" I gently pushed her hair out of her eyes and saw the streaks from tears down her cheeks.

"A bunch of guys came and they had g-guns. They… they… t-took Mia and Parker's mom." Her words came in bursts, like she'd been holding them in and they'd finally fought their way free.

"How long ago?" My tone was no-nonsense, and it occurred to me, fleetingly, that Parker would've been gentler. But I was running out of time, and whenever I looked at the clock, I panicked a little more just thinking about the short time I had left to save him.

He could teach me how to deal with people all he wanted... *after* I saved his life.

"They were here for a little while before they left with them. Asking questions about you. Not long since they left—an hour maybe?" She looked down at the broomstick she'd attacked me with. "I thought you were one of them. I'm sor—"

"Don't be." I shook my head, quick and firm. "You did the right thing. Why didn't they take you?"

"I was in the bathroom when they came, and when I heard them ... " Addie stopped and looked down, shame written on her face. "Parker's mom was yelling questions like she wanted me to hear—she was warning me, so I hid."

"Good. That's exactly what you should've done, Addie." I reached out and lifted her chin until she looked straight at me. "If you hadn't, then we wouldn't know what happened. Now we can try to save them. They won't catch us off-guard on this... and that's all because of *you*."

Her eyes filled with gratitude and she gave me a shaky nod.

"Did they say how they found you here?" I frowned, glaring at the not-so-safe house around me like it was to blame.

"I heard one of them say it was the first place on the chemist's list ... "

I swore. "My mistake. I picked this one because it's the house we never used, but that's also probably why Dad would choose it as a piece of information to give the Takers when forced." I felt like an idiot. I should've considered that possibility. "I'm sorry, Addie."

"Stop." She shook her head and put an arm around me. "You were only trying to protect us, Jack. No one expects you to be able to predict every move they make."

I appreciated her trying to make me feel better, but she was wrong. Predicting every move the Takers made—that was exactly what I'd been working so hard to do for most of my life. It was what I expected of myself—what Dad expected of me.

As we walked out toward the van, I saw Finn pacing next to it. When he saw Addie, his worried expression broke into a wide grin and he ran over to hug her. His eyes met mine over her shoulder, and it was obvious I wasn't hiding my own worry as well as I'd hoped.

"Where's Mia?" he asked.

Addie shook her head and closed her eyes.

"They took her and Parker's mom." I spoke the words so she wouldn't have to. Chloe sagged back against the van like someone had knocked the wind out of her. Libby's face twisted into a pained grimace. She knew exactly what it felt like to have Takers kidnap people you cared about.

"Why?" Finn's face went from fear to anger and caught

me completely off guard. "Why do this? They already have Parker. Isn't that enough?"

I swallowed hard and simply shrugged, because there were only two reasons I could think of that they would need more hostages. And I couldn't bring myself to say either of them out loud.

First: they needed some leverage to convince Parker to do something.

Second: their first hostage hadn't survived.

Fighting back the tight ball of fear in my stomach, I focused on the only thing I could control. It was a Hail Mary pass at best to hope that Cooper would exchange Parker for something other than Eclipse, but I'd take almost anything over sitting here and worrying. "Come on—let's follow the plan. We'll go back to my lab at Parker's house and finish this formula while we still have a shot at it."

———

Parker's house was worse than the safe house. They'd been through here thoroughly. The lock on the back door was busted, chairs were turned over, desks were emptied. They'd probably been looking for a clue about where his family was.

A wasted effort, since apparently they'd had the address they needed already.

I walked through the house, feeling hopeless. At every turn, the Takers seemed a step ahead of me. I hated it with every fiber of my being—I wasn't used to being outmaneuvered. Bending down, I picked up a broken picture frame.

Shattered glass jutted out and sliced my finger. I turned it over and saw the smiling faces of Dad, Mrs. Chipp, and a very young Parker. I set it carefully back on the table and moved on.

Every room was the same: everything wrong, broken, and out of place. Every room except my lab, anyway. It was pristine—because God forbid something prevent me from making the precious Eclipse Cooper wanted so badly. I felt a sudden urge to smash up the lab myself. I wanted to break it all, the way they kept breaking my whole life.

I heard a scratching noise and turned to see Chloe with a broom and dustpan. She had her back to me as she swept up the shards of glass from the floor. I didn't think she'd spoken a word since we left the safe house. When she turned and caught my eye, her gaze was full of apologies that I didn't expect or want from her.

Drawing in a deep breath, I moved into the lab and started prepping to make the formula that would save Chloe—because even if no other Taker was worth saving, she *definitely* was.

———————

Libby sat very still as I drew out a small vial of her blood. She kept looking at me like she wanted to say something, and then looking away again. Once I finished putting a Band-Aid on her arm, I met her eyes and then held them as she tried to look away.

"What do you want to say, Lib?" I sat down across from

her and put my hand on top of hers. "Something to confess? Any blood-borne illnesses I should warn the Takers about?"

A real smile spread across her face as she replied, "I wish."

I chuckled and shook my head.

She hesitated as she watched me, but then apparently decided to go for it because she dove in full-speed. "How can you be doing this?"

I groaned. "Not this again. Not now. It isn't helping."

"Don't you see?" Libby gestured down to her arm. "They're still feeding off of us. Still using us for their own needs."

Holding the vial of her blood in my free hand made it hard to argue her point. Still, I shook my head.

"They're parasites, Jack," she hissed. "Always have been, always will be. When will you see that changing the way they use us doesn't change who they are?"

"This is different," I said.

Libby shook her head. "She's skewing your mind and you can't see anything straight."

"Maybe she is. Maybe she should be." I raised my voice a fraction before immediately lowering it again. "How can we lump all of them in one box and say they can't be different? They can't change? Would it be fair to say that you're exactly like *all* other Builders?"

Libby groaned and tried to pull her hand free from mine, but I held tight.

"Fine," she said, "but how can you even trust her? How can you be sure Chloe isn't part of everything Cooper is doing?" She gestured with her free hand toward the kitchen.

"How do we know she didn't tell them to go after Parker's mom?"

"I trust her." I squeezed her hand and willed her to believe me while at the same time hoping like mad that my gut instinct about Chloe was right. "She wants to help. That's all I can say."

"I just hope you know what you're talking about. I hope she hasn't sucked you into some lie that'll cost all of us." Libby didn't sound like she was hoping for anything good.

"Do you?" I dropped her hand and placed the vial on the table, standing up in frustration. "Because you sound more like you hope Chloe's lying. You sound like you hope she proves you right. What you're hoping for... it would cost me everything. *Everything*. I hope you understand that."

Libby looked like I'd slapped her. "Y-you really feel that strongly about her?"

"I might..." I turned my back on her and closed my eyes, rubbing my hands across my face. "It's confusing. I don't know."

When I moved back to my seat across from her, she had her eyes down, focused on the vial of her own blood. "Why a Taker, Jack? That doesn't make sense. You're a Watcher... you should be with someone who can help you. You should be with... a Builder."

I smiled and put my hand over hers. "If only the best ones weren't either my best friend or the girl who's in love with my brother."

Libby leaned back in her chair and sighed, watching me with her huge dark eyes before finally speaking again. "I'm sorry. I know I've been awful to you lately. I needed someone to blame and you're here and I knew you wouldn't hate me for it. I needed someone to kick and you just let me kick you."

"Stop." I interrupted before she could go any further with this train of thought. "You don't need to be sorry. I understand. I miss Marisol too. Keep kicking me if you need to. I can take it."

"I don't know how I'm supposed to just keep going without her. She was like a mom to me, way more than my real one. How can I just let people that I love go?" Her eyes filled with tears.

I nodded without speaking, trying not to interrupt her now that she was finally letting some of this venom out that had been poisoning her from the inside for so many days now.

"I just—I hate them so much, Jack." She let out an angry growl and then looked surprised at herself. The fury she felt seemed to bubble under the surface. I could see it poking through even when she was trying so hard to control it. "I know I shouldn't. They can't control what they are, but it doesn't matter. I still do. I hate them all and I don't care if they all die. I want them all to die."

It was hard to hear this coming from Libby, not only because she'd always been so happy and bubbly, but because she'd been the rational one of the two of us. Still, I couldn't pretend not to understand it.

"I know you do. I felt that way for so long too." I heard a noise from someone moving through the hallway and lowered my voice. I rubbed my thumb along the back of her hand and tried to think of the right words that wouldn't offend her but would explain what I was thinking. "What you're feeling right now is fuel. You're *so* mad, and that anger is what's holding you up and keeping you moving. I get that. I've felt it. But at some point you're going to need more than hatred. You'll need something more because this isn't who you are."

She watched me with an expression I couldn't read. I wasn't sure if she really understood what I was saying or not.

"It's never been who you are, Lib. And Marisol wouldn't ever want you to become that."

Libby thought that over for a minute before she got up, gave me a hug, and then walked out. All I could do was hope that at some point my words might eventually sink in.

I started carefully preparing the ingredients, and Mason came in to assist. We had the adenosine from Mason, and Chloe had gotten the second ingredient, the acetylcholinesterase inhibitor, by slipping into the back room of a small pharmacy to pick up a bottle on the way here. Thankfully, that compound was commonly used on Alzheimer's patients and wasn't considered a controlled substance or kept locked up. Last were the vials of Libby's blood.

Now we just had to make sure we mixed it all exactly right.

It was clear from five minutes into our work that Mason knew exactly what he was doing and that Dad had trained him. The way he hummed as he ground an ingredient with the mortar and pestle, squinted with one eye as he adjusted the Bunsen burner, smiled as he held up a beaker of liquid into the sunlight—it reminded me of working with Dad.

The reassurance it gave me was a welcome relief when every time I thought of the time ticking away I felt sick.

The lab work put me into a kind of focused frenzy that enabled me to zone in on following one step of the preparation after another. I forgot where I was, who I was with—everything but what I was trying to do.

It was a reprieve from the torture of worrying about my brother and if I might already be too late to save him.

"Hmm." Mason looked over the ingredients list again. "So it's not an injection?"

"No…" I double checked my measurement. "For mass consumption purposes, I think Dad designed it to be easy to take. Some of these chemicals should absorb into the bloodstream almost immediately. I think on the whole it should be pretty fast-acting."

His only reaction was a simple grunt before he went back to work.

Mason and I made sure to triple-check every measurement and every step carefully before taking any action. I'd just mixed in the final ingredient and poured the liquid into single-dose glass vials when I turned around and realized that Chloe was sitting in a chair a few feet behind us. I knew she hadn't been in here the entire time, but from the way she slouched down in her chair with her feet up, it looked like she'd been sitting there awhile.

"I think I'll get some fresh air," Mason muttered, stretching his back as he walked out of the room.

Moving back, I sat in the chair beside her, trying hard not to stare at the blue liquid in the vials waiting on the lab table.

She shifted in her seat, leaning away from me. I wondered if I'd offended her somehow. The dark circles under her eyes were even more pronounced than they had been. Her eyes looked wilder and her skin and lips were paler, making her bright gray eyes stand out in stark and alarming contrast.

"Are you feeling okay?" I asked, keeping my voice low.

"Is it ready?" She ignored my question and her voice came out hoarse, like it was rough with exhaustion.

"Nearly, but I'm not sure what to do with it now." I pushed my hand up through my hair. Should we just trust Dad that this was his new formula and show up at the Takers' base with it? If we got there and somehow convinced Cooper to take it—a nearly impossible feat all by itself—and then it *didn't* do what we claimed, Parker's life would be on the line. Could we risk that? What other options did we have?

"What else do you still have to do to it?" Chloe sat forward and tucked one knee up under her chin. Her hand hung loosely across her knee and I saw it trembling. She was worse off than I'd thought. I wondered if the experience with Eclipse and being separated from Finn last month had worn her down in ways we didn't understand. Maybe she had even less time than I thought.

Just the idea made my hands sweat with panic.

This drug would work. It had to.

"It just needs to sit a minute more, and then it'll be ready." I tried not to focus on her shaking hand and how small and vulnerable it looked.

Finn poked his head in the door. "So now that we have a completed formula ... "

"It really does need a name," I finished for him, crossing my arms over my chest.

"What about something tough, like Terminator?" Finn spoke the last word with his best Austrian accent before crossing to stand by us.

"Not that I haven't loved all of your ideas, Finn…" Chloe stood up and walked to the table. Finn took her seat as we watched Chloe kneel down so she was at eye level with the blue liquid. Light from the setting sun outside shone through the window across from her, bounced off the glass vial, and left a rainbow pattern of light across her hand. "But how about…Spectrum?"

I looked at Finn and we both nodded. From the Night Walkers to the normal Dreamers, a "spectrum" represented us pretty well. And all of us working together toward something better. Just like we were right now. It was what Dad had wanted…it was perfect.

"Spectrum it is," I said.

"And how many doses is this?" Her voice sounded stronger now, and she stood up beside the table.

"Each vial is one dose, so we have five doses, but I can make more." I gave her a feeble smile. "Just wanted to make sure this first round didn't explode or something before mixing up more."

"Good. Because I'm taking this one." Chloe turned to grab one and I stumbled out of my chair at her words, getting there just in time to move the tray of vials out of her reach. Finn sat forward in his chair but looked like he wasn't sure who to help.

"What are you doing?" I hissed, trying to keep my voice low as I placed the tray on the table behind me.

She looked at me like I'd lost my mind. "This was the plan the whole time, Jack. Who did you think we were making this formula for?"

"No, Chloe." She tried to reach around me and I grabbed her wrists, holding them against my chest. "I want to use this to save you, but I'm not like your brothers. I won't let you be a lab rat this time."

She stopped struggling for a minute and looked surprised. "Thank you for saying that," she finally said, yet then added, "but I need to take this *now*. Not for them or for you ... but for me."

"Why? Why can't you wait until we've tried it out on Cooper?" I relaxed my grip on her hands, now just rubbing my hands along the back of hers, enjoying the feel of my warm skin against her hands, which never seemed to be anything but chilled.

"We don't even know if we can convince Cooper to take it," she said. "We have to *know* it works if we want to have any chance of getting him to listen to us. These are my people, and my father messed everyone up." Her voice was soft and pleading. "This is the best thing I can do for them ... maybe the only thing. You want to save your brother. I want to save my kind. *Let—me—help*."

"Chloe, you've already helped." I saw Finn slip out of the room and hoped he might be going for reinforcements.

"No ... it isn't enough." Her palms went flat against

my chest, like she wanted to push me away but couldn't quite bring herself to do it.

"It's completely untested. We have no idea what this could do to you." I looked straight into her swirling gray eyes and my throat tightened. "It could *kill* you, Chloe."

"Here. Take it." I heard Libby's voice speak from behind me, and saw her move quickly to the other side of Chloe, holding out a vial.

"Libby, what are you doing?" My alarm showed, even though I was fighting to stay calm.

"I'm helping her," Libby stated simply. She went on to say the exact words that would make certain Chloe drank the formula whether she was really ready to or not. "If she doesn't, she's going to die anyway. Chloe says she wants us to believe we can trust her, that Takers can be more than just murderers who use everyone to get what they want. Let her prove it."

Chloe blinked, like the sting from Libby's words had momentarily stunned her. As I tried to move closer, she grabbed the vial from Libby and stepped into the hallway. Turning, she gave me a weak version of her tough smile and lifted the liquid like a toast before bringing it toward her lips.

"Chloe, no!" I shouted, but before she could drink it, the vial was lifted from her fingers. We all watched in shock as Mason downed it in one gulp.

He grinned down at her. "You can't expect to go first when I put in all the work fixing this up. I've been waiting too long for this, girly."

We all watched in stunned silence as he cleared his throat and said, "It's got a bit of a strange aftertaste there,

Jack." Then he stumbled against the wall. Chloe only managed to slow his descent a little as he fell down hard onto the hallway carpet.

"Mason!" By the time I got to him, Mason's entire body was convulsing. Finn helped clear some space and we dragged him into the living room. While Libby and Finn were trying to help me, Chloe stood frozen in the corner, watching. I couldn't blame her. Her face paled, and her fingers clutched in tangled knots against her chest as the drug that was supposed to save the Takers ravaged through Mason's body like a tsunami across the shore.

He took one long, ragged breath ... and didn't take another.

THIRTY

PARKER

The smell of rubbing alcohol, plastic, and medicine surrounded me. All I could hear was the thrumming, beeping, and humming of machines. Something was on my face and I wanted to push it off, but I couldn't move either of my arms. The machines were medical, I realized, and the sound was my heartbeat. I was in some kind of hospital-type room now.

I struggled against whatever was tying me down, feeling stronger than I had in days...and so confused. Drugged—I recognized the feeling. I'd been drugged, but it wasn't with the black goo. It was something more normal—painkillers. I struggled more forcefully against whatever was binding my hands down and pain shot through my entire body.

Apparently, not enough painkillers...

There was a metallic sliding sound, and then Dr. Rivera

was bent over me. He looked in my eyes and shone a light in them. He looked at a couple of the machines by my bed before injecting something into the I.V. bag hanging next to me. Immediately the haze of sedation washed over me. This was *much* better. Whatever they had me on, it was strong and felt amazing.

I stopped fighting the rest that my body so badly needed and floated off into oblivion again.

————————

When I woke up again, my back hurt from being hunched over a desk. I sat up straight and stretched, amazed at how good everything else about my body felt. A paper from the desk was stuck to my face and I brushed it away with a yawn. I heard a voice and spun in a quick circle, but there was no one there.

I shook my head, but something felt different. No... everything felt different. My hair didn't fall against my neck. I reached up with my fingers to touch it, but it wasn't there. It had been trimmed in a short, straight line against my neck. They'd cut my hair?

And my arm... didn't I get shot? I reached up with my left hand for my right shoulder, but then I saw my left hand and froze. It was older... wrinkled, with sunspots on it. My chest felt so tight it ached. I heard a voice again, but the words weren't clear. I spun out of my chair and stood up, backing toward the wall in a full-on panic. I couldn't think. I couldn't breathe. What was happening?

When I got to the wall, I waited, trying to sort it out. Could this be a dream? Were the painkillers making me dream? That couldn't happen, could it? What was going on? I glanced over at the silver side of the desk I'd been sitting at and caught a warped image of my reflection ... only it wasn't me. It was Dr. Rivera.

I held up one hand and waved, and the reflection waved back.

Then I remembered what Cooper and the doctor said they'd been trying to do with the black goo injections. My stomach sank and my thoughts spun through this new reality. It had finally worked ... they'd succeeded in flipping the switch in my brain.

I was now a Taker—and I'd just taken over Dr. Rivera's body.

The voice came through clearer this time, and I realized it was Dr. Rivera's voice. If I focused in on it, I could hear his thoughts, dreams, and memories. I imagined that if I practiced, I could find out almost anything I wanted from him. He was like a puppet and I was pulling his strings.

I shuddered and felt suddenly, violently sick.

"Well, this is different." My own, normal voice spoke up, and I lifted my eyes to see myself standing across the room. From the way Darkness faded in and out, I immediately knew it wasn't my actual body. Even though I looked like I'd been to hell and back, I was pretty sure he didn't compare to the way the real me looked right now.

I'd become Divided again.

I sat back down in Dr. Rivera's chair and laid my head

down on the desk, trying to process all of this. "What the hell am I supposed to do now?"

Even though Darkness kept his voice soft, there was a growl to the edge of it. "Well ... I'd say we don't waste another second of time doing *this*. What do you think?"

"It's surprisingly nice to have you back." I smiled for the first time in what felt like forever.

"I knew you'd miss me." He gave me a dark grin.

"We have to find a way out of here—or at the very least, try to call Jack. To tell him if he can't get here quick, then it might be useless to come at all ..." I got to my feet and looked around the room, but it looked like it was mostly a place to take notes. There wasn't even a phone in here.

Darkness stood up straight and took a step forward. "Finally, you're starting to make sense to me."

"I'm not sure if that's a good thing, but for now I'll take it," I muttered as I moved toward the door, but hesitated and turned back toward Darkness.

"Wait. This is exactly what they've been trying to do— turning us into a Taker, right?" I gestured back toward the door and lowered my voice even further. "So why didn't they set up any safeguards against it? Why aren't they prepared for their plan to work?"

Darkness nodded like he was thinking. "Even if they are ... what can they do? Make sure no one makes eye contact with our body? Then they wouldn't know if it worked. And if there *are* people in the hallway keeping watch ... they won't be able to tell that you aren't the real thing."

"Not if I don't clue them in." I took a slow breath and

hunched my shoulders just slightly the way Dr. Rivera always did. "Here we go."

Walking into the hallway, I gave a slight nod to the guard across from the door, who looked directly at me but didn't react. Mimicking the way I'd seen the real Dr. Rivera behave, I moved further down the hallway. Anytime there was no one around, I checked every hall for an exit and every room for a phone. The place felt like a maze. Who knew all this was underground here? After a few minutes, I finally found a room with a phone on the desk.

Keeping the light off, I went in and picked up the receiver with shaking fingers. Darkness watched me, looking almost as nervous as I felt.

"This is bizarre. It's crazy watching you . . . when you look like that," he finally said.

"Tell me about it." I punched in the last digits of Finn's number and waited as it rang once—twice—and I heard him pick up.

"Hello?" He sounded the way he always did when he answered calls from a number he didn't recognize.

"Finn!" The relief in my newly nasal voice was extremely clear. "I know this doesn't sound like me, but it's Parker. I need to talk to you and Jack. Are you with him?"

"I—I don't—" Finn sounded beyond confused, but apparently he decided the best move might be to sort it out with Jack's help because I then heard, "Hang on and I'll get him."

There were footsteps and muffled conversations in the background. I caught a few words like, "doesn't sound like him" and "no clue" and "thought you might know" before it sounded like Finn put me on speaker phone and I heard Jack's voice.

"What was the name of the first person we were sent after?" His completely and utterly flat voice sent a chill through me.

I looked up at Darkness and he returned the same panicked expression. "I, uh...I'm trying to remember."

Jack's voice went cold. "Nice try."

"Wait!" my voice squeaked. The line was still live, so I kept going. "I've been through a lot here, Jack. I don't remember the name anymore. But I can tell you something else maybe..."

"Last chance. Where was the hidden message Dad sent you?"

"In the lining of Dad's wallet," I spat out the words as fast as I could. "It was behind the stitching that was different and I never would have noticed it, but you did."

"Parker..." Jack's voice was so full of emotion now that I began to wonder if I should be testing *him* to be sure he wasn't someone else. "What's going on? Where are you? What did they do to you? Libby lost you in the dream and I was so afraid that...that..."

Someone yelled Jack's name in the background and I heard him cover the mouthpiece and say, "Yes. You stay there with him in case he needs CPR again."

"What's going on there?" Everything in me went cold. "Who's hurt?"

"It's no one you know or need to worry about. It's

nothing..." But Jack didn't sound like Jack. He sounded more like me than ever—he sounded terrified. Then he pushed on without leaving me time for more questions. "Why do you sound so strange, Parker?"

"It's been rough. They've been giving me drugs, Jack, awful drugs." I tried not to worry about what I'd heard on the phone. I spoke the words as fast as I could, knowing we could be interrupted at any moment. "They said Dad gave them the idea. They figured out how to flip a switch in our brains and turn us into a different kind of Night Walker. It isn't that easy, because it took them a while with me... but they did it."

"What do you mean?" Finn asked, his voice coming from the background now; I realized Jack must have put me on speakerphone. Finn sounded on the verge of a full-blown panic attack. "A different kind... they turned you into something... oh my god."

I could tell that my meaning sank in for everyone on the other end of the phone, and it was silent for seconds that felt like they stretched on forever. Finally I spoke again. "Yeah. I took over the doctor who was experimenting on me. That's how I'm calling you."

"We've got the new formula now, and we'll figure this out too." Jack's words were quiet and fierce. "I promise to find a way to turn you back."

"That doesn't matter!" My voice cracked with desperation and I clutched the phone with both hands as I heard footsteps coming down the hall. "I don't care about that right now. Don't you see? None of that will matter if I'm not alive—if I don't get out of here. I won't survive much more of this, Jack.

They've shot me, they've been torturing me. They have me at some abandoned amusement park called Funtopia. In tunnels that run deep underground. But I don't know anything more than that. I can't do this anymore. I can't … *I can't*."

Cooper pushed the door open and two of his thugs came to pin my arms to my sides. The phone fell, swinging beside the desk. I heard Jack yelling my name. I considered pretending to really be Dr. Rivera, but it was clear from the smile on Cooper's face that he'd heard enough to know their black ooze had finally done its job. He lifted the handset and smiled as he spoke into it. "You hear that, Jack? Now you have even more reason to get back here with the Eclipse right away, because believe me, he's right … he won't live much longer without it."

Cooper sat down on the desk and turned to stare at me with a smile. "I've made certain of that."

"We have what you need, Cooper," I heard Jack say into the phone. "We're ready. If you touch him again, I swear I will kill you first and then destroy the drug second."

"Ah, brotherly love. How tender. The amusement park is an hour outside of Madison. If you don't know where to look, just ask Chloe." He hung up even though I could hear Jack still swearing into the line on the other end. He looked at me. "Well, I couldn't have worked that out better if I'd told you *exactly* what to do."

I stopped struggling and Cooper nodded for the guards to release my arms. "What do you mean?"

"There were questions I couldn't get the answers to: How close was Jack to having Eclipse ready? How could I get him to speed things up a bit?" He rubbed his eyes, and it took him a few seconds to open them again. "You're running out of time...so am I. I needed answers about Eclipse and I need him to hurry, but letting you call him makes everything simpler. He wouldn't lie to you." His smile was positively triumphant but his tone dripped sarcasm. "Thank you so much for your cooperation."

Darkness stood just behind Cooper's shoulder, looking halfway terrified and halfway like he wanted to kill him with his bare hands. I wished he could. If Darkness could do that, at this point, I absolutely would let him.

Like he knew my thoughts—and he probably did—Darkness said, "Cooper is so tired, and we're currently in Dr. Rivera's body—we're healthy. We have more energy right now. We have the advantage... *right now.*"

Jumping forward, I broke the grips of the two thugs, plowed over Cooper, and bolted for the door, but I only made it five feet down the hall before I heard a yelp of pain and turned to see four more guards—with Mia and Mom between them.

"Where is my son?" Mom grunted out, her hair a mess and her eyes on me.

It took me a minute to remember that I didn't look anything like myself.

"Don't hurt them!" I demanded, raising my hands in surrender. Mom looked at me in confusion as they marched me past her toward the office where I'd woken up. Part of me wanted to explain, but I barely understood it myself.

Instead, I just whispered as I passed them, "It's going to be okay."

Before I got very far, Cooper ran out after me with an obviously broken nose. Darkness walked beside him, chuckling and taunting him with words only I could hear. Joey was the only thing that kept Cooper from attacking me in Dr. Rivera's body. I smiled grimly at him and waved. Enjoying the fact that right here, right now, Cooper might be able to stop me from escaping, but he couldn't hurt me.

The guards tied me to a chair, and Dr. Rivera's assistant gave me a shot to sedate me. They'd have to wake up my body and force me to make eye contact with someone else before they could break my connection with Dr. Rivera.

As the sedation started to take over, I looked up at Darkness and did the only thing I felt could give us—Mom, Mia, and me—any hope to get out of here alive. I gave Darkness total control. In my mind, I told him we both knew that in this situation, he was our best shot.

If there was ever a time to have my desperate will to survive operating at full capacity, this was that time. So I relaxed, and felt Darkness step in and take over.

It was the most welcome release I'd felt in as long as I could remember.

And then there was nothing.

THIRTY-ONE
JACK

Finn's phone was still gripped tight in my hand long after Cooper had hung up on me. I couldn't make my fingers release it. They had turned my brother into a Taker? How was that even possible? Dad had never mentioned anything like that to me. Then again, he'd never mentioned the possibility of hiding things in dreams ... let alone in the mind of a Taker. I should've been used to discovering the important things that he'd been hiding from me by now ... but I wasn't. Each new discovery felt like it was telling me again and again that I hadn't known him at all. How was I supposed to figure all of this out when he had so many secrets?

My mind was moving so fast my body couldn't catch up.

"Jack?" Chloe loosened the phone from my fingers and

handed it to Finn. She moved around in front of me until I looked down at her.

"Cooper said you know where they are—the abandoned amusement park near Madison?" I finally said, my voice almost non-existent. "Did you know they were capable of turning him into a Taker, Chloe?"

She winced and looked away. My heart ripped inside me, like she'd reached in and torn it in half herself. It was the only answer I needed.

"Jack, wait…"

I pushed past her and stalked to the living room couch, where we'd put Mason's body once he finally stopped having seizures. His heart had stopped twice, but luckily Addie and I both knew CPR and we were able to bring him back. The battle for his life had felt like it went on forever, but in reality it had been about fifteen minutes. Since then he'd been sleeping peacefully, for over twelve straight hours. It was after ten in the morning now; the rest of us had slept—or tried to sleep—in shifts, making sure someone was watching him at all times for any other problems.

But there hadn't been any. Twelve hours of sleep appeared to be enough for us to determine an answer…as long as we could actually wake him up and make sure he'd really slept.

With only four days left to save Parker, it was time to wake Mason up.

"Mason." I spoke his name loud enough to wake a normal person, but he was definitely in a sleep that was deeper than could be considered normal. Reaching out, I grabbed his shoulders and lifted him off the pillow, releasing some of my pain, fear, and anger by giving him a tense shake and shouting, "Mason! Mason, you need to wake up! I *need* your help!" My voice cracked, reflecting the way I felt like I was shattering inside, but I didn't let go.

Libby came in and put one hand on my shoulder. "Jack, I'm not sure—"

Finn took a more direct approach. He ripped one of my hands free until Mason fell back into his pillow.

And then Finn yelled at *me*. "Knock it off! This isn't helping! You can't stomp around here taking your anger out on everyone. It doesn't do Parker or us any good. But you *can* come up with a plan to save your brother, Jack. He needs us now—he needs *you*. You are the only one who can help him ... and you need to do it *right now*."

"Maybe you two should stop yelling in an old man's face," Mason muttered as he blinked his eyes up at us. We both forgot about each other and turned all of our attention on him.

"Are you okay?" Finn asked.

"Do you think Spectrum worked?" I wasn't trying to be callous, but there were more lives that depended on this answer than just Mason's.

Mason yawned as he sat up, but the color in his cheeks was better than I'd ever seen and there was a spark of life back in his eyes.

"Well, I just had the most amazing dream—for the first

time in forty years—so I'd say yes." His face crinkled up into the biggest grin I'd ever seen on him.

Finn let out a loud, startled whoop of joy and then turned to me, his smile sobering slightly. "We need to get moving."

Chloe grabbed my arm as I moved toward the kitchen.

I jerked my arm away. "Not now, Chloe." I gathered the remaining vials of Spectrum from the fridge and looked around for something stable to transport them in.

"Yes, now!" She grabbed my arm again and then pulled hard until I looked down at her. "You need to listen and believe me. We went to the amusement park a long time ago. They've mentioned it once or twice since then, but I had no clue that would be where they'd end up. As far as the other part, I've heard Cooper mention the idea that maybe they could turn one type into another … but it was all just talk." She looked desperate to convince me, but I wasn't sure I even wanted to listen. "I didn't think it was real, let alone that they could be doing it to Parker. If I'd even suspected, I promise I would have told you."

"It doesn't matter. I don't have time to talk about this now." My voice was tight and angry in spite of my words, but my attention was entirely focused on the vials in front of me as I tried to find a way to be sure we wouldn't spill a single drop of the precious liquid. "I have to focus on Parker. How to get him back, how to save him—and then how to turn him back."

"But even if he's a Taker for good, at least he's still alive.

Right?" She looked up at me and gave me a tentative smile. "And we've worked so hard. Now, with Spectrum, all the Takers could live long normal lives—"

"You think I'd let my brother remain a Taker like you?" I spun on her and had to move fast to catch the vial my movement had knocked to the edge of the counter. My voice lowered. I looked her straight in the eye and uttered the next word like a solemn vow. "Never."

She recoiled violently, as though I'd hit her, then nodded and silently backed out the door into Parker's backyard. My heart ached that she was gone, while my brain was furious with me for *ever* trusting a Taker.

Searching for anything else to think about besides Chloe, I searched again for something in which to transport the twenty vials I'd now made—I'd finished fifteen more while Mason was sleeping. On one corner of the counter, I saw one of Mrs. Chipp's plastic containers with separate compartments. That would work perfectly, and it also offered the added bonus of reminding me that Parker wasn't the only one depending on me anymore … I had to save his mom and Mia too.

"I think these will work. Help me pack the vials into these?" I asked.

It took me a moment to realize that no one was moving. When I looked up, Finn and Mason were both looking at me with disappointment, but when I saw Libby looking out the door after Chloe with a hint of triumph in her eyes, the guilt seeped in and I knew I'd gone too far.

I'd have to sort it out with Chloe later. For now, I had to get to Parker before they did anything more to hurt him. "Just help me pack this stuff up," I grumbled. "And we need a cooler from the garage."

Finn shook his head in disgust and walked out after Chloe.

"I'll get the cooler." Libby sounded reluctant, but I was still grateful for her help.

"Your dad was always proud of you, Jack." Mason walked over to help me pack the vials. He tilted his head toward the door Chloe had disappeared through. "Don't make me think he was wrong to feel that way."

His words stabbed straight through me. Chloe was so brave and strong that it was easy to forget what she'd sacrificed. She'd given up everything and everyone she'd ever cared about simply because she believed it was wrong. She was incredibly selfless and probably braver and stronger than anyone I'd ever known...definitely more than me. And half the time I'd treated her like she was no different than her father.

But maybe I was the one who was too much like him. Maybe I was the one who thought other people were less than me just because of what was in their DNA.

Parker would be lucky to be more like Chloe.

Libby and Finn helped pack everything into the van as I wrote down exact directions for making Spectrum.

"I imagine this wears off, but I don't know how long it will take. We still have a lot to learn." I handed the paper to Mason but didn't release it yet. "We've sacrificed a lot to get this. My dad trusted you, and so do I. You have to protect Spectrum, because whether we survive today or not, all this fighting has to stop. You can't let the formula fall into their hands. We have to make certain they need *us* to get it. We have to give them something to lose. Promise me you'll make this available to any Taker who wants help and is willing to live peacefully from here on out. That will go a long way toward ending this war."

"I promise." Mason took the paper, folded it carefully, and stuck it in the front pocket of his flannel shirt. His brow creased with worry. "What do you plan to do when you get there?"

"I'm running out of options. It's kind of a Hail Mary, but I guess I'll offer Spectrum to Cooper and hope he's desperate enough to take it." I massaged the knotted muscles at the back of my neck with my right hand. "I figure either it'll cure him and he'll help us just to make sure he can stay alive, or he'll have an even worse reaction than you did and it'll kill him. I can't say I'll be disappointed if it turns out to be the second option."

"Well, good luck." Mason gave me a grim smile. "You do what you can to get out of this alive, because celebrating when everyone else is dead ain't my idea of a good time."

"You've got it." We shook hands, and I swallowed back the sinking fear that this could be the last time I saw him. Then Addie, Finn, Libby, Chloe, and I got in the van, and I started to drive.

————

It was midday before we got to the abandoned amusement park where the Takers had set up their new camp. I could see immediately why they'd picked this place. Cooper might be going crazy, but he wasn't stupid. There would be no sneaking in unnoticed around here.

Before I'd even parked the van, I saw a watchtower set up in the highest cart of a massive Ferris wheel in the dead center of the park. It must've been one of the newer rides when the park closed, because it didn't look nearly as rickety as some of the others. The rest of the park was nightmarish. Even staring too hard at the creepy bones of the white roller coaster to my left felt like it could get me infected with rust and decay. The whole place felt like a graveyard where the happy dreams of children came to die.

A perfect new home for Cooper and his thugs, but I was oddly relieved that Chloe hadn't ever lived here—even if it was because they wouldn't take her back after she'd helped save Finn. I glanced in the rearview mirror, regretting my words once again.

Chloe was sitting in the very back seat. She hadn't said a word or even looked at me the entire drive.

I definitely had some apologizing to do.

Once I parked and got out, I took two vials of Spectrum from the cooler in the back of the van. I left the rest where they were. Reaching for some extra knives, I paused with my hand on the hilts. I would keep the knives I always carried on me, of course, but I figured any noticeable weapons would only lead to more people dying...so I left the rest there.

I turned back to face the others as they climbed out, and Chloe immediately looked away. "I think our best bet is for all of you to stay here. Maybe if I go in alone, then—"

"No." Finn looked at me like I'd just told a very unfunny joke.

"Absolutely not." Libby rolled her eyes.

Chloe just started walking toward the park entrance.

"Fine," I grumbled, closing the back of the van.

I stood behind the van, taking a deep breath. The last time I'd gone to face the Takers, I'd lost my dad. Now I was here to save my brother, and this time I refused to leave anyone behind. Being here now, it felt like some part of Dad was here beside me.

And instead of weakening me, it made me feel stronger.

I stepped out and took a look at the huge rusty building near the front. The weeds on the path in front of it were trampled. That little detail, plus the sheer size of it, were the only things I needed to see to know that this was the main part of the park the Takers were using.

The structure must have originally been some sort of fun house, because there was a huge discolored clown on the sign hanging above the door. The eyes of the clown had been blacked out and the once-red hair had faded to a sickly orange-yellow color.

I shivered. Clowns were something I'd never understood. I'd seen more of them in other people's nightmares than in real life. How could something so many people found nightmare-worthy also be considered fun? I didn't get it.

The two large doors on the front of the fun house suddenly squealed open. Cooper walked out, backed by a virtual militia. There were twelve heavily armed men behind him. Different ages, heights, builds, body types … but they all had the same telltale signs of exhaustion. The same pale, gaunt skin. The same dark circles beneath their eyes.

They were an army of Takers here to do his bidding.

Perfect.

"Welcome! It was so nice of you to let us know you were coming, Jack." Cooper kept trying to look at me, but the sunlight was too bright and he was obviously in pain, trying to use his arm to block out the sun. He gestured with his free arm toward the group behind him. "As you can see, we've been able to organize a better welcome party to greet you this time, since we had a little notice. Come on in."

"Where's Parker?" I walked slowly forward into the shadows, giving my eyes time to adjust. I was still tired, but soon my eyes were fully acclimated and I got a real look at Cooper. He looked far worse than anyone else—he'd lost noticeable weight since I'd seen him just eight days ago. His eyes wandered and he was struggling to focus. His body suffered from one tremor after another.

Chloe must have recognized the same thing because I heard her inhale sharply behind me and whisper her brother's name.

Cooper glared at us. "Didn't anyone ever tell you it's rude to stare?"

"Cooper, I think you need what we brought more than anyone." I spoke the words quietly and sincerely, despite the fact that I'd be utterly satisfied if he just fell over and died instead.

Cooper waved one shaking hand toward a couple of his heavily armed escorts and they stepped aside to reveal three metal chairs behind them. I had to squint into the shadows until someone closed the doors to the outside and flipped on the lights. The room we were in was immense, the walls covered in dusty mirrors. Many were cracked or broken. This must've been a maze at some point, but all the mirrors and walls in the center had been taken out, leaving just a few support beams.

People of all ages stared at us from their spots around the room. Many were standing, but some were seated on triangular concrete platforms that were spaced evenly around the room, which must've been part of the original design as well. The kids in the room were quiet and looked hardened; the adults ragged and tired.

These weren't people who were living it up like the gods Steve Campbell professed them to be. They were just people, many of whom had to be as tired of the endless fighting as I was. A slight spark of an idea wiggled its way to the top of my thoughts. Maybe Cooper wasn't the one I needed to convince ...

There was movement near the back corner of the room, and the people stepped aside to let someone through. Two guards dragged something behind them. My hands flexed into fists and I suddenly wished I'd brought more weapons. They were dragging Parker.

My heart stopped and my chest felt like a sucking pit of agony. He had bandages on his arm and leg. His eyes were closed when they lifted him into a chair. A hand squeezed my arm and I turned to see Addie looking as pale and terrified as I felt.

They bound Parker to the chair and gagged him. Even though I wanted to kill everyone around him ... my chest felt lighter because I knew he must be alive. No point in tying a dead body to a chair.

Then Parker's eyes opened, his face barely registering recognition as he looked at us. His eyes met mine before closing again. I didn't even care anymore if he ended up getting stuck as a Taker—I was just so relieved to see him. Other guards marched Mia and Mrs. Chipp in at gunpoint and tied them to chairs beside him. They both looked relatively unharmed, which was a relief to see. Parker's mom only lifted her worried gaze from Parker long enough to give me a pleading look.

Chloe growled and stepped up beside me. "When does this stop, Cooper? Does it ever end? Why did you have to take them too?"

"Shut up, you traitor!" he screamed at her, with such fury that he stumbled to one side and someone behind him stepped forward and steadied him. I recognized Joey before he stepped back into the shadows again. "I needed them here to keep Parker in line. He was becoming ... difficult to control."

"You didn't *need* them, Cooper," Chloe argued, but I

put a hand on her arm to signal her to stop. Arguing with an obviously unstable person was never a good idea.

"Just give me the Eclipse." Cooper's words slurred slightly and he sounded almost as tired as he looked. I was beginning to wonder whether if I just gave him a few more minutes he might die on his own and save us a lot of trouble.

I held up one of the two vials I'd brought. The blue liquid sparkled under the lights. A guard took it, holding it gingerly as he carried it over to Cooper.

My eyes traveled back to the hostages and stopped on Parker. I studied him closer; he now was hunched forward in his seat. Not sitting up like Mia and his mother. Still, even without seeing his face, I could tell he'd lost significant weight too. He was dirty, and dried blood covered his clothes.

Fury bubbled up inside me and I didn't even care about all the guns or heavily armed men anymore. All I wanted to do was smash Cooper through the wall for what he'd done. My hands curled into tighter fists and I had to blink away the red haze threatening to take over my vision. Shadows were lifting up from the ground and snaking around the bodies of the people casting them. It was horrifying... terrifying. My entire body shook and I wondered if my shadow was about to ensnare me as well.

"Easy," Chloe whispered beside me. "You have to calm down, Jack."

Her words drove back the images and I realized they were all a trick of my mind. I was more exhausted than I'd thought. I needed to stay calm. Parker needed me at full strength right now. I shook my head and looked away from him, focusing instead on Cooper.

A doctor in a white coat stood beside him. He whispered to him as he examined the vial of Spectrum. Finally, he shook his head in a firm and undeniable no.

"This *will* help you, Cooper. I promise you that ... " I tried to speak up before Cooper had a chance to react.

Cooper's lip curled up and he smashed his fist down across the guard's fingers, causing him to drop the vial. The whole room seemed to hold its collective breath as the vial fell and shattered into a million pieces on the concrete floor.

"Nice try, Jack." Cooper's voice wavered between disappointment and pure hatred. "The doc here says that Eclipse shouldn't be blue. So I'm going to guess you're lying to us—just like your daddy."

"It isn't Eclipse. It's something diff—"

Before I had a chance to say any more, Cooper grabbed the gun of the guard closest to him and pointed it at me. His hands shook worse than ever and he screamed in rage and frustration. Before I could even think to react, he shot Finn in the thigh.

Finn cried out and fell to the ground, clutching the wound as blood soaked his pant leg.

Cooper smiled and kept shooting.

"Please, listen!" I yelled, ducking low and pulling Chloe down behind the nearest triangular platform with me. People behind us seemed more confident than me that Cooper was only shooting at us, but they still slid a couple feet to

331

either side. My heart pounded in my ears as I peered around one end of the platform, scanning the room to find some way to fight back, to make Cooper stop.

For right now at least, he was the only one shooting. His guards were looking at each other like they weren't sure if they needed to stop him or pull out their guns and start shooting with him.

Parker lifted his head and looked at Finn. There was still no emotional reaction in his eyes as he watched Finn before looking away.

His best friend, shot and bleeding on the ground, and he had no response.

Everything was happening so quickly. I crouched, getting ready to move toward Finn. He was bleeding too fast. If I didn't stop it soon, he could bleed out and it would be too late.

I slipped out toward Finn, but the moment I was visible, Cooper adjusted his aim on me. Just before another gunshot shattered the quiet, Chloe somehow saw what was going to happen and did what Chloe always seemed to do.

The last thing I expected.

She dove out over my back, wrapping both arms around my neck. I fell forward with the impact and we both sprawled on the ground. The gun went off at the same time and her eyes went wide. Time felt like it was spinning out of control, and I couldn't force it go backward like I wanted. My heart pounded so hard in my chest that I was afraid it might hurt her. How could she do this? I hadn't even told her how sorry

I was yet. I hadn't been able to tell her how she'd changed my mind about Takers…about everything, including myself.

I carefully lifted her away from me in slow motion, looking for the blood, trying to find out exactly how much Cooper was going to steal from me in one day. And then Libby made a small, surprised sound and crumpled to the ground behind me.

Chloe ripped her waist free from my fingers before I fully understood what had happened. And then I saw the blood spreading, too fast, across the bottom right of Libby's light green shirt.

My heart felt numb and I leapt to my feet. Chloe helped me ease Libby onto her back behind the protection of the nearest platform. Addie ran past us to help Finn, completely ignoring the bullets Cooper was still trying to hit me with.

He'd completely lost it. The tremors in Cooper's hands had already cost him a couple of his own people. They'd lost whatever faith they had and were now rushing for cover in a mad panic around us. The last I saw of Addie, she'd grabbed Finn's shoulders and was dragging him back behind one of the platforms, out of sight of both me and Cooper.

The shooting stopped temporarily and I heard Joey and Cooper yelling, but every bit of my attention was on Libby.

Libby's hands trembled as she reached for my arm. Chloe handed me her jacket and I pressed it against Libby's already blood-soaked shirt. She'd lost so much blood in seconds. I couldn't look at her. I couldn't let myself feel what it would be to lose her.

Not here. Not like this.

"We have to stop the bleeding," I said, to myself as much as anyone.

"Jack." I heard Libby's whisper.

"I know, Lib. It's going to be fine. Just hold on." I hoped against hope that if I said it out loud, somehow it could be true.

"I'm sorry," she wheezed, and then coughed.

"Don't talk, Lib." I squeezed one of her hands in mine as I used the other to press the jacket harder against her wound. She winced.

When I looked at her, her eyes were on Chloe. "She saved your life…" Her voice sounded shocked.

"I'm so sorry, Libby," Chloe whispered. "I only thought about moving Jack out of the way…I—I didn't realize you were right behind h—"

"No." Libby shook her head firmly, her tone leaving no room for argument. "You did the thing I should've done when I saw the gun. You tried to save him."

"Shh, Libby." My voice was raw with emotion as I looked at the jacket quickly becoming soaked with her blood.

"Jack." Libby moved her head a bit to look at me and her coughing turned to a wheezing sound. She lifted my hand up to her lips and kissed it. "I want you to know. You were always my favorite dream…"

She took one last ragged breath, then went still. Chloe choked out a soft sob and smoothed her hand through Libby's hair.

I squeezed her fingers tight between my hands, afraid to let her go. Another shot was fired and it hit a stranger several feet behind us. I climbed slowly to my feet, meeting my brother's eyes as I stood. For that moment, I wished I could feel empty of emotion and pain—the way his eyes looked right now. Loss was so heavy on my shoulders I had to fight under the weight of it. I'd finally lost too much. Grief coursed through me like a living being.

Chloe started trying to pull me through the crowd.

I watched Cooper yelling at Joey and then kicking Parker's chair. It fell over. I saw my brother's head hit the ground and his eyes closed immediately. Jerking my arm out of Chloe's grasp, I pulled one blade from my boot without even thinking and threw it straight into Cooper's shoulder.

It was a rare miss for me. I'd been aiming for his heart.

Cooper yelled out and pointed his gun at me again. Chloe grabbed my arm again and pulled me forcefully back through the crowd of escaping Takers. She jolted me along in her wake toward the door.

"Stop them!" Cooper yelled to his guards.

A few of the guards ran toward us, but all the Takers in the room were now running around in absolute chaos. Even many of the guards on our side of the room were hiding in an attempt to escape Cooper's mad rage. I saw one guard against the wall behind us. He was bleeding from the stomach.

Cooper didn't even care who he hurt. All he cared about was the power that Eclipse could give him.

I gritted my teeth together and picked up my pace behind Chloe. Right now, no matter how much all my emotions were screaming at me to go back for Parker, to help Finn, to save Addie and the others—to be with Libby—my instincts told me it was no use. The way Cooper was shooting at me with complete disregard for those around me . . . everyone in that room was safer with me out of there.

I had no choice but to get to a safe place where I could figure out a new plan.

Because I was done trying to convince Cooper to take Spectrum.

Now, my only option was to kill him.

THIRTY-TWO
PARKER

Everything that was happening around me felt like it should matter. I knew that it did … but at the same time it felt too far away to worry about it. Since Darkness and I had woken up back in my exhausted body, I wasn't in charge anymore. I'd given that responsibility to Darkness and it felt great. It was oddly relaxing, especially if I tried not to pay attention to everything outside my head. It was better that way.

When the guards came to drag me into this large room, Darkness had actually seen an opening and head-butted the first guard. My head ached, but the guard's nose had bled enough that he'd been replaced by a different guard. I knew right then that I'd made the right choice. I didn't have any fight left in me. Fight was all Darkness was made of.

Fight was what we needed right now.

They pulled me onto a chair. I knew they were setting up chairs next to me, and I could hear someone making noise to my left, but Darkness had his attention focused on the rope that was securing our wrists. He was bent forward, eyes closed, as he wiggled one hand and then the other, trying to find the weakness that might allow him to slip one hand free.

A whimper came from my left and I wondered if something important was happening, but Darkness didn't care. From far away I heard my brother's voice. Even Darkness couldn't ignore that. He barely moved, but he peeked out through the curtain of dirty hair and we saw Jack, Chloe, Finn, Libby, and Addie standing about fifteen feet in front of us.

Darkness felt like snarling at Addie until her worried eyes met mine and I saw the fear in them. This wasn't the nightmarish hallucination that had been making our life hell. This was my *Addie* ... it was really her. She was here.

But Darkness didn't care. All he cared about was that no one was watching me. The doorway to the outside was only twenty feet away. He moved his attention back to the ropes on our wrists, no matter how much I wanted to watch my friends and brother—to make sure they were okay.

A glass vial of blue liquid exploded a few feet in front of us and brought our attention back into focus. Darkness let out a low growl around the gag in our mouth and started working on freeing our hands again, his motions growing more frantic.

Then Cooper had a gun in his hands. Darkness's rage bubbled up inside and his focus on freeing our hands was lost. He just wanted to kill Cooper. His attention shifted to seeing which weapons were within reach and imagining how he could use them to make Cooper bleed.

But I saw Cooper point the gun at everyone I loved, and my entire world stopped.

I fought wildly to wrestle control back from Darkness, but he was in full-on adrenaline-driven panic mode and didn't budge. His eyes settled on a knife in Cooper's boot just a couple of feet in front of us. If he could reach it, he could cut the ropes.

I couldn't force him to listen to me—or maybe I was too weak now to fight hard enough.

A gunshot went off and Darkness jerked back before finally taking a good look around. I was brought back to complete awareness as I got my first view of the whole picture. Mom and Mia were tied up next to me, and on the other side of the room, Finn had just been shot in the leg. My heart pounded hard against the wall of my chest.

Darkness looked up into Cooper's hard, cold eyes. The madman smiled and the message was clear. Cooper liked what he'd just done. The killing wasn't over.

Then I felt something coming from Darkness that I'd never expected. He felt remorse.

It only lasted an instant and then it passed, but it was something. He'd experienced one of *my* emotions without me trying to push it on him. He was changing…and if it could happen once, maybe it could happen again.

Cooper started shooting again. Darkness watched as chaos spread across the room. For an instant, we made eye contact with Jack. I saw pure fear in his eyes. And then he started to run.

This, for some reason, kicked Darkness back into action. He started working on freeing our hands from the ropes again, but I didn't want to run anymore. I wanted to help. Jack needed me, and I wanted to help my brother finish this—for him, for me, for Dad.

Joey was so quiet beside me he almost seemed to be holding his breath. Finally, he stepped forward and spoke soft enough that I only just barely heard him.

"Enough," Joey said, putting his hand on Cooper's shoulder. "This has to stop, Cooper."

Cooper jerked out of his grip and kept shooting. I saw Libby fall down, over by Jack, and my heart ached for my brother. Darkness kept working on the ropes and I just tried to stay out of his way. If he could get our hands free, then we could take the gun away from Cooper. That was the only thing that mattered right now.

Across the room, I saw Chloe trying to pull Jack to safety. His eyes rested on mine, and even from here I could see how badly he wanted to stay, to fight. But instead he backed away, following Chloe slowly toward the crowd of terrified people.

Was this it? Was this where he left me...again?

Joey put his hand on top of Cooper's gun and force-fully pushed it down. "You have to stop. You're putting your own people at risk. Don't you see how crazy this is?"

"Get out of my way. You've never belonged here. You don't have a clue what it's like to be this way," Cooper growled, jerking the gun out of Joey's reach. "You've been going soft ever since we captured Parker. If you're too weak to help me, just stay out of my way."

In a rage, Cooper screamed. Darkness lifted my head and Cooper met my eyes, stepped toward me, and kicked over my chair. The world tilted and then my head exploded with pain as everything went dark and silent.

THIRTY-THREE

JACK

Chloe and I darted across Funtopia trying to find somewhere to hide. I could hear Cooper's guards coming out of the funhouse behind us, but they were just trying to get organized in the chaos and we'd made it out fast enough that no one saw us cut a quick right behind the de-mirrored funhouse. We sprinted deeper into the carcass of the amusement park, running left and right until we finally found a haunted house. The entire front was boarded up.

Grabbing Chloe's hand, I ran around the back and found a small, partially broken window into what seemed to be storage room. Ripping my leather jacket off, I wrapped it around my fist and pushed in the remaining glass. I spread the jacket over the bottom of the pane and reached out for Chloe's foot. She wasn't even an instant behind in understanding my plan.

Immediately, she used me to boost herself up and inside, then moved out of my way as I jumped up onto the windowsill and rolled into the room.

"Here," Chloe whispered as she lifted my jacket out of the window, shaking the bits of broken glass off before handing it back to me.

I didn't speak. I pulled my jacket on, willing my dad to somehow inspire me through his old piece of clothing. Then I took Chloe's hand and ducked out of the storage room, into the haunted house. I could hear the guards closing in on us.

Everything inside was dark. I took my phone from my pocket and turned on the flashlight, shining it around us. An old coffin—a prop—sat half-closed a foot to my right, a skeletal hand still reaching out for anyone who came within reach. Fake spiderwebs now mingled with real ones as they stretched across the ceiling.

I moved quickly into the next room, instinct driving me to get as far into the center of our new hiding spot as possible. My brain flew through option after option as we walked from one nightmarish room to the next. I tried desperately to construct some sort of plan to save all the people I'd grown to care about. No, it was more than that—they'd become my family.

Everything in me ached at losing Libby. We'd left Finn bleeding, and all of them were now in Cooper's crazed hands. If Finn died, I knew Parker would never be the same. If any of them died . . . but how could I possibly save them all?

My heart burned and ached in my chest and I wished I could stop myself from feeling. I couldn't let the grief, panic, and fear paralyze me right now. I had to fight through it and find a way to think in spite of the pain overwhelming me.

I didn't realize I'd circled back to the same room three times until Chloe gently tugged on my hand for me to stop. I finally held still but kept my back to her, afraid that seeing sympathy on her face would break me.

"Jack." She spoke my name and then came around to face me. But I studied my feet, shuffling them through the dirt as I suddenly remembered how many things I'd wanted to say to her. The tightness in my throat made it even more painful to push out the words.

"I'm sorry." I whipped the apology out fast, like ripping off a bandage and hoping it wouldn't sting as much. My shoulders caved in under the weight of everything I felt I'd been trying to carry on my own. "I'm so, so sor—"

I stopped because Chloe was shaking her head. In an instant, she closed the distance between us. Reaching both hands up behind my neck, she pulled me down and kissed me.

It was so sudden and unexpected that my mind seemed to explode in response. Any words I'd wanted to say floated away. Logical thought was gone, but my body knew what to do without it. I wrapped both arms tight around her waist and pulled her in, so close against me it was like she was part of me.

I kissed her the way I'd wanted to for so long now. I took every terrifying emotion that filled me and poured it into showing the one person who was still with me exactly how I felt about her. I kissed her until she was breathless and clinging to me... the same way I was to her.

"I need you to hear me and know..." I pulled her tighter against my chest as we both caught our breath. "I was wrong to say what I did before, about not wanting Parker to stay a Taker. I'm so sorry."

"I know. And you can make it up to me later." Chloe ran her thumb across my jaw. The smile in her voice slipped away as she continued. "For now, we have to find a way to help all the people we just left with Cooper—starting with your brother."

"I'm pretty sure that isn't my brother." I sighed as I rested my chin on top of her head, taking comfort in the warmth of being so close to her. "I could see it in his eyes back there. The way he reacted to Finn being shot—it would be hard to convince me that was really him."

"You think he's Divided again?" Chloe shook her head and put her forehead against my chest. "How can you be sure?"

"I'm fairly certain, but I don't know if anyone could be one hundred percent sure unless they were in his head." I stepped back and was about to look at her when an idea clicked into place and I pulled her in close again. Reaching into the pocket of my leather jacket, I pulled out my sunglasses and put them on.

"Jack... what's your plan?" Chloe took a step back and squinted at me in the darkness.

"The last person I made eye contact with was Parker." I

was thinking out loud at this point, developing my plan as I went.

I looked around the room, studying it closely for the first time. Any old props that used to be in here had been removed, and I had to admit I was relieved about that. Planning to go into a Divided mind was a scary enough prospect.

"You're going to try to go into his mind?" Chloe looked beyond skeptical. "Is now the best time for that?"

"If we're going to stand a chance, I need Parker back, to help me." I turned to face her, willing her to agree that this plan had a chance of working. "I need to figure out what's going on in the funhouse. Maybe Parker can tell me. Give me an idea of where they keep their prisoners, or a weakness I can attack. Hopefully I can help him break free of whatever is going on in his head while I'm at it."

"How do you know you're still connected?"

"Because Cooper knocked him out." I spit out the words, not trying to hide the venom attached to them. I turned to face her. "Chloe, I don't think we can plan to help Cooper anymore…"

She took a step back from me involuntarily, but then studied the floor. Her back slouched forward a bit in defeat and I wished I could help her, but this was a realization she had to come to on her own.

"The Cooper who I'd hoped we could find is gone." Her eyes were sad, but she shuddered slightly and then nodded. "We can't let him get the chance to hurt everyone anymore. Do what you have to do."

Reaching out, I squeezed her hand, knowing there was

nothing I could say to make this situation any better for her. The only way to help was to try to stop Cooper from hurting anyone else, as quickly as possible.

I cleared a spot on the floor near one of the doors. There was only one entrance and one exit from the room; we could escape if they came in looking for us, but they'd have to know we were here in order to ambush and surround us. And disturbing as our location was, it was our best option. There must've been some truly creepy props in here at one point, because the faded red paint on the wall and floor was obviously intended to look like blood splatters. Huge windows had been painted on the opposite wall, their cracking paint displaying naked tree branches and creepy, elongated shadows.

I rolled my jacket into a pillow and settled down on the only spot on the concrete where it didn't look like a massacre had occurred.

"Wait, Jack." Chloe moved over to the place I'd cleared and sat down. "Are you sure you can handle this? I've been in Parker's mind when he was Divided. He's incredibly powerful. A strong Divided mind can crush a regular Watcher. After what I saw, I'm certain he's strong enough. And if he isn't the one in control..."

I made certain my own concern about that didn't show on my face. "He wouldn't hurt me, Chloe."

"As I said, you might not be dealing with him."

"He's still in there. I'll be okay." I kissed her once more, softly, and then handed her one of my knives. "If someone comes while I'm out... you know what to do."

She gave me a stiff nod and turned her gaze to the opposite door.

I closed my eyes, hoping Parker was the one I found in the Hollow.

THIRTY-FOUR

PARKER

I was in a haze of blackness. Not sleeping, not awake, but it comforted me and held me like a blanket. I felt like I was wrapped in a cozy cocoon where nothing could get to me. So this was what the mind of a Taker was like for a Taker. It wasn't nearly as hostile as it had been when I was a Watcher...

Until something started fighting it.

It felt like someone was hacking away at pieces of my warm cocoon, and I wanted them to stop. Bit by bit, one piece of me felt exposed, then another, then another. It was awful and terrifying.

"Parker!" I heard Jack's voice yell my name again and again, but I didn't answer. This could be another cruel trick my mind was playing on me. Like fake Addie ripped apart my reality, fake Jack was now tearing apart my mind, and I wished he would stop.

"Please, please…" Jack was closer now, and he sounded so tired. "I need to know you're okay, Parker. You're my brother and I can't handle losing you too. Please help me find you!"

There was another noise now, and it actually sounded like he might be fighting back his emotions—mixed in with the occasional string of curses. I was so shocked that I listened for a minute more, just to be sure I'd heard right. Jack didn't ever get emotional like that. I was pretty sure he didn't have feelings, let alone allow people to see them.

"Jack?" I said his name tentatively, unable to resist the idea of my tougher-than-nails brother possibly in pain. All noise stopped.

"Parker?" he screamed, and it felt like he was yelling into my brain.

"Shhh…geez, I'm right here," I mumbled, rubbing my hands against the sides of my head where my migraines always started. Jack continued to bash through toward me until I could see him through cracks in the hazy shell.

"I'm here too," I heard my voice say, and Darkness showed up a few feet in front of me, protecting us even from a possible hallucination.

Jack finally broke all the way in, looking like he'd been fighting a war. His eyes were watering. His nose was streaming blood and it trickled from both his ears. When he got through to me, he took three steps forward, but skidded to a halt when he saw Darkness sitting a few feet away from me.

"I'm so sorry I couldn't get you out of there." He looked sincerely remorseful, but I still wasn't sure what to think.

"You left me there?" I asked, ready for the Jack hallucination to attack me at any moment.

Jack sighed. "After Cooper knocked you out, he was shooting wildly and too many people were getting hit. I had to leave."

"He hit Finn ... " My voice faded as I remembered that my best friend could be dying in the real world and I couldn't do anything to help him.

"I could see that it wasn't you, Parker. Even from across the room, I could tell." Jack looked unsteady and dropped onto his knees on the ground. "Last time, you thought you might get taken over by him permanently—do you remember what you asked me to do if that happened?"

I did remember, but it felt like a completely different time and place, a different world even.

Darkness looked over at me and then answered for us both. "I asked you to make sure I couldn't hurt anyone else. But we haven't hurt anyone."

Jack nodded, panting slightly, and then said, "But I don't know if you're hurting Parker."

"I *am* Parker," Darkness snarled. I could feel his anger growing. "Why does no one understand that? We are the same."

"You aren't the same." Jack shook his head, but his voice didn't sound like he was trying to attack. He sounded sincere. And everything he said and did was making sense. Could this be the real Jack? I'd never hallucinated in the Hollow as a

Watcher, so why would I do it as a Taker? Maybe it was better to just assume Jack was real, until he proved he wasn't...

"You are different and opposite," Jack went on. "Together you're Parker. But separated like this—and locking each other up in the corner of your minds—you'll never be everything you could be if you don't figure out how to live and work in here together."

"It doesn't matter, Jack. We're both going to die anyway." I rolled away from them and toward the dark corners of my mind. "Who cares who is in charge when that happens?"

Darkness spoke to Jack too, keeping his voice lower this time. "*This* is why I've been in charge..."

"It's still my mind too," I muttered. "You can't whisper so quietly that I can't hear you."

Jack cleared his throat, and when I rolled to face them, they both were watching me with expressions of deep concern on their faces.

"I need you to help me," Jack said.

"I can't." Arguing took a lot of effort, so I just left it at that.

Unluckily, Darkness knew my thoughts and spoke for me. "He's giving up, Jack. He thinks we're probably better off dead than living as a Taker. You told us how terrible they are and now we've witnessed it firsthand. He thinks our dad would probably rather we die than choose to live like one of them."

"No!" Jack's voice rang out with authority. "I know I haven't told you much about Dad yet, even though you asked me again and again. I'm sorry. I made mistakes and I want to fix them, but you're robbing me of that chance."

He scooted across the floor toward me, his expression desperate.

"The first thing you should know about Dad is that he would *never* want you to choose death over being a Taker. Never, Parker." Jack seemed so positive that it made me begin to question all the things I believed. "You think you want to know Dad? Let me tell you what he would say if he could see you doing this. He would say he'd rather you die than give up in the way you have—the way you are right now."

Outrage shot through my veins and I sat up. "You have no idea what this has been like. What we've been through."

"Then he'd say, 'You're tired?'" Jack shrugged, but there was something nervous in his eyes as he continued. "'Big deal. So is everyone. Look around, Parker—you're in a Night Walker camp. Stop whining and fight!'"

"*Now* you decide to start telling me about Dad? Great timing, Jack." Pure anger fueled me and I moved closer. "Cooper has been putting me through hell. Do you have any idea what it takes to turn a Watcher into a Taker? It takes torture—a full-on, constant attack to the body and mind. You think I'm just tired? You can't even begin to understand..."

Darkness had no use for my words. Instead, he dove straight for Jack, but Jack was ready. He sank down into the black haze and then floated back up again as Darkness landed on his other side.

Jack turned to face me. "*You* are the real Parker. You need to work with your angry other half over there—"

"He calls me Darkness," Darkness said, eyeing me warily.

"You need to work with Darkness to find some of that fight left in you. I think that right now, he's your best asset. You both need to help me if you want to save yourself. And Finn, Addie, Mia, your mom—everyone you care about."

Then Jack moved closer and wrapped both arms around me. He hugged me tight against his chest. "You're my brother, Parker. You're the only family I have left, and ... I love you. I want to tell you everything you want to know and probably some things you don't—about Dad, about me—but you *have to stick around.* I expect you to fight by my side. Don't give up on me, because I will *never*, ever give up on you."

It was what I'd always wanted from Jack. His warmth flowed through me and filled me with new life. This was no hallucination. My brother was here, and he wanted me to fight. I wrapped my arms around him and hugged him back.

"How do you think I can help?" I asked, and my fear was evident.

"I don't know ... you're inside their prison. Can you tell me how to get to you? Where are they keeping you?" Jack sat back and looked at me.

"It's deep underground. That's all I really know." I shook my head, remembering something.

Darkness sat in the same spot where he'd landed after his failed tackle, but he was watching us now and all signs of his anger were gone. Instead, he looked intrigued ... even excited at the prospect of us taking action to get out of this mess. But something was making him hesitate. "This is all great and good," he said to Jack, "but I don't think you're real."

"Why not?" Jack shot me a look of confusion.

"Because the last person we made eye contact with wasn't you." Darkness looked back and forth between Jack and me meaningfully. "It was Cooper."

Jack opened his mouth to respond, but then closed it, thinking. He was quiet for a minute before slowly nodding. "So both Cooper and I are connected to you, Parker...like we were with your mom. Remember how the two of us connected to her and went into her dreams so I could teach you to be a Watcher? This is like that, only Cooper is still awake, so it's just us right now."

Darkness looked like he was piecing it all together, and then he nodded. "I prefer you to him anyway."

Jack's face broke into a small smile. "Thanks...I think."

"So, I'll soon be in Cooper's head?" I groaned, thinking of the times I'd been in there as a Watcher.

"Yes, if you don't wake up. I'm not really sure how a Taker-to-Taker connection would work." Jack shook his head and frowned, muttering, "I should've asked Chloe."

"You're still with Chloe?" I asked, realizing I'd been too busy worrying about whether Jack was real to ask what was happening in the real world. Jack hesitated, but then filled me in on all the details. I felt sick with each piece of information. Libby dead, Finn shot and possibly bleeding out, Addie, Mia, and Mom all in the hands of the Takers. Chloe and Jack hiding away in some spooky haunted house...it seemed too much to overcome.

"How do you expect us to help you fight this?" I groaned,

not sure whether to panic or go back into hiding again. Even Darkness looked like he'd consider giving up to be a viable option at this point.

"I—" Jack looked determined for an instant before his face fell. "I don't know...but I'm open to suggestions. Anything that can get everyone out of here alive would be great."

"Well...I think I *used* to support staying alive." I tried to smile for the first time in what felt like forever. It felt surprisingly good. "I could probably get on board with that again."

"Good. I'm very happy to hear that." Jack waved his hand to gesture to Darkness and me. "I honestly don't think it's safe right now to try to put Humpty Dumpty back together again. But as the more complete side, Parker needs to be in primary control—then maybe you two can try to figure out how to work the both-sides-as-one angle a little more effectively."

I'd gotten used to the dulled sensations of the backseat, but I knew Jack was right. As much as I'd been acting like it, I really didn't want to give up. "I think I can handle that," I said, and then looked over at Darkness. I saw Jack's shoulders visibly tense while we waited for his response.

"I'm game. It turns out that being in charge all the time is way more tiring than I ever expected it to be. I would've turned this whole mess over to Parker already if he'd been at all up for it." Darkness flopped onto his back. "God, I need a nap."

Jack laughed...then stopped abruptly and sat up completely straight, looking back and forth between Darkness and me with his mouth hanging partially open. It took a full ten seconds, and me lifting my eyebrows at him, before he said, "I think I might have a crazy idea."

"Then you're in luck." Darkness lifted his head with a bit of a wild grin. "According to Parker, crazy is my forte."

THIRTY-FIVE

JACK

My mind whizzed through the possibilities. I wasn't sure if this would work, but since Parker had made eye contact with Cooper last, and I was here in his mind ... then he definitely had to be connected to us both.

"I think we need to try to take Cooper down ... from the inside out." I spoke the words slowly, knowing this went against everything I'd ever taught Parker about being a Watcher. We always tried not to hurt anyone ... but this time was different. It was Cooper.

"You mean, from inside his mind?" Parker asked, and then looked at Darkness. They both seemed doubtful.

"Cooper has tons of neat drugs to play with, Jack." Darkness's frown deepened. "One of them has supercharged his mind somehow. He's insane ... but very strong."

"I think the drug is part of why he's so messed up." Parker rubbed his hands over his knees. "I think it might have made him the way he is."

I lay on my back, thinking about alternatives for a few seconds, but came up empty. "I think this is our best shot. There are three of us…"

They looked at each other and Parker said, "Not really, though."

"No, you're right. But your mind is so strong with you Divided, even after all they've done to you, that I can literally feel it vibrating in the dream around me, Parker." I couldn't keep my voice from sounding a little impressed. "When you two work together, you're formidable—even without me." I tried to infuse my voice with all the confidence I could gather. "And *with* me—we can do this."

Parker and Darkness looked at each other and then back at me. "So now what?"

That question had been bothering me too. What if it was hours before Cooper went to sleep? What if the Takers found Chloe before we even had a chance to do this? What if Cooper started killing other people because he got bored waiting?

"I'm not sure," I said. "I guess we hope he goes to sleep sooner rather than later."

Darkness gave a short, barking laugh. Parker shot me a dark look and said, "Cooper's even more tired than me. Half the time he falls asleep standing up."

"While torturing us," Darkness added.

"So it shouldn't be too long."

"Good." Except for the mention of torture, I felt mostly

relieved by what they'd said. "All we need is an instant of Cooper dozing off. I can trap him while we fight."

"Before that happens, tell me what to expect." Parker sat forward. "Don't we need a plan for what to do in there?"

"Well…" I wanted to give him some idea of what we should do, but I really didn't have that answer.

"What will it be like when we're all connected to the same dream?" Parker asked.

I tried to scramble together something to tell him… a starting place if nothing else. If Cooper was as strong as Parker said and we went in there unprepared, we could be in serious trouble.

But the truth was, I had no clue what to expect or how to attack in a situation like this. I'd never heard of anyone doing it.

The next instant, I knew that any time for preparation was gone. It was now or never—the dream around us was vibrating so hard my head started to hurt. Cooper must have been falling asleep.

"Just keep fighting him, Parker," I said. "Giving up in here could mean dying. Keep fighting and I'll find you."

———

The suffocating blackness of Parker's mind melded with a new layer that felt thicker and firmer than the rest. I immediately felt around for the new presence. It wasn't hard. Cooper's mind felt so intense it clashed with every dream layer it touched. It seemed like sound waves in an echo chamber, bouncing against everything remotely close to it.

Focusing every ounce of energy I had left, I fought through the layers and closed in on him quickly. Reaching out my hand, I phased my fingers out and jammed them roughly into Cooper's leg. He cried out in pain and I heard a bashing sound nearby as Parker and Darkness broke into Cooper's cocoon too.

"What the hell are you doing?" Cooper looked down at me, thrashing his leg, trying to free it from my grip, but I held tight. I focused all of my energy on tying his mind here, keeping him bound to this dream and to me. If he was going to get free, he'd have to rip me apart. Which, from the excruciating pain I felt every time he tried to pull free, was absolutely possible.

I hoped Parker was ready for this.

"I'm keeping him here," I yelled to Parker, and Cooper pulled even harder, realizing what we were doing. "You have to hone in on his mind and do the opposite of everything I've ever told you. Get in his mind and tear each bit away. Any kind of damage you can do will help."

"You can't do this." Cooper laughed and yanked away again. My mind felt like it was exploding with every tug. "You're not strong enough … even together."

"Parker!" I screamed, trying to get him to move before I lost my ability to fight altogether.

He and Darkness flew into action. They dove toward Cooper's back and I felt a physical shuddering in the dream world around me as Parker slammed his fingers into Cooper's body.

Now Cooper was the one screaming.

Darkness stepped directly into Parker and disappeared—they were working as one. The shudders of the world became strong as an earthquake. Cooper stopped moving. He stopped pushing me away. He raised his hands to his head and pressed them against his forehead.

Suddenly his thoughts and memories flooded into me. He was using them to push me away. I saw him torturing my brother as if I were the one doing it; I felt his joy at seeing him die and bringing him back. I saw a white room with unbelievably bright lights where they'd injected Parker with a black, sinister-looking drug. I jerked my hand out of him like he'd burned me, and Cooper closed the cocoon of darkness around me.

"Jack!" Parker yelled, and I knew he was now both holding Cooper and trying to attack him.

I dug into the dream space, heading that direction, and broke through after a few seconds. In that short time, Cooper had already gained so much ground. Parker was still holding on, but he was down on his knees and looked like he was having convulsions. I dived forward, steeling myself again as I stuck my hand back into Cooper.

Parker stopped shaking and got back on his feet. My heart ached as Cooper bombarded me again with the horrifying memories ... but I held on, realizing Cooper's whole plan was to make me let go. Because Parker was winning his battle—and Cooper wanted desperately to run before it was too late.

Parker attacked viciously, going through behind the memories Cooper was hitting me with and tearing them to pieces with terrifying ferocity. Cooper howled in pain with each one.

Then new memories came to light, unbidden. I saw Cooper punishing Takers for as little as noticing his exhaustion. I saw Cooper killing people he only suspected of being Builders and Watchers—the way he'd seen his father do, except—as Cooper was committed to being more than his father was—he was willing to do anything.

And I saw Cooper screaming at Joey for helping my brother.

Then he stopped paying attention to me, and Parker yelled out as Cooper started to fight him. Darkness reappeared, like Cooper had somehow managed to separate them. He fell to the ground, struggling to get back up. Parker screamed in pain and my heart filled with panic. Cooper was winning again...

But only because he'd stopped fighting me.

Refocusing my energy, I only used a tiny piece of my mind to chain him here. With the rest, I did exactly what I'd asked Parker to do. I began ripping Cooper's mind apart.

I started with his memories of all the Night Walkers he'd murdered. Using my mind, I pictured shattering each memory like a piece of glass, smashing them into a million pieces. Cooper reacted violently, but I held on, tearing through him as quickly as I could.

Every move I made damaged me. The effort it took to break one piece of him away was unbelievable, but I kept fighting. I left shredded memories in my wake—of his father, of his brother. I realized that the memories of him being cruel to Parker and Chloe were the easiest to destroy. Others were harder. The one of him finding his father dead was the hardest. It was tied to an emotion I recognized too well—grief.

Then everything got easier, faster. I looked up and saw that Darkness and Parker were united again, and they were plowing through what remained of Cooper's mind faster than I could keep track. Parker looked ragged, staggering to his knees again as he kept fighting through the pain I could see in his eyes.

"No! Please!" Cooper cried out, and then the last piece of what made him Cooper exploded, along with the dream around us. The last thing I saw before I woke up was Parker sinking into the black swirls and out of sight.

THIRTY-SIX

PARKER

I sat up straight in my chair and moaned out loud. It felt like my veins had been filled with glass. Every heartbeat sent slicing shards of pain throughout my body. My head was the worst. It was excruciating. I could barely think beneath it.

"Cooper?" I heard Joey's voice say, and lifted my head to see where he was.

He stood directly in front of me, staring right at me. I blinked and looked down at my hands. They were smaller than mine, and I wore Cooper's ring…

"*What the hell!?*" Darkness stared at me from a spot on my right. He'd expressed my thoughts exactly. I'd somehow taken over … a Taker.

But when I honed in on my body and thoughts, the way I had with Dr. Rivera, there was nothing.

Cooper was gone, destroyed... and so I'd taken over *just* his body, because that's what Takers do.

"Are you okay?" Joey's words sounded concerned, but his voice was anything but. "When I came in, you were asleep in your chair, and then you started having some kind of seizure."

"I'm... okay," I answered slowly, then looked up at Joey as I tried to figure out what was happening. We were in an office, and it was just the two of us. No one else was here. I needed more information. "Did we find Jack and Chloe?"

Joey frowned deeply and then sighed. "You aren't hearing me. I don't know why I'm still surprised by that. I'm not just saying that *I* won't go out looking for them—I'm saying I'm not going to let *you* do it anymore."

I couldn't keep the surprise from my voice. "You won't?"

"No. This has to stop, Cooper." Joey lifted a gun from the desk beside him. "I don't want to hurt you, but I will *make* you stop. I'm not a Night Walker. I'm not a so-called god, as Dad called your kind—and maybe I *am* less than you, just like he always said. But this..." He gestured toward the office door and his face showed genuine remorse. "You killed people out there today—people from both sides. This is war, and that's nothing new. You have to stop this now. Let's talk to Chloe and see what she has to say. She's our sister, Cooper."

I grumbled a little, mostly buying time to figure out how to respond. Cooper would never agree to Joey's proposal. My hands grew sweaty; I could see in Joey's eyes just how serious he was about this. It seemed like I kept jumping out of the fire and into—another fire. "You're going to shoot me?" I asked.

Joey nodded without hesitation, and this time he pointed the gun at me. "I've wondered for a long time if Dad finally killed himself because he couldn't handle one more day of living the way he did, destroying people that way. I've been hoping you might figure that out before it was too late. But it's like you're only determined to outdo him. I'm done waiting."

"Okay," I answered slowly, trying my best to sound reluctant. I'd had no idea Steve Campbell had killed himself. I was pretty sure even Jack didn't know about that.

Joey dropped the gun to his side, shock registering plainly on his face. "Okay?"

I thought about how to carry this charade on, but the truth was that Cooper would go down swinging in this situation ... or he'd survive through deceit. He might agree to Joey's demands, and then have one of the guards shoot Joey the instant they were out the door. This family had so many secrets ... just like mine. It was time for the truth. My only chance was to tell him everything and hope Joey was the kind of guy, deep down, that I was starting to suspect he was.

"I need to tell you something." My speech was slurred

and my eyelids drooped. I raised my hands, signifying surrender, and Joey's eyes narrowed.

"What?"

I climbed painfully to my feet to make sure I could stay awake. Who knew what would happen if I fell asleep again and disconnected from this body? "I'm not Cooper. I'm Parker."

Joey lowered his chin in obvious disbelief, raising his gun again.

"We were in a dream, and we fought ... I'm not sure how, but apparently I've taken over his body." I stared Joey straight in the eye, trying to show him that I was telling the truth. "You brought me food and water. I know you aren't a Taker."

Joey shook his head. "Cooper knows all those things. This doesn't make sense. Why are you trying to convince me that ... "

"Because it's true, Joey." I fought back another wave of exhaustion and continued. "But I'm not sure how long I can stay awake and in control here, so maybe we should take advantage of the moment. I can tell all of the Takers that Cooper has—that *I* have—changed my mind. I'll tell them I'm putting you in charge. You know that blue vial Jack tried to give Cooper earlier? It's a new drug that could save the Takers. But it won't allow them to hurt other people, so in that way it's far better than Eclipse. It's called Spectrum. We *have* a way to help—I just need to convince the other Takers it's worth a try."

Joey stood there staring at me, his forehead deeply furrowed, watching me closely.

Darkness shook his head. "I'm not sure he's buying it."

"I need your help to do this, Joey." The pleading tone in my voice came through loud and clear.

"How do I know this isn't some elaborate lie so you can get to your guards and then tell them to kill me?" Joey's gaze was so hard, it felt like he was trying to read my mind. He probably wished he could.

"Isn't the fact that you have to ask that question proof that your brother *has* to be stopped?" I yawned and leaned back against the wall behind me.

Darkness showed up at my elbow and clapped his hands loudly in front of my face. "We have to stay awake, and hurry. It will be very bad if this body finally gives out while we're still in it. We don't want to go down with this ship."

I nodded slowly and stood up straight.

"What position did I play on our soccer team?" Joey asked, his eyes focused on mine.

It took me a second to answer because I was so surprised at the obvious question. "You were a fullback. Cooper wouldn't know that?"

Joey stuck the gun into the back of his pants and his expression was heartbreakingly sad when he replied. "He never cared enough to pay attention to anything I did."

I stepped forward and shook my head. "That was a mistake ... one of many that Cooper made. But I made that one too."

Joey's expression was part surprise and part suspicion.

"I should've tried harder to get to know you before now," I said. "Maybe we could've stopped this sooner— before it got so terrible." I extended my hand toward him. "But we have a chance to stop it now. Are you in?"

He stared at my hand for a few seconds before shaking it with his massive one. "I'm in."

THIRTY-SEVEN

JACK

I sat straight up, gasping for breath at the pain in my head, and Chloe slapped a hand across my mouth. She stared at me, her gray eyes wide as she pointed across the room to the doorway on the opposite wall. She lifted one finger to her lips to signal me to be quiet.

Then I heard them. There were Takers inside the haunted house with us. I climbed silently to my feet, my head pounding, and Chloe mimicked my motions. From the amount of noise the Takers were making, it was clear they didn't know we were here. Reaching back for Chloe's hand, I led her into the next room. Thankfully, it was empty.

We made our way silently through a couple of additional creepy rooms, but when we got back to the one we needed to leave through, there was a single guard posted in the doorway. Chloe tapped me on the shoulder and handed me the blade I'd given her to protect herself.

Then she whispered, "Please don't use it unless you have to."

I nodded slowly before peeking out again into the outer room. The guard stood there looking bored. He seemed pretty young... younger than us. I had to find a way to get us out of here without killing him. Gesturing for Chloe to stay behind me, I crept out. The guard didn't realize I was there until I had my knife at his throat. I placed my other hand over his mouth and his eyes went wide.

"I don't want to hurt you... but I can't let you stop me," I whispered low in his ear. Chloe came around in front of him and pulled his gun from his belt, pointing it at him. She looked like she knew how to use it. I put my knife away but kept my hand over his mouth.

"Do you have something we can tie you up with?" Chloe asked him.

He didn't respond immediately, but apparently decided he'd rather be tied up than dead. He pointed to a pair of zip ties he had in his belt. Chloe took them out and we walked him back to the room where we'd just been hiding. We moved him to a corner and secured his hands and feet.

I leaned down close. "I need you to give us thirty seconds. If you start yelling before we get far enough away, then she might have to come back and shoot you. Neither of us wants that. Okay?"

The poor guy looked terrified as he nodded his head furiously. He didn't make a sound when I removed my hand—and he gave us a full minute, at least, before we heard the commotion and knew he'd alerted the others.

Smart kid.

By that time, Chloe and I had run across the amusement park and were circling around to the funhouse entrance. I desperately hoped that all the friends we'd left here a few hours earlier were still alive.

As we crossed the park, I filled her in on what had happened in Parker's mind.

"So you were just thrown out?" she whispered, her face pale. "Do you think he … do you think Cooper is dead?"

I shook my head and squeezed her hand. "I don't know yet, Chloe. I feel like we did a whole lot of damage … but I won't know until I see him myself."

"Do you think Parker is okay?" She squeezed my hand back.

I held my breath and pulled her low to the ground as one of the guards passed twenty feet ahead of us, heading into the funhouse. Climbing to my feet, I shook my head without speaking. The fact that I couldn't answer that question was eating me alive. How could I have asked Parker to do something so dangerous? What if it killed him too? What if I'd lost him—not because of what Cooper had done, but because of what I did?

As soon as the coast was clear, we made our way to the funhouse entrance and slipped in, hiding in the shadows.

There was a big crowd on the other side of the room but they all had their backs to us. No one saw us slip in.

I scanned the area, looking for an opportunity to somehow get to my brother. But then my eyes stopped and my gut wrenched with unexpected pain. There, on the same spot where we'd been shot at earlier, I could still see a red tinge to the ground. Libby had been shot right there. She'd died there.

I hoped Finn hadn't met the same fate.

Then I heard Cooper's voice, and all the blood drained from my head down into my feet.

"I need to talk to all of you. Something has to be done, whether you like it or not..."

I knew that his voice alone would make these people afraid enough that they would agree to anything he demanded. As long as he was leading them, it would be nearly impossible to build up an opposition.

Then I saw him. What we'd done in the dream hadn't worked. I released Chloe's hand and slipped out my knife. Taking a few steps closer, I waited for the right angle.

This time I wouldn't miss.

Cooper kept talking, but I was so focused on his movements that I didn't listen to his words. I raised my hand to throw the blade just as he turned to face me. His eyes widened, and I realized I'd stepped up into the light. I pulled back my hand—and Chloe hit me hard from behind.

My blade fell to the floor as I staggered forward, but I immediately picked it up before spinning to face her. I couldn't believe she'd just betrayed me after everything we'd been through. Guards rushed over and pinned my hands behind my back.

Chloe's eyes were huge. She kept looking back at where we'd seen Cooper, and then at me like she was trying to signal me in some way. I didn't understand. How could she have stopped me? I knew he was her brother, but I'd thought she'd agreed this was the only way. Then she gave me a hard look that seemed to question my intelligence and mouthed one word: *Listen.*

I whipped my head around, trying to see Cooper again, but there were guards blocking my view. What was she talking about?

"Bring them up here." Cooper's voice rang out above the noise, and everyone quieted down.

The guards pushed us up to the front of the room and then released us once we were surrounded. Cooper stared hard at each of us, but I saw that his hands were trembling. Up close he looked more like an animated skeleton than a person.

"As I was saying"—his gaze fixed on me like he was trying to pierce through me with his eyes—"I'm near my limit. I can feel it. And we've lost too many people."

I felt my eyebrows raise until Chloe kicked my foot, and I forced myself not to respond. I didn't understand how or why, but either Cooper had had a change of heart, or ...

"Joey has been helping me come to a decision, and I'm going to put him in charge. I think he and my sister, Chloe, should work together to come up with the best solution to avoid even more of our kind dying." Cooper looked hard at me again, and I thought I caught the slightest twitch as the corner of his mouth. "Unless you just want to keep fighting, Jack, because this truce has to come from both sides."

It was an expression that was so clearly Parker's that I felt like the wind had been knocked from my lungs. Parker had taken over a Taker? How?

Then I realized that was exactly what had happened when we'd destroyed Cooper. Parker was now a Taker, so he'd been sucked into what was essentially an empty shell. Now he was using it to our advantage—brilliant.

And I'd almost killed him with my blade.

Thank God for Chloe.

I realized Parker was still waiting for my response. "I will agree," I said, "if you agree to release my brother and the others you've been holding captive."

"And give me the chance to talk to you and the rest of your people about a new drug called Spectrum," Chloe added before Cooper had a chance to respond. "I honestly believe it can save us all."

Cooper looked like he was considering this for a moment before he let out an exhausted sigh. "Fine." Then he looked over at Joey and his guards. "Get his brother and friends."

Joey stepped up beside him as the guards walked off, confused expressions on their faces. Joey's face betrayed one other emotion, though—sadness. He looked at Chloe and she gave him a slight nod. He knew.

And he'd helped us anyway.

"I think I need to go rest for a little while." Cooper looked up at Joey, his legs shaking beneath him. "You know what to do."

"I do," Joey said, and Cooper gave me a look before Joey helped him toward the door.

It was surreal to watch this walking, talking, living person and know that in reality he was just a shell. He disappeared from sight, and I knew that as soon as Cooper went to sleep, his heart would stop. It would only be minutes until his tired and sick body would be as empty of life as Parker and I had made his mind.

THIRTY-EIGHT
PARKER

The instant we woke up back in my body, Darkness told me he was done. I was back in charge, and he ordered me to stop bothering him so he could rest. That worked just fine for me. When I opened my eyes, I saw guards standing over me and cringed ... half because I wasn't supposed to know what had just happened, and half because it was kind of an instinct now.

"We're here to bring you to your brother," the closest guard said. He looked uncertain, and I wasn't sure if he was uncomfortable with releasing me ... or with everything they'd done to me before this.

They escorted me to an office, where Jack and Chloe were waiting.

I limped toward Jack, but I was so tired that even staying upright was a serious challenge. Jack walked straight up and hugged me.

"I was worried. Glad you made it out all right." Jack shook his head. "Also, you're a genius," he murmured.

It was still surprising to have Jack acting this way, but I hugged him tight, whispering, "We did it."

"*You* did it." Jack pulled back and shook his head with a wry smile. "I helped, but this would've been impossible without you. Dad would be so proud."

"It wasn't just me. But, he would?" The weight of everything I'd been through eased a little and my voice cracked with emotion.

"Absolutely." Jack walked me over to a chair Chloe pulled out and I sat down. "And I can't wait to talk your ear off telling you all about him."

"Does that mean you'll come live with us?" I tried not to show on my face how much I wanted him to say yes. I knew now that he had enough pressure on him without more coming from me.

Mom came rushing in with Addie and Mia in her wake. She hugged me and then reached out with her free hand for Jack, tugging him in too.

"I'm so happy you're both okay!" Mom pulled back, looking both of us over and wincing at how tired I looked. She turned to Jack.

"First, I heard what Parker just asked." She actually looked nervous. "Will you?"

Jack looked between us both and then he smiled. "I would love to."

Mom hugged us both tight again and her grin was as bright as I'd ever seen it.

Addie and Mia hugged me next, but I pulled Addie away and looked into her eyes. "I know Finn got shot..." I couldn't even voice the question.

Addie had tears in her eyes, but her smile widened. "I had some help." Then she walked back to the door and held it open.

A guy a little older than Jack came in, pushing a wheeled office chair. Finn was slumped down in the seat. His pants were torn and there was a clean white bandage on his leg. His face was pale, but other than that he looked okay. He grinned up at me even though he was having a difficult time keeping his head up.

"Parker! I haven't seen you in forever, man. Where you been?" His words were heavily slurred and his head fell to one side. I hugged him as he tried valiantly to lift it again.

"I'm glad you're all right," I said, clapping him on the shoulder.

The man escorting Finn had clean hands, dirty clothes, and was carrying a large medical kit with him.

Addie gestured his way. "This is Shawn. He was that crazy doctor's medical assistant."

"You're real?" I blinked at him, and Shawn laughed at the look of complete shock that must've been on my face.

Jack threw me a confused look, so I explained how Shawn had talked to me through the wall of my cell.

Shawn extended his hand to me. "I'm so sorry for what Cooper and Dr. Rivera did to you. I wish I could've helped more."

"You did." I rubbed my hand against my neck and stretched. Every muscle ached and I was so tired. "I would've lost my sanity without you there to talk to me... well, even more than I did, I guess."

Shawn smiled. "I'm just happy to have done something good for a change."

"You helped Finn?"

Addie answered, "I managed to slow the bleeding, but they threw us into the same cell as Shawn. And then Thor—"

"Joey," Jack, Chloe, and I corrected simultaneously, and then laughed. Chloe reached out and Jack took her hand.

Both Addie's eyebrows shot up to match mine, but then she continued with a small smile, reaching down to squeeze my hand. "So then *Joey* brought in a medical kit and Shawn got out the bullet and stitched him up."

"As you can tell, the kit had a painkiller in it. The bullet just missed his femoral artery."

"The feral artery is a big one." Finn stopped trying to hold his head upright and just rested it against the back of the chair with a huge grin. "It missed it because I'm so lucky!"

I laughed. "Sure you are." Then I pulled Addie in for another hug and shot Jack and Mom a smile. "And so am I."

THIRTY-NINE

JACK

We all waited while Joey went to gather the Takers together so Chloe could talk to them. So far, there had been very little resistance to the new plan. Chloe said she wasn't surprised by that, but I stayed on edge, waiting for something to go wrong.

Joey had locked up Dr. Rivera and a couple of the guards who'd started to disagree, but on the whole the transition was going smoothly. I had a feeling they were all just waiting to hear about Spectrum before they made their decision. I could only cross my fingers that our new drug wouldn't be as dangerous for people who weren't as old as Mason.

He'd survived, of course, but if the Takers witnessed someone's heart stop multiple times, it would really be bad for morale at this point.

I looked over at Parker and noticed his eyes twitching before he leaned forward and covered them with his hand.

"You look pretty rough. I think we should ask Joey and Shawn if they can look for the drug that'll switch you back to a Watcher … assuming it exists. Or would you rather just stay a Taker and we could try Spectrum on you?" I asked, watching him carefully for his response.

"I'd like to be back to normal again at some point, but right now I think I'm up for anything that will let me get some sleep." As Parker slumped farther down in his chair and closed his eyes, Addie stepped up to me.

"I can't help him through my dreams anymore?" she asked, the sadness clear in her eyes.

"Not if he remains a Taker." I squeezed her shoulder. "But we'll help him. I promise we'll figure it out."

Addie didn't respond, just walked over to Parker's chair. She smiled when he looked up at her, kissed him on the cheek, and took his hand in hers.

Joey was behind me in the doorway when I turned around. "I'm sorry about Parker."

"You didn't do it, but you can help us make it right. We need Chloe to show them about what this new formula can do." I looked at him and then back at Chloe. "That's all I want."

"You sure this Spectrum stuff will work?" Joey looked genuinely nervous.

"I'm sure they'll die without it." I tried to sound as confident as I wished I actually were. "It's worked for one

Taker already, and he's much older than all of you. His body was long past even normal Taker limits. I hope that means it will be a smoother process for everyone else."

"How did he live that long?" Joey frowned.

"Some kind of herbs and meditating all day," Chloe answered. "Probably not our best option, but still good to know about."

These details seemed to make Joey feel better. "Then let's get started."

He led the way back toward the main room, but I grabbed Chloe's hand and kept her with me as the others followed him.

"Are you sure about this? We saw how hard it was on Mason." I spoke low in her ear. "We're trying to be positive here, but what if his reaction was the good option? Yours could be much worse..."

"Yes. I'm absolutely sure." Chloe looked me in the eyes and put her hands on each side of my face. She gave me one more kiss. "All we can do is hope it goes well. If I don't take it, I'll die anyway, and I'd rather go down fighting. You of all people should understand that. This war has to stop. You know that. We've only paused it for now, but without convincing all the Takers to take Spectrum, this truce won't last. This is the first real chance I've had to make it happen—I can make a difference here. I have to end it, Jack."

I kissed her again and then crushed her against my chest, smelling her hair and feeling how good it was to hold her close. I felt her breathe; I kissed her neck and felt her heartbeat; then I spoke low, my voice unsteady. "You fight to live. You hear me?" I pressed my forehead against hers and stared in her beautiful eyes. "You fight to come back to me."

She gave a fierce nod and a tear fell down her cheek. "Always."

————

We walked out to the main room of the funhouse. It was packed, but there was a spot in the center where a mat had been spread out for Chloe. Addie had retrieved a vial of Spectrum from the van, which she handed to Chloe as she sat down on the mat.

Shawn walked up behind me. He had a defibrillator in one hand and a pack of needles and a medical kit in the other.

"Go ahead. We might need you." I stepped aside and put my hand on the blade of the knife in my belt. "I'll make sure no one interferes."

Shawn looked me in the eyes and smiled. "Changing the way everyone thinks isn't going to be easy. I never expected it would be. Just don't use that unless you have to."

I'd been thinking about nothing but finding a way to stop the fighting for months now ... but holding still, with Chloe at risk, was one of the hardest things I'd had to do. Fighting came much easier to me than having faith or trust. I wasn't sure why I hadn't recognized until now that this might be a challenge for me.

"I won't," I answered quickly. "I've fought too hard for this to get in the way of it now."

"Good."

Chloe spoke to the Takers. "This is going to look scary at first, because it's a huge change for our bodies. I'll have some tremors, and there may be some more serious reactions." She gestured over to Shawn. "That's why we have someone with medical training ready. But those initial reactions should only last a few minutes."

Chloe moved like she was trying to display confidence, but I knew her better. She was scared . . . and I was terrified.

"After that part, I should sleep," she continued. "Really sleep, with dreams and everything. That's it for now. Any questions?"

Everyone in the room watched her intently, but no one appeared ready to ask anything yet. Chloe turned to look at me and winked, but I saw her hand tremble as she downed the blue liquid in one swallow.

———

Chloe's heart never stopped. She had a seizure, and stopped breathing for a few seconds, but then it was over. She looked so peaceful in her sleep it helped me feel like everything might just be okay. When she woke up the next morning, eight hours of precious sleep later, Shawn said her vitals were stable. You could already see a bit more color in her cheeks.

The next week was a blur of activity and planning. Except for a small altercation at Cooper's funeral, the Takers seemed eager to embrace the idea of a new future. Nearly all of them had signed up to take Spectrum, and Shawn had been put in charge of the schedule and administering the drug. Randall volunteered to donate his blood, as a Builder, to make more Spectrum and end the war, and a few other Builders joined him. Since we wanted to give it a few days before bringing any other Builders into the Taker camp, Shawn and I went to Cypress Crest to collect it.

One of the things we'd done the first day after Chloe woke up was to bring in two doctors that Mason knew and trusted, to check her and Mason out for any possible negative side effects from Spectrum. So far, there were none. From the early blood work we'd run, it looked like the drug's benefits would last for roughly one month. Not bad, but Mason had already come up with some ideas for herbs that could be incorporated into either the Takers' diet or the drug itself, to make it last more than twice that long.

Dad's formula was everything he'd hoped it could be.

The majority of the Takers had agreed with "Cooper's" decision to appoint Joey the new leader of the NWS. He only agreed to do it if the groups would select one of each type of Night Walker to act as advisors. Joey had initially pushed for an actual Night Walker to be the leader, but Chloe convinced him that it would be better for someone who wasn't biased toward a specific type to unite and lead this very broken group. Mason was selected as the Taker advisor, Randall was the Builder advisor, and they chose me to advise on behalf of the Watchers.

I wished Dad could be here to take on the role he deserved, but in his place, I agreed to do my best.

Parker's body was healing well from all the physical abuse it had endured. He'd taken Spectrum for himself shortly after Chloe had woken up, and his body had reacted more violently. We weren't sure whether it was related to him not being a true Taker or the exhausted state of his body, but he suffered through the convulsions for over an hour. I wondered so many times during that hour if I'd made a huge mistake in agreeing that he should take it. But since then he'd gotten several solid nights of sleep and looked like a different person.

Actually, since Parker was back in charge all the time instead of Darkness... he *was* a different person.

Since Dr. Rivera wasn't answering my questions, I resorted to my tried-and-true method. It only took me one night in his dreams to sort out where he kept his experimental vials, and which one could help turn Parker back into a Watcher. We'd given it to him three times now with no results, but Parker said it had taken time for them to turn him into a Taker, so we shouldn't expect the opposite to be any different.

At the end of the week, as Randall, Joey, and Mason walked me out of the amusement park to say goodbye at the van, we passed an old, kid-sized bumper car ride that I hadn't noticed before. Each cart sat still and silent, vines and weeds threatening to eat the metal alive. Even in full daylight, the whole place just creeped me out. I was happy to hear that Joey had no intention of staying here permanently.

Randall chuckled at something Mason said behind me. Those two had hit it off from their first meeting, when Randall and the other rebels came to officially meet Joey and the other new NWS leaders. Since then, Randall had been at the Taker base more often than not. The leadership had even discussed moving some of the rebels from Cypress Crest to a new permanent base ... once we found one.

I'd been thinking a lot about the old one, Benton Air Force Base. It hurt so much to think about it or even look at—it was the place where Dad had died. But that base might feel different to me if we were moving back to set up an organization that would honor him instead of imprison him. That idea felt right.

"I've been thinking ... I went back to visit the old Taker base a couple of weeks ago. It's huge, and more than two-thirds of it was completely undamaged." I could feel all their eyes on me, and I deliberately didn't meet them because I was fighting off difficult emotions already. "The buildings are sound, and it would fit so many more people than anywhere else I can think of. Plus, I think my father would—I think Dad would like to know it eventually ended up as a place that helped Night Walkers, like he'd always hoped it could be."

Joey nodded, then extended his hand and shook mine. "That sounds like a good plan ... we have so many things to fix after all the fighting. I would be the perfect place to start. Many mistakes were made there, including what happened to your dad. I'm sorry for that."

"Thank you. But we need to stop looking back and move forward. Now seems like the right time for that." I smiled and Joey smiled back. It was the first time I'd ever seen him look happy. It was nice. I hoped in the future he'd have many more reasons to smile.

"Are you sure you're not interested in coming back to Cypress Crest, Jack? It will be safer there now..." Randall looked a little hurt, expecting I'd again reject his suggestion. I knew he missed Libby as much as I did, and that was part of the emotion behind his question, but me moving back there wouldn't bring her back.

What I was planning to do, I did in honor of everyone I'd lost. I was trying to move forward with a normal life—the life we all might have had if we hadn't been surrounded by war. It felt like the best way to thank those I loved for what they'd sacrificed.

"Thank you." I clapped my hand on his shoulder. "But I think it's about time I lived with my brother permanently. We'll come and visit. I'd like to bring flowers for Marisol and Libby—and my mom."

We both knew that the graveyard across the street from Cypress Crest was too full of people we'd known and loved—even more so for Randall than for me.

He gave me a sad smile. "You'll both always be welcome."

I missed Mom, Dad, Libby, and everyone else I'd lost. They'd left holes in me that wouldn't ever go away, but I knew that losing Parker too would've been more than I could have ever recovered from. Now that I knew he was going to be okay, I was learning that those holes don't have to be left vacant and gaping forever. Every step toward new people I cared about filled them up just a little bit.

When we got to the van, Parker and Chloe were already there, just finishing loading up their stuff. Mrs. Chipp had driven home yesterday, with a plan to set up a room for me. I'd told her I would be just as comfortable in a sleeping bag in the backyard. She'd given me a hug and shook her head before carrying on with her "new bedroom" planning.

Joey dropped one big arm across Chloe's shoulders and she fell against him under the weight of it with a laugh. "You sure you don't want to stay here?"

"No." She shook her head and gave him a hug before ducking free. "I have school this fall, remember? I'll stay at the house in Oakville and come out whenever I can."

Joey rubbed the back of one hand with the other, looking distinctly uncomfortable with the idea. "Maybe I should go with you?"

"I'll be fine." Chloe put one of her hands on top of his giant ones. "They really need you to stay with them. You need to make sure they don't go back down Dad's road." Joey had said from the beginning that the Takers didn't have to take Spectrum unless they wanted to.

He still appeared to be thinking about arguing with his sister's plans. "Promise me you'll keep me updated and I can come visit?"

She stood on her tiptoes and lowered her brow as she gave him a stern look. Even at that, she still only came up to his shoulders. "I promise."

He sighed in resignation and then shot a look over at Parker and me. "And you two will keep her out of trouble?"

Chloe winked at me, then grinned.

I laughed and said, "Your job leading the Takers might be the easier one ... but we'll do our best."

Parker pulled out his phone and checked the time. "If we're going to make it home in time to beat the others over there…"

Ever since he'd taken Spectrum, he'd been talking every day about going to see Finn, Addie, and Mia. Their parents had ordered them to come home immediately the instant they'd found out Finn had been hurt.

I lowered my chin and looked at him. "Because they will do *what* if we aren't there on time? You know they'll just be sitting there waiting for you even if we're hours late, right?"

Parker's expression changed to mock dismay at my comment. "Well, we obviously have a lot to teach you about manners now that you're moving in. Being punctual is the same as being awesome."

"I really think I should reconsider staying here…" I turned my back on my brother, but he slipped up beside me when I wasn't looking. Before I knew it, he hit my elbow hard enough that my keys flew out of my hand. Then he grabbed them from midair and jogged back toward the driver's side of the van, yelling over his shoulder, "Come on—I'm driving!"

Chloe and I said quick goodbyes to Mason, Randall, and Joey before hopping into the backseat of the van. I was privately grateful that Parker had insisted on driving because I felt like I hadn't had any time to really talk to Chloe alone since she'd taken Spectrum.

My brother seemed intent on giving us some time, too. Before we were even all the way out of the Funtopia parking lot, he had the radio turned up a bit on the front speakers and the rearview mirror was angled so the only thing he could possibly see out of it was the ceiling.

Wow, he was smooth ... and not at all subtle. My neck felt oddly hot and I hoped Chloe wasn't paying too much attention to what Parker was doing. If she noticed, she didn't say anything, and I appreciated that.

She sat close enough that our legs and arms touched every time the van went over the slightest bump. It was distracting and fantastic in the best possible way. The color had returned to her face and cheeks slowly over the last week. She now looked positively vibrant with life. If I'd thought she was beautiful before, she was flat-out stunning now. We hadn't kissed since before she'd taken Spectrum, but now my brain didn't want to think about doing anything else.

"I think we need to talk about it," Chloe said abruptly.

"You do?" I asked, sitting up a little straighter.

"Yes." She shifted slightly until her body was angled toward me.

"Okay." I shifted too before following up with the all-important question. "What are we talking about?"

"Drugs."

I frowned ... definitely not even on my remote possibility list for what I'd thought she could be talking about. "Drugs?"

"I've been thinking a lot about doing it." Chloe reached out and took one of my hands in hers. "I want to know what you think."

"About drugs and doing it?" I repeated, then realized that this had come out very wrong. The corner of Chloe's mouth quirked up and she put an extremely appalled look on her face. Before she could go any further with teasing me, I decided to cut her off.

"You're messing with me," I said. "Tell me what you really mean."

She smiled, and with a slight bob of her head, clarified. "I've been thinking about taking the drug that would turn me into a Builder." This time, the nervous expression on her face was completely sincere.

I wrapped my fingers tighter around hers. "You're a Taker and you're healthy now. Why would you want to mess with that?"

"Because if I was a Builder, I could help you." She rubbed the back of her thumb across my knuckles but wouldn't meet my eyes.

What she was offering was huge. It was sweet and generous... and dangerous.

I lifted her hand to my lips and kissed each knuckle. "Thank you, but I'm not willing to risk you for that. We have no idea if any of those drugs are safe. It isn't worth it. Besides, you just spent several days teaching me how cool and useful Taker abilities actually are. You don't want to give that up completely. Regular Builders can help me, and now that you actually have dreams, I can always visit you there."

Chloe looked half disappointed and half relieved, then looked up at me with a mischievous smile. "Maybe Mia could teach me a few tricks about self-hypnosis?"

A surprised laugh escaped my chest. "That sounds like an idea worth trying."

Wrapping my arms around her, I pulled Chloe in close and kissed her—first her eyelids, her nose and cheeks, and then down to her lips. We could be as soft and as slow as we wanted, because now we both had all the time in the world, and we were determined to take full advantage of it.

The End

Acknowledgments

Finishing a series is such an amazing thing. You realize how far you've come since the beginning, and sometimes how little you knew before you started. Right now, the main people I want to thank are the readers. You've read and stuck with this story through it all. You've loved it. You've emailed me to talk about your feelings for the story, how it kept you up reading, and then you asked for the next one.

You are incredible. This has become your story. You are the Night Walkers.

Thank you for reading. Thank you for telling other people to read. Thank you for loving Parker, Jack, Finn, Addie, Mia, and hopefully now Chloe. Their stories only became important when you read them and cared about them.

And a special shout-out to all my international readers from around the globe. Your unbelievable support has helped me learn that this world is a smaller, friendlier place than I'd ever believed.

I also want to thank my amazing agent, Kathleen Rushall, who supports me through literally everything. This journey would've been nothing without you! Thanks to Taryn Fagerness, who helped this book get into the hands of publishers and readers around the globe. Thanks to Brian Farrey-Latz, Mallory Hayes, Sandy Sullivan, Lisa Novak, and the rest of the Flux team for making these books stand out in such great ways. You've made this ride so exciting.

Thank you to all of the other amazing writers that help me mold an idea into something that actually makes sense, starting with the Seizure Ninjas, my weekly critique group (long story on the name, don't ask): Janci Patterson, James Goldberg, Heather Clark, Cavan Helps, Heidi Summers, Lee Ann Setzer, Sandra Tayler, and Alex Haig. Massive thanks to you all! You're the reason this book was finished.

Thank you to the writing community, both here in Utah and across the country, as well as to online groups like my lovely YA Scream Queens and the Lucky 13s. You're all so wonderful. Thank you for accepting me with all my quirks.

Also, thank you to my oldest and truest writing friends: Michelle Argyle, Natalie Whipple, Kasie West, Candice Kennington, Renee Collins, Bree Despain, Sara Raasch, and Nichole Giles. You're fantastically awesome. You know how much I love you.

Thank you to my family and friends who read my books: Mom, Krista, Bill, Eric, Grandma Maurice, Nick Whipple, Dave Cutler, and everyone else who helps and supports me in so many ways. You're the best!

Lastly, to my incredible husband, Anders, and our boys, Cameron and Parker. You inspire me. I'm excited to wake up to any day that has all of you in it. Thank you for putting up with my late nights and hectic schedule. I couldn't have written a single page without you. Thank you. I love all three of you with every little piece of me.

© Michelle Davidson Argyle

About the Author

J. R. Johansson is the author of the Night Walkers trilogy (Flux) and *Cut Me Free* (FSG/Macmillan, 2015). She has two amazing sons and a wonderful husband who keep her busy and happy; in fact, but for the company of her kitten, she's pretty much drowning in testosterone. They live in a valley between huge mountains and a beautiful lake where the sun shines more than three hundred days per year. She loves writing, playing board games, and sitting in her hot tub. Her dream is that someday she can do all three at the same time.

Visit the author online at www.jrjohansson.com.